The She-Wolf pricked her ears and filled her lungs. The wolf beside her whined. "Soon" the chieftess soothed. Rahnee seldom rode her wolf-friend. She said her legs were too long and her hips too narrow, but that was only a half-truth. She would not have sat on an elf's shoulders either.

"Are you all right?" Fastfire sent. He received a menacing growl for his pains. When his lifemate had prey-scent at the back of her nose she was always more wolf than elf, regardless of wolfsong.

Ice caught his mother's scent with his nose and mind. He knew what bait she'd take. Leaning forward, he locked his mind with his wolf-friend's and unfurled his plan.

"This is the way" he sent triumphantly. "This is the way *Wolfrider's* tribe hunts!"

Other Elfquest titles
published by Tor Books

The Blood of Ten Chiefs
Wolfsong: The Blood of Ten Chiefs vol. 2

ELFQUEST

Winds of Change

Vol. 3

The Blood of Ten Chiefs

Edited by
Richard Pini

TOR
fantasy

A TOM DOHERTY ASSOCIATES BOOK
NEW YORK

This is a work of fiction. All the characters and events portrayed in this book are fictitious, and any resemblance to real people or events is purely coincidental.

WINDS OF CHANGE: THE BLOOD OF TEN CHIEFS VOL. 3

Copyright © 1989 by WaRP Graphics, Inc.

A Tor Book
Published by Tom Doherty Associates, Inc.
49 West 24th Street
New York, N.Y. 10010

Cover art by Wendy Pini

ISBN: 0-812-50700-2

First edition: March 1989
First mass market printing: April 1990

Printed in the United States of America

0 9 8 7 6 5 4 3 2 1

ACKNOWLEDGMENTS

Contents

Timmain ─┬─ true wolf
         │
         TIMMORN ─┬─ Valloa / Murrel
                  │
                  RAHNEE ─┬─ Zarhan Fastfire
                          │
                          Prunepit / PREY-PACER

Wreath ─┬─ PREY-PACER ─┬─ Softfoot
        │   │
        SKYFIRE   Swift-Spear / TWO-SPEAR

SKYFIRE ─┬─ Dreamsinger
         │
         FREEFOOT ─┬─ Starflower
                   │
                   TANNER ─┬─ Stormlight
                           │
                           GOODTREE ─┬─ Lionleaper
                                     │
                                     MANTRICKER

MANTRICKER ─┬─ ?
            │
            BEARCLAW ─┬─ Joyleaf
                      │
                      CUTTER, Blood of Ten Chiefs

Prologue

Sometimes the Holt was called Goodtree's Rest, for that was the place the eighth chief of the Wolfriders had chosen to settle with her tribe. She had begun the shaping of the forest giant that everyone called the Father Tree there, and for untold turns of the seasons Tree and Holt had been home to the elves.

Longreach sighed and rolled his shoulders, trying to work out half-imagined kinks. For three hands of days the Holt had been anything *but* a place of rest. The season of new green had given over to the long, bright days; the daystar was hot and full and high in the sky. It should have been a time of ease and laziness, for neither elf nor wolf felt much urge toward exertion during the day. In past turns days like these would be for tongue lolling and wolf-naps, for huge stretches and great yawns—and the warm nights for hunts and dancing beneath the moons or amid clouds of fireflies and warm leaf-scent.

But lately, for three hands of days at least, there was no languor, no relaxation. Even Joyleaf, normally one of the calmest, most serene of the Wolfriders, was snappish, and that was having its own effects, particularly on Bearclaw. Something had come into the Holt and set nerves on edge, something that had ridden in on an ever-so-subtle breeze that stirred not even the smallest leaf. Whatever it was, it was not felt on the skin, but rather within the skin—like an itch that would not stay in one place long enough to scratch. Like the finest of hairs blown into the eye, impossible to rub out—or like the high, reedy whine of insects in the tall grass, impossible to pinpoint, always there.

There had been no stories told since the strangeness had settled like a mist over the Holt; no one had been in the mood to ask, and there had been no reason or desire for a howl. Longreach didn't quite know what to feel; if there was any rejection of his talents, he concluded, it was too well hidden to be bothersome.

Besides, the tribe seemed more occupied in trying to cope—however badly—with whatever was irritating them all. If it had been meat, they would have been able to say that it was spoiled. If it had been the sky, they could say, "It will storm soon." But it was more intimate than that. It was a part of them, their spirit, their magic responding to the taint of decay and the fear of events and change out of control. And for that they had no name, nor any way to talk about it, nor any memory of anything like it.

Or do we? Longreach wondered, as he shook his head to clear it of the soundless buzz, and went to find his cache of carefully dried dreamberries . . .

Ice

by Lynn Abbey

Winter gripped the taiga. The bright stars of the sky hunter stood high above the trees. The two moons, the Mother and her Cub, showed silver faces that sparkled like frost or laughter, but cast little light on the open forest below. There was a certain beauty to the night—a certain beauty to all the cold, clear nights of a wintry world. It was a subtle beauty, filled with grays and silver, well suited to wide elfin eyes. Colors were for the brief summer with its bright, hazy nights.

Rahnee's tribe of elves and wolves, half-elves and half-wolves, enjoyed the warm comfort of thick fur and close friends. Their lives revolved around an immense herd of deer whose hooves clicked and snapped as they marched. They called the beasts clickdeer and, with their wolf-friends, they culled the herd in the manner of all predators.

The clickdeer dictated the tribal rhythms. Spring was migration time, when the herd followed the retreating snows to the treeless tundra. By summer the herd had grown sleek on gray-green grasses and stretched from one horizon to the other. In late summer the antlered stags divided the herd, sometimes fighting to the death for a choice clutch of does. Then mating was over. The air turned icy; the stags shed their racks onto frosted grass.

Does led the autumn migration back to the sheltered taiga. They grew antlers as they went, and dominated the now-bareheaded stags. For in the end, in the winter, it was a matter of survival, and the does with their unborn fawns claimed that right as the herd scattered into foraging families for the long, dark winter.

Other rhythms were longer than the turning of the

seasons, but neither the herd nor the tribe knew those names. Wolfsong admitted no question that could not be answered by the steady march of the seasons and the herd.

During the winter the tribe lingered by open streams and let the foraging deer come to them. Their snug, sturdy lairs were dug into the ground, covered with branches, then layered over with insulating snow. They hunted when the weather permitted, rested when it didn't, and came together at the start of each night to sing by the amber glow of a small fire.

Rahnee could scarcely recall a time when she hadn't been chieftess. She had watched her tribe grow from a handful of wolfless, desperate hunters. Like the others of her generation, the cubs of Timmorn Yellow-Eyes, she was content to savor the present and disregard the past. The old ones, including her lifemate, Zarhan Fastfire, remembered everything, but they were outnumbered by wolf-blooded elves now and wisely kept their memories to themselves.

Life proceeded without undue dissonance. The clickdeer were healthy; the wolves were healthy. Cubs nestled in warm skins between their parents; mates nestled in each other's arms. The gentle voice of Samael Dreamkeeper carried a wondrous and familiar tale to a full-bellied audience. It was wolfsong without care or thought—and that was just the way the chieftess liked it.

"Hear me! I am *Wolfrider*. Hear me, mothers and fathers, elders of the *kinds*, mates and cubs. Hear me and know my name!"

Rahnee's serenity was shattered. She sat mute and frozen, and grew wary long before her mind had reformed itself from the shapeless now of wolfsong into the cold, sharp discomfort of *now*.

A clickdeer pelt fell at her feet.

"Hear me, Chieftess. Say my name!"

Caught in the fugue between wolf and elf, Rahnee watched a cloud of ice crystals billow around the offering.

Why am I the one who gives out names? she asked herself with a voice she hadn't heard in many turns. *How do I know if the name is right for a cub or a mate?* The ice motes reached their zenith. The She-Wolf could see the rainbow in each crystal, and hear its music. *This one was my cub once. When did my cub grow up?*

The fugue ended. The ice crystals vanished on a cold wind. Rahnee stared up into the fire-amber eyes of her son.

All her cubs were called Brighteyes. There had been three, and this was the third. Something within her, something elfin, cried out that there should be something more between a mother and her cub, but the wolf said there was birthtime, and there was milktime, and then the cub was a cub no longer.

Rahnee remembered her first cub—and how he had died beneath clicking hooves before the tribe had mastered the hunting of this herd. The second cub had been a daughter —the red-haired, green-eyed image of her father. That one had a touch of her father's magic, and a full measure of her mother's recklessness. There had come a spring when she would no longer follow the herd, or her chieftess. With her mate and cub, she had set off toward a different horizon.

***Mar? Mar?* Where are you? What became of you?**

Rahnee's sending escaped unwillfully, and went unanswered. She shivered in her furs as seasons and turns cascaded past her mind's eye. Then she faced her third cub, a son full of strength and fire. He was a stranger to her, yet a piece of herself nonetheless.

"Hear me!"

His voice was both pleading and angry. Rahnee took her time, gathering her legs beneath her and gathering the thoughts of her tribe as well. She couldn't remember when she had first performed this ritual—the old ones could tell her, if she ever needed to know—but she had performed it many times in wolfsong and knew how to do it now.

A sharp knife hung in a sheath between her breasts. Once it had been part of the skymountain that had brought Timmain and her folk to this world. Once it had been a gift to a shy wolf-daughter who had no other link to her elfin inheritance. Now it was their only relic, and if the chieftess used it to divide the pelt among the *kinds,* then the tribe accepted *Wolfrider* as this hunter's chosen name.

3

But if she did not draw the knife from her breast—and as she absorbed doubt upon discomfort from each mind in the circle, she knew that she would not—then he kept his old name.

What has been his name? the elfin chieftess asked her wolfish self. *He looks too old for a milkname . . . too old to be a Brighteyes. What have we been calling him?*

The youth endured her hesitation. She was the chieftess, he told himself while tension twisted his gut. She treated everyone alike. Rahnee She-Wolf, Rahnee the tribe's first chief after Timmorn Yellow-Eyes, but never Rahnee his mother. The anger, the need for something more than she gave him, had been with him forever. Not the now-and-forever of wolfsong, but a precise, nurtured forever that left him no peace.

This son set himself apart from his agemates and his *kind*. He cultivated notions that were meaningless to the rest of the tribe: ambition, pride, and perfection. He had studied the clickdeer for a moondance before selecting one to be his offering. He'd stalked her by himself. He'd killed her with a single spear thrust through the eye so the pelt was unmarred. He'd scraped the skin, dried it, then kneaded it back to suppleness with pungent oils.

She had to accept it. It was a gift worthy of . . .

The chieftess looked away from the pelt. She got to her feet and left the firelight, leaving her son to seethe in the ashes of his pride.

You'd be gone, She-Wolf. You'd be driven out to die. You'll see. Just wait. Your time will come. Not that he was ready to challenge her, not yet. Abandoning his gift, the disappointed youth retreated.

He escaped into a stand of dense, needle-branched trees where elves and wolves alike were reduced to groping through the darkness. Crouched on the ground, chin resting on his drawn-up knees, he nursed his injuries with salt. The world shrank until it began and ended with the pain in his heart. He bounded like a startled doe when a warm hand closed over his shoulder.

Rushwater? he sent, reaching for his lovemate's mind. But Rushwater was with the others around the fire.

"I am your father. Don't you recognize me?"

The youth did, and proved it by twisting away. "Why did you follow me? Couldn't you tell I didn't want to be followed?"

"I thought you might want to talk."

"I don't want to hear any more excuses for *her*. You can't bear her most time yourself, even though you're Recognized."

"That's not true—"

"You have no time for mindless wolfsongs."

"Is that what you want to talk about?" Through the darkness Zarhan could hear his son trembling with rage and rejection. "Do I make you so angry? Does the wolfsong?"

"I want my name, Father. Four times I've come to her. How many more times do I have to ask her for my name? She looked at me tonight. She saw me—she knew what I wanted—and she denied me just the same."

Zarhan Fastfire hunkered down. He swept up a small mound of fallen needles and brought sparks to them with his magic. The young hunter hid his face behind his knees until Fastfire reached across the flame. He lifted his son's chin with a strong and gentle hand.

"It wasn't your mother who turned away. She is the chieftess; she does the tribe's will. You have asked for a name she cannot give you, don't you understand that? The tribe, all the *kinds* together, oppose you in their gut. You cannot choose the name that belongs to all of them. The tribe is—or is becoming—Wolfriders."

The youth snorted derisively. "My hind foot they're Wolfriders. When has Samael Dreamkeeper ridden a wolf? When have *you*?"

"The She-Wolf brought the wolves to us from Timmorn, her father—"

"But she rides like tripe in a sack! She bruises their ribs. Her feet drag on the ground." Zarhan stared silently at his

5

fire and the youth savored his triumph a moment before continuing. "I was the first to *ride*. I taught myself to throw my spear from my wolf's back, to draw and aim my bow while he held the wind in his teeth. There were no Wolfriders before me.

"It's my name, *mine!*"

Zarhan raised his head slowly, fearing he'd get caught in challenge. His son's eyes glowed in the firelight, but there was no warmth in them. The tribe had given a name to this nearly grown cub. They called him Ice for the chill winds that fanned his passions. But they did not call him that when he could hear.

The young hunter had done all that he claimed. In the short turns since his birth he had taken the bond between elf-friend and wolf-friend and made it into something none of them had imagined possible. He taught his mates, those cubs his own age or nearly so, his tricks as he learned them, and from his mates the knowledge had spread through the tribe. Hunters seldom came home empty-handed anymore. And even the old ones were beginning to forget the taste of famine.

Ice had changed the tribe as surely as Timmain, Timmorn, or Rahnee, but they denied him the name his heart craved.

"It's not *fair!*"

Zarhan cringed at the sound of the old elfin word. He saw the world in terms of right and wrong, fair and unfair. All the old ones did when they looked back through their undimmed memories. But fair was a notion Timmain had shapeshifted out of her offspring—and that had been, in Fastfire's thinking, one of the fairest things she'd done.

Now there was Ice, who never stopped comparing this with that, whose mind was full of first and best. Yet he was wolf as well, and all the more dangerous.

"There has never been any use in naming what's fair and what's not," Zarhan said slowly. "That's what wolfsong is for."

"How would you know?" Ice demanded.

"I speak with your mother about these things."

"Easier to talk to a tree."

"The firstborn are different from me and from you. It is true that when she listens to the wolfsong, your mother hears little else, but she would not be chieftess if she were not much more than that. It is . . . *unfair* for you to think of her as you do—"

"And it's fair for you to wander from lovemate to another mate? How convenient for you that you were not with some other when I called her out tonight. It all stops and starts with Recognition for her, or is that why you're content to leave her in wolfsong from one turn to the next?"

There was challenge in Ice's eyes. Challenge—that primal, wolfish answer to all things right or wrong, fair or unfair. It raised the short hairs at the base of Fastfire's neck. The elf's back stiffened, his lips parted, and he drew upon everything he'd learned from his wild lifemate. He could break this challenge if he let Ice plead his mother's cause long enough. But, in the grander sense, that itself would have been grossly unfair.

"She knows more than you imagine," Zarhan said softly. The fire winked out and he left his son in darkness.

The moons were gone by the time Fastfire made his way to the woven-branch shelter he shared with his lifemate. Her mindtouch was strong and wild, but also fully alert; he began to walk faster.

The firstborn were the eccentrics of the tribe. As cubs they had been completely dominated by Timmorn's inbred offspring, and almost as ignored by their elfin mothers. They showed their wolf-blood through long, hollow faces; coarse, many-colored hair; and their stolid endurance. Yet they were elfin, too, as subtle and refined as any of Zarhan's star-faring ancestors.

Privately Zarhan considered that his lifemate was most remarkable for the dissonance between her elfin and wolf selves. Her mind and body were too small for her soul. If Rahnee was under the sway of her wolfsong, which happened whenever life became unsurprising, then she had a wolf's contentment with an endless cycle of hunting, eating, frolicking, and sleeping. But when the wolfsong subsided, no elf was so compelling or magical.

Her hand locked over his as he drew the hide curtain back from the entrance to their lair. She pulled him closer and they submerged into their own intimate world until long after the daystar had risen and sunk again below the horizon.

"It has been so long this time," Rahnee whispered as she combed the tangles from Zarhan's hair.

"Long—yes, but only because the tribe has prospered."

"It would be better for us if every night brought some new danger, something I could not face without you . . . without all of me."

"We would wear ourselves out," Fastfire replied, trying to make light of a painful subject.

The hair fell from the chieftess's hands. "That would be new, wouldn't it?" There was a hint of bitter anger in her voice. "Perhaps you would hear your own wolfsong if there was only me in your life."

I don't think so. He took her hand between his and pressed her fingertips against his forehead, to assure her of his sincerity.

Thought and experience flowed naked between them, bridging the turns that had elapsed since the last crisis. While it was true that wolfsong blended seasons and turns into a seamless whole, it was not true that it completely inhibited memory. Rahnee had noticed the times when he wandered from her side, but in wolfsong she was more often chieftess than lover or lifemate. Her blood seldom quickened with passion, and she needed no one beside herself.

The She-Wolf pulled away. Elves had several words for madness; even wild wolves had a taste and scent for it. Not that wolfsong was madness, nor the dizzying sweep of elfin memory, but the unstable mixture of both natures in one mind touched close to madness.

"It was worse for my father," she assured herself. "For him it wasn't wolfsong, it was *wolf.* When I saw him last it was as if a great cave had opened in his life and the better part of him was lost in blackness. It is like day and night for

8

me, but night isn't as dark as a cave. No, more like
dreaming and waking, and each is the shadow of the
other."

She might well have added that the transition out of
wolfsong was like waking suddenly from a brilliant dream.
There was a moment of disorientation when the dream was
more real than wakefulness. And when the dream had
lasted a double-hand of turns, that moment could last a
long time.

"It was not the first time he came to me for his
name . . ." the chieftess murmured to herself as memories
rained through her consciousness. "Always he wants that
name; always it is denied. Tonight, I think, was no different
from the other times. Yet something must have been
different, else it would not have aroused me this way. What
can it be if it is not Ice who would be Wolfrider?"

Zarhan did not gainsay her. "We have done well
enough," he said cautiously.

"Yes." She tapped her fingertips together, counting each
face in the tribe. A hand of hands, and that again—a
number too large to have a name. A number that was
almost too large to feed. Somewhere in the midst of
wolfsong, that supposedly unchanging rhythm, she had
divided her tribe into a hand of *kinds:* smaller groups of
pairs, cubs and elders who watched over each other and
shared the hunt.

It worked well enough, as Fastfire said. No wolf or
Wolfrider hunted every night—nor did the whole tribe
come to every feast—but there was always hunting and
eating.

"The clickdeer herd grows vast," Rahnee mused. "And
the winter is hard this turn."

Zarhan's spine stiffened. For many turns the winters had
been mild and the summers lush—at least a mildness and
bounty were known in this place. The herd had never been
larger, nor had the tribe. This winter, though, had fallen
early, and promised to run long. Trees and shrubs were
stripped to the bark as high as an elf or deer could reach.

One did not need the names of numbers to understand
what was happening.

"It is the quiet before the storm," Fastfire confirmed. "And something in Ice's offering told you."

Rahnee nodded. But knowing that a storm would come was not the same as facing it. She would have to wait, and waiting was something the She-Wolf did poorly.

"Let's hunt," she announced, throwing her concerns to the back of their lair. "I'm hungry."

She surged outside, filled her lungs with cold air, then fell back to her knees, clutching her gut. Zarhan crouched beside her, holding her tightly while she trembled and grew wild-eyed. She writhed in his arms and vomited froth onto the snow.

"Hairballs," she muttered weakly as the attack subsided.

Zarhan reached for one of their sleeping furs and draped it over their shoulders.

"My gut's alive," she moaned as a second attack began.

Her lifemate nodded. He brushed a stray wisp of silver hair back from her face. **It will pass,** he assured her, and warmed her cheek against his chest.

But it would not pass quickly. Fastfire held his mate through that night and into the next day. He left her only to climb the prickly evergreen trees and chop branches the clickdeer could not reach. He packed away their sleeping furs and made a new bed of pine boughs. He kindled a fire to keep her warm, and she was too bedraggled to complain.

The high ones, Timmain and the other ancestors, had come to this world from some unimaginable other place. Their four fingers were their most apparent alienness, but not their most profound. Timmain had claimed they'd knowingly made their bodies proof against the ravages of time and such things as she called *viruses.* Though the high ones drew sustenance from the foods of this world, they were not a part of it. Though they could be killed, their souls were not part of this time and place.

Timmain had not shared her immortality completely with the wolves; perhaps it was impossible; certainly it would have been unwise. It was no good to be healthy if you were also cold and starving. Some of Zarhan's kin had withered slowly and mercilessly. Timmain's wolf-shaped children were of this world as she and the other elves could never be. They could thrive where high ones barely survived, but, in consequence, they were prey to mortality. True, they had some large measure of elfin vitality; their lives could be very long, and they were rarely ill, but they needed young Willowgreen's healing as the old ones never did.

Fastfire huddled in the furs and waited for Rahnee to return from another trip to the bushes. As usual it seemed that the firstborn suffered more than all the others. They did not seem to fight small skirmishes against sickness while wolfsong held them, as the young Wolfriders did, but when they emerged, that part of them that was elfin fought everywhere at once.

"I would rather *die*!" Rahnee moaned from her concealment.

"Come back where it's warm."

Weary and disheveled, the chieftess staggered back to the lair. Her lifemate handed her a cup of steaming tea. She drank the liquid, then scooped the soggy pine needles from the bottom of the cup and ate them with a grimace.

"Why do I crave the very things that make me retch?" she demanded. "And why does the thought of fresh, bloody meat make me even sicker?"

"If you ate your meat cooked . . ."

She gave him a look as dark as a bear's cave and hurried toward the bushes.

For four days and nights her body purged itself of all that was unwanted or unwholesome. Her skin was mottled with ugly bruises. There were raw places above her forehead where her hair had fallen out. Zarhan had begun to believe that her own health had brought her out of the wolfsong. On the fifth day he had brought Willowgreen to see her, but the healer refused to intervene.

"She might die," Fastfire argued. "Mosshunter died."

"Mosshunter died because he would not leave the wolfsong behind long enough to heal. The She-Wolf is twice as stubborn, but not half so foolish. Leave her be, she's doing it all herself anyway."

Zarhan shook his head and heard Willowgreen laughing

11

as she left. The healer was a full-blooded elf, but hardly an old one, being but a fraction of his age. She got along better with the Wolfriders than her full-blood kin. Where healing was concerned, she was seldom wrong, but Zarhan did not take her advice. He stayed beside his lifemate, fussing over her comfort, and by the ninth day she felt well enough to complain.

Ice listened to her caustic comments from a pine tree overlooking their lair. He bared his teeth when she refused to drink the teas Fastfire brewed, but he bristled at his father as well when the old one persisted in offering help when none was wanted.

Listen to them! Whining and bickering. And they don't even have the sense to be ashamed! Suppose something happened right now. Suppose the tribe needed the chieftess. What would happen? His thought spread out from the tree until it touched the mind of his lovemate.

I don't know, Rushwater sent from her snug den. She had been an outsider—a feral adolescent who had lived by her wits and strength until the tribe crossed her path. She didn't remember her parents, but she could bond with the wolves and so they had accepted her. **If the tribe needs a chief, it will have a chief. If not the She-Wolf, then someone else. And *now* I need nothing more than your arms around me.**

The tribe needs a chief with pride. A chief who doesn't sicken herself with wolfsong. She should have been driven out long ago. The tribe has lost its way with her! One of these nights—

A wave of revulsion flowed back into his mind, then Rushwater closed herself to his thoughts. Ice's face grew as sour as one of Zarhan's teas. He loved Rushwater because she was different from the rest, but she was not different enough. She had survived by wolfsong; she had no time for brooding and revenge—only for deeds themselves.

I won't wait any longer. I'm strong enough. Strong enough to use the wolfsong, and not be used by it. It's time she got out of the way. It's time all the firstborn were gone. They aren't as good as the old ones, they aren't as good as

12

the wolves, and they aren't as good as us. It's time they got out of the way. It's time for Wolfrider to be chief of the Wolfriders.

Ice's thoughts were completely absorbed by the need to be first within the tribe as he climbed down from the tree. He didn't notice Rahnee watching him from the bushes, or Zarhan watching from the lair.

He will leave soon, Zarhan sent to his lifemate.

He will challenge first, she replied, and frowned as she flexed her weakened muscles.

The hunters of the watercave *kind* gathered by the stream with their wolves. Treewalker, a firstborn hunter, scratched a map across the snow.

"There're clickdeer beyond the rocks here. Lapwing, Badger, and Dawn will come with me. Snowflower, you take the rest with your wolf-friends to the fallen oak and wait. The clickdeer will be spread out by then. Bring down two of the stragglers."

There were no questions; each *kind* hunted in virtually the same way. They hunted as Ice had taught them, riding their wolves and using heavy thrusting spears for the kill. Half the hunters harried the deer, separating the strong from the weak. The rest of the hunters hid farther on and rushed in from the flank for the kill. It was the way of the pack and it worked very well.

Treewalker straddled his wolf and led his harriers across the stream. Snowflower lingered a few moments before leading her group to the huge dead tree. She caught the scent of something with her mind—a stray sending, perhaps, or someone thinking strongly about her—but she could not make it come clear. After shaking the distraction from her thoughts, she gave the signal for the others to come forward.

Masked from sight and scent, they waited until the underbrush shook with sound of running. The howls of wolves and riders came down the wind. Their wolf-friends snapped at the air in anticipation and toothsome grins fixed on the faces of the hunters.

13

Treewalker and his harriers had done their task well. The clickdeer ran flat out, their breath spilled in steamy clouds. And the stragglers, the weakest ones, were easily marked: great shaggy stags who had spent themselves in the mating season and who now were exhausted to their bones. Snowflower tipped her spear and the final chase began.

It was the *way*, taken from the precepts Timmorn had laid upon them from the beginning and from the natural inclination of the wolves. A strong, healthy clickdeer had nothing to fear.

Until now.

While the *kind*'s hunters trapped the heaving clickdeer between fangs and spears, a lone hunter burst from nearby cover with an ear-splitting whoop. Brandishing a flint knife above his head, he urged his wolf-friend at an antlered doe. The wolf leapt at her flank, throwing her off stride long enough for the hunter to leap onto her back.

Snowflower blinked once with disbelief, but no more. She carried a killing spear and the hunt's success depended on her. She urged her wolf-friend into low attack, as much in danger from her own comrades as from the stag, and thrust the spear into its breast with a powerful twist. The normally voiceless beast gave one cry as its heart broke, then crashed to its knees. The wolves finished it.

The huntress got to her feet. There was a general touching of minds as they assured each other that both attacks had been successful, and that no one had been seriously injured. Someone always got hurt—that was the way of the hunt. Snowflower's shoulders burned and her ribs ached where something had struck them. One of the wolves had blood on its flank. Everyone, hunter and wolf alike, was breathing hard.

Who? Treewalker sent to Snowflower, filling her mind with an image of the lone hunter.

Ice.

No spoken communication could match the subtle complexity of directed thought. Every shade of emotion was carried in the word—the name the youth rejected. Treewalker looked at his panting wolf-friend, looked away,

14

and set off on the clear trail. Snowflower took a step after him.

Leave it be, Badger urged her. **Leave it be between them, not us.**

The downy hair between Snowflower's shoulders tingled. Ice's bold hunt was an act of challenge to which any of them could have responded. Indeed, if none of them responded, it was as if they had all submitted, so someone had to respond. She had chosen the prey; she had wielded the killing spear, but Treewalker was the eldest. The firstborn had taken the challenge upon himself, and that, in a subtle way, was also a challenge.

Snowflower advanced another step.

Stay out of it, Dawn lock-sent. **Have a thought for you and Badger. It's stay or go with Ice. Let Treewalker take the challenge, unless you're ready to raise your cub apart from the tribe.**

Snowflower turned away. The tribe was everything to her: a community of blood from the aloof old ones to Dawn's cuddly cub—to the cub she would bear before the snows melted. The *kind* was her family. Treewalker was her grandfather; he had raised her after the hunting accident that had killed her parents. The mates were the friends and lovers with whom she shared everything.

Not all questions of precedence needed to be settled by challenge.

Treewalker did not return, nor did his wolf-friend. The hunters butchered the clickdeer in silence, dividing the carcass among themselves and the wolves. The firstborn hunter was in all their thoughts, but they shared nothing. They took a bit longer than usual to complete their task, but when the kills had been reduced to neatly tied burdens and red splotches across the snow, they headed home without a backward glance.

Ice appeared at the height of the feast. He was bare-chested despite the cold and glowing with pride. The doe's bloody antlers were slung over his shoulder, and that was all he brought back from his kill. He cast a glance at Fastfire, who sat in the chieftess's place behind the fire.

Everyone felt the thoughts traveling on that glance, but the old one did not look up and, after an uneasy pause, Ice settled beside Rushwater.

Treewalker returned long after the fire had blackened. He sat by himself at the edge of his *kind*. He bore no wounds, or none that could be seen, but he turned away from Snowflower's compassion and was gone by morning.

The watercave *kind* would not hunt again for several days. Snowflower had time to bind her ribs with soft leather, and time to watch Ice slink away each afternoon. There were no more challenges, no more bloody entrances to the feast, but when her *kind*'s day came again, it was Ice who led them.

Snowflower bit through a knot in her auburn hair, then went off to the chieftess's lair. She had not seen the She-Wolf since Ice had asked for his name. The young huntress was dismayed to see the dullness of the She-Wolf's hair and the hollows beneath her shadowed eyes as she slept.

"Is she . . . *dying*?"

Fastfire shook his head. "No, though she has wished it often enough in these past days. Actually she's almost better now, and eating bloody meat again."

"Ice. Ice brought her the meat he didn't share with us . . ."

Zarhan could not answer her aloud. **Why would you think that?** he sent gently.

You know . . . You must know! Snowflower wrested away from him to crouch on the ground beside Rahnee. "Chieftess, Chieftess! Wake up! I must speak with you."

Deep violet eyes opened slowly—befuddled, irritated, then, finally, responsible. The She-Wolf waited for the Wolfrider to speak.

"You must do something, Chieftess. It's gone all wrong. Treewalker, Ice, the *kinds*, and everything. Ice has changed the hunt. He teaches a new way. We need you."

Fortunately the young woman sent thoughts beneath her speech, or Rahnee would never have understood. Even with the images, and the emotions, very little was clear.

"There have always been those who were better hunters

16

than others, and those who were content to let others hunt. Treewalker was always better with his bow than with a spear, and Ice has changed the hunt before—"

Snowflower shook her head violently. "But Treewalker's gone—not even Frost can find him. And Ice . . ." Still trembling with frustration, Snowflower shared her memories of the young hunter vaulting onto the doe's back and entering the feast circle with the bloody antlers. "Ice does not *hunt*."

The chieftess absorbed the images slowly, sharing them with Zarhan when his mind inquired against hers. She felt the wrongness, but Zarhan found the words first.

"No one, not even Threetoe, has taken trophies."

The name meant nothing to a young Wolfrider like Snowflower, but it opened a flood of dusty memories for Rahnee. Timmain had set them all on a poorly marked trail to survival. Threetoe had wandered down a blind path where wolfsong was never-ending. He had been strong, and arrogant in his strength, but he had been a hunter, not a killer.

"Trophies." Rahnee rolled the unfamiliar word across her tongue. "Trophies. The pelt he brought into the circle, that, too, was a trophy. Trophies shattered my wolfsong—they have no place in wolfsong, but why?" Rahnee asked Zarhan.

"Wolfsong is the way to survival, but sometimes some elves must do more than is necessary for survival. A basket is just a basket—it needs to be nothing more—but New-Wolf must always make hers differently from Changefur or Rellah. Even you prefer one spear over another."

Rahnee shrugged. "It must be balanced just so, for the strength in my arms and the way that I throw."

"Ah—but why do you always seek the blackest flints for your spearhead, never white or gray or any other shade? Is black flint better?"

"Because I *like* the black flint. It is my way," the chieftess snapped, blind to her lifemate's logic.

"Having your own way, and having a different way, is what our cub does best. He is bringing pride to his hunting. The hides, the antlers, they are his art, his trophies."

Snowflower and Rahnee shared a distrusting glance. Timmain's descendants perceived beauty in the spontaneous disorder of nature; they understood preference, and the need to add something personal to a spear or a basket; but they were less certain of art made from blood.

Rahnee worried her lower lip until it bled. "I do not understand this taking of trophies, the why or how of it, but in the end, that is no matter. What matters is that Ice makes his trophies from does with unborn fawns, and that he does not share his meat. I will not gainsay what I don't understand, but I will not permit him to hunt in this new way."

The chieftess pushed upright, spreading her feet wide, testing her strength and balance before taking a purposeful step. She grabbed her black flint spear from its place by the lair and strode off showing no sign of her previous weakness. Zarhan took a second spear and, with Snowflower beside him, followed in her wake.

He recognized his lifemate's head-down, shoulders-up walk. The She-Wolf would go forward now, courting challenge until either she or it was victorious. She was right, of course. The balance between the herd and its predators was precise, and the predators doomed themselves if they hunted the strongest animals—much less the does, who carried life from one turn to the next. Pack or tribe, the group had the right to drive a renegade hunter out.

It was twilight, the shadow that passed for daylight in the winter when clouds hid the daystar and the fullness of one's belly was the most reliable measure of time. The *kinds* were scattered in private lairs, rock dens, trees, and clearings as far as the mind could feel.

Wolfriders! "Wolfriders!" the chieftess sent and shouted, summoning the tribe to the empty feast circle.

Most of them had not seen her since the night when her son had tried to claim a new name. They took her measure as she stood there with the erect spear beside her and they did not for a moment think she was simply announcing her recovery from wolfsong purges.

18

The She-Wolf's eyes glazed while she polled her tribe. "Where's Ice?" she demanded. She sent the same message to those who had not yet arrived. "Have him show himself."

"There is no *Ice*," a voice snarled from the periphery.

Rushwater pushed through the bare branches. She stood square before the She-Wolf and planted her killing-spear hard against her foot. "There is only my mate, Wolfrider."

The defiant woman barely cleared Rahnee's shoulder, but she was a sturdy huntress with a grin that showed all her teeth. Her stance was a gesture short of insolence, her eyes a scant hair too low for challenge.

"It matters nothing to me what he calls himself, only that he show his face when I call," Rahnee said in carefully modulated tones. "Can you call him?"

A soulname was the most powerful sending. It crossed the greatest distance, and it crossed barriers that were not distance in any ordinary sense. All those who bore elf-blood had a soulname locked within them. Lovers shared soulnames when they became more than lovers. Parents knew the names of their children. Timmorn Yellow-Eyes had somehow known everyone's name, declaring his kinship with the whole tribe. Rahnee denied kinship with her son.

The youngest cubs whimpered as tension snarled the air. The elders stiffened, but Rushwater shook her gray-metal hair over her shoulders with nary a twitch of nervousness.

"He hunts," she replied. Her shoulders stiffened; her eyes lifted that last small fraction; and she placed herself between her mate and her chieftess.

"Then I shall go to him."

The She-Wolf broke contact with the young woman and strode out of the clearing, certain of her destination. Rushwater slumped forward. Her spear slipped from her fingers, clattering across the ice-crusted snow before it came to a halt some distance away. With her mate's soulname foremost in her mind, Rushwater had risked everything in a challenge that was not her own, that her chieftess had not deigned to accept.

19

Lynn Abbey

A few of the Wolfriders, including Willowgreen, the elfin healer, came to Rushwater's comfort, but others went after their chieftess. Snowflower hesitated a heartbeat longer than the rest. She had no special bond with Rushwater, but she shared that young woman's empty anguish. A challenge made and lost—even unintentionally, even for another— was a wound that scarred and crippled.

In the end the tribe was more important than any single hunter or cub, and the chieftess defined the tribe. Snowflower turned away and followed the broad trail the others had made.

Ice felt them move through the forest, just as, moments before, he'd felt the stab of Rushwater's despair. He was not without compassion for the woman who had defended him—risking everything, losing everything—but such feelings ran cold in him. Very cold.

He flexed the muscles between his shoulders. The tension flowed from him to his wolf-friend, and among the wolves to the hunters waiting beside him. He thrust his spear into the snow and left it shuddering there.

No spears, he sent to his hand of comrades. **No cowards.**

The tension had spread to the other hunters. They, too, stretched and filled their muscles with strength and cast their spears aside. **No cowards,** they chorused.

It was an ancient word, one that harkened to a time out of time, a time before Samael Dreamkeeper and his firelight stories. An empty word. Had they guessed what lay behind Ice's hard-edged sending, they might have objected. Badger might have protested that there was no cowardice on this world—only survival. But Badger and the others tasted only the excitement.

All the hunters had sensed Rahnee's summons. They'd felt the strong pull of her leadership, of the habit that kept them all together, and they would have gone to her had their newfound leader not forbidden it. They hadn't felt Rushwater's aborted challenge, but they'd watched the change come over Ice. They followed him now with the

20

exhilarating knowledge that whatever happened next would be something that had never happened before.

The clickdeer weren't far away. A double-hand of the beasts, mostly females, led by a shaggy doe who bulked as much as any hand of Wolfriders. She carried a winter rack of antlers that would have looked fine on a three-turn stag.

Mine, Ice sent, his fingers stiff and clawlike. **Mine.**

It was not unusual for the hunters to declare their prey. Two spears hurling toward the same mark could be more dangerous for the Wolfriders than the clickdeer. But the hunt-leader did not always choose the prime target, much less claim it like it belonged to him alone.

While the other does and yearlings browsed, the leader lifted her leathery nose and sucked the air. Her ears flapped; her eyes rolled white; and she coughed a warning from deep in her chest. With a cloud of ice crystals she broke from the brush. The other deer bounded after her.

Ice cursed. They'd hunted this part of the forest too long. The deer ran from only one scent, feared only one predator. He'd kept his hunters carefully downwind but his worm-riddled mother had crossed upwind with the rest of the tribe.

Another score to settle.

With a shrill whoop he locked his legs around his wolf-friend's ribs and began the chase.

The She-Wolf pricked her ears and filled her lungs. The wolf beside her whined. **Soon,** the chieftess soothed, then adjusted her course through the trees. Rahnee seldom rode her wolf-friend. She said her legs were too long and her hips too narrow, but that was only a half-truth. She would not have sat on an elf's shoulders, either.

Are you all right? Fastfire sent as she smiled. He received a menacing growl for his pains. When his lifemate had prey-scent at the back of her nose she was always more wolf than elf, regardless of wolfsong.

Many of them were panting as the She-Wolf led them arrow-straight toward some destination only she could

imagine. She went through brush even the wolves would
rather have gone around and floundered once hip-deep in
unmarked snow, but she did not slow down. Like a wolf
that could always find the straight path to its pack no
matter how they both wandered, the chieftess knew where
her hunters would be.

Ice caught his mother's scent with his nose and mind. He
knew her well enough—knew what bait she'd take, and
knew she was good enough to find him where *he* chose to be
found. Leaning forward, he locked his mind with his
wolf-friend's and unfurled his plan, then he shared it with
the other hunters behind him.

This is the way— he sent triumphantly to all those
who waited beside the chieftess. **This is the way
Wolfrider's tribe hunts!**

The clickdeer entered the clearing where Rahnee waited
with the tribe. The hunting wolves were flat out, but the
deer—especially the doe Ice had chosen—had stamina to
spare. It was time for the flank wolves and riders to join the
chase, but no one did. Both the She-Wolf and Ice restrained
them, though Rahnee was unaware that she did so.

"Ayee-e-e HAHHH!"

Ice's wolf squandered its last strength leaping for the
doe's throat. It fell short, barely escaping the flint-hard
hooves, and it fell away bare-backed. Ice tightened his
thighs against the doe's shoulders. He shouted his pride
once again and grasped the points of the doe's antlers in his
fists. Drawing strength and leverage from deep within
himself, he hauled her head back and gave it a mighty
wrench to the side.

The doe's front hooves lifted momentarily from the
snow, then she crashed to her side. Air emptied from her
lungs in a steamy cloud. Ice stood over her lifeless neck and
stretched his arms wide.

"Ayee-e-e HAHH!"

His hunt-cry echoed through the trees. He was victorious, but Badger had not been so lucky. That Wolfrider had
never before leapt from wolf's back to deer's back. He had
not fallen, but neither had he clamped tight with his thighs,

22

and when he tried to imitate Ice's death-twist he found himself without the necessary leverage. The doe had tossed Badger aside like so many leaves. Face down, shoulders twisted, he lay unmoving in the snow. The clickdeer clattered out of sight.

"*Ayee-e-e! Ayee-ah!*"

Ice exploded with pride, but no one seemed to notice. And he did not notice Badger. He did notice several small stones resting in the lee of a larger boulder. He raised one above his head, then smashed it against the doe's skull.

Celebrate with me! Feast with me! he sent as he dipped his fingers in the warm blood.

A shadow crossed his hands. "There is nothing to celebrate."

His mother's voice—rough and menacing, but still according to his plan.

"Celebrate or not, it's all the same to me. Stay or go, that's the same, too—but your turns have passed, She-Wolf. Let the tribe choose."

"Look at me when I talk to you!"

The young hunter, the would-be chief, had not truly expected that she would go quietly into the twilight, but neither had he expected his neck muscles to tighten cublike as they did. It took strength, and courage, too, to stand erect before her, meeting her deadly eyes.

It is over for you. He no longer trusted his voice.

"It is over for Badger. It has only begun for you."

Long ago, when the She-Wolf had been a nameless whelp, she had lacked confidence and every other attribute of leadership. Zarhan knew there were still sluices of doubt that drove her through thoughtless wolfsong, but now—a now of both wolfsong and elfin memory—she was Timmain Shapeshifter, Timmorn Yellow-Eyes, and herself, Rahnee She-Wolf, with one relentless will.

Ice felt waves of unnatural power pummel his inner being. He had not thought she had such reserves, but he was her son and he was strong, too.

**I . . . have . . . shown . . . the . . . new . . . way . . . ** he gasped into the intangible wind she set against him.

23

"Surrender Timmain's knife!" His concentration wavered just a bit and his glance swerved away from hers. It was scarcely a heartbeat—not enough to end the challenge, but enough that he saw Badger's inert form. He gathered his strength for another assault.

**The weak have . . . always died. This . . . is . . . This . . . is . . . the . . . way . . . **

Rahnee battered him, using her will to drive him onto himself. His head drooped; he sank to his knees.

"This is not the way . . . This is not the way." Tears flowed freely down his cheeks. The She-Wolf relented, but Ice could not take any advantage. "Rot take your eyes, *Mother*." The beaten hunter thrust his hands into the snow, made fists, and squeezed the snow into ice. "Rot take you forever." He pressed the lumps against his face and let the cold restore his senses.

It's not about Badger, he lock-sent. **It's about you, and me, and which way the tribe should take!** But she was gone and he was left beside the cooling body of the doe.

The chieftess heard him, and understood that he was right. Badger's death had been a star-crossed arrow carrying her to challenge at an instant of her own choosing rather than her son's. She hadn't broken him—not as her wolf-friend, Wind, would have broken such a dangerous challenger, not as she could have broken him had she not drawn back at the last heartbeat. And because she hadn't driven him away, she hadn't really broken him or his influence at all.

Tyr, Tyr. Rahnee had denied her son to the tribe, but she could not deny him in her heart. Challenge was rite and ritual, the way to the soul. The She-Wolf had plunged deep and seen Tyr's spirit burning knife-sharp, ice-bright. His way was different, but having seen and felt it, Rahnee could not say that it was wrong. There was too much of herself in Tyr. His choices were closed to her, to the firstborn, and to the elves. His way had killed Badger, but even that did not make it wrong to challenge the world. *Tyr, Tyr*.

The She-Wolf called a halt. They laid Badger across his wolf-friend's back, then she opened her throat to the sky.

The fine, translucent hair on her arms and back pulled taut as she called the taiga to commemorate what it had lost. The wolf-friends who had paced beside them added their voices to her song. The old ones stood transfixed, unable to join a song they could not resist.

Soon all the naked trees echoed as the Wolfriders at the camp, their friends, and the wolves passed the song among themselves. Only one voice was missing; only Rahnee heard that it was absent. She brought the song to an end.

By the fire-pit, she sent to all those who still sang or listened. **Now.**

The tribe and its wolf companions had gathered by the time Badger's corpse was laid on the chieftess's snow-cat furs. Snowflower was numb with anguish, unable to approach his corpse. Halfmoons, his mother, led the others of his *kind* to see his bloodless face and lay small tokens of memory at his side. The chieftess moved quietly to the edge of the clearing. Fastfire was there waiting.

"Are you well, beloved?" he asked, holding her close and feeling an unnatural lassitude in her limbs.

"It must be done," she whispered, not pulling away, yet not absorbing the comfort he offered, either.

Between lifemates it sometimes happened that the sending of thoughts, images, and emotions was accomplished spontaneously—without premeditation, without conscious desire. Rahnee's turmoil bridged into her lifemate's mind.

Fastfire saw how it would be if their son led the tribe. Wolfriders would dominate the taiga as the great cats and bears did, but they would be a tribe, not lonely individuals. They would shape the land to their will as Timmain had shaped her body to the wolf's. It was a way as far from his lifemate as the high ones were from the pack. **I cannot help you,** he sent as he released her.

She hadn't expected that he, or anyone else, could. What a chief had to do, a chief had to do alone. The tribe came first. The chief could not follow the flame in his soul—or in her soul—without thinking of the tribe. Parting the bare branches and the mourners, the She-Wolf took the chief's place beside Badger. She inhaled the frigid air until her eyes were wide and bright and she had gathered the thoughts of her tribe.

"He was Badger, born to Halfmoons and Slider. He was a hunter, swift and brave, bold and strong. He found his soulname in the place beyond wolfsong. He shared it with Snowflower, who will share it with his cub, but he died too young to take a place in our dreaming memories. We grieve with his *kind* and his mates. No one can say who he might have been, what he might have done . . . and when we remember him we will not remember who he was, only the reckless folly that was his death."

Halfmoons fell to her knees; Snowflower began a thin keening. Samael Dreamkeeper, who nurtured their inheritance with his dreamberries, gripped his staff with whitened knuckles. The Wolfriders, unlike their five-fingered enemies, made few rituals and no religions. Their grief was simple and natural, yet the words the chieftess spoke over a fallen tribesmate were the lessons of a life, the limits of future memory.

"Badger need not have died," Rahnee continued, fully conscious of what she said. "He strayed from the ways Timmain laid down for Timmorn Yellow-Eyes; he strayed from the ways of his wolf-friend. He followed one who has no wolf in his heart. He hunted for pride and he died with none.

"The high ones came here with magic and pride, and this world rejected them. Only Timmain knew what must be done. She gave us the wolfsong so we could live in harmony with the world that had become her home; to give us the strength to resist the calls of magic and pride.

"The wolfsong shows the way. We hunt as the wolves hunt: working together. We hunt what the wolves hunt. Our strength is the strength of the herd and the pack. It is our way—the wolves' way—to take the weak who run behind the herd. We do not hunt the strong."

Her words were as sharp and cold as the silver knife glinting against her shirt. Slowly members of the tribe looked away from her, submitting to the force of her will.

26

Badger's parents and siblings resisted, then they, too, began to bare their necks. Slider held out the longest, withstanding the She-Wolf's glare until his face throbbed with the effort. **Was *your* cub who led him off the path,** the old hunter lock-sent in the heartbeat before she overwhelmed him.

Weak in the knees, Rahnee surveyed her tribe. It was the wolves' way to rule the pack through strength, to winnow not merely the weak but also the eccentric. She had acted in harmony with the wolfsong—she had followed the way as she understood it—but there was no comfort when no one, not even her lifemate, could meet her eyes.

"Take him deep into the forest. Sing his name and cover him with love." She did not linger to see how they obeyed her.

That should have been the end of it: a stern rebuke, a night of mournful song, a feast circle that no longer included Badger or Ice. The *now* of wolfsong washing over the grief, anger, and pain until only the dreamberries remembered. That was how it should have been—and was not.

Ice returned wearing the doe's raw pelt over his shoulders. Her antlers balanced above his head. The sick-sweet smell of death hovered about him. A miasma of doubt covered them all; no one forgot what had happened; and the blissful *now* of wolfsong remained just out of everyone's reach.

Rahnee moved the tribe through the taiga, seeking new lairs, unwary clickdeer, and peace, all to no avail. Something larger than the Wolfrider tribe, something they could feel but not name, hung over the dark green trees. The clickdeer were as restless as the Wolfriders. They fought with each other as they foraged ever deeper into the taiga. The weak were very weak and came to bay before the hunt had barely begun. Meat was abundant; the wolves grew sleek but the Wolfriders grew irritable.

"Look at this!" Willowgreen exclaimed, holding a bone up in the firelight. The youngest of the pure elves, her

27

agemates were the Wolfrider hunters, not the old elves. She ate bloody meat at the feast, but she was also the tribe's healer. The bone snapped when she twisted it. "Twigs! It's got bones like dead twigs!" She threw the pieces onto the fire and stalked away.

The feasters watched her leave in silence. Instinct said to be glad that there was one less mouth to feed, one less stomach to fill, but something more than instinct made them look more closely at the half-devoured carcass. It had been a great stag. Last autumn it had carried a dangerous rack; probably it had gathered many does to its harem and sired many fawns, but winter—not the Wolfriders—had been its undoing. Its hide was rough and bald in places, its hooves were cracked, and its bones, as Willowgreen had noted, were dark and withered.

Wolfish instinct, and the clear memory of times when the hunting was very hard, kept the feasters at their task, but there was meat left to be buried in the morning.

Rahnee had not witnessed Willowgreen's outburst. She heard about it from everyone who had, and twice as many who hadn't. Meat was meat where she was concerned, and easy hunting was to be relished not questioned, but they gave her no peace. She gathered the tribe and struck out again for fresh hunting.

The situation was the same wherever they went: easy hunting, uneasy feasting. Often they found an animal that had floundered and died without a hunt. Occasionally they found a carcass left half-eaten by other sated predators.

"Is it because the meat's bad, as Willowgreen says?" Rahnee asked her lifemate as they stared at the frozen remains of a stag. With the purges well behind her now, the sight of meat made her mouth water, though she'd eaten each of the previous eight nights. Even now her belly wasn't quite empty, yet there was a strong urge to bash a rib free and chew on it as they walked. "Is it something about the meat I can't sense?"

"No, not exactly. That is, there is something wrong with the meat because there's something wrong with the clickdeer first. A stag isn't just weak all of a sudden, it got

28

weak slowly, and it got weak because of something else. Whatever the something else was, well, Willowgreen says it's still in the meat, and then it's in whatever—whoever—eats the meat."

The chieftess got down on her hands and knees, peering into the stag's belly and hindquarters. "I don't see anything that isn't supposed to be there. It doesn't even have black bones like the other ones did."

Zarhan rubbed his forehead and stared at the sky. "I don't know, Rahnee. Maybe this one was healthy. Maybe Ice brought this one down. Can't you understand? The things that weaken the deer, the things that make you sick when you come out of wolfsong, the things that make the wolf-friends die—they aren't things that you can see."

"I don't believe in things I can't see."

"Can you see the wind?"

"I can feel it. That's the same."

"All right, then, everything's in Willowgreen's over-heated imagination. Clickdeer just die when they feel like it, so will the wolves, and sometime so will the Wolfriders!"

Fastfire headed back the way they'd come. He'd only gotten a short distance before the She-Wolf was back at his side, tugging him to a stop.

"But the wolves are healthier than they've ever been at this time of winter. Wind's fur is thick and shiny. I can't feel his ribs at all. How can it be bad to not be hungry?"

"Beloved, we're not hungry because the clickdeer *are* hungry. Look around you—what's left for them to eat? They've stripped the taiga bare. They're starving, but first they're dying from other things, the things that Willowgreen feels like the wind. Only the strongest die of starvation—Timmain knew that. It will take a long time, and neither we, nor the wolves, nor anything else that lives off the herd as the herd has lived off the forest, will go hungry while it is happening. But soon the herd will be smaller, small enough that *they* won't starve, and then what happened to the herd will happen to the meat-eaters. There will be too many hunters, too many cubs—"

"Even our cubs? The cub within me now?"

29

Fastfire did not answer. He did not need to explain survival to her.

Unfocused anxiety was a poor substitute for wolfsong. When their chieftess was restless, the Wolfriders were restless; when she was irritable, they tried to stay out of her way. The She-Wolf led the hunt herself. She studied every stumbling deer they brought down, never finding what she sought. Willowgreen examined each carcass for the deadly things that could not be seen, separating meat from rot. They left a few warm carcasses in the snow, but the feasting went on.

Wolf ways could not heed elfin caution. Rahnee might well have fought the wind . . . or Ice.

The proud young hunter insinuated himself back into the tribe. He still hunted the strong—the antlered does. His kills always found Willowgreen's approval. He marked his feast circle alongside his mother's and invited them all to choose. Conscious of the cub growing within her, the chieftess found it impossible to challenge those who did not feast with her.

We can roast our meat over the fire, Zarhan suggested. **Willowgreen says that the flames drive the weakness out.**

Rahnee agreed, and picked at steaming, tasteless, and discolored meat in the company of fastidious old elves. After each joyless feast, back in the lair with Fastfire sound asleep beside her, she would stiffen with silent, aching sobs. Bitter tears seeped from her eyes.

Father, what would you do? Grandmother, which is the way you meant for us to follow? But neither Timmain nor her son would answer.

The time came to begin the spring migration but winter kept its fist closed tight. The moons danced, but the thaw did not begin. A blizzard roared in from the tundra and for a hand of days no one budged from the lairs. When the daystar finally overcame the clouds, the feast circles were hidden by a mountain of dazzling snow.

Wolf and Wolfrider alike sank to their chins in the

powder. Walking was an adventure; hunting almost impossible. It could have been a dangerous time, a hungry time, but it wasn't. The clickdeer huddled in wind-carved hollows and could not flee when the predators approached.

The wolf-friends gorged and whined. The bitches plunged into the snow, desperate to reach the open tundra before their cubs were born. Ice stood beside Snowflower when she presented her sable-crowned cub to the tribe.

"I call him Plenty," she said, shielding his sensitive eyes from the light. "Because he is born when we have all that we need and more."

Plenty was a healthy cub with strong lungs and a piercing cry. The chieftess rested a hand over her belly. Timmain's descendants weren't like the wolves or the deer. Their cubs came randomly throughout the turns of the seasons. It would be winter before the chieftess's cub saw the daystar. There was plenty now. Would she call her own cub Famine?

Rahnee leaned low over the cub, fixing his shape in her memory, drawing the scents of his body and soul into that place where she held all the other members of the tribe. Her metal knife flashed in the daylight. A chubby four-fingered hand grasped for it. Before Ice or anyone else could comment on a possible omen, Rahnee swept the cub into her arms and held him aloft for everyone to see.

"Welcome the littlest Wolfrider!" the chieftess proclaimed. "May his days be long, his arm steady, and his stomach never empty."

She arched her neck and began the howl. As the chorus swelled, the little bundle wiggled in her hands. She lowered him to her breast and looked deep into his clear, gray eyes.

His mother would have him back, Ice sent with no warmth at all.

In the heartbeat before the She-Wolf's eyes met his, she meant to tell him he would have a sister, to share with him the name she and Zarhan had heard beyond wolfsong. But there was nothing in Ice's face to encourage sharing. She returned Plenty to his mother.

"As we have all been cubs, so the cub belongs to us all,"

Rahnee said in a voice that was less strong than she would have liked. "All shall teach him. All shall protect him."

I shall protect him. I shall teach him, Ice responded, not in challenge but in simple fact, as if the question had already been decided.

The blizzard had taken winter's last strength. The day-star marched above the treetops and the thaw began. White snow gave way to clinging brown mud. The clickdeer turned their heads toward the north once more. Abandoning all but their lightest or most cherished possessions, the Wolfriders prepared to follow.

There were still many clickdeer in the taiga. They merged daily into larger and larger groups, swimming across swollen streams, trampling the fords into vicious quagmires. The wolves' thick fur was clotted with mud, and even the old ones were a sorry, pitted sight. Legs ached from battling with the soft, pitted ground. Everyone longed for clear water that did not taste of clickdeer.

"Sleet and slush, I can hardly hear myself think with all their noise," Laststar complained.

She rubbed the deep furrows of a two-night headache and leaned wearily on her spear. The herd was deafening as it plodded along. The animals were always moving and each step produced the distinctive snap that had given them their name. The deer seemed to be comforted by the sound, the wolves seemed not to notice it, but it had become oppressive to the tired Wolfriders.

"They've turned the world into a bog," another hunter added.

"And where they don't trample, they dung," the chieftess observed while picking dark suspect globs from the rough hide of her boots.

All day she'd pushed the tribe: now they were abreast with the herd leaders, now they would find the high ground, now they would rest—and tomorrow it would begin again. They would have liked to rest longer, they would have liked to have a little more space than this hillock afforded. They would have liked many things, but the wolves and the herd had the spring grasses of the tundra in their narrow, relentless minds, and the tribe came along like a squirrel's tail.

"It's been worse," New-Wolf said to no one in particular, and not gently. The migration fell hardest on the old ones, the elves who lacked stamina, whose blisters healed but did not build callus.

"Oh yes, much worse," Rellah agreed. "In the autumn they turn around and go the other way. The mud's not so bad, then, but the *flies*!"

"A herd of flies for every clickdeer. A buzzing, black cloud over each of them . . . and us. Oh, you'll miss your precious wolfsong then."

Slider's fist clenched. "If it's so bad, why do you come with us? None of this would be so bad if we didn't have to listen to you as well."

"But you never listen, you're always off in your own little world with your wolves . . ."

Rahnee jammed her hands over her ears, shutting out voices that no longer belonged to individuals but to the tribe as a whole. Was it worse this turn? No, probably not—maybe even better. Zarhan insisted the herd was smaller, and a smaller herd made less mud. Still, there wasn't a Wolfrider who could hear the wolfsong. They were all swung away from their wolf-blood, their wolf-friends. All were exquisitely aware of the journey's discomforts— and acting as if they'd never been aware before.

And perhaps they hadn't been. Every other spring she'd been one of those who put her head down and *went*. Life was hard on the world of two moons—hadn't that been what Timmain meant when she took the wolf's shape for her own? Live for today, and if today was hard, then forget today. And if it weren't . . . ? Well, forget that, too, because it would be hard again soon enough.

The Wolfriders were still sniping at each other when Rahnee edged down the slope. They were her tribe, all of them—her responsibility—and she wanted nothing to do with them right now. The She-Wolf found Wind, her wolf-friend, in the darkness and trod carefully through the sleeping pack to reach her. She scratched the wolf's forehead, made contact with his wordless thoughts, then sighed.

Even Wind was irritable. Two bitches were ripe. Their legs and backs ached and they were always hungry. They wanted the summer dens dug. They wanted the cubs out of their bellies. They wanted to keep moving, but were too tired to walk another step. And it was all there in Wind's thoughts. Rahnee left off scratching and settled that much closer to the mud for whatever rest she could wring from the night.

The chieftess was more tired than she'd imagined, or more inured to the din. She slept well into the overcast morning. She awoke quickly with a yawn and a stretch, ready for anything and aware that something had changed while she slept. The pack was crowded together out in the mud. They were on their dawn kill and the tang of blood was in the air. Rahnee thrust her senses deeper into the morning, examining the pack and their kill more closely.

Milk. Milk-smell below the blood-smell . . . and coming from the herd itself, not the pack. The does were dropping their fawns!

The She-Wolf was on her feet, headed up the slope, her mouth watering. Most of the tribe was already awake and tending their weapons. The bickering of the previous night had vanished. There was simply no better hunting than this hunting; no better meat than fawn . . . .

Rahnee stopped short, her hand dropping to her hardening belly. Her gaze raked the mud plain, noting the does who had not dropped, the fawns nuzzling their mothers, the red splotches where the pack had killed already, and the frantic does who searched for fawns that would never taste their milk. She saw Wind at the center of the pack, his storm-cloud fur streaked crimson. Their minds touched; the chieftess felt, and for a moment shared, the excitement, then she pulled back.

Where have I been? she asked herself, knowing the answer. Wolfsong hunted as the wolves hunted, and the wolves were single-minded about fawns. The does with their antlers were dangerous, but the blood-and-milk-nurtured meat of the fawns was a short step below ecstasy. A smaller pack might not dare follow the deer so close, but this pack—their wolf-friends—were stronger and smarter than the herd.

Oh, Grandmother, how can this be the way? Fawns and cubs; wolf cubs and Wolfrider cubs. What is the difference? The old ones will know. Zarhan will know.

She raced up the hillock—and stopped short. Her lifemate had used his magic to make a fire. New-Wolf or one of the others had erected a spit. And there was no mistaking the flayed little creature they were happily roasting.

Zarhan!

For a heartbeat Fastfire thought the world was ending. He looked over his shoulder expecting the worst, but what he saw in her face was beyond his understanding.

Rahnee?

How can you do this? How can you? How? How? How!

The question swirled around him with angry intensity—and left him dumbfounded. His hands were empty. She knew his fire magic well enough and had never objected before. The tribe was united by purposeful activity as it hadn't been in moondances. His mind crafted an inquiry of its own, but she was surrounded by impenetrable disquiet.

"How what?" he said with exasperation. "What's wrong with you this morning?"

She shared what she had seen and how she had seen it until Fastfire felt the shadow of life growing within her and the life shadow of the roasting fawn.

Why else do the wolves follow this stinking herd? Why else do *we* follow them? He refused to see the connection.

But not this . . . This is the life of the herd, the future of the herd. If there is weakness in the herd, then the fawns must be protected.

Fawns are the weakest of all, Zarhan replied defensively. **Stars in the sky, you're usually the first one out!**

35

No. Rahnee's lips trembled and drew back from her teeth.

She raged because he was right. Through the pleasant haze of wolfsong she remembered uncounted mornings like this when she had tracked some big-bellied doe away from the herd. A morning when she had watched a new life blink at the daystar. A morning when, inevitably, her spear had found its mark.

"This is not right!" she shouted to the tribe. "We do not hunt cubs!"

They stared at her. Their thoughts radiated doubt and suspicion. Snowflower clutched her cub one-armed and reached for the spear lying across her feet. The others made gestures that were less obvious but no less defensive. No one hunted cubs. No one thought of the fawns as cubs.

An anonymous thought swept through the tribe: **She's gone *mad*.** On the other side of the hillock Ice set aside his knapping stones. He could hear the chieftess's voice, but with the constant clatter of the herd, he could not make out her words.

***Cha?* Lifemate?** He called Rushwater away from the tribe's thoughts. **What's happening? What is *she* doing?**

I don't know . . . I don't understand—but she's very upset and saying that we hunt cubs.

Ice joined the rest of the tribe, careful to stay out of his mother's sight as he did. He pumped air through his lungs, filling himself with strength and vitality.

"Never a mother with her young—if there's another to be had," Rahnee shouted. "That is the way I laid down for you. It is not our way to take a cub before it sees the daystar. Have you all been so lost in wolfsong that you do not remember the way?"

"There have been many ways," an old Wolfrider hunter said defensively.

"We do not live as we once lived—"

"Or hunt as we used to hunt—"

"We have the wolf-friends now—"

"We follow the way of the pack now—"

"Everything has changed. Ask Samael Dreamkeeper."

Ask Samael Dreamkeeper . . . ask Samael Dreamkeeper . . . The Wolfriders made a chorus of the request. The old elf held their memories in his sacks of wrinkled berries and seeds—the only possessions which they would never leave behind. Whenever there was a question, the tribe turned to Samael for the truth.

The old one came forward, looking only at the chieftess. He locked his thoughts with hers. **I will tell them—**

"Does our firstborn chieftess set her ways above those of the wolves?" Ice shouldered tribesmates aside and thrust himself between Samael and his mother. "Does she forget, herself? Is she blind—unable to see what the wolves choose?"

Jubilation swelled in Ice's heart. He had taken the chieftess by surprise, as she had taken him. She was mesmerized by the challenge implicit in his voice. For a moment he dared look away from her to touch the minds of the Wolfriders.

"Look at our chieftess!" he commanded. "Look at our chieftess who twists the way of the wolf-friends. Hunt like the wolves, she says when the snow is deep. Do not hunt like the wolves, she says when the doe drops its fawns. Do not scavenge, but neither take your meat from the strongest, the healthiest. Make your feast on the weak, the stragglers, even though Willowgreen says their meat is rotten. Will we hunt only what pleases our chieftess?"

Rahnee's mouth worked silently. **Can't you see?** she sent desperately to her son. **We must be very careful. We aren't wolves. We aren't elves. Our way is only as wide as the edge of my knife . . . ** But his mind was impenetrable.

It was the opening the young hunter had craved for dances, seasons, and turns. **Then give me the knife and see if I may safely walk its edge!** He spun around, confronting her, digging his hands into her shoulders before anyone could stop him. **It is over!** his soul thundered at hers.

The She-Wolf had never lost a battle—no chief did, and

remain a chief. Her best defense was the prelude to her offense, but Ice denied her the offensive, and she was trapped.

We must be careful. We are less than the high ones, but more than the wolves—

As I am more than you. *Give me the knife!*

Cold fear wove through Rahnee's heart—not so much fear that she would no longer be chieftess, but a deeper fear that Ice would lead the tribe to catastrophe when she was gone. The fear was enough that she violated the ways of challenge that set one will alone against another, also alone. She reached out to the tribe and sucked their minds into the vortex.

Through our ancestress, Timmain Shapeshifter, we became part of this world and through our ancestress we are not part of this world. We have always been too weak, but we could become too strong. We could become a plague upon the land if we stray too far from the narrow way between wolf and elf. We could become all that the five-fingered ones are—

And worse.

She flooded them with memories of Threetoe and the hunt, with Zarhan's memories of his father being consumed by the madness of his fire magic. She called Samael's ancient memories and showed how the five-fingered ones had driven the high ones into deeper exile, then she imagined what vengeful Wolfriders—skilled hunters, linked by magic with the wolves—could do to their enemies. She thought the images would fill them with revulsion.

She was wrong.

Our future! Ice exulted, taking her fear and making it his triumph.

Frantic, the chieftess chose a narrower focus—the weak, helpless fawns. She drew an imaginary line through all life and said it was across that line to prey upon cubs or fawns. She thought she knew her kin and her tribe. She thought that their generations of suffering had taught them compassion in their bones. And perhaps she did know them. She felt them sway toward her, then she felt her son haul them back beyond her reach.

We will not be ground down, Ice told his tribe. **If we have strength, we will use it. If we are hungry, we will eat. If we are harried, we will strike back. If our way leads to the top of the mountain, we will not turn aside.**

He held them all, and none escaped.

Discarded, Rahnee She-Wolf slumped to her knees and felt an emptiness more profound than any she had ever imagined. In the desolation she remembered all the challenges she had pursued and won—all the rebels she had cast down. A wave of nausea crashed over her and she doubled over.

Her son flipped her hair aside, baring her neck and wrenching the leather thong over her head. He slipped the metal knife from its sheath and brandished it above his head. He shouted his triumph. Rahnee could hear his words, but not his sendings.

It is the way, she shouted at herself.

The wolves showed the way in this as in all other things, and, among the wolves, the winnowing of the pack through challenge was constant. Those who had lost their strength, or had too little strength, were cast out and forgotten. They did not necessarily die, the She-Wolf reminded herself—not immediately—but they never came back.

It is the way.

Feeling returned slowly to Rahnee's arms and legs. She pushed herself upright and glanced around, careful not to see any of the Wolfriders. It was migration time and she possessed very little: a spear, a fur blanket, knapping stones, and the clothes she wore. Nothing she hadn't carried yesterday; nothing she couldn't carry today or tomorrow. She threw the knappers on the blanket, then rolled it up with thoughtless expertise.

"Where do we go?"

I don't know.

"Will we follow the deer?"

Rahnee sat back on her heels, thinking. **No . . . No, not the deer. Not in the Wolfrider wake. Not alone.**

"But you aren't alone."

Her heart skipped a beat. Zarhan's shadow lay across her still-trembling hands. Her mouth worked soundlessly. **It is the way . . . ** It was worse to have him standing there, to feel his soul and be not quite alone. **Go away. Leave me to my shame. Please?**

Fastfire tried to insert himself into his lifemate's field of vision, but she would not look up. In the end, he knelt on the opposite side of the tightly lashed blanket. **The tribe has fractured. Some go with Ice, the rest will go with you—**

It is not the way.

It has never happened before, that's all. Now it has. Now it has become the way. Can you understand that, beloved *Chieftess*? The tribe was becoming too large. You saw that when you organized the hunting *kinds*.

Rahnee shook her head. The *kinds* had come to her in wolfsong. They simply happened; she did not remember organizing anything. **Go away,** she repeated, turning away once again.

A chieftess does not abandon the tribe. Fastfire's sending contained the essence of an ice-choked stream. It was enough to rouse her to her feet. "Where do we go if we do not follow the herd?"

Retracing the migration would be the quickest way to place the greatest distance between herself and the Wolfriders, and that was the way the She-Wolf chose. Not that she gave any orders or reasons; she merely set off, not caring if anyone—wolf or rider—followed. Zarhan and the others with him exchanged anxious thoughts, but they followed her. She was their chieftess.

The day was the longest in Rahnee's memory, the antithesis of wolfsong. Yet, in other ways, not so different from wolfsong. She nurtured only two thoughts: right foot, then left foot. Head down, shoulders slumped, plodding along without vigor or interest, the She-Wolf was blind to the lay of the land and squandered her strength breaking a crude trail. At the end of the day she did not so much stop as collapse, ignoring the water and jerky her companions offered.

40

"We have made a grave error," Rellah whispered to Zarhan.

The auburn-haired elf tucked the fur blanket beneath his lifemate's chin. "How so?" he asked, leading the other elf away. "How can you tell so soon?"

"Look at her! She isn't aware of anyone or anything. She doesn't know we're with her—how can she lead us?"

"Perhaps she can't." Zarhan shrugged. "But we weren't about to stay with Ice and we all agreed that we'd be best off returning to the taiga. Where else would we be, if not right here?"

"We would not have come so far. We would have sought safer, easier passages than she's chosen. We would—"

"Then she *is* leading us, Rellah."

The old elf walked away with a grimace that conveyed equal measures of despair and irritation. Zarhan shook his head and smiled. The old ones—among whom he rarely included himself—would complain, but they wouldn't leave. Timmain's sacrifice had bound them inextricably with the Wolfriders. And his lifemate would return to her senses—being chieftess was a more comfortable burden than being alone.

Rahnee awoke when dawn was a faint glow in the eastern sky. Wind was beside her, thrusting a cold nose under her arm and concerned images into her mind. The bond between elf-friend and wolf-friend was private, not tribal. Wind would follow her to the end of the world. So long as Wind and the pack endured, the She-Wolf could not be alone.

Rahnee scratched that elusive place at the center of Wind's forehead where neither paws nor teeth could reach, then she studied this ragtag collection who called her their chieftess. A hand of old ones, another of cubs, three hands of hunters—none of them outstanding. But, then, Ice had won the challenge and these were the ones who had chosen not to stay with the victor.

The She-Wolf knew Timmorn's way, Timmain's way. Her mind told her how much they would eat, how often they must hunt, their strengths and weaknesses. Sharpears, Frost, Laststar, all firstborn like herself; Cloudclimber and

Flint, Wolfriders who harried but seldom closed for the kill; Shadowdancer, their best spearthrower, but her cub was still milk-fed. Rellah, Zarhan, New-Wolf, Changefur among the old ones, but neither Willowgreen nor Samael —neither healer nor storyteller. They would have to be careful—just as well they were headed back to the taiga; just as well Changefur knew herb lore. Just as well Wind was the undefeated chief of the pack and all the unbonded wolves came with him.

Strengths and weaknesses, taken and measured. She was chieftess again before the daystar showed crimson on the horizon.

"Wake up, you sleepyheads! We've a long way to go! Look at the sky—there's rain coming. You don't want to trek in the rain, do you?"

They all muttered against her as they rubbed their eyes and stretched their limbs, but then they always did. The despair of the previous day lessened and a trace of laughter could be felt as blankets were rolled and boots carefully laced. The She-Wolf set a gentler pace and chose a winding path that skirted both bogs and briars. When the storm rolled over them, she let them take shelter.

In time the She-Wolf brought them back to the taiga. The scars of the harsh winter were plain to see, but the small prey that slept and fed underground had not suffered as the clickdeer had. Her hunters were equal to the task of feeding her tribe. Spring became summer, and summer brought an abundance of ravvits, maskeyes, chuckers, and pouchrats. If the little band did not exactly prosper, neither was it diminished.

Rahnee found more consolation in her reduced state than she dared admit to herself or anyone else. She led each hunt herself, and the hunt was the best part of life. Racing through the brush, heart pounding and lungs burning, she could hear the wolfsong again. The haunted look left her face, and she began to relax—to forget what the Wolfriders had been like, or at least the pain of leaving them.

Her belly began to bulge, as was the way with all creatures who would soon become mothers. The She-Wolf loosened the laces of her tunic and breeches, adjusted her spear-throw to her changing shape, and intended to do nothing more. This was not her first cub, nor would it likely be her last. She would be active until the labor pangs began and, after that, she expected someone else would provide the greater portion of her cub's needs—as someone had always done with her other cubs.

It was her way, and she was unprepared for the ring of long, disapproving faces between herself and Wind.

"I'll hunt if I want to," she warned them, changing her grip on the spear as she did.

They remained silent, eyes downcast, not offering challenge, yet not moving.

"We need meat—"

"Sharpears can throw," Rellah interrupted. "He's been practicing with Shadowdancer."

Rahnee settled back on her heels. Rellah speaking for the tribe—now, *that* was unusual. Not totally unexpected, as the old one remembered Timmain and had never been completely convinced that Timmain's shapeshifting had been necessary, but unusual for exactly the same reason. Shadowdancer teaching Sharpears to throw. Well, they could use another thrower, but it was her responsibility—the chief's responsibility—to see that knowledge and skill were shared.

"Am I not your chieftess?" Her voice came from the back of her throat, with more than a hint of a growl underriding the words.

They exchanged rapid, anxious thoughts that she sensed but did not understand. They looked to Zarhan, but he was never a leader; they looked to Shadowdancer, but neither was she. Rellah cleared her throat.

"You are indeed our chieftess, She-Wolf, and that is why we must insist that you do not hunt until your time is well past and your cub welcomed to the daystar."

Rahnee was surprised past coherent speech or thought. "I do nothing that has not been done—"

"No," Rellah insisted, coupling her mind to her words as mothers did when teaching their cubs the safe ways of the world. "Our place is precarious . . . no, you have said as much yourself, Chieftess. We have not seen a winter; we have not seen a turning of the seasons. It is a time when the survival of the tribe is more important than any one hunt, or one huntress."

"The tribe will survive—"

"Not without its chief, and you are both its chieftess and the mother of its chief."

Timmain had meant her son to be chief, but Timmorn's daughter was not so confident. She had met every challenge, dominated every time save once, but she had never considered it inevitable that one of her cubs would become chief after her. "Timmorn was Timmain's only cub," she said slowly, as much to convince herself as them. "It was the way for him to become chief, as it was the way for one of his children to become chief after him. And it is the way for all cubs to be loved the same. My cubs are no different."

She sent as well as spoke, putting her wishes—a chief's command—into the thought. But its echo was hollow, even in her own mind. Could Ice have been anyone but her cub?

"It is *not* the way. It need not be the way! Any one of you could be chief instead of me!"

Zarhan could not contain a snorting laugh. He knew her best. "I think not, beloved, not so long as there was breath in your body—and you'll have to forgive us if we choose to keep our chieftess safe and healthy."

"We have no healers," Changefur added unnecessarily.

"Birthing has never troubled me."

"You won't let us take risks while hunting," quiet Flint reminded her. "Why take risks now?"

How old am I? the She-Wolf asked herself, and had no notion of the answer. *How long was I chieftess of the Wolfriders? How many challenges did I face? Did I think I had learned all I needed to know? Oh, my son, there is so much more to being the chief than you or I can ever know.*

Rahnee surrendered her killing-spear into Sharpears's keeping, warning him that she would reclaim it as soon as her cub felt the light of the daystar, hoping it would be true.

It wouldn't be long, she told herself, before the summer turned to autumn. The cub would be born in winter, and she would be free.

The She-Wolf was hunting for dreamberries with Rellah when Sharpears brought back the first mottled white ravvit. The hunters flayed it, divided up the flesh, and scraped the hide clean before she got back. No one told her about it, and it was doubtful she would have thought anything of it if they had. There were always a few animals whose fur changed while it was high summer and the cold of winter shut deep in memory.

In another moondance, when the nights had just begun to cool, almost all the ravvits were mottled, and the pouchrats, too. The hunters came to their chieftess with their fresh kills.

"What does it mean?" Cloudclimber asked.

Rahnee felt Samael's absence. The old storyteller would have brought out his sack of dreamberries and led them down the trails of memory until they all found the answer. Rellah had gathered the berries. She'd dried them, just as Samael did, and put them in a brightly painted waterproof sack, just as he did, but she wasn't Samael Storyteller. The chieftess felt the pangs of inadequacy that had, long ago, plagued her leadership.

Closing her eyes, she buried her face in the thick fur. She searched her senses for its secrets, but found only a soft scrap that might be the start of a cub's bunting.

"I don't know," she admitted.

"Isn't it early for ravvits to have mottled fur?" Zarhan asked. It was his way to make an opinion into a question, and often it annoyed Rahnee to the brink of rage.

This time she took his notion gratefully, using it to focus her own thoughts as Samael would have used the dreamberries. She tumbled back through the long turns of her life, and never encountered a summer when the ravvits had changed color so early. Never.

The She-Wolf returned the pelt to Cloudclimber. "Gather your things, as much as you can carry—especially the pelts. It's time to move."

"What's wrong?" one of the young hunters asked. "What does the ravvit tell you?"

"It tells me nothing, and I do not intend to stay where my memory is blind."

There was no autumn that turn. The trees were still green when the gray wall of winter howled down from the tundra. Paper-bark trees exploded as their sap congealed. Other trees collapsed as snow collected on their leaves. Some unfortunate animals froze with wild flowers still in their mouths—but not the ravvits, and not Rahnee's tribe.

The She-Wolf kept her tribe moving southward, slowly, steadily. They took time to hunt, and time to scrape the skins into rough-cured pelts which were swiftly worked into blankets, leggings, cloaks, and hats. No one suffered, but they looked over their shoulders toward the tundra— where the clickdeer were still on migration and where others, whose names were never mentioned, might not be so fortunate.

Once winter had arrived, it did not relax. There was no respite from the cold, yet the snow came fitfully, in small squalls that added only a finger or two to the ground accumulations. Rahnee sent her scouts out to find a cave large enough to shelter them, but they were beyond their familiar ranges and the scouts had no luck. The snow wasn't deep enough to dig a cave, nor crusty enough to sculpt into a wall. Knowing nothing better, Rahnee kept them moving, hoping that something better would appear.

The wolves came to their rescue, as they had done uncounted times since Timmain had shifted her shape. Shortly after dawn, they'd go through a frenzy of digging and shoving, piling old snow atop the new. Most times the She-Wolf put a good hike between one night's camp and the next, but one day she called a rest. At twilight the wolves went digging again, hollowing out the mounds they had made at dawn.

Flint was the first to heed his wolf-friend's urging. He lined the cavelet with blankets and curled up to sleep in a shelter scarcely larger than himself. Morning found him stiff, but warm.

Thus it was that Rahnee's cub was born in a snow womb late on a gray afternoon, after the hunters had left for the evening hunt. It was not a difficult birth—Timmain had wisely seen to that. Cubs were very small at first, and very delicate—far more delicate than either of their brethren. For several days the girl cub's eyes remained closed, her ears crimped down close to her soft skull, which retained the elongated marks of its passage into the world.

The She-Wolf tended the cub herself, totally absorbed by mote of life which had been a part of herself for so long. Zarhan Fastfire brought food and water to his lifemate, but unlike the previous birthings, he was unable to lie beside them, sharing the birthsong. The snow womb was only large enough for mother and cub. Dreamy-eyed, he leaned against the hard snow and listened at a distance as the single syllable was repeated in his mind in infinite inflections:

Kree, Kree-e-e, KREE!

Their daughter's soulname was radiant in the emptiness of time and space. For a hand of days, while she still drew strength from her mother, her world was small but perfect. Then the cub opened her eyes and saw . . . darkness. The birthsong ended, taking her soulname until the future time when she would be old enough to find it again for herself.

The cub mewed, and Rahnee thrashed her legs against the prison of the snow womb. With help from Zarhan the hardened snow was chipped away. Both mother and daughter were blinded by the light. Wind was there, his nose against the She-Wolf's cheek, taking the cub for his own, giving it the wolf pack's protection. The other adults—old ones, firstborn, and Wolfriders—touched the girl cub with their minds and were pleased with what they found. But the chieftess simply blinked and stared at the bundle in her arms.

The magic was gone, lost with the birthsong, and with it the instinct that made her mother before chieftess. All cubs looked remarkably alike once the birthsong had ended. They had downy hair and big eyes, but what she noticed most of all was their mouths—already open, waiting to be filled. She remembered the last newborn she had held, Snowflower's cub . . .

And what shall I call you, with that always-empty belly and the bright, asking eyes? Are you a gift of plenty or of famine, eh? The cub looked deep into her mother's anxious eyes. *We won't know until it's too late, will we?* The She-Wolf lifted the cub high above her head, into the light of the daystar. "I call her Brighteyes!" she proclaimed, changing her hold so the cub looked down on everyone. "Welcome the newest . . . the newest member of our family."

They knew their chieftess, and her flaws. Fastfire was there to take the newly named cub from her arms, and Shadowdancer, too. Though Shadowdancer could only hold the cub; her milk had dried and there were none beside Rahnee herself who could feed the cub, unless they gave her to the wolves. The chieftess said nothing.

Does it bother you so much? Zarhan asked gently, guiding her away for a moment's solitude.

I remember Selnac, and how she despaired that there was no birthsong at all. Then you showed me where to find my soulname, and I thought everything would be all right . . . What did you hear?

It was difficult to dissemble while sending, and impossible to lie to Rahnee when she put an edge on her thoughts. **I heard what you heard.**

Where is the other half? What have I done wrong that none who have been born since I became chieftess have heard the full measure of their name?

He took her in his arms, pressing her head against his shoulder, but he did not answer.

The chieftess tended the cub herself. She watched as the gray eyes became flecked with violet like her own and the glimmerings of independence and temper flashed in those same bright eyes. The old ones fashioned a sling for her and she carried the cub above one slender hip. The infant learned to be quiet while her mother hunted, and learned not to move when the spear was thrown.

The She-Wolf pushed the tribe south again and again, retreating a little farther as each storm loomed on the northward horizon. They were below the brush forest of the taiga where the deer wintered and into high canopy forest where branch-horns were the largest deer and white-tails the most numerous.

Very little time passed before the wolves accommodated themselves to the smaller, more agile white-tails. They forgot that they had grown up chasing the vast herd of clickdeer. The wolf-bonded hunters followed the same course, slipping into wolfsong as patterns reestablished themselves in their lives. Each dawn Zarhan looked into his lifemate's eyes to see if the fires of perception had been banked.

Rahnee felt his curiosity, and bore it without explanation. The malaise that had begun when she and her cub left the snow womb held the wolfsong at bay, and she allowed it to dominate her thoughts. Where had *Kreanne* gone? Why had *Kree* appeared in her place? The names she and Zarhan heard in creation between them were always elfin names, but cubs were born knowing only half. And they didn't find the other half on their name-quests, either, if Samael's gentle probings on her behalf had discovered the truth.

Wolfsong was a mystery to those who never heard it, but it admitted no mysteries within its chorus. It sang of contentment, of a wholesome lack of variety, of a healthy ignorance toward that which could not be known or explained. But so long as Rahnee felt her cub riding on her hip, wolfsong had no place in her life.

The wind shifted, bringing storms from a different quarter of the horizon. It was still cold, but the silhouettes of the trees changed as the tips of their branches swelled.

"We will find the clickdeer," Rahnee said when she had gathered her followers for the feast. "We will find the Wolfriders."

She was their chieftess. There was no way she could not feel the relief and joy that spread around her. The rift between herself and Ice had shattered *kinds,* families, and friendships. Everyone had left someone behind. Everyone

49

hoped, even within wolfsong, that the tribe might still be put to rights—though no wolf had ever rejoined the pack.

There were no laggards when the She-Wolf took her bearings to begin the journey. It was as if a storm-dam had finally burst and a stream allowed to resume its age-old course. Rahnee knew she was not truly leading them.

Ice would not be glad to see her, nor would she have the strength to take the tribe away from him. She did not—and she knew it—desire to lead the tribe again. All she desired was the answer to a single question: Do your cubs know themselves completely? If the answer was yes—and she prayed that it would be—she would leave all her followers, including her cub and her lifemate, behind forever.

The fires of perception burned very bright each time she took her lifemate in her arms or held her cub at her breast. She would not lose their last moondances together to the vagueness of wolfsong. Her need for sensation was ferocious, her appetite for love was insatiable. Fastfire, who knew her well, began to suspect, but she held him off.

The old ones were the first to touch the Wolfriders. All were alive, all were well, they reported, but they would say nothing more. The younger ones were satisfied with this, and content to wait until eyes and hands could mend the tattered edges of their friendships. Rahnee, though she traveled in the bleak silence of exile, knew there was more, but as she kept secrets from Zarhan, so he and the other old ones kept their secrets from her.

They entered the open forests of the taiga. Dormant instincts awakened and the She-Wolf broke their journey to hunt the clickdeer again. The tang of the herd tickled their noses, but they had been gone too long for anyone to say if it was stronger or weaker than it should have been in the last dance of winter. It was enough to set the deer to flight, separate the stragglers, and bring down the weakest. The meat was as potent as dreamberries.

Each night brought Rahnee's band palpably closer to the Wolfrider camp. Each twilight she expected to meet their hunters and scouts. They found and followed a trail that was well marked by both elf and wolf. The night breeze brought the scent of meat being smoked for the migration journey. But Ice held his tribe close and no one came out to greet them.

Wind sank on his haunches and howled, another wolf answered with a clear warning. The packs would come no closer to each other. Rahnee's fingers were bloodless and trembling, but she rubbed her forehead against the wolf's and told him she would be safe while he waited.

Ice kept a dark camp. There were no fires or lamps to define its edges, and it nestled in the shadow of a high escarpment. An ice-free torrent stream protected its front and sides. By moonlight it was difficult to tell anything more, but had the former chieftess of the Wolfriders felt the need to protect her tribe from enemies, she could not have chosen a better place. There was no easy entrance.

Call them, she ordered her followers. **Surely they do not soak themselves after every hunt.**

Activity erupted on the far side of the stream.

"There's a log crossing far to the left, against the rocks. They say we may use it," Rellah said in a carefully neutral voice. "Do you want to go first?"

"Shouldn't I?" the She-Wolf snapped back as she stomped across the snow. Fluidly she unslung her second-best spear and held it upside down just above the flint. **Make me a fire,** she sent back to Zarhan. **I want to see their faces.**

A globe of foxfire flared at the butt of the spear. Her son was waiting, a black force that held her in exile, and she was glad of the light. Still, she could not see the far end of the log when Ice ordered her to stop.

"Why have you come?" he demanded.

"I have a question—"

"I will give you your answer: The others may stay, but you may not."

She felt the log shift as someone stepped on it, then the chief came into the light. It was Ice. Even estranged and locked in silence as she was, she would always know him, but it would have been easier without the light. His face was covered with dark scars that could only have been

51

deliberately inflicted. His hair was stiffened and stood out from his face like a menacing cloud. Rahnee recognized her son, but there was nothing familiar about him.

"That was not my question," the She-Wolf said, mastering her heart's pounding.

He took the question from her mind. His lips twisted into a smile that revealed his teeth. "I am called Wolfrider now, as is my right."

Rahnee risked no reply, but deep within marveled at his strength, and the madness that had overtaken him. She longed to see the others, but any move, even a hint of curiosity, would be a challenge, so she lowered her eyes and acknowledged his name.

"You may return when the moons are dark and I may give you your answer."

The rest of her band was behind her now. They could see what she saw, feel what she felt, and perhaps a bit more. Whatever, they weren't pressing forward. The stalemate lasted a few heartbeats, then the foxfire in Rahnee's spear exploded. It reappeared on the leveled spears of the hunters who stood behind her son. For a moment she saw their hard, scarred faces, then, like a spark in the wind, the fires vanished.

"You can leave now," Ice's voice came through the darkness.

The chieftess felt the doubts and apprehension of her band, and, despite that, their desire to share with those they had left behind. "We have come a long way, surely you will share your hunting and feasting with old friends?" There was no answer. "I shall return at moonsdark," Rahnee said as she took a careful step backward.

Her own band parted. Their hands and minds brushed against her as she slipped through them. *You are our chieftess. Wait for us. Guard our wolf-friends. Do not leave without us.* They filed across the logs until only Zarhan stood on the far bank beside her chief.

"Does my father not wish to sit beside his son?"

The She-Wolf's breath caught in her throat. She caught her hand and held it, lest it betray her by clinging to

Fastfire's sleeve. In their long turns together she had never taken his loyalty for granted, but neither had she told him how much she needed him.

"I would have my father sit beside me!"

Go! Rahnee lock-sent.

I would rather not—

I'll be safe enough until moonsdark. Go—

What of *my* wishes?

Not now, beloved. Please, not now!

He left her, and the darkness became total.

With the cub, Brighteyes, still snug and sleeping against her hip, Rahnee trudged away from Wolfrider's camp. Wind found her before she'd found a resting place. She told him she could not stay with the others, but must return when the moons were dark. He understood the leaving— instincts had already told him to take his pack far from this place—but he could not understand the return.

The wolf could not use words, but his sendings were eloquent without them. What had been, was no longer. Where there had been self, there was no longer self. Where there had been pack-friends, there was nothing. It was time to leave.

But I must have the answer to my question. If my son's tribe knows its name, then I can accept that my time is over, but if they don't—

Wind took her wrist between his teeth and shook it gently but firmly. He was no less a chief than she. The wolfsong sang his rights and obligations. An ordinary wolf heard only the wolfsong from one end of his life to the other. Wind could feel his elf-friend's doubts, but, though she was the center of his life, he would not let her draw him into her agonies. Wolves did not try to guess the final chords of their song.

A wolf's jaws could crush her bones to useless pulp. Their wolf-friends had never hurt them, but when Wind growled deep in his throat, Rahnee heeded the warning. She could not think of anything else, but she could—and did—stop thinking altogether.

He led her to the pack, where they crowded around her and the cub. They kept the She-Wolf warm through the long, cold night, and calmed her with the unity of their thought. At dawn he nipped their flanks and got them moving away from the territory of a pack he no longer recognized as kin.

Leaving her spears behind, the She-Wolf lost herself with the wolves. The moons danced among the stars. They grew full faces, circled each other, then the Mother Moon turned away and the Cub began to arch inward. Rahnee shook the snow from her clothes and pushed her tangled hair away from her face.

We go now, she sent to the wolves.

Wind pawed the snow. His elf-friend went against wolfsong. His shoulders hunched, his lips curled back from gleaming fangs, and his head thrashed from side to side. Wind's instinct could not choose between challenge and submission, so she made the choice for him by walking slowly away. He let her get out of sight; then, when it was his decision again, he led the pack after her.

They came to Wolfrider's camp by full daylight. From another part of the escarpment Rahnee could see how much larger it was than anything she had ever felt necessary. It was orderly, structured, and abandoned. A few figures were huddled in the pit of what had been a good-sized den. She recognized her lifemate by his flaming hair.

What's happened? she sent across the valley.

A bolt of relief too heartfelt for words shot back at her. Zarhan's thoughts blended with a dozen others. Images blurred in her mind's eye, and for her own well-being she walled them off until she could sort them out with her other senses.

The crossing logs had been upended. Rahnee was obliged to pick her way across the stream, straining her concentration between the slick stones and the clamor in her mind. She slipped and was up to her knees in cold water before regaining her balance.

"Silence!" she screamed with her voice and mind.

Shamed by her outburst, they huddled closer together, like orphaned cubs. Only her lifemate had the confidence or courage to approach her once she reached the bank. He took her in his arms, holding her as though they had been separated by far more than a moondance. And because the unity of his elfin nature was as soothing as wolfsong, the chieftess surrendered to him . . . for a moment.

Her back stiffened and she pushed him thoughtlessly away. That sorry lot she could see beyond his shoulders needed her. They were followers and she was a chief; nothing could be simpler.

The silence she had commanded remained unbroken even while she stood in their midst, looking down on their faces. There were Rellah and Changefur, cowered against Talen, who had been with Ice, and the three of them looking like they'd lost their names. There was Samael Dreamkeeper, pale and ancient-seeming. Indeed, all the old ones were here, except for Willowgreen, the healer. Lapwing had joined her, along with Sweetbark, Weaver, and a hand of others whom—the She-Wolf realized with a shudder—she could not recognize in the silence.

She had led her tribe through hunger, storm, and myriad disasters, but she was two generations removed from the despair that had led Timmain to seek new vitality among the wolves. Her imagination could summon no catastrophe sufficient to account for these hollow faces and empty eyes.

Brighteyes woke up. In a flash of inspiration, Rahnee loosened the sling and thrust the youngling into Samael's limp arms. She tucked his soft, gray hair behind his ears and looked into his eyes. The balance shifted within him; faint life returned to his eyes. He held the cub close in his arms.

Then the chieftess saw Flint. Short, stocky Flint who was best at nothing, but who never ceased from trying. Flint, whose soul was fragile and with whom a chief must tread carefully lest it shatter beyond all repair. Flint, whose chest was bandaged, whose leg was bound with a splint, whose right eye was swollen shut, and whose cheek was slashed with an ugly black line. The She-Wolf knelt before him and cupped his ravaged face gently in her hands. Her mind touched his with the gentlest caress—and found only a brittle shell.

Who did this! Who? How? Why was this done to one of mine!

Fire blazed in violet eyes, but none could, or would, answer her until Samael rose stiffly to his feet.

"Wolf . . . Your . . . It was Ice's honor to the hunters, to mark their face with the juice of dreamberries so . . . so they would not forget . . ." His voice was weak, as well it might be. Only he knew how to make the potent beverage; this could not have been done without his help.

"And Flint?" The She-Wolf allowed none of the mercy she felt in her heart to emerge in her voice.

"He wanted to be accepted. He . . . he went out to hunt with them . . . as you had hunted with wolves and spears. But that is not the way now—not Ice's way. The hunter . . . killer now . . . must stalk the proud ones, the antlered ones, and kill with his hands alone." There were tears in the old elf's eyes as he handed the cub back to her mother and turned away.

"Rotting, dung-eating fools!" she shouted past the camp, then she remembered the web of scars on her son's face and on the faces of the hunters who surrounded them. Fools—yes, but successful fools. These were the losers, the ones who had fallen from her son's way. These were the ones who would follow her as the hunt had followed her father.

She threw back her head and howled until the rage left her and she collapsed in the midst of her forlorn tribe. She would have followed Flint into nothingness, but the wolfsong called her back. Wind did not *choose* to be pack-chief; he *was* pack-chief. As long as there was a tribe beside her, Rahnee would be chieftess. She pulled herself upright.

"What of my question?" she demanded. "Did he answer my question?"

They stared at her with uncomprehending eyes, then Zarhan was behind her, his hands resting on her shoulders. **He laughed, and said it did not matter.**

But did he answer?

Beloved, he no longer hears his own name . . . Isn't that answer enough?

Before she could reply, someone else touched her arm.

"May we leave this place now?" Shadowdancer asked.

Her face was marked, too, though the cut was almost healed—or as healed as it would ever be. Rahnee touched the other woman's face where the black line crossed her cheekbone. There were many things she would never know about the days and nights her tribe had spent here; many questions her wolfsong would not allow her to ask. Another hand touched her. The She-Wolf looked down into a cub's eyes.

"*Wolfs?*" the cub asked brightly, pointing across the stream where Wind had brought the pack. "*Wolfs!*"

"Wolves," the chieftess agreed. She settled the cub above her empty hip and headed for the bank.

They returned to the deep forest where there was little to remind them of vast herds. The trees grew green and the hunting was good. Samael scoured the clearings for dreamberry bushes, but though he gathered and dried the berries in the warm sunlight, he told no stories. Those who could escape their sadness in wolfsong did so—putting empty memories between themselves and what had happened in the northern taiga.

The leaves turned scarlet and gold, then fell and were buried by the first snows. Rahnee led her tribe into an abandoned cave where they could wait for spring's return. She listened to the wolfsong now, and Zarhan passed his time with the old ones or Shadowdancer. Both Rellah and Changefur were brooding, and those who could not cling to wolfsong hoped a healer might be born the next summer.

The old differences reemerged. Wolves and Wolfriders were active at dawn and dusk; the old ones tended their crafts by daylight. Without Samael's stories to bring them together, they drifted apart, yet the wounds were healing and the old elf had amassed three fat sacks of berries for a brighter future.

It was midafternoon. Weak light made its way to the

center of the cave, where the old ones were scraping pelts from the most recent hunt. The chieftess and the other hunters were napping with the wolves deeper in the cave where the light would not bother them. Fastfire sat just outside the cave, one arm around Shadowdancer and the other tending his fire. With two of their own kind breeding, the old ones had returned to cooking everything they ate.

Everyone was caught in private thoughts or dreams when the soundless scream shattered the peace in every soul. It transfixed them with its horror. There were no adults in the cave who had not felt Recognition's tug; there were no strangers to death among them. But this was more than the agonizing moment of a soul's departure. The patch of light crept out of the cave, and the scream continued. The wolves nudged their elf-friends, then left reluctantly to hunt.

Day had ended before the rending stopped. The ensuing silence was almost worse. They reached for each other in the darkness.

What was that?

Are you there? **And you?** **And you?**

Who was that?

Chieftess . . . ? Chieftess . . . ? *Chieftess!*

The She-Wolf swallowed the bile that had collected in the back of her throat. She dragged her stone-useless body to the center of the cave where Zarhan had ignited a small fire. Her tongue was thick and the water was too bitter to bring relief. Planting her spear against the rock, she pushed herself to her feet. Her blood fell and the flames swirled before her eyes.

"We must leave," she gasped, steadying herself with the spear. "Now."

They could not leave, not that night or the next. Rellah and Changefur could not stand, much less walk, and the two whose faces were marked with black stared straight ahead without seeing anything. Rahnee alone had the strength and the desire to trek north to the scream's source.

Wind went with her, and all the unbonded wolves, so she was hardly alone or in danger as she plowed ahead. The dense forest offered some protection from the storms that rolled down from the north, but all too soon they were into the sparser growth of the taiga. They skirted snowdrifts that were as tall as the trees, and hunted with ease. It was a sorry feasting. There were clickdeer carcasses in the lee of almost every tree, each skeleton-gaunt, empty-gutted, and riddled with disease.

Rahnee's heart ached each time they came upon a staggering doe, though she knew it was a mercy to put the creature down before starvation did. If there were healthy deer, she did not see them. But it wasn't the death of the herd that had reached down to her tribe in its cave. Arrow-true, the chieftess and her wolves kept to their course.

Snow was blowing in their faces when they reached the bluff overlooking her son's camp. A hand of storms had blurred the outlines of the catastrophe, but enough could be read by one with the eyes to see it. As the clickdeer herd had shrunk, predators had grown fat and lazy. They had also been forced closer together.

Timmain's descendants could face down any wolf pack, but there were other predators whose challenges were not so easily met. Great bears and long-tooth cats were solitary hunters who, though they gave no ground, would not usually attack first. Still, even a winter-turn ago, something had made her son claim this shelf of land for his camp.

The She-Wolf flared her nostrils, drawing the snowy air into her lungs. Wind circled around her legs and the other wolves broke into short, anxious howls. She ruffled the coarse hair behind his ears.

Wait here if you wish. I won't be long.

Wolfrider's tribe had not gone quietly. Snow-covered mounds on the far side of the stream leaked death-scent. An ice-crusted paw the size of her head thrust out from the boulders in the middle of the stream. Rahnee crossed carefully, without looking into the dark water. There was no way, though, that she could not see the carnage of the camp itself, not if she were to find what had drawn her here.

Bears had found them, by the way the dens had been crushed and swept aside. More of the awesome creatures than the She-Wolf ever wished to see in one place. She could only guess what had bound them together in an attack; perhaps the neat rows of meat-drying racks had proved irresistible. She could not eliminate the chance that her son had challenged them as he had challenged everything else.

Tears froze on her eyelashes as she stumbled toward the middle of the camp. She could feel them now, the lingering traces of soul-spirit that had not been swept away in the scream. Tamsen, Jerem, Olwun, the infant, Kara. The names sifted through her fingers as she dug through the fresh snow. One name, of course, was not there, but her son was proud, even in death. He was a chief, too. He had led his tribe to death, and led it beyond death.

Rahnee's numb fingers found the unyielding mass they sought. She yanked with all her strength and brought Ice's mangled body into the fading daylight. There was no soothing the blue-lipped snarl on his lips, or closing the whitened eyes. Timmain's knife was frozen to the great wound that had killed him. Her hands closed over it, needing it, yet unwilling to break it free as she must.

"Grandmother! How could you let this happen? Where is your way in this?"

"There was no stopping it once it had begun—once he had been born."

Utterly startled by the voice, the chieftess fell forward. The little knife came free. She saw Willowgreen, but could not shape the healer's name with voice or thought. Like a frightened cub, she scrambled backward when the apparition reached out to touch her, then she mastered her fear and froze with wide, distrusting eyes.

"I'm not like you," Willowgreen insisted, kneeling down in the snow. "I'm no fighter. When the bears came, I drew my scent in and hid beneath the snow. I haven't the courage to face death."

"You knew I would come?" Rahnee asked, and felt foolish as she did.

"No. I knew you were coming, but I didn't know you would come. At the time I just didn't want to be killed. I didn't think how I would die once I was alone. Once there was nothing left to scavenge."

"There are . . . no others, just you?"

The healer nodded. "It was a challenge, Chieftess, you should know that, at least. Wolfrider would never be content with what he had. Never. That was why it had to end this way. I had hoped—even Samael hoped at the beginning—that we could steer him." She shook her head and stared down at her hands.

"You mean heal him, don't you? You thought you could have what Timmain had gotten from the wolves, but heal us from the wolfsong."

Willowgreen did not need to answer.

"Without the wolfsong, we're not elves, and we're less than wolves."

"But the Wolfriders are not whole, either. You must know that. Zarhan took you beyond the wolfsong to find your name. You *know* what they're missing."

Rahnee shed her fear in a single sigh. She reached across her son's body to take the healer's hands between her own. "You didn't listen, did you? You heard them die, but you did not listen."

"I heard the pain, the dying . . . The failure of our hopes."

"There was no failure. My son found what he was searching for, but it was not here, not on the world of two moons." She stood up, bringing Willowgreen with her. "Come, it is time for us who belong here to go home."

61

Wind Warning

by Katharine Eliska Kimbriel

Wind curled along her forearm, its touch tingling in the aftermath of evening rain. Inhaling deeply, relishing the sharp, heady aura of the source of her tribal name, Windwhisper reached for her spear and soundlessly rose to her feet. Sinking Child moon cast fitful light through the ragged clouds, stippling the trees with silver as a shadow detached itself from the surrounding hollows. A cold nose touched the elf's hand momentarily, and a crystal thought caressed her mind: **Food.** Nightshadow's sending was very clear, an image of a fat wattle-neck with neck broken by powerful jaws.

Smiling faintly, Windwhisper let agreement filter through the wolfsong as she started down the trail, facing into the wind. It was the half-light before dawn, her favorite time for stalking, and dreams would not let her sleep. With the deer hunters still days away, the others would be grateful for whatever she brought back to the caves. No Wolfrider ate small game when deer was available, but almost anything was better than fish . . . and it had been fish for many days now.

It was spring sickness that drove her into the damp ground cover. Several children and old ones had finally succumbed to the fevers and aching that seemed to arrive with the thaw. The healer had done what she could for them, with her powders and teas, but there had been little improvement. Finally Windwhisper had swallowed her shyness and asked the aloof elf-woman if different food might help.

Dealing with the old ones and their children was hard, doubly so when Prey-Pacer was off with the hunters.

Willowgreen had turned a hard eye on the delicate Wolfrider, a calculating eye. *She does not forgive*, Windwhisper thought to herself, even now, days later. But whatever her private anger, Willowgreen had admitted that variety in diet would tempt appetites. Convincing a cranky child to eat was a battle, and the cubs did not have much flesh to lose, not at the end of the long cold.

Yesterday it had been ravvit, thin after a hard winter, but more than acceptable. She had caught two hands of the rodents, seven mature and one second-winter, and they had made a nourishing stew. Although she wrinkled her nose at the memory of the meal, Windwhisper was grateful that New-Wolf was skilled at stretching a kill as far as it would go. This time she was determined there would be hot, fresh meat for everyone—enough for them to roast old Talen his own bird, for the ancient elves liked their meat singed by fire. Yes, despite the troubles, the forest blushed with the promise of spring, and she rather thought today would be good hunting.

Moving slowly, silently, the wolf Nightshadow paused, ears alert. Familiar sounds reached the pair of hunters. Suntails. Not as big as wattle-neck, but easier to kill, if they could be caught on the ground. If only they were busy feeding . . . Peering through a bush studded with pale green leaves, Windwhisper shoved back a long lock of black hair that had escaped her braid and searched the clearing for her prey. Ah, many of them, all males, scratching for new bugs and old seeds.

Not scratching. Milling, more like, as confused as deer when skyfire struck a tree. This gave her pause, her sending clamping down on Nightshadow's eagerness. No, there were no big cats, and certainly no five-fingers, not this far north. The wolf seemed oblivious to whatever had frightened the birds. She could sense nothing that should give them unease—except the wind. It smelled different, a difference she could not give a name to.

Nightshadow's churning hunger thrust itself into her mental ramblings, disturbing her musings. Owl pellets.

Letting her mind drift, her wolf's intent woven about them both, Windwhisper cast her spear with fine instinct, her accuracy matched by few among the Wolfriders.

Suddenly her world came apart. The lurch to her stomach was real, not dream, even as a familiar nightmare feeling raked across her consciousness, drowning her in a sensation of swirling heat. Force slammed into her mind, actually knocking her off her feet, and as the birds rose in frenzy before her, she heard Nightshadow's howl echo through the trees. Windwhisper lashed out blindly with her arm.

Finally she could see again. Thrashing form resolved itself into a struggling bird, elf fingers tightly clasped around its neck. Her spear had also struck true—the impaled suntail was dead. Startled, Windwhisper twisted quickly, breaking the neck of the creature she held before it could scratch with its talons. Only then did she lift her head, seeking Nightshadow.

A darker presence within the gloom, the black wolf came toward her, whining a protest. Dropping the bird, Windwhisper reached for her, wondering if her dreams had finally reached her wolf. But dreams could not knock a person to the ground . . . Trembling, Nightshadow pressed close, almost crawling into the elf's lap. Worried, Windwhisper let her thoughts touch her wolf-friend, radiating calm and safety. This was out of character for the big female; Windwhisper could not remember ever seeing her wolf disconcerted, much less frightened. Nightshadow recently became alpha female of the pack upon Foxtail's ascension, and feared little short of a long-tooth.

Still standing. Bright images filtered into Windwhisper's mind, and she realized the wolf had a different understanding of what had happened. Unease, masked by hunger but now foremost in her mind. Sound even an elf could not hear—Windwhisper knew by the tilt of the animal's head she was hearing *something*. Nightshadow had not lost her balance during . . . during what? More rain coming, the sky rumbling with it? Had skyfire struck close by?

Motionless, they waited as moments passed. Nothing.

64

Finally Windwhisper slowly stood, grabbing the two birds as she rose. A third suntail lay dead, its throat ripped. Windwhisper indicated that Nightshadow should eat the bird. Maybe food would calm her.

They shared the meal, as they shared everything, but food did not noticeably relax the wolf. Her agitation was no greater, no less. The mood growing on Windwhisper was not comforting. She had reason to fear; Prey-Pacer did not like her hunting alone, but both striplings who enjoyed haunting her tracks were ill.

You are not strong enough. Her chief's blunt words came back with brutal clarity. A death sentence, that—she was too fragile to join the hunters, too frightened to learn from the elders. More elf than wolf—much more; only her mother's mother, Rahnee the She-Wolf, had claimed a share of Timmain's sacrifice. Part wolf—not much, but enough. Enough that three previous wolves and now Nightshadow had chosen her, though the choosing had surprised both the old ones and the Wolfriders.

Not enough of either. The thought nipped at her, darting among other musings and disrupting them. Thinking to submerge herself in the comfort of wolfsong, Windwhisper strung the remaining suntails on a thong and slipped it over one shoulder. No one could deny her skill with a spear, and right now skill, not brute strength, was what was needed. The leaders of her tribe were far away, which meant there were only the old ones to deal with . . . and silence could deal with them. It was a fine veil of silence, like Willowgreen's pride; but a poor mask last winter, and growing weaker every day.

It was elf magic, these dreams, Windwhisper felt certain of it. What to do about it? Suddenly nervous, she sprang to her feet, nostrils wide and seeking. No, no danger. Why did the wolfsong not soothe? Shaking off a sudden impulse to return to the camp and seek Talen or New-Wolf, the elf seized her spear and moved on through the clearing.

Surely the spirit of Timmain hovered over them that morning. Even after stuffing Nightshadow's belly, a full three hands of kill remained: more suntails, a few wattle-necks, and a fat cackler, newly arrived from the south. Most of the pack had gone with the hunters, and there were no litters at present—twelve birds for the tribe! Ignoring her own exhaustion, she exuberantly lifted her low voice in a howl, crowing their success at the hunt. That odor again, what was that . . . ?

The ground shrugged beneath her, and Windwhisper collapsed into a tight ball as vision flared in her mind. Like the old ones' fires, only more, much more, filling her sight, swirling and rolling like New-Wolf's cauldron. Twigs peppered her delicate form as the trees exploded from motion. Hysterical birds and squirrels careened in all directions, the air heavy with the chaotic vibrations of mass exodus. Windwhisper felt an odd sensation within, as if her stomach had flipped over, and then everything returned to normal.

Enough. Although the forest looked as it should, the birds were still distressed, crashing madly into things as they avoided touching anything solid. Projecting an image of the Wolfriders' cave to her frenzied companion, Windwhisper heaved her line of birds across her back and started for the stream.

She speared two more suntails that were flopping aimlessly along the trail—protecting nests? No, they were first-winter males, and she did not hesitate to take them along. Only the strongest should father the next generation. There was a wolf remaining in camp, Mist's companion Darkwater, for Mist had been gored by a stag during a desperate stalk last Mother moon, and she was not yet strong enough to rejoin the hunters. The she-wolf would not leave her chosen rider, not even to join Windwhisper and Nightshadow on their journeys. Surely Darkwater was tired of eating the rodents near the campsite, and would appreciate a suntail of her own.

Despite the clouds, daylight had finally come, though the path was still in shadow. Pausing by the source of the stream, a gurgling spring, Windwhisper dropped her burdens and reached into the water to wash away both dirt and

66

exhaustion. What swirled across her palms surprised her, and she stared. It was muddy! But the spring itself was never muddy, not near these rocks. This was underground water, coming from deep within the land. Prey-Pacer himself had sought the beginnings of its flow, and in vain. The source was never muddy, whatever happened to the stream itself.

Fear stabbed through her. This was bad, very bad, and the chief was not here to deal with it. Leaving the final suntail impaled on her spear, realizing with a start that she had broken off the point of her flint, Windwhisper seized the string of birds and rushed toward the cave.

Darkwater greeted them at the foot of the path, eager for the company of others of her *kind*. Pulling the still-warm bird from her spear, Windwhisper tossed the wolf the kill. At first the female would not touch it, deferring to Nightshadow's superior status, but Nightshadow, her belly full, ignored the suntail. Only then did Darkwater gleefully seize the bird, carrying it up the path.

Mist—Darkwater brings you a surprise. Amusement tinged Windwhisper's sending as she momentarily pushed aside the disturbing morning.

A shriek erupted from the path above, and Windwhisper quickly started for the cave. "It's all right, I gave it to her," she called, certain she knew what had provoked the cry. Rounding the turn, she saw New-Wolf at the wide mouth of the cave, on her feet and looking within.

"A suntail! Darkwater has a suntail!" the elf-woman blurted out, sheer envy in her eyes. Windwhisper could not resist; moving up next to the willowy New-Wolf, she pulled the string from her back and held it out. Carcasses hung its entire length, as long as Windwhisper was tall. New-Wolf could only stare.

"We won't miss it," Windwhisper assured her, and was engulfed in a rare elfin hug.

"Child, it's a feast! I can use a whole one for broth, for Talen and the little ones!" **Rellah, come help!**

As New-Wolf sent her clear thought in search of the

elder, Windwhisper knew it was time to retreat. Taking one of the suntails from the string, she started into the cave. She and Mist would eat as they preferred, fresh from the kill, and the others could simmer and roast as they—

Vertigo seized her. A terrifying impression of falling stone flickered before her eyes, and with a shriek Windwhisper threw up her arms, waiting for death. Several moments passed before she lifted her head. New-Wolf was suddenly next to her, offering an arm in support.

Did you slip? The stones are wet— The first-comer knelt beside her, offering familiar comfort. New-Wolf had raised her after her mother had died, and still seemed fond of her former charge, even despite the wolf-blood that separated them.

"No," Windwhisper croaked. "I am fine. New-Wolf, did anything odd happen here this morning?"

"Odd?" The elf frowned slightly. "No, nothing I would call odd—except that I noticed the stream has stayed muddy. Usually it clears a few hours after light rain. But I heard thunder earlier; it must be raining nearby."

"Thunder." Her voice sounded stupid to her own ears. Windwhisper reached for the suntail she had dropped, and climbed to her feet. "Of course. Just thunder."

"Dry warning, perhaps. It is more common in the hot season." This was from regal Rellah, coming from the depths of the cave. "We need more wood in back, Murrel. Talen is cold again." Then she saw the dead bird.

"Windwhisper had a *very* good hunt," New-Wolf told her, answering to her true-name without comment. "I'll need help plucking. Treehopper will get you some wood, I am sure. We'll promise him a cackler leg!"

Aware that Rellah's eyes were still upon her, Windwhisper slipped around the tall elf-woman and penetrated the darkness of the cavern.

Ask Willowgreen which bird would make the best broth for Talen. Rellah's crystal thought followed Windwhisper, scratching her mind. The young Wolfrider suspected that she bore up under the true elves' sendings better than any of her Wolfrider kin, but even she winced from Rellah. There was a hardness about her, as if her heart was made of stone.

She found the invalids to one side of the cave, behind an outcropping of rock. Talen and Mist were behind the small fire, Willowgreen at the old one's side, while the children snuggled closer to the niche's entrance. Darkwater had actually brought the bird to Mist and was helping her devour it. Strange that the wolf would enter the cave; Nightshadow had remained outside. The wolves did not like the big cavern shared by the elves, preferring their own dens in the rocks above the stream.

Opening her mouth to speak, Windwhisper thought better of it and sent a private, narrow thought to Willowgreen. **We have suntail, wattle-neck, and cackler. Which would be best for the broth?** No sense in exciting the children, she decided.

A toss of golden hair, and the healer's willow-green eyes met Windwhisper's black ones. Lifted eyebrows meant that Willowgreen had been interrupted while in a healing trance; her relaxing spine meant that Windwhisper would be forgiven the intrusion. **Wattle-neck makes a richer, more nourishing soup, but suntail is most flavorful.**

Suntail? Even in his weakened state, Talen's strong mind grasped the quiet thoughts. Windwhisper's eyes narrowed as she looked at him. Thin, more than ever, but holding on to life. Surely he would recover. The true elves were eldest—the old ones, Wolfriders called them—but Talen never changed. He looked no older than the chief, and Talen was an elder before Prey-Pacer was born.

Yes, Talen, suntail. Do not wake the children! Windwhisper glanced at Willowgreen again, but the healer had unfolded her long legs and walked away without a word. Sighing, Windwhisper sat down next to Mist and savagely began plucking feathers. They made lovely patterns on the tunics . . .

"Don't mind her," Mist whispered, offering her a leg of the other suntail. "I really think she is jealous of you. You aren't that much different, but the wolves like you."

Accepting the leg with a nod of thanks, Windwhisper bit

into it, teeth holding it tightly as she continued plucking. Setting her fair head against Darkwater's flank for comfort, Mist seemed not offended that Windwhisper did not answer.

We should be friends. Windwhisper could not say it to Mist, for Mist would not understand. But there it was; could Mist be correct? Windwhisper was only an eighth wolf, while fair Willowgreen was the healer's daughter, and no wolf-blood ran in her veins. Dark and light, they were, Willowgreen as blond as Windwhisper was dark, but the difference ended there. Thinking hard about it, Windwhisper decided that the healer was a half head taller; otherwise their delicate, graceful forms were the same. *I am Wolfrider, and she fears the wolves. She embraces the teachings of the old ones, while I merely fear what they might teach me.*

Would the wolves abandon her if she grew to understand what was churning within her? Clearing a large patch of feathers, she tore off one suntail leg and returned Mist's offer, which the maiden eagerly accepted. *Willowgreen and I are more alike than different. I thought it was because I shunned Rellah's words.* Why would anyone favored by the healing power envy another of the tribe?

Discarding the jumble of thoughts, Windwhisper leaned over and asked Mist's opinion about her broken spear point.

Once more that day the stomach-churning sensation struck Windwhisper, but she did not speak of it. Even if it had resembled illness, she would have had to be very sick indeed before she approached Willowgreen. Not one to turn up her nose at prevention, though, Windwhisper did drink some of the smelly tea the healer was foisting on the tribe. Perversely annoyed at the others, Windwhisper chose to spend the day with Nightshadow, seeking sleep where the wolves laired.

Darkness found her wide awake as the true elves sought their rest. Now was the time she missed the Wolfriders most—the long hours until moonrise, and then longer until the sun returned. There was no denying her irritation; she was angry because the others seemed oblivious to what was troubling her. If this was elf magic, then why didn't Talen or Rellah notice it? If it was natural, why didn't the wolves have some buried knowledge of it? Both Nightshadow and Darkwater seemed aware of her bouts of vertigo—anticipated them, even—but now quietly lay by her side at the entrance to the cavern.

It was a puzzle.

You cannot run from it. The thought was faint, but very clear. Windwhisper lifted her head, startled. It was Talen, his sending stronger than she had expected. Perhaps his fever had broken. Standing, Windwhisper moved into the cave.

Huddled bundles of darkness were barely outlined by the banked fire which glowed by Talen's feet. Windwhisper sat near his head and took his wrist, as she had seen Willowgreen often do. Blood pulsed normally through his veins, and the skin was no longer damp. Windwhisper knew enough about illness to understand that Talen's fever was fading.

Shall I wake Willowgreen? she asked the elf courteously.

Not necessary. But you could put a few chips on the fire.

This was not to her liking; Wolfriders avoided fire whenever possible, except when they were very damp, but Talen rarely asked for favors. Windwhisper blew carefully on the fire, setting a few dried leaves upon it. Only when a tiny flame burned brightly did she lay sticks across the pit. Talen's handsome smile indicated his pleasure with her efforts.

It will not go away, you know, Talen sent abruptly, not looking at her.

Windwhisper considered silence, but his thoughts were too close to her dilemma of recent days. **How do you know?**

Your mother fought it, and so did her mother—Rahnee expended *her* talents in leading us. But it sleeps within, the elfin strength. I think in you it will erupt. This time Talen looked at her, his light gaze questioning. **Will you control this power, or will you be its prey?**

His choice of imagery caught her thoughts, as he must have hoped. *He is right. If I do not hunt down the truth of this, I will be hunted in turn. Then I will have scorn, not tolerance from the tribe.* That they might come to fear her was a concept Windwhisper did not dare explore.

Do you know what it is? She felt momentarily dizzy; the Wolfriders rarely sent involved conversations.

Talen shook his head, and Windwhisper felt a prick of disappointment. **It is true power rising within you. You are of the right age; Timmorn's line matures quickly. I have not kept track, but you have seen more than a hundred cycles. Exactly what is it? That I cannot tell you.**

How will I know? This was sharper than she'd meant, but Talen did not take offense.

If it was something we knew came from the blood, like healing or fire starting, you could try to use it. All Rellah and I are sure of is that it is strong; you disturb our sleep with its birth. The elder's thoughts were compassionate but firm.

So lessons from Rellah would not have helped . . . Rising swiftly, Windwhisper moved toward the entrance to the cave, away from the smoke and flame. Tears threatened, but could not fall; she would not let them. Dropping next to Nightshadow, she put her arms around the she-wolf and hugged her tightly. Aware of her chosen Wolfrider's distress but not understanding its source, Nightshadow shoved a cold nose against her neck in sympathy.

Is there no answer? She sent her cry into the forest, a narrow projection to whatever lurked within the damp leaves and mud. **Mother of us all, is there no answer?** Timmain might have known, self-shaper that she was, and there had been a tree-shaper among the Wolfriders at one time; what was his name? She was tempted to wake Owl, the new Dreamkeeper since Samael had left them, but something stopped her. A drifting of thought; a response from the forest?

No, it was familiar thought. Had the hunters returned?

Three does not a hunting party make. The thought was faint but approaching. Windwhisper leapt to her feet, lunging for her spear and its new flint, a dark flame in the muted firelight. **Wait on us, it is misting here.** Impatient, Windwhisper leaned against the rocks and crossed her legs.

They were only half a night away; they had feared to wake the camp by announcing their return. As the trio drew closer Windwhisper recognized the sending: Starfall. Only three? There had been at least seven in his hunting party, which left before the one led by Prey-Pacer or the one led by Wreath.

We are well, Windwhisper. We met in the south, following the deer and the spring. Prey-Pacer sent us ahead with a few haunches in case you were tired of fish. He had sensed her anxiety; his sending was as much a caress as his touch.

Pulling away from such thoughts, Windwhisper settled for a spark of pride. **Fish and suntail and ravvit and wattle-neck and cackler.**

In that case, you can feed us. We're tired of deer!

Laughing aloud, Windwhisper moved to the elders' poles, pinching the remaining birds that were being smoked. Still fresh enough for enjoyment.

Hurry up, then, before the smoke dries them. A touch of haste met and tangled in her thoughts, and Windwhisper laughed again, resolutely shoving her problem away. Starfall was back, and for now that was enough.

They arrived well before dawn, deer meat strapped to their backs. Shimmering like a star darting among clouds, Starfall looked more elfin than many of the Wolfriders, although three or four generations stood between the silver-haired elf and grandsire Timmorn. As tall as Willowgreen, with eyes touched by frost, he was Windwhisper's favorite among her age-mates, although she

73

did not let him know it. Beside him were tiny, tough Yarrow and also the leggy youth Wasp, Rellah's most recent child.

His tongue stings like a wasp, Windwhisper thought absently, hoping the elf was too tired to chide her over their successful hunt. Sometimes his teasing (and it was teasing; he had a good heart) went too far, and Windwhisper could not forgive his immaturity. At other times his flower-yellow hair and black eyes made her impatient for him to finish growing. Yarrow, on the other hand, caused no divided reflections. The elfin maid was a steady hunter, willing to do the dirty work of flint-knapping and even wood-gathering so long as the chief required it. Except that *she* thought Windwhisper should be allowed to hunt deer.

If asked, Windwhisper simply would have called them friends.

Perhaps Prey-Pacer is right. I am not as sturdy as you. She gave them time to reach the top before moving out into the drizzle to greet them, relieving them of bows and sleeping skins while they set the meat near New-Wolf's cooking supplies. Each was impartially given a hug, for they had been away a dance of Mother moon and more.

"We saw so much game in the south, even you could have come, Windwhisper!" Wasp looked mischievous. "You could have sat in a tree and speared a deer as it passed!"

"Huh. I was needed here. We have spring sickness in camp."

Good humor turned to concern, and the group huddled just within the opening of the cave, well wrapped against the cold, while Windwhisper related how the remaining elves had occupied themselves while the three hunting parties were away. She did not speak of her dreams, however—perhaps to Starfall, later, but not the group. Wolfriders disliked magic, and disliked change even more. Why burden them with her dreams?

Desire for speech, for company, swept away her concerns. All three hunters were very tired, tired enough to sleep the rest of the night and into daylight. Windwhisper sat near their fur-wrapped forms, losing herself in the wolfsong, absently waiting for the magic to come again. Worrying a strip of dried wattle-neck, she chose not to speak when New-Wolf came upon the deer haunches. Fortunately the elves were accustomed to occasional odd behavior from their hunters, and no one pressed her with questions.

The hunters are close—only a few days away. They have been successful, Windwhisper finally told New-Wolf when the sun had reached its zenith.

"Good. The stream is still muddy. Did it rain hard last night?"

Windwhisper scarcely heard the elf-woman. She was concentrating on something *different* about the morning. A sound. No, a . . . *tone* . . . that was not familiar. There was that horrible smell again; could New-Wolf smell it? With a start she realized that the wolves, who had spent the morning sunning themselves at her feet, were no longer there. Where was Nightshadow?

Something gave way in her mind with a jerk, shoving her off balance. Throwing out an arm, Windwhisper leaned back against the pile of furs, gasping for air. Her actions woke Starfall, who leapt to his feet in response.

The world snapped back to normal, and Windwhisper was huddled on the ground, Starfall's arms around her. A distant voice was saying: "But I heard thunder. There must be a huge storm coming. Someone find Owl and ask him."

Windwhisper? Finally opening her eyes, the elf-woman saw Starfall's lean, pale face. She reached to smooth his cheek.

Did you feel it? Her thought was narrow, private. The effort echoed in her head, and she winced.

Feel what? The thunder? The ground actually shook—a big blow must be nearby. Puzzlement and concern warred across his face.

Struggling to sit, Windwhisper pulled herself up by grasping his shoulders. Shaking her head slowly to clear the confusion within, she continued: **No. Not a storm. It has been going on for days, the vibration. The shaking. And other things—the game in these parts is distracted, confused. The waterfall is muddy—from the source, Starfall!** The force of her sending made her faint; she leaned against him, drawing on his strength. **The wolves know something is wrong, but they can't tell me. They . . . hear something. And that strange smell—** Her thought winked out as the exhaustion of the past days clawed at her.

Starfall held her close. "You must sleep, you have worn yourself out." Then a whisper of thought came from him. **Do you think all those things are connected?**

Windwhisper did not answer for a long time. Finally she told him, "Yes. Because I am the only one who has noticed. I and the forest."

Tugging her to her feet, Starfall led her back into the cavern, near the niche holding the invalids. "Sleep. I'll hold you." He was plainly worried.

There was no point in arguing; Windwhisper settled herself on a pile of furs. Maybe another's warmth would help.

Dreams came, the same dream, but this time stripped of its terror. Windwhisper realized that the image was in vivid color, tossing like a field of wild flowers, swirling like roaring autumn leaves. Yellows, reds, oranges, blacks— amazing that black could be more than one color—even flecks of silver, like Starfall's eyes. Heaving and coiling, a raging river out of control, but not water, not fire.

Stone. How she knew this she had no idea; was it like the effect of dreamberries, the memories of elves both living and gone beyond? That stone could be fluid, could flow like water, ooze like mud, glitter like flame? She swam in the fiery stream, passed through it, beyond it, rising through solid rock, slipping through it as easily as a ravvit burrowed. Rock moved beneath her hands, matching the curve of her palms, taking the prints of her fingers and then freezing once again. These mountains knew her, responded to *her* knowledge, obeyed her will.

Rain began somewhere, the sound of tiny droplets intruding on her sleep, sizzling on hot rock, soothing the fever of her body. Windwhisper opened her eyes to see that it was sprinkling once again, water washing the path outside clean of mud and debris. Starfall was now standing near the cave opening, shaking his head at the damp, but equally leery of the cooking fire New-Wolf was trying to build up.

Was she still dreaming? Confused, Windwhisper wriggled her way out of the furs. As if in a trance she moved past the niche to the wall of the cave, laying her hands gently upon its cold, smooth gray flanks. Once it had been liquid, this ridge of stone . . .

Deep within the heart of the mountain, Windwhisper felt a tremendous snap, as if a great bone had fractured.

GET OUT! GET OUT OF THE CAVE! Her sending buffeted the minds of all who heard it. Starfall and New-Wolf were literally thrown out of the cave into the rain as Windwhisper's unvoiced screams filled their heads. There was pain here, pain that she was causing; but she could not stop, she *had* to force them outside, because the mountain, too, was in pain, heartpain, and its writhing would reach the surface. Soon. Now.

This time they all felt it, a thunder so great it was deafening, vibrating through body and soul. It should stop, this thunder, but it did not. It went on and on through the wolves howling and children screaming and elves trampling each other to get out of the cavern . . .

Time ceased to have meaning. Windwhisper knew this convulsion was nothing, nothing in the stretch of time this range had known, a flicker in the eyes of the true elves. But still it was death, this shifting terror, for something was moving at the heart of the hills, and her people would be buried alive if she could not drive them out of this stone womb. They were leaving, even as she realized she was restraining the avalanche, forcing a great spur of rock to hold its boulder children tightly, hanging on with a death-grip to the cones of stone dangling above their heads. *No one can hold back a mountain.* The thought was almost blinding in its clarity, like the fiery veins of her granite home.

She remembered the invalids. There were seconds, only seconds; no matter that it was an eternity of thought, it was now, the terribly real now, and she could stop only so much. Futility swept through her as she dug deep into herself, dragging forth raw power to shore up walls and brace arches. *If only I could have understood, could have learned*— Some tiny kernel of awareness nipped at her, drawing her hands out of solid rock, and as the great tremor swept outward and beyond, Windwhisper felt herself slip after it, following it down into darkness.

Something cold and moist finally drew her back to her body. It was painful, the return; she was one large bruise, both in flesh and in spirit. She felt coolness on her face and warmth against her body. Arms tightened around her fragile form.

Windwhisper? The word itself was no more than a whisper, as if the sender feared treading into the moonless night of her mind.

But I am back. Where had she been? Gone away, she had definitely gone away . . .

"She is waking up," someone said softly. New-Wolf. The elf-woman was alive; she *had* escaped. Windwhisper had been afraid she had imagined it. The others?

Windwhisper? Starfall, of course.

What happened? So soft. She tried to put some strength behind it, but there was nothing. She felt like clay squeezed out to dry.

Several tribesmates started chuckling. Protesting, Windwhisper's eyelids finally opened when the cool cloth wiping her face became a warm, rough tongue. Knowing the touch of Nightshadow's mind, Windwhisper tried to reach to scratch the wolf's ears. She had no strength; she felt as if she had been ill for seasons, and was finally contemplating healing. Her body was slightly tilted, raised so she could see those gathered near her. Odor told her it was indeed Starfall who held her, and she could see Willowgreen at her feet, tensing at Nightshadow's presence. A blur beyond that, maybe New-Wolf bending over them, but—

"The others?" Her voice sounded husky to her ears, her throat as raw as after a howl.

"Safe. All safe, thanks to you," came a calm voice.

She knew that voice. Stirring, she tried to look around, to see the source. Prey-Pacer stopped her with a touch to her arm as he squatted down beside her. "My chief? You are back?" Her words were so faint, as if she had no voice left at all.

"We have been here two days," he said gently. "You have been . . . gone . . . a long time. How do you feel?"

Windwhisper considered the question. "Like I tried to wrestle a deer to the ground *before* the final thrust," she admitted.

"It does not surprise me. You had a mountain by the tail, child." Prey-Pacer looked like he might say more, and then he stopped before any words came out. "Rest, mountain tamer. There will be time for questions later." Standing again, the chief gestured with a lean, sinewy arm, and the group crowding around them began to move away.

"They are all right? The children, and Talen, and Mist—" It hurt her throat to talk, and Windwhisper stopped abruptly.

"They are. You *shaped* a den for them, a room within the cavern, and a spiral path which led out to the trail. We moved them afterward," Starfall added, embarrassed. "We did not know if the cave was safe."

I will check when I get up.

"When you *can* get up," Willowgreen corrected, offering her a hollowed gourd full of water. "At least the waterfall is clear again."

Keep watching the water! Windwhisper's thoughts were laced with alarm, and several of her elders looked over at the small group. **If the water turns muddy at the falls, the land may move again.**

Flesh twitched against her back as Starfall shuddered. "I hope not. You are in no condition to deal with it again."

Water trickled down her throat, soothing the rough soreness. *I wonder.* Her left palm was against the stone beneath them; Windwhisper spread her fingers, feeling for the smooth interlocked crystals, slowly, lovingly caressing the coolness locked within, reaching for the heart of fire—

"Stop that!" Starfall sounded frightened and exasperated. And amused?

His words drew her back to the surface of her mind, her hands free of compulsion. Gently her mind traced her handprint in the rock, the fingertips bent, reaching. Her lips curved in a smile.

For now. Windwhisper agreed mildly, relaxing against him. **For now.**

A Friend in Need

by Mercedes Lackey

The clearing sky and glimpse of sun after that first bad storm, thought Willowgreen. *It looked so hopeful, so promising. Oh sky and stars, what a cruel lie.*

The promise of sun and better days had not been fulfilled. There was a day, perhaps a hand of days, in the time that followed the storm when rain had not poured from the lowering clouds. But that run of days was the exception.

Rain, rain, and more rain—that's all they'd had ever since, from dreary drizzles to frighteningly powerful thunderstorms like the one moving in now; the river ran high and swollen, rising a little more every day. Not one single elf could get to any of the normal springtime hunting grounds; they were blocked out of the wilder lands by the river, by swollen creeks, and by new watercourses through valleys that had been dry for as long as the elves had been here. Willowgreen and Talen, the latter stirred by a vague memory of a long-ago time even before the fall of the skymountain, stirred perhaps by one custom of the despised humans, had done what they could. Working together, they made some attempt at planting a food garden. That, too, came to nothing.

It was ironic that Talen originally feared there would not be enough water. There was *too much*. And too much was worse than not enough; if it had been dry they could have brought water to the young plants, in their bare hands if nothing else—but the rains washed half of the seeds and seedlings away before they could take root, and rotted the ones that remained in the ground before they could sprout or grow.

81

Finally the elves fell back on the old expediency of their first days on this world, and gleaned plantlife from the forest. But now, after hands and hands of days since the rains began, days of nothing but downpours and floods that kept them from foraging very far afield, they'd eaten all the edible plants they recognized. And at this point even the most feral of the halflings would gladly bolt any of that "messy green stuff" they used to scorn in preference to meat. The river was too angry and roiled for successful fishing, everything but the young and the mothers of the game animals were hunted out, and the wolves themselves were subsisting entirely on mice. Graywolf, showing his teeth and enforcing his will on all the wolves, had turned on the pack only that morning. He flatly refused to allow any more hunting on the grounds that it was breeding season and they'd deplete the game for the future. And without the pack, there were few elves capable of successful hunting even in good weather. In this mess, with tracks and scent washed away as soon as they were laid down, it was impossible.

If this goes on much longer, there isn't going to be *a future*, Willowgreen thought fearfully, her eyes burning.

The situation grew desperate. Their bellies flattened against their backbones, and faces took on a pinched and desperate look. Shelters that stayed warm and cozy in snow were not adequate in rain, and the ever-present cold and damp were nearly as hard to bear as the constant hunger. The high ones had taken to losing themselves in dreams to escape the perpetual gnawing of hunger and chill.

Of course, while they were lost in dreamtime, they did nothing useful—which infuriated Two-Spear.

Willowgreen curled herself up as small as she could in a corner of the pine-bough shelter she and Two-Spear shared. He seemed to her stranger than ever after going off on his own; stranger even than Graywolf. He frightened her now, as he had not done before; he was cruel and caring by turns, and, most frightening of all, he did not seem to notice the difference between cruelty and love. He clung to her in despair one moment, then mocked her with her uselessness

82

in the next. Worst of all, he blamed *her* for the way the high
ones lost themselves, sinking into themselves and their
dreams, as if *she* could do something about it. His temper
grew shorter day by day until little or nothing would set it
off, and his sister did not help matters . . .

Skyfire used the current crisis as reason to press for
moving out, moving on, and not coincidentally, moving
far away from encroaching humans. That infuriated Two-
Spear even more, as did the fact that more than half of the
tribe agreed openly with her. Even worse, so far as he was
concerned, those in agreement with Skyfire were an equal
mix of high ones—when they could be brought out of
dreaming—and Wolfriders.

And Graywolf sided with Skyfire, at least in this. That
defection cut Two-Spear deeply. More deeply, Willowgreen
suspected, than he would ever admit.

Not long ago Skyfire came slogging through the calf-deep
mud to the shelter Willowgreen shared with Two-Spear, on
the excuse that she thought Willowgreen might be able to
rouse Talen out of the state of apathy into which even *he*
was sinking.

But when he heard Skyfire's reason for coming, Two-
Spear snapped something calculatedly harsh about
Willowgreen's inability to do anything requiring forceful-
ness.

Willowgreen collapsed, retreating into tears, and Skyfire
leapt joyfully to her verbal defense, ever eager for an excuse
to bait her brother into a fight. And now the siblings were
arguing again; sky and stars, they fought at least once every
day. The storm within the pine-scented shelter was worse
than the storm without. Willowgreen crouched and covered her ears and sobbed soundlessly, but though she could
block the shouting, she could not keep out the hate-and-
anger-filled sending.

"Fool, fool, fool, and *worse* than fool," Skyfire lashed,
"you're killing us by thumb lengths with your madness!"
And sent: **Why don't you cursed well go off and lead your
humans *right here*? Then at least we'd die cleanly! *You can't
fight starvation with a spear!* You're a mind-bent rabid

83

beast, with no thought but death, and you'll bring us all down with you!**

"*They aren't* my *humans!*" Two-Spear raged back.

"Oh no?" she taunted. "You're wedded to them in a death-dance, dear brother, as wedded as if they knew your soulname!"

He ignored the taunt. "And I *won't* give up the territory *we* won back to them! Run, that's all you can think of, run and hide like a treewee, afraid of your shadow, afraid of a storm, afraid to stand up and fight for what's yours!" And *he* sent: **Coward! Gutless, spineless, cry-in-the-night! By Timmorn's Blood, you're as fear-sick, as weepy, and as much of a burden as—**

He caught himself before he let the thought slip, but Willowgreen sensed the echo of the words in her mind— *you're as much of a burden as a high one, as worthless as Willowgreen.*

That was too much. Willowgreen uncoiled from her crouch, sprang to her feet, and pushed past them, bursting through the woven pine branches out into the storm. She ran.

She didn't know where she was going: she didn't much care.

And she couldn't see more than an arm's length in front of her, anyway.

While the argument built, the storm built up, too, and now it was at its shrieking height. The rain lashed her, more than half blinding her, plastering her hair down over her eyes. It was as dark as thick dusk; the clouds were a jumble of absolute black, and lightning tore open the sky while thunder roared at the wounds it made in the heavens. Willowgreen wept openly now, without shame; her sobbing tore within her chest, just as her heart was torn. It didn't matter, no one could hear her in this tempest. She let her bare, cold feet find a path; it was the one that led to the river.

For one instant she felt Two-Spear's mind touch hers, but she closed him out with hysterical anguish. She couldn't even bear the merest thought of him, his cruelty, his occasional kindness. She loved him, and that made his cruelty hurt all the more. She couldn't bear it any longer.

Her aching feet splashed through ankle-deep puddles; the water was frigid as snow-melt, and soon it numbed her legs to the knee. She began shivering, her teeth chattering, but she didn't stop in her aimless headlong flight; she just hugged herself and ran on.

Below her now she heard the raging river, a constant roar against the intermittent boom of the thunder. One step to the side and she'd tumble down the slope into the water to an unpleasant death by drowning.

And who would care for more than a hand of days?

Her side began to ache, a sharp pain that she cherished as a distraction from the pain in her heart. She stopped shivering, passed from chilled to numb, and still she ran on.

Suddenly, with a sound like the end of the world, lightning lashed down out of the angry sky. It split the tree beside her in two. She skidded to a halt, slipping in the mud and tumbling to her knees, frightened witless by the fury that had missed her by a hair's breadth. Her heart pounded, her breath stopped. She felt only stark panic; the scent of smoke and sharp tang of ozone were overwhelmingly near.

Too late she heard the scream of the wood of the tortured oak, heard the shriek of it tearing itself along the lightning-wound—far too late to dodge out of the way as half the tree came down on her.

She cried out, or thought she did. This was worse than her worst nightmares. She saw the massive branches coming at her, and she stood frozen, unable to move though her mind screamed at her paralyzed body to *run*.

A branch cracked her on the head, another struck her upraised arm. Gnarled twigs snatched at her, scratched at her, raked her with wooden talons, beat her half-senseless, and caught her up within a clawlike embrace. The pain was overwhelming; it sent her unconscious and conscious again, the world flickering about her in a way that had nothing to do with lightning.

And the destroyed tree continued to fall, picked her up, trapped her, and tangled her in its limbs.

The world plunged sickeningly about her; she tumbled end over end within her cage of branches. The tree crashed over the edge of the path.

As her mind screamed in an inarticulate and wordless cry for help, as she reached in panic for the mind of her lover that she had only moments before blocked out, she felt the tree plunge down the slope of the bank and hurl itself into the raging river, taking her with it. And all she could do was wail in utterly helpless fear and pain.

The universe held nothing except pain and numbing cold. Existence was only the struggle to keep her mouth above the waves, the gasp for each breath. Reality narrowed to the fight to live: *now* breathe, *now* hold tighter, *now* inch a little higher on the bough. There was nothing else, nothing but dark and a roaring that numbed the mind and sent it retreating down into a state of not-being.

Thoughts came and went with the lightning-flashes of pain, and the explosions of real lightning.

He only wants me when he needs me. Need isn't love.

She fought to breathe, cough water, breathe again.

Her chest was a mass of hurt, punctuating the end of each breath with a stabbing pain that meant that something was broken inside.

Graywolf means more to him than I do. He wouldn't have cared half as much if it had been me siding with Skyfire.

She cried out as her left leg struck something unseen. Her head went under a wave; another struggle to breathe, to cough.

She wiggled a little higher on the bough, then lost her grip and slipped under again.

She felt the cold come to claim with dark, silent fingers.

She fought it. Fought with pain when will began to fail.

Unbidden came the memory. *Graywolf*— A memory of yellow eyes. A moment of wonder at what might lie behind those eyes.

She shied away from the thought, but it returned.

86

There was a hunger there, a strange and aching hunger to touch. And be touched.

No!

What if it had been Graywolf who was chief—who ruled the elves—and Willowgreen . . .

No!

And still the insidious thought returned.

Then she jolted against something, a shock that nearly loosened her hold on the branch; a swirling of the water around her that nearly tore her off it—then she was drifting. Then stopped.

Moaning deep in her chest, she pulled herself fully up onto what was left of the trunk. She had to do it with only her right leg; her left was useless, hanging limp. In the errant flickers of lightning she saw the riverbank, and her heart leapt.

Then she saw the dark *shape* that waited on the bank, where the trunk of her tree had lodged.

But that was all she saw before an interior darkness blacker than the night claimed her.

She woke warm, cushioned, cradled. Her mind was a little fogged, still sunk in the lassitude that follows injury, illness, or healing. A dull headache throbbed away behind her eyes, a headache that sharpened when she moved her head slightly. She was too weary to open her eyes, too weary to really think, other than vaguely—*They must have found me; he heard me and came for me,* without wondering which *he* she meant.

Then her mind suddenly recognized some of the strange smells about her.

Woodsmoke, cooked meat—and *human!*

Her eyes snapped open, and she struggled to rise; struggled in vain, for not only was her left leg splinted and bandaged, but she was bound hand and foot beneath the tanned hides that had been placed over her. And whoever had tied her had known how: she was bound in such a way that she couldn't get at any of the fastenings with her fingers, or even with her teeth. Yet—

87

Yet she was *not* uncomfortable; her bonds were carefully padded so as not to hurt her. She was warm, and whatever she was lying on covered something yielding that kept her from the hardness of the rock floor beneath her.

For she saw now that she was in a cave of some kind, tucked into a little alcove off to one side of a larger chamber. There was a small fire somewhere out of sight; she heard the crackling flames, scented the smoke, and she saw the light dancing on the cave wall opposite her. There were bunches of dead plants hung up on that wall; some looked vaguely familiar. This was a well-lived-in cave, from the smell . . .

Yet that was a strangeness, too. Most humans Willowgreen had scented *stank* of rancid grease, dirt, and sweating bodies left too long unwashed. This—well, it wasn't strong; it was different, but not unpleasant, and it was overlaid with a fresh hint of herbs.

Sound. A soft footfall off to Willowgreen's right. A shadow loomed up on the wall, then the shadow-maker herself moved into Willowgreen's vision.

It *was* a human; undersized, from what the elf knew of humans. And it was female; the simple, knee-length tunic of leather, beaded and decorated with shells, clung to her body and revealed her sex by her meager, high breasts. Her eyes, dark, brooding with some past hurt, and small by elfin standards, met the frightened eyes of her captive.

Willowgreen panicked, thrashing so hard she threw off her blankets, straining against her bonds as fear rose in her throat and choked it shut. *Never* had she come this close to a human. Humans *hurt*, humans *killed*.

Surely, surely this creature had saved her for some awful purpose; for a sacrifice to one of the horrible, bloodthirsty human spirits, perhaps. There could be no other reason for a human to succor an elf!

Willowgreen screamed, shrieked, threw herself hysterically again and again against the thongs holding her in the bed-place—

Until the human reached out calmly, quietly, and

slapped her once across the cheek so hard that her teeth rattled.

The blow shocked Willowgreen into a kind of temporary calm. She fell back onto the bedding, her hair straggling into her eyes, her breath coming in hard, painful pants, and she stared at the human with benumbed wonder.

The human stared right back at her, quite calm and unthreatening, humming softly under her breath.

The woman was not young, Willowgreen could see that now. And she *was* cleaner of body than any human she had ever known before, just as the scents in the cave had hinted. She had hair as long as any elf's, done up in two long, raven braids that held streaks of silver. She was thin for a human, but not gaunt. Willowgreen noticed now that the decorations on her tunic were carefully worked, and included shells, feathers, bits of rock, beads—but no bones. She racked her memory for what Talen had told her of the humans he called *shamans,* and recalled that he had said that since their cruel rites involved many sacrifices, they reinforced the fear caused by those sacrifices by *wearing* the bones and skulls of previous victims.

Not a shaman, then. But what?

The woman reached for Willowgreen again, but this time slowly, carefully, every movement half-mimed well in advance. The elf shrank away from her touch—

But all that the human did was to free her right hand.

Willowgreen sat shocked nearly senseless, as much by the woman's touch as by the fact that she had been freed. Then another movement on the human's part caught her attention again, and she saw that the human held out a wooden bowl, signing that the elf should take it. When Willowgreen did not, the woman reached forward with it, put it on the floor of the cave between them, and signed again that she should take it.

Cautiously Willowgreen did so. It contained tepid tea of various herbs; she sniffed it, trying to identify them. Some she recognized as for healing, some she knew, but only that they were harmless.

Mercedes Lackey

The woman snapped her fingers, catching Willowgreen's attention. This time the mime show she made was quite elaborate, and quite clear.

Willowgreen was expected to drink this, or else the woman was going to sit on her chest, hold her nose, and pour it down her throat.

The woman may have been small by human standards, but she was still heftier than Willowgreen—and *she* was not handicapped with bandaged ribs and a splinted leg. And she looked as if she had been eating regularly as well. Willowgreen had no doubt who would win in a struggle.

She mewed with fear, but she obeyed. The woman took the empty bowl from her numb fingers with every sign of satisfaction. And as sleep stole Willowgreen's sight away, the elf wondered in despair if she would awaken again, or if she would *want* to.

The second time she woke, her headache felt less painful; other than that, nothing much seemed changed, at first.

But when Willowgreen took a second look at the odd shapes in shadowy corners and nooks about her, she saw that she was not as alone as she had thought.

Perched like a carving in a hollowed-out place halfway up the wall was a great raven. His eyes were closed, and he seemed to be asleep. Willowgreen wondered why he hadn't tucked his head beneath his wing as birds usually did to sleep. Then she saw that the wing was splinted as neatly as her own leg and was bound to the bird's side.

Beneath the bird was a vixen nursing a pair of kits; after the illness that had nearly killed the wolves, Willowgreen could recognize the symptoms of *her* sickness, but could also see that the fox was more than halfway to recovery. Willowgreen was astonished that the kits were still alive; that fever had killed the wolf cubs before striking the adult wolves.

In another alcove, four sun-yellow eyes blinked at her; as her own eyes adjusted to the flickering shadow-shapes, she could see the spotted coats of a pair of treecats. They were heavily bandaged.

What amazed Willowgreen was that all these creatures were normally enemies; all were predators and competed for the same prey. Yet here they were, all apparently being healed, and all seemingly under some kind of wordless truce. Willowgreen could even hear purring from the treecats' nook.

While she was still trying to grasp this, the human returned, letting Willowgreen know, with deliberately loud footfalls, that she was coming. Of this, the elf was certain; the human had been able to move quietly enough before, and these footsteps had a kind of studied sound about them.

This time the human did not come alone.

Wound about her shoulders, black eyes glinting with mischief from behind his black mask, was an unusually quiet ferret. Willowgreen could not for a moment imagine what was holding him so still, until she noticed that he had only three legs. This time the human wore her long braids wound into a knot on the top of her head, and there was a lizard coiled inside the larger coil of hair.

The human woman knelt down beside the elf, and slowly, searchingly, examined her; she peered into Willowgreen's eyes, checked the bindings on the splint, laid her hand as lightly as a leaf on the aching leg. Finally she nodded, as if to herself, and released Willowgreen entirely from the bindings that held her to the pallet.

She reached into the shadows, then brought out what could only be food.

Willowgreen's mouth suddenly watered at the scent of the hot graincake and the meat broth the woman held, and her stomach growled and ached with emptiness. It had been at least a hand of days since she had had even half a bowl of broth.

She reached out beseechingly, no longer caring if the human was hostile, if the food might be poisoned. The woman smiled tightly, and handed her the cake, and then the bowl.

Willowgreen couldn't help herself; she bolted both, nearly burning her mouth on the hot broth as she gulped it down. It was wonderful; the Wolfriders didn't like fire, and Willowgreen didn't get cooked food nearly as often as she preferred, even when times were good. And now—this was a feast.

But she was still hungry when she finished every crumb and drop, and she looked up at her rescuer, hoping for, but not really expecting, more.

The woman took the bowl, rose to her feet, and moved out of Willowgreen's field of vision. But she returned again almost immediately, and again the bowl was full, and she carried not one, but *two* cakes, as if some of the elf's hunger reached into her mind to prompt her.

She knelt again, but this time kept the food just out of Willowgreen's reach. Before the elf had more than a moment to wonder if this was some new kind of torture, the human set the bowl and cakes down and laid her hand on her own breastbone.

"Shayana," she said.

Then she touched the ferret. "Whist." The lizard, still in her hair, was "Green." Then she leaned forward just enough to touch Willowgreen's hand, and raised her eyebrow in an obvious question.

"Willowgreen," the elf replied, startled that the human was actually trying to communicate.

The human repeated the name, frowning with concentration; Willowgreen corrected her pronunciation (trying to ignore the fact that her stomach rumbled loudly), then countered by repeating the human's name, and her animals'. Shayana nodded, clearly pleased.

Then, to Willowgreen's intense relief, she seemed to decide that the elf had worked enough for one so ill and hungry. With a smile of satisfaction the human gave the elf the food she longed for so much, before Willowgreen disgraced herself by snatching at it.

Shayana waited then, with her hands folded, while Willowgreen ate—more slowly this time, taking time to savor the salty broth. Willowgreen could tell that she was watching-but-not-watching, a technique the elf used her-

self, often, when trying to avoid frightening a wild bird.
When Willowgreen was nearly finished, the human raised
another eloquent eyebrow, plainly asking if Willowgreen's
hunger had been appeased this time. Willowgreen handed
back the bowl with a sigh of content; seeing that the second
helping satisfied her, Shayana gave the elf another bowl of
the herb tea, and left her to drift again into slumber. This
time the elf drank the concoction without fear, feeling
somehow certain that whatever Shayana wanted, it wasn't
to harm her.

And this time, as she sank back into sleep, the human left
the bindings off.

Willowgreen sat in the sun, sheltered from errant breezes
by a cluster of boulders at the cave's entrance. The heat felt
wonderful; to see the sun again seemed almost miraculous.

I should try healing myself soon, she thought, *when this
stupid headache is gone, so I can concentrate. I'll have to
leave eventually, but by Timmain's sacrifice, I'm not certain
I want to!*

The human Shayana—surprisingly strong for one so
small—had actually picked Willowgreen up and carried
her here. After several days of nearly constant interchanges
whenever Willowgreen wasn't sleeping, the two were beginning to understand each other fairly clearly. Their speech
was a pidgin of human and elf, with a liberal dose of mime
thrown in whenever needed.

So when Shayana said this morning that she had work to
do outside, and that she was going to get Willowgreen out
there for some fresh air, the elf hadn't fought or struggled
when her human friend scooped her up. Though what
Shayana had actually *said* was, "Got work out-cave. Good-
air out, bad-air in. You go, too."

Willowgreen also hadn't tried to argue. She knew already
that Shayana could outstubborn an allo.

Shayana was right; the hot sun seeped into all the little
aches and bruises Willowgreen hadn't noticed in dealing
with the greater pains in her head, ribs, and leg. She leaned

against the smooth, sun-warmed rock at her back, felt the gentle heat penetrate and loosen muscles that had been tensed far too long, and watched Shayana work.

What the human was doing really couldn't be done in the cave, not without making a mess and a stink, and Willowgreen knew that Shayana was fully as finical about cleanliness as any high one. She occupied herself scraping hides that had been soaking in some concoction or other, removing every last trace of hair. The work was very sloppy, so, the day being warm, the human stripped off her tunic and was working clad only in a couple of scraps of hide. This was the first time Willowgreen had seen her friend without the garb that covered her neck to knee.

When Shayana turned, Willowgreen gasped to see that her entire back was disfigured by a lacework of scars.

The human looked up at the gasp, and her eyes and mouth went bitter and angry.

"Your back—" Willowgreen gulped.

"Old hurts," Shayana replied. "My people did."

"But how? Why?"

But the human only shook her head. "No right words. Later. Hard say now, need more words."

"Are you—"

"Shayana all right," the human interrupted. "Willowgreen eat sun, rest. Shayana got work."

And she turned back to her scraping without another word. Willowgreen sensed that further attempts on the subject would be met with silence, but she was intensely frustrated.

Still, for all that she was injured, for all that her head *still* hurt, this was, in some ways, a better life than she had shared lately with her own kind. For although she longed to be back with the others with all her heart, still she could not deny that there was peace here that she had not enjoyed much, of late. No one mocked her, no one forced her to choose between two equally unsavory paths. Shayana cared for her with what seemed a genuine and nonjudgmental affection.

This was certainly unlike all the other tales of human

behavior Willowgreen knew. And it sat very ill with Two-Spear's assertion that all humans were utterly evil.

And the way Shayana lived sat equally ill with the common wisdom held among the Wolfriders that no human could live *with* the world; that it was in them only to *conquer* it. Shayana had built herself a little nook here that was, if anything, far more a part of the forest than the Wolfriders' home.

Willowgreen found herself wondering about one thing, though. Shayana never left the cave long enough to do any real hunting, yet there was always fresh meat in their broth. And those hides she was scraping had once adorned the bones of a fairly large branch-horn, but no single hunter could ever hope to take down a branch-horn by herself.

No sooner had Willowgreen framed the question in her mind than her answer appeared.

The bushes to the right of the clearing in front of the cave rustled; Willowgreen started to cry out a warning. Shayana sat up on her heels just as a rangy, pale gray wolf shot through the greening branches, the carcass of an old buck-leaper dangling from his mouth.

The wolf—a young male, Willowgreen saw, with half a tail, one ear missing, and a slight limp—did not slow his rush, but launched himself at Shayana, bowling her over. Willowgreen nearly cried out in alarm and scrabbled for a stone to throw—then saw that Shayana was laughing so hard that tears streamed from her eyes.

The human and the wolf wrestled for a few moments, until Shayana got the upper hand, pinning the wolf to the earth. He crouched and she straddled his back, although she was far too large to be able to "ride" him. She worried his remaining ear playfully with her teeth, mock-growling along with her laughter.

Willowgreen froze.

She heard—there was something, sending, just at the edge of her perception—coming from the wolf.

Then it was gone; the wolf was up. He shook himself and dropped the leaper at Shayana's side, his jaws stretched in a panting, lupine grin of mischief. Shayana jumped to her feet again and dusted herself off, muttering good-naturedly at her attacker.

But there was no doubt of it; the sending *had* come from the wolf. And now that Willowgreen thought about it, there had been a similar sort of tickle at the back of her mind when Shayana had dealt with her injured animals. Only in those cases, it had been Shayana doing the sending—hadn't it?

If that was what it was. It felt a good bit different from what Willowgreen knew as sending; it was both stronger and weaker, and it was surely not so finely tuned. It was like the difference between the way a dreamberry and a blueberry tasted. There was something *more* in the taste of the dreamberry, something that hinted of its power over the mind. There was something more in the elves' sending—yet both were berries, and both were sending.

Still, that would explain Shayana's power over her animals, though it gave no hint where that power came from.

But this wolf—from the size and the sending—could easily have been one of the Wolfriders' pack. Yet it glanced at Willowgreen, then away again, with no sign of interest or recognition. Another mystery.

Could it be that there were other wolves, other packs even, with some of Timmorn's blood in their veins, wolves that had never seen an elf in all their lives?

The question became an academic one within a heartbeat, for Shayana turned to face Willowgreen again, right hand dangling the dead leaper, left buried in the wolf's short ruff. The human and the wolf together came toward the elf, and Willowgreen had always feared the wolves of the tribe because she could not, had never been able to, reach their minds properly. There was too much of the high ones' blood in her; she and the wolves mistrusted each other equally.

Yet Willowgreen fought down her fear until it was only a cold lump in the pit of her stomach; this wolf showed no sign of that mistrust. He did not expect her to mesh her mind with his. It was to a human, to Shayana, that he turned for a pack-leader's guidance. Without any expectations on his part she realized it might be possible to meet in friendship. It was certainly less unlikely than the fact that a human and an elf had done so.

She swallowed hard, and held out her hand timidly, as they drew near. The wolf sniffed it with a certain amount of interest, then grinned, wagging his tail slowly.

"Willowgreen," Shayana said, "this One-Ear, hunter. Friend." Then her eyes narrowed a little in concentration, and this time, perhaps because she was prepared to sense it, Willowgreen actually received the gist of the human's sending.

It came in images and feelings, not words, and not particularly aimed at the wolf's mind; it was more as if Shayana was sending openly, for any mind to hear that could.

Image-of-Willowgreen—a strangely attenuated and delicate thing, *much* more delicate than Willowgreen had ever pictured herself. There were overtones of protectiveness and a certain wry envy, an envy that connected to a feeling of awe at the elf's beauty. There was also warmth, caring, near-kinship. **Feeling-of-hurt,** Shayana was projecting now. **Cub-feeling. Need to guard this one.** It was a wild, feral mix; a sending that could never have been mistaken for an elf's.

The wolf looked directly at her, in the way wild wolves so seldom did unless they were challenging a pack-rival, a look which the elf-blooded wolves *did* wear in imitation of their elf-friends.

Agreement, came the image from One-Ear. **Cub-thing.**

Willowgreen blushed with shame, for the wolf's thoughts were tinged with amusement bordering on contempt. She was a weak thing, his thoughts implied, born and bred to be protected.

Shayana ignored the blush, and ruffled the wolf's fur. **Hurt-thing,** she corrected. **Guard while hurt.**

The wolf only grinned again, then sent a thought at Shayana, something that just brushed by the edges of

Willowgreen's reach. Shayana cocked her head to one side, eyes widening, then turned to Willowgreen.

"One-Ear say you . . ." The human hesitated, groping for the word.

Willowgreen shook her head and spread her hands apart, the signal the two of them had settled on as "I don't understand."

Shayana tried again. "Words here"—she touched her head—"go here"—she touched One-Ear's—"but no mouth."

"Send?" supplied Willowgreen.

"Send? How? What you? *Where* you?" the questions spilled from the excited human. "Only my people do. You not Shayana's people—what you?" She pounded the rock of the cave entrance with an impatient fist. "Not enough words! Not enough words!"

Now her excitement infected Willowgreen. "*Give* words," the elf urged. "Use words, use send—"

"*Yes!*" The human dismissed her wolf with a hug and ran back to her work site just long enough to shove her half-finished hides back into their pit. Then she returned at a run to Willowgreen's side, her face bright with excitement. The wolf didn't seem to mind being ignored. The beast seemed just as pleased to go flop down on a sun-warmed rock for a nap as the pair of two-legged fools began frantically searching for a way to augment their mutual vocabulary.

By nightfall they had quadrupled their limited store of words; by the middle of the following day they had done far more than that, and questions could be asked and meaningfully answered. Their hybrid language held nearly equal numbers of elf and human concepts, for there were some things, it seemed, that could only be expressed in one or the other tongue.

They were inside the cave; Shayana did not want to chance the weather today, and Willowgreen agreed. Besides, it was easier to concentrate in the quiet.

"Questions now?" Shayana asked Willowgreen when their energy flagged and they decided to break for something to eat.

Willowgreen nodded.

"I think we can understand each other fairly well now. Since it's *you* that's been helping *me*, it's only fair that you go first," the elf said, after a pause to sip at one of Shayana's herbal brews. The strange sending that the human had been doing made her constant headache worse, but this stuff did seem to dull the pain. "Try what you wanted to know when One-Ear told you I could send."

"What are you? Where are you from?" the human asked eagerly. "No one like you, never saw anyone like you—not human, could see that, but not spirit, either. And you mindtouch! Only the Handmaidens can mindtouch!"

Slowly, and with many pauses to grope for words, Willowgreen tried to explain the skymountain, the high ones, the Wolfriders. The latter seemed to make a certain kind of sense to Shayana, but she only shook her head at Willowgreen's fumbling attempts to explain the former.

"I can't—I don't—not got half that. No sense in words. 'High ones'" (she used Willowgreen's word) "like spirits seem." She looked wistfully at the elf. "You seem spirit, so pretty, so small. Not much like spirit in river, though, like drowning leaper!" They both laughed. "Spirits not have broke bones, either. Why fear Shayana?"

That provoked an outpouring of how humans had greeted the elves—and how the conflict still continued.

To Willowgreen's concealed alarm, her words had a powerful effect on the human.

"No surprise, not to me." The human's eyes turned hard and cold during the discourse. "My kind, they fear strange, fear different, fear strong; will control strange, or else—" She slashed her hand down in a chopping motion.

She brooded, and Willowgreen wondered at the change in her mood. "Maybe Bright One brought you here, maybe She be angry, tired of death, tired of little-minds, of no-think. Maybe She set elves against them; make them

99

change or die." Her eyes brightened with an eagerness and an anger Willowgreen could almost feel as heat. "Maybe She let elves take their place!"

"You *want* that?" Willowgreen felt appalled at the barely controlled violence within her friend.

"You saw." Shayana gestured angrily at her back. "I be Handmaiden, Bright One's priestess, healer. Then Gotara priest come, say war and death stronger than life and healing. Chief listen. Chief say I make too much trouble, say I make women not-obey; say I not useful like Gotara priest, not make sun, not make rain, only tell when rain come, not-come. Chief's son get sick, get Wasting Fever. I angry with Gotara priest, not go to boy while priest there. When I go, it be too late, he die. Chief say I kill him. Gotara priest say I kill him, on purpose, use bad magic make him sick." Her hands clenched and unclenched in her lap, her gaze far away. "They beat me. As you see. Throw me into forest, wait for beasts to eat me. Hah!"

She grinned ferally. "They not know I get mindtouch with beasts when become Handmaiden. I wait till dark; go home, get things, come here. Heal. Not go back, not ever. Even if they all dying of Wasting Sickness, I spit on them. Wild ones come, when they be sick, hurt. I heal. Some stay, Whist, Green, One-Ear. *They* good to friend. *They* not lie, not cheat, not steal. *They* should live, not humans."

"But why did you help me?" Willowgreen asked in bewilderment.

"I dream of you, three, four nights; then I hear pain in storm. Not human pain, not beast pain. Not know what, but know not-human. I help not-human. If you human I push you back in, let river take you. But you have look of spirit, hands strange, eyes strange, ears strange. Not-human. Help you."

The hate in her voice chilled Willowgreen's heart. The only hatred she'd ever touched that was *that* intense was Two-Spear's hatred for all things human.

Timmorn's Blood! If he could get over the fact that Shayana herself is human, those two would match like two halves of a nut!

Shayana shook her head. "Not-human, know that even in dream. Other—you mindtouch strange, but like Hand-maiden. You know herbs, could see you careful with herbs. Be you healer?"

"I try to be. But I don't heal the way you do, with herbs and things, at least not mostly. I heal with magic—" It occurred to Willowgreen then that she was finally strong enough to do some of that healing on herself. And if she could, she could knit the bones of her leg fast enough that she could set off on her way back to the elves within two hands of days. Suddenly she was almost sick for the sight of them. Shayana was kind, but very odd, and the violence that lurked now just under her surface thoughts made Willowgreen no little afraid. "Just look, I can show you!" she said. "Watch—"

But when she put her hands over the broken bones of her leg and reached for the healing power, it was gone.

Gone without a trace; as if she had never had it. Groping for it felt like the time she had tried to shape trees; there was simply nothing there to work with.

And her healing was the only thing she *had* that was hers, the only thing that made her useful to the tribe. Without it she was nothing.

Her panic must have shown on her face, for Shayana asked sharply, "What wrong?"

"I—can't—heal. I *can't* heal! It's *gone*! I—I—" She sobbed, unable to cope with the loss, all control gone.

"Stop that—" Shayana said, a little angrily; and when that had no effect, she took the elf's shoulders in her hands and shook her until her vision blurred. "I say *stop* that! Stop that right now! What be you, baby, wailer, cry-in-the-dark? What wrong with magic gone? You got life, hands, mind! You *alive*!"

"But—" Willowgreen whimpered, no longer hysterical, but empty with her loss, "without the healing, I'm nothing! I'm useless! I should be dead!"

"Turds! Mindsickness! Foolish! Stupid, stupid, stupid!" the human replied with mordant disgust. "What I, tree stump? Dead bone? *I* not got magic, I heal! I heal good! I heal *you* good! You got complaints—look at leg, straight! Ribs, straight! No rib in lung! So you lose magic—maybe when you hit head. Hit head loses things, sometimes. Maybe magic come back, maybe not. You not want be a big rock on neck of elf people, you learn *my* kind healing! Takes only hands, and memory, and thinking, lots thinking, *smart* thinking. I think maybe you not got smart thinking. I think maybe you dumb like dirt, way you cry! You say you woman grown, you look like woman grown, but you not act like woman grown! I think it be time you act like you grown up, not weepy baby with wet bottom!"

And with that, the human rose abruptly. "*I* got things do, not waste time on woman-big baby! You want, you take care self today, else rot like dead branch. Hah!" And she turned on her heel and stalked out of the cave to take up some chore, leaving Willowgreen to brood alone, watched only by the wary eyes of the treecats.

At first she was angry. *How dare that—that—human talk to me this way? What does she think she is?*

She raged on in her mind for some time, her anger hot within her, frustrated, scared, longing for something to rage against. Finally Willowgreen started grabbing every twig and branch within reach of her pallet, snapping them into smaller and smaller fragments. Over and over she snarled to herself: *Who does she think she is? Just who does that human think she is?*

But that thought triggered the answer, and her anger cooled to nothing. *She's a healer, and one that can still heal, that's what she is. I insulted her. She's more now than I am. Without my magic—*

She thought about that, soberly. *I've been acting—like she said—like a baby. And I've been getting away with it with the elves because they couldn't do without my magic. Talen and Rellah are so fragile; and half the Wolfriders don't trust them, anyway, at least not enough to let them inside to heal them. When I left the tribe, they were starving, but I was more concerned that Two-Spear was unkind to me! Timmorn's Blood, why did they let me get away with being such a fool? No, I'm not as strong as the Wolfriders, but I still*

*have a brain, I could use it. Softfoot was weaker than I,
Prey-Pacer was just as weak. But Shayana was right, I
haven't been using my mind; I've been too busy wallowing in
self-pity, too busy trying to find someone to take care of me.
No elf should be so dependent as that! Graywolf was right
about me.*

Willowgreen found herself looking into the mirror of her
own soul, for the first time in her long life, and she didn't
like what she saw. For what she saw was a coward: a woman
too fearful to stand up for herself, a creature that would
rather cry than fight, rather let others take responsibility
for making decisions, rather submit her will to that of
anyone stronger than think for herself.

*But I can change, I can learn, I must. Two-Spear needs
my help—he's been crying for it without words, and I've
been ignoring him to nurse my own little heart-bruises. And
the tribe needs all the help any of us can give. And right now
I'm the only one that hasn't been trying to give that help.*

Something deep inside her shut forever—a dark little
place of selfishness and weakness—and something else
opened. She didn't think she would miss what she'd just
closed away.

It was after sunset when Shayana returned to the cave;
she found Willowgreen waiting for her.

Willowgreen had discovered a way to move about the
cave without disturbing the splinted leg: she crawled. Once
she knew she had a practical, if painful, sort of mobility,
she kept the little fire on the hearth alive, shuttling back
and forth to the woodpile, carrying a few sticks at a time.
She'd watched Shayana, so she knew how to make the
graincakes that were a part of each meal and how to bake
them on a smooth stone. So when Shayana returned,
graincakes waited next to the hearth as well. Willowgreen's
cakes were a little burned at the edges where she'd patted
them too thin, but were otherwise just like Shayana's. The
broth had been cooking when Shayana left, so Willowgreen
left that alone except to stir it occasionally, but she
straightened up the cave, a little at a time, and she made
her *own* medicines when she needed them. And she

103

discovered one reason why Shayana liked having Green
and Whist around; when she disturbed the pile of wood she
rousted out a mouse and a few insects. Whist pounced on
the first, never seeming to mind his missing leg, and Green
licked up the bugs with a long, sticky tongue. Willowgreen
laughed, and then thought, *I wonder if I could seduce
lizards into our shelters—*

Now she sat by the hearthside in weary, smudged
triumph, meeting the surprised gaze of her rescuer with a
smile.

"You're right, I'm a fool," she said without preamble.
"Will you help me become less of one?"

There was more—much more—to learn than Willowgreen had guessed. And Shayana was far from being an
experienced or patient teacher.

They began with the treatment of wounds, because the
very next day a half-grown and badly mauled bear staggered into the clearing before the cave and Shayana needed
more than one pair of hands to keep it alive.

Willowgreen threw up at the sight of it, and once again
got the sharp goad of Shayana's tongue. Flushing beneath
the sting of that scourge, Willowgreen learned quickly to
control her revulsion and her trembling hands.

She also learned how very much she missed her lost
magic. Wounds that she could have knit in heartbeats were
pure torture to mend, and for all concerned. Shayana
laboriously pinned the edges together with boiled thorns,
but only after dusting the gashes with an unsavory powder
of mold and pulverized herbs, then coating them with
spiderwebs to make the blood clot.

Then, once the wound was pinned up (and the thorns
had a tendency to break at just the worst moment), she
coated the whole seam with a smelly paste of more herbs
until there was no raw flesh showing.

"How did you do this alone?" Willowgreen gasped when
their bawling patient squirmed away from them for the—
well, too many times to keep track of.

"Not easy," Shayana replied laconically, wiping some of the paste out of her eye. "You lucky. Elf not run away."

"I don't know," the elf replied, looking dubiously at her paste-covered hands. "This stuff might *scare* them away."

Shayana just snorted.

Finally another decoction had to go down the unwilling patient's throat. More of it ended on Willowgreen and Shayana than in the bear.

That turned out to be Willowgreen's job, because of her splinted leg—that, and a great deal of the picayune work. Since the elf couldn't move much, Shayana pinned the struggling bear down with her own weight while Willowgreen followed her panted directions.

One thing the episode *did* prove: Shayana's powers of the mind might be cruder than an elf's, but in some ways they were much stronger; the bear never once turned on them, not even when their ministrations made it bellow in pain.

The whole process took nearly a day, and left them both as exhausted as their patient.

Then there were the herbs to learn—and not just memorizing what they looked like and what they did.

No, Willowgreen discovered that Shayana expected her to be able to identify them not only green and growing but also dried or even powdered. In the dark, if need be, by smell and sometimes taste.

"What if it be dark night, and no fire, hey?" the healer scolded her when she failed the last test, and waved her hands helplessly in the air. "What you do, let friend die? Bet you would, it easier to cry for dead friend than make head work!"

That made Willowgreen angry, and anger gave her the energy to try again.

Shayana taught her not only herbs but every plant in the forest that could be used for food. Willowgreen was appalled to discover that the Wolfriders had passed over any number of plants that were edible when immature just because they were inedible when fully grown. *That* mistake

105

couldn't be undone, but Shayana drilled her unmercifully to learn plants and parts of plants in various stages of growth and maturity—until Willowgreen was certain that the elves would never face the danger of total starvation again.

More than once the human so lost patience with Willowgreen that she stalked out of the cave and into the forest without a word, leaving Willowgreen alone. Shayana's temper was fiery; her patience was inexhaustible when dealing with something helpless, but nonexistent with the elf, whom she considered perfectly capable of learning or doing.

So when Shayana stamped off to cool her temper, Willowgreen coped with whatever was left to be done. It was not quite fair, however, to say that Shayana left the elf alone, for she never took One-Ear with her, and the wolf hovered around the elf until his human returned, taking his orders to "guard" with absolute seriousness.

That turned out to be a benefit that Willowgreen never expected.

Hurt thing— the wolf sent at her one day, after watching her from his favorite sunning rock.

**—I—One-Ear—* she replied tentatively.

The wolf wagged his tail slowly. **Hurt thing not fear?** he asked. **No fear-smell.**

At that, she sat up straight and realized that the wolf was right; she *had* lost her fear of him. She still could only touch the edges of his thoughts, but neither what she sent nor what she heard was clouded with her own fear.

Not fear, she replied firmly, and with a tentative stirring of content.

One-Ear put his head back down on his paws, and shut his eyes. **Good.**

There was yet more to learn. Sicknesses were actually the easiest to deal with, for Shayana could use her own strange sending ability to put an image of the symptoms in Willowgreen's mind. But there were often several treatments for each . . . depending on season and what was or was not available. So not only must Willowgreen memorize her herbs, she must learn *when* they were at their best.

There were times when she wanted to give up, but Shayana's taunting drove her on. It occurred repeatedly to her that Shayana's scolding mockery sounded a great deal like Graywolf's, and she wondered more than once if the strange wolfling elf had been trying to goad her into developing a little more spine, and not just trying to hurt her. In time, she began snapping back at Shayana, and to her astonishment, her human friend was pleased rather than further angered.

"Hah!" Shayana crowed, the first time Willowgreen made a scathing retort about stupid humans who expected a person to be able to cram a lifetime of learning into a few moondances of days. "Hah! There be fire, finally! There be backbone! Shayana wonder if Willowgreen got spirit like rock, or spirit like green twig! Now—*when* bladderwort be good, hey?"

Bonesetting nearly made her want to give up; Shayana made her practice on injured birds, whose fragility made her afraid to touch them. Normally the healer didn't even bother with injured songbirds, unless they happened to flutter into her clearing. Usually she healed only the larger animals and the predators. ("We got eat," she said pragmatically. "What we do, heal leaper, not eat? So, heal hunters, like us. Hunters bring meat, sometimes once, sometimes lots. We heal leaper, what it bring, leaves? Heal hunters, I. When good times, heal branch-horns, tree-horns—bad times, give them clean death, eat them. That life, that death.") But now, with a pupil to teach, she went out into the forest searching for injured birds and bringing them back to Willowgreen to practice on.

"I set elf bones," the healer said implacably. "You got bones like bird, light, easy break. You want help your people, you learn on birds."

It gave her nightmares sometimes, nightmares in which she dragged herself from friend to dying friend, unable to help any of them.

Rockfall!
Talen was dying, snapped nearly in half by the boulders that rained down on them. Willowgreen read his death in his eyes, and tried to hold it off, but he was gone before she even touched him. And the others—Two-Spear, Skyfire beside him, screaming in red agony, clutching a shattered arm to his chest, an arm so ruined that splinters of bone stuck through the mangled flesh. Skyfire lay close, ominously still, her upper body twisted at an unnatural angle. Behind her, around her, Willowgreen heard moans, calls for help, and she could do nothing, nothing—
She woke, crying, tears streaming from her eyes.

Then Shayana was there, the comforter that Willowgreen remembered from the first days, rocking her in her arms like a child and soothing away the tears.

"I know," she crooned. "I know. I got dreams, too. Healer *knows* she healer when she get dreams."

Sometimes Shayana frightened her, with her implacable hatred of her own human kind. Such hatred was even more mindsick than Two-Spear's, because it was directed at what Shayana herself was. Willowgreen could not imagine how she sustained it, and often wondered how long the healer could endure such a deadly hate without tearing herself apart.

And when Shayana now and again began to ramble about her "Bright One," Willowgreen really didn't know *what* to do. It almost embarrassed her, especially since Shayana once admitted that she had only encountered this being once, at something she called her "ordeal." But when Willowgreen ventured a tentative question about that occasion, the human became silent and secretive.

It was the one point on which they had no common meeting ground. Willowgreen understood Shayana's scorn for the incompetent, the pride in her hard-won abilities, even the hatred for those who had rejected her. But this, this was alien, beyond Willowgreen's comprehension— and no little peculiar. Willowgreen was forced to wonder if the whole thing hadn't arisen out of Shayana's long isolation.

The day arrived when the splints came off, and Shayana declared that she had no more to teach.

"You go home now?" the healer asked, as Willowgreen flexed the newly liberated leg and tested it with her full weight, then, in sheer delight at her new-won freedom, crossed the clearing in a series of exuberant leaps. "Time— more than time. You be ready."

Willowgreen stopped dead. "I—I hadn't thought about it, not for a long time," she faltered. "I—Shayana, how can I face them with my power gone?"

"You heal with hands now, you know how."

"Yes, but will they trust me? And there are too many times when—"

"When need magic." Shayana nodded slowly. "Hah. Heal elf not like heal bear. Bear die, well, bear die. Elf die, lose friend."

"Yes," Willowgreen said after a long pause. "That—I think that's where the nightmares are coming from."

"Bright One teach in dreams. Maybe trying teach you. Head still hurt?"

"Not any more—"

"But magic not come back. Ssss—" The human paced the clearing, deep in thought, as if trying to make a decision about something. "How bad you want magic? Take chance Willowgreen die?"

Two seasons ago Willowgreen knew her answer would have been negative, but now . . ."Yes," she replied simply. "I want it back that badly."

The human gazed deeply, searchingly, into her eyes, and seemed pleased by what she found there. "So. Got backbone, eh? Hah. Sit."

Willowgreen found her favorite flat rock; Shayana sat beside her. "I tell you only Handmaidens mindtouch, yes?

I not tell you how. Comes from Bright One, at ordeal. Handmaiden not eat, at dawn walk far, far, walk until find good place. Sit. Then eat . . ." She spoke another gibberish word.

"What?" Willowgreen asked.

"Is plant—" Shayana jumped to her feet and vanished into the cave, emerging a few moments later with a single dried mushroom, which she handed to Willowgreen. "That. Eat it, wait, Bright One come. Bright One look at heart, head; decide if live or die, then give gift. Mindtouch gift. With people, with beast, sometimes. See spirit, sometimes. See ahead maybe, see far off, sometimes. So; Bright One come, gives gift, you live, you go home, be Handmaiden. Heal with herbs, use gift."

As Shayana had taught her, Willowgreen touched her tongue cautiously to the mushroom, analyzing what that brief taste told her. *Something like a dreamberry,* she decided after a moment, *only much stronger. Well, this won't kill me—* "So this might give me back my magic?"

"Bright One give back magic," Shayana corrected. "This make Willowgreen see Bright One. But Bright One maybe not like Willowgreen—"

"I'll take that chance," the elf said, lifting her chin.

Shayana nodded again. "Then—Willowgreen want start now?"

Willowgreen was light-headed from the three-day fast, but she was in better physical shape than she had ever been in her life. Shayana had forced her to do things while she'd been healing that had toughened and strengthened her, chores she had been kept from doing for the Wolfriders on the grounds that she did them too slowly. She still wasn't as strong as a Wolfrider, but she had lost much of the pale languor of a high one.

"Follow river," Shayana advised. "River bring you, river show you way home, river be good omen. Bright One be with you—friend."

Then she embraced the elf's thin shoulders, tears in her eyes for the first time in Willowgreen's knowledge.

110

"Are you saying—goodbye?" the elf faltered.

The human nodded, scrubbing the tears away with the back of one brown hand. "You live, Bright One send you home. This not Willowgreen's home. Willowgreen's home with her people, yes?"

The elf nodded reluctantly.

"So. We be different outside. I think we same inside, some. Go. Bright One with you, healer. Go heal your people."

So Willowgreen departed, walking slowly beside the river, her every sense sharpened. The river was no longer at flood stage, and tumbled over boulders below her in a way that no longer seemed threatening. The bank was thick with moss, cool and soft to the feet. Willowgreen wandered on, keeping no particular track of time. Shayana had told her to wait until she found "a good place," and no matter what Willowgreen thought about the human's superstitions, that seemed to be eminently sensible advice. A "good place" could mean many things, including a cranny secure from predators, since without Shayana's protection, Willowgreen knew she'd be fair game. And no one but a fool ate dreamberries in a place likely to induce nightmares or bad memories; how much more must this be true for this strange mushroom.

Willowgreen heard the gurgling of the river below her change, become wilder; and she heard a new note in the music of the water, for up ahead was a sound of thunder—

She emerged abruptly from the trees to find the river had become a waterfall, plunging many hands of elf-heights to rocks below her feet. She saw now that the land all around dropped sharply at this point, that she was standing on the brink of a precipitous cliff. The thundering of the river was exhilarating, not frightening. The entire vista spread out before her, great spans of forest, with the river resuming its meandering course, a silver ribbon glinting through the green of the trees. It was intoxicating.

Looking down, Willowgreen saw a path beginning near her feet at the edge of the cliff, winding down the face of it, to disappear into the forest below. It looked safe enough.

111

Keeping one hand on the rock at all times, she began to edge down the narrow path.

She didn't have to go far before she found what she was looking for. Just below the cliff's edge, but invisible from above, there was a shallow cave. It was empty, and commanded a splendid view of both waterfall and landscape below, as if the viewer were suspended in the mist of the falls.

A "good place," indeed. Willowgreen wondered for a moment if Shayana knew about this place, and concluded with wry good humor that she probably did.

No matter. The elf made herself comfortable, with her back against the wall of the cave, and with a tiny twinge of apprehension, swallowed the blackened bit of fungus.

For what seemed a long time, nothing happened.

Then—

She was light and fire; she was sun and starshine and moonglow. She was homey firelight, reflecting on the faces of elves and humans alike, and the longings in their hearts were not so terribly dissimilar. Nor were their fears. She was lightning, lashing the ground below her. She was a forest fire, started by skyfire, exalting in her terrible destructive power, rejoicing as life crisped into ash beneath her. Willowgreen shrank from that; not denying it, but vowing that nothing so negative would control her. *No,* she said to it, *that is part of me, but that is not me. I am—*

She was water; everywhere, in rivers and ponds, in rain and fog, thundering over the falls, or dropping gently on a thirsty flower. She was. That was all she needed to be. Just as water was.

But that wasn't enough, either. *Water is directed,* she told it. *I am not that passive, not any more. I am, but I also do.*

She was wind, all action; the tempest tearing the land, the breeze spreading the seeds, flinging herself against mountains with a shout, coursing down canyons, forming the clouds, unmaking them, then forming them again, all at random.

No, she said sadly, for the freedom of the wind was something she only wished she had. *I act, but I act with*

112

purpose. I used to act without thinking, but I have left that time behind me.

There was a pause, a moment in which she was nothing, and after a moment, she realized that this was a test as well. *No*, she said. *I have things to do. I can't give up, not yet, not now.*

A swirl in the dark nothingness.

Then—

She was earth, then she was more. She was the world.

She saw herself, sitting oblivious in the cave, but not alone.

She could never be alone, for she was connected to all things, all life—to her own kin, far off, fey flames in the great net; to the wolves that coursed the forest; to the forest itself; even to the humans, in a strange way. All things were joined in the net, all things living; the power moved through them and with them and was affected and effected by them. Anything she did would ripple down the net, making changes, some small, some large. Some changes would be negated, but others would cause still more changes, for that was the way life was. The net formed a shining whole; parts of it blazing with life and light, parts of it sick and dark with disease.

She realized that this was what Shayana had perceived as the "Bright One," experience and perceptions limited by knowing only life in the human village had caused her to personify it and deify it. Not that it didn't deserve deification, but this web of life was indifferent to worship, because the worshippers were already part of it. It was indifferent to prayer because prayer made no changes. Only actions changed anything, and those changes might not bear fruit for generations.

She could see what Timmain must have seen; how the high ones, the first ones, did not fit. How they were making empty places within the net, and would ultimately be eliminated from it. She saw what Timmain had done, and understood why. And was saddened by what was thus lost, but gladdened by what was gained. And for a brief moment, she could see the shapes of other answers that might well

113

have worked—and could see some of what would come of Timmain's answer. And she realized with a deep sadness that Two-Spear was right—for all the wrong reasons. And that she would have to support him.

Then she remembered why she was doing this, and asked herself (for that was obviously the only place where she would find an answer about herself) what had happened that she had lost her magic.

It was never lost, she saw. *It was blocked. As Shayana had said, it had been the blow to her head that had blocked it off from her use. But now, with the strange mushroom coursing through her, another kind of shock was being applied to her system—*

She held up her hands, and could *see* the healing power flowing through them again, and rejoiced. Even more, she felt the coming of a new gift, a strengthening in her sending. She rose to her feet, and went lightly up the trail, laughing at the rainbow forming in the mist over the waterfall. Still caught up in the edge of the life-web, she could see that Shayana had been right; all she needed to do to find her way back to her people was to follow the river.

As she thought of Shayana, she found herself *seeing* the human. The healer was seated in the sunlight beside the mouth of her cave, clean hides stretched out on pegs to dry beside her. Pensively she scratched One-Ear's ruff, but she suddenly looked up, seemed to see Willowgreen, and grinned, a wide smile of congratulation and shared triumph.

Then Willowgreen was back inside herself, running easily along the path beside the river, the song of all life giving her feet new grace and speed.

She was going home.

It was Rockarm who saw her first, as she walked along the path beside the river. She sensed him before she saw him, sensed, too, his wolf, and sent both of them greetings that surely confused them.

Wolf and rider came crashing down off the ridge, both in too much a hurry to care about the amount of noise they made. Willowgreen waited for them; tired now, and feeling it, with most of the mushroom purged from her blood in that long, exalted run.

"Willowgreen?" came the incredulous shout from above, and **Willowgreen? Is it really you?** the sending that followed.

Well, it certainly isn't Timmain! she sent, laughing, as they tumbled down onto the path in front of her. **Hello, Whitetip. Is your mate better?**

The wolf stared at her, and whined, then began wagging his tail; slowly at first, and then with such enthusiasm that he threatened the stability of his rider.

And *that* made Rockarm stare even harder—especially when she went down on one knee and exchanged gentle ear-bites in greeting with his wolf. She could sense his mind-blank astonishment, and nearly giggled out loud.

"Don't you think you ought to call the others, O scout?" she asked, reminding him of the reason he had been watching the trail.

She nearly drowned in greetings, engulfed in a wave of elves. Two-Spear nearly went out of his mind with joy, so much so that Willowgreen finally had to block him out. The high ones, Rellah and Talen in particular, were almost as overwhelmed, but had their minds under much better control. Only Graywolf held back from the celebration.

Almost before she could blink, an impromptu party began; she was seated at Two-Spear's side, the center of all attention. Even Skyfire seemed disinclined to pour rain on the proceedings. But still Graywolf held himself away.

Willowgreen had gotten much more than her magic back; she seemed now to be able to sense others' thoughts without their knowing she had done so, just as she did with Graywolf. How long this ability would last, she had no notion, but as she shared the welcoming feast (meager, but now that the rains were over, the Wolfriders were hunting again) she probed his mind.

She smells like woodsmoke—and human, the elf thought broodingly. *That isn't the same tunic she was wearing,*

115

either; it looks like it, but it doesn't smell the same. And look at her—

She got an odd glimpse of herself through his eyes, surrounded by both elves and wolves, she who had been frightened sick of the wolves before.

She talks to the pack now—she likes them. I don't like it. She won't say where she's been.

Then she lost his slippery thoughts in the press around her. But it made a cold spot in the bottom of her stomach, wondering how—or even if—she could explain what had happened to any of the others, even Talen.

And as for Two-Spear—

She took a thin strip of meat from him, looking up into his eyes with love, hiding the worry she felt. How could she tell Two-Spear that she'd been helped and healed by a *human*? How could she tell him that same human had saved her life?

Willowgreen snuggled against Two-Spear's shoulder with a contented sigh. He stroked her hair, but it was an absentminded gesture. She could sense the question long before it came.

"Where were you?" he asked. "I—"

"I told you, told all of you, I was swept down the river. I was hurt, and it took a long time before I could travel. It wasn't pleasant"—she finished, and put an un-Willowgreen-like force behind the final words—"and I'd really rather not talk about it."

She felt him tense. He was startled, and resentful. "I don't understand why not! We've always shared everything until now!"

No, my love, she thought sadly, looking up at the stars and moons above them. *I always shared everything—you only shared what you chose to.*

"Perhaps I've changed," she replied. "I ended up relying on myself a lot. I guess I've gotten used to it."

"Huh." He let go of her, but at least he didn't pull away. "You *have* changed; everyone's noticed. I thought it was

116

wonderful. At least you get along with the pack now, but—"

But you don't like the new independence, do you, beloved? she thought, when his words trailed into silence. *I wonder what this will mean to the two of us; I never thought about that. And I wonder what you'll say to Graywolf when he brings you his questions. Will you still trust me? Will you trust me when I side with Skyfire, about running from the humans, even though I believe she's wrong about the high ones and I know that you are right? Will you believe me then when I side with you if it comes to a real conflict with her?*

She sighed, as his breathing slowed and deepened, telling her he'd fallen asleep. *It doesn't much matter; I've made my decisions. I can't go back.*

I can never go back.

Song's End

by Janny Wurts

The wolf's jaws snapped shut with a sound like the crack of new ice. Deadly teeth slashed nothing but empty air, and the beast's frustration could be felt, hot as the spurt of fresh blood. On damp earth barely one stride distant, Huntress Skyfire rolled and evaded the edge of the stone knife which stabbed down to kill her. Breathless, sweating, bleeding from three previous challenges, she scrambled into a crouch and leapt while her opponent recoiled from his lunge.

On the sidelines the wolf whined. Its lips lifted into a snarl, and its haunches bunched, quivering. But this combat was a thing between elves. The pack was forbidden to intervene.

Skyfire struck her attacker solidly in the chest. He overbalanced, and both of them rolled with the throw. The knife grated against dirt. Skyfire took a knee in the ribs; air left her lungs with a grunt. The scent of her opponent filled her nostrils as she gasped a fresh breath. His odor carried a tang of fear. This, because she had bested two stronger challengers before him; those defeated had not lingered to watch her fight again. Both had retreated to the wolf lairs to lick wounds and nurse resentment.

Skyfire caught the new challenger's knife-hand and bore him down in swift and merciless attack. Fright made him dangerous, even desperate. The chieftess clung grimly as the Wolfrider thrashed beneath her. Anger lent her tenacity to match his fear. She barely felt the blows as he kicked and punched to win free. She twisted the wrist in her grip, felt the sinews tighten. Bone grated beneath the pressure of her hand. While pain distracted her opponent, she kicked away the knife, and sought his throat.

Abruptly the Wolfrider went limp under her hands, chin lifted in submission. Skyfire released his wrist and neck. Wearily she gathered herself to rise, to turn, to face the next of the challenges that had inevitably followed her return with the Dreamsinger to the Holt.

Only that morning, she had shouted to the first dissenters who crowded round. "He is an elf, and a Wolfrider, and by the Way, I say that he stays in this tribe by right!" Now, in her exhaustion, the words seemed still to ring in her ears.

At some point during the second fight the Dreamsinger had faded into the forest. With him had gone the scent of dreamberry blossoms, and soft south winds of spring. His leaving changed nothing. Wolfsong gripped the tribe like lust, and the open outbreak of rivalries had upset order within the pack. Skyfire barely noticed Rellah's hostile glare. These fights made distasteful work, since the challenges themselves were an indulgence of wolfish instincts. That Skyfire did battle to temper those same instincts mattered little. Bites and wrenched joints and knife wounds demanded exhaustive concentration and energy drain, and Rellah had none of Willowgreen's natural gift. Still, with the healer gone away with Two-Spear's exiles, only Rellah remained to fill that responsibility. She carried on with a learned knowledge of herbs and bandaging, and an uncompromising sense of duty, ancient as she was.

Dreamsinger, Rellah sent, **is spell-blind, mad. Not worth this bloodshed, desist.**

Skyfire refused the reprimand. Scuffed, stinging, sticky with the blood of conflict, she shook back tangled hair and snarled.

Rellah failed to flinch; and that lack of reaction by its very incongruity raised Skyfire's hackles. Prompted by distrust, she spun, her snarl changed to a growl of rage. The sudden movement spared her. She took the knife thrown by treachery from behind in the shoulder instead of the heart, where it was intended.

"Murder!" screamed Rellah. "A curse upon Timmain for mingling the seed of the beast in our children."

But Rellah's outburst reflected only ignorance, and anger

119

at things she could never understand. Skyfire gripped her shoulder, hot blood dripping through her fingers, eyes narrowed with a rage only Two-Spear might have equaled. This assault had not arisen from the blood of the wolf; pack hierarchy was a discipline ritualized to minimize deaths. Stealth, subterfuge, attacks calculated to catch the victim disadvantaged were subleties reserved only for the taking of prey.

Ready now to kill out of hand, to discipline in the manner of the pack, the Wolfriders on the sidelines crowded around the offender. They caught his hands and feet, splayed him helpless upon the ground that, wolflike, they might rend him limb from limb.

First in their longing to tear out his throat was Huntress Skyfire; yet she did not. She shivered and overran instinct and kicked the nearest of the scufflers, who happened to be Skimmer, with her boot. "Stop! Let him go." When others were slow to listen, she jerked the knife from her flesh, then dove in and hammered them all with her fists, her elbows, her knees, and sent the offenders rolling away in surprise. Dizzy now, and caked with clinging dust, she glared around the circle of her following. "No elf must die."

She remained upright until the knife-thrower had shambled to his feet and fled ashamed from the circle. Then the dizziness took her, and she staggered . . .

. . . and awoke, sweating in noonday heat, to scratch at a scar that seemed endlessly to itch, and to wonder just why this dream should return to trouble her. The tree hollow was stifling. Skyfire brushed damp hair from her eyes. She rolled for a breath of fresh air, and as her hand brushed empty space, realized. The Dreamsinger had left her. In the dance of moons since the fights had ended, this was not like him.

A chill roughened her skin, a premonition of something amiss. By reflex, Skyfire reached out with her mind for her mate.

His sending cut her awareness, sharp as a knife's edge with danger. One with his mind, she felt a blow strike his

120

shoulder, then a sensation of falling, falling; and then pain, sudden and shattering and violent. She recoiled in shock, and slammed hard against the tree wall. Her mind rang with the Dreamsinger's sending, and the last, whispered syllable of her soulname.

"*Kyr!*" Her own scream snapped the link. "Dreamsinger!"

She scrambled in a rush from her nook. Down the tree limb she slid, without bothering to reach for handholds. Bark scraped her skin. When she reached the main trunk, she leapt outward.

And reexperienced the rush of the Dreamsinger's fall for an instant of shared memory.

Then she struck ground. Rolling, banging into roots and the detritus of last year's leaves, she reached out to recapture the link. She received not the smallest spark from the Dreamsinger. Where once the air itself sang in echo of his magic, emptiness remained. The song, the life, the vitality, all had ceased in a terrible, smashing fall from the heights.

Skyfire fought her way to her feet. He was dead; she knew this beyond doubt. The wolf pack sensed the kill through her distress. They gathered already, restless to dispose of the remains. Such was the Way, and not a thing Skyfire would forbid. Her mate was beyond help. Reason more dire than sentiment caused Skyfire to spring into action. With the weight of the Dreamsinger's cub heavy within her belly, she broke and ran from the clearing.

Only Sapling saw her go. But though Skimmer was soundly sleeping, and Pine was busy with a lover, and Owl absorbed by another of his enigmatic weavings, Skyfire's emotions cut through with an urgency that would not be denied. One by one the Wolfriders arose from their hollows, or abandoned the thread of their activities. In silence they gathered to follow their chieftess; of them all, only Rellah was obliged to ask where to look.

The ravine lay in the direction of sun-goes-up from the Holt. Trees did not grow near the rim; only the toughest

121

lichens could garner a foothold upon the jagged, flint-black rock that stabbed like teeth through the soil. Below, the stream carved a course like knotted thread, frayed at intervals into waterfalls that threw drifting curtains of mist. The sound of water tumbling and frothing over stone had fascinated the Dreamsinger. Many an afternoon he had lingered above the ravine, perched on an outcrop with his feet dangling.

Now Rellah stood on that same formation, her hide skirt pinched in nervous fingers, and her skin roughened by the moist chill that eddied off the falls far beneath.

"The Dreamsinger's song is ended," she said. Unlike the Wolfriders gathered at the site, she avoided looking at the shadowy forms which darted like ghosts along the streambed. Years had done little to accustom her to the ways of the wolves. The fact that the mangled rag of flesh and bone that had once been a living elf was now only meat to sustain the pack revolted her. Curiosity alone brought her to the scene of death. The attraction for many of the others was similar. But Skyfire was not among the few who clustered with Sapling out of concern.

Apart from friends and Wolfriders, the chieftess knelt on the earth at the forest's edge. With a diligence that brooked no interruption, she examined the ground for sign, and found none. Now, more than ever, she missed the companionship of Woodbiter, who had hunted his last ravvit soon after the coming of the green season. Without the guidance of her wolf-friend, Skyfire could not unravel scents too faint for her nose. That such clues existed only fueled her frustration. Here she could smell the rancid leather track of a sandal, and there, clinging to ferns, the musky hint of sweat; just enough to know that an elf other than Dreamsinger had recently trodden this path. But the subtleties escaped her. Precisely *which* elf Skyfire had no way to determine.

Absorbed by the problem, the chieftess did not look up as the rest of the Wolfriders began to disburse. Sapling slapped her shoulder in sympathy, and Pine offered condolences. She acknowledged both with a nod, but made no move to return to the Holt. Rellah's insistence that companionship might ease her grief was ignored.

"He was mad," the older female said in her infuriating, superior way. "His presence caused dissent, and if he chose to end his life, the whole tribe is better for it."

Skyfire arose then, so suddenly the taller elf started. Pale with anger, the chieftess said, "*Kyr* did not choose to die."

Rellah recoiled a step. The Huntress's wrath was a palpable force, dangerous as the wolf crouched to spring. The first elf dared not argue, but retreated quickly, breaking into a clumsy run just beyond view in the forest.

Skyfire heard her departure as a noisy crashing of sticks, an inept intrusion that rankled upon nerves already overtaxed. Lips drawn back into a snarl that was all wolf, the chieftess returned to her task. She quartered the ground in relentlessly widening circles until twilight stole away the light.

Summer night fell, loud with the voices of crickets. The water crashed down its course, misting the air, and dew beaded the rocks over the precipice where the Dreamsinger had fallen. Huntress Skyfire straightened, aching in ways that had nothing to do with the fact she had spent hours on her knees. She perched in the niche her dead mate had left vacant, eyes closed in misery. No longer would the trees wear blossoms out of season, or brambles blaze with the colors of autumn during spring. The Dreamsinger was gone, his magic reduced to a memory. Only one legacy remained: the cub in Skyfire's womb quickened and steadily grew toward its birthing. As much for that unborn life as for her own grief, the Huntress could not let the father's death rest. The tragedy that had overtaken the Dreamsinger might one day happen to his offspring; as surely as she breathed air she knew that another elf had dealt the blow that precipitated the fatality. The act was a poison, a danger hidden as a snake among the tribe; a Wolfrider's mindset was trusting by nature. The Way of the wolves had no analog for murder.

Skyfire kicked irritably at the moss-caked stone of the ravine. To search out Dreamsinger's killer posed almost insurmountable problems. The sending she had shared in the instant before annihilation had shown no face; just the roughness of the hand that pushed, and the terrible plunge, and the pain. A wolf might unravel the scents, but by now the trail was cold. The tribe had crossed and recrossed the paths to the ravine, and Skyfire's own search had further obscured the evidence. Even without these complications, no other rider's wolf-friend could be trusted to investigate in her behalf. Pack members who bonded to an elf owed their first loyalty elsewhere. Should her request fall on a tribesmate who was involved, or in sympathy with the killer's cause, she would learn nothing but lies. Dreamsinger's madness had been feared, distrusted, and at the last resentfully tolerated because she had fought and bested every Wolfrider who had dared to challenge his presence. But dissidents remained, too timid or too crafty to fight. Of the many who had licked wounds in defeat, some might whisper for retribution. Factions lingered yet from the days of Two-Spear's chieftainship; Skyfire sensed them at the hunts like tangles in the continuity of the pack. Though most Wolfriders were not capable of intrigue, any one of them might be led by conspiracy.

Half lost in his song and the visions woven by magic, the Dreamsinger had never thought to take precautions. For that, Skyfire blamed herself. From the head of the ravine she listened to the howl carried out in her mate's memory. She did not return to participate. Alone on the height that had killed, she listened, straining to determine which voices were missing, and which sounded uncertain.

Her suspicions knotted uselessly into confusion. The howl for the Dreamsinger ended quickly. His brief stay with the tribe had largely been misunderstood. Skyfire alone had been able to temper his madness, and see beyond to the shape of Timmain's dream. Only she had seen promise of a future where the gentleness of elvish heritage might coexist with the hardy cunning of the wolf. Yet now, with one who murdered magic at large among the tribe, that future and that dream lay threatened.

Night deepened. The two moons lifted over the trees;

light through the leaves dappled the forest floor, and touched the rocks at the precipice with a glint like dagger steel. The larger of the moons led the dance, silvering the spume which veiled the head of the gorge. The place where the Dreamsinger had fallen lay lost in black shadow. Brooding, sad, and uncertain what to do, his grieving mate shook back her bright hair.

"Which of us wished you dead?" she asked the empty air, the faces of the moons, the soft sigh of the wind. Only crickets answered. Their song of summer's plenty held nothing to console an empty heart. Restless with loss and frustration, the chieftess cursed.

At the sound, something at the forest's edge started back. Alarmed, Skyfire ducked low in the niche. Carelessness made her cross. She had been as trusting as her mate to linger here, and certainly as foolish. Now the rushing water at her back held threat enough to raise the hair at her nape. She carried the Dreamsinger's cub. If she could sense its gift of magic as it grew, so might others; so might the killer who had destroyed its father. A push from the same hands might send her to share his death. Memory of that plunge and the agony of its aftermath returned with a force like premonition. Skyfire shivered.

Cautiously she hugged the stone. A leap to safer ground might provoke a retreat; already this elf had proved his lack of courage. Yet she chose a more dangerous course. If she could tempt an attack, make her situation seem more precarious than it actually was, she might emerge after a scuffle with Dreamsinger's killer held captive.

But time passed, and the tunes of the crickets continued undisturbed. Skyfire listened until her ears ached. The forest night revealed nothing. At last forced to conclude that the movement had been an illusion born of grief, she raised her head and looked.

The angle of the moons had changed, plunged the trees in deep shadow. Yet the dark beneath the branches was not empty; there shone a pair of silver eyes, eerily identical to the Dreamsinger's.

Skyfire gasped. At the sound, the eyes flashed and

125

turned, lost in the forest's dark. Shaking now, and fighting tears, Skyfire scrambled up from the precipice. She rested her cheek on cold rock. Her mate had not turned spirit to haunt her; she had seen only his gray wolf, who shared the color and intensity of his eyes. While the rest of the pack retired to sleep off gorged bellies, this one restless beast sought a master who would never hunt again.

Deprived of Woodbiter's company, and robbed forever of the Dreamsinger's mad passion, Skyfire longed to reach out to the wolf, to sink both hands to the wrists in his luxurious silver pelt. She wanted to weep in his warmth, and then to run, fast and strong, into the heat of the hunt.

"Song," she called, though she knew the wolf would not come. Wolves who lost elf-friends did not bond to another tribe member; so said Owl, who sometimes, after dreamberries, remembered such things.

The appeal of Huntress Skyfire to her Dreamsinger's wolf brought only a flash of white brush as he turned and retreated into the trees. For a moment, she almost let him go.

Reason why she must not snapped her mood of brooding heartache. Skyfire started up from the rocks. Her brow furrowed with a determination the rest of her tribe knew better than to cross. Song was more than a wolf who had lost a master. He was the key to the identity of Dreamsinger's killer. For that one name, Skyfire was willing to undertake any difficulty, no matter how impossible.

Huntress Skyfire raced into the forest. The wolf fled ahead of her. Running hard, she glimpsed his form as a flash of silver through the glades where the moons' light struck through. She heard him as a rustle of leaves, the scrape of claws on stone, and the soft, disturbed breath of air as he sniffed his back trail for pursuit. Song was fleet, young, and clever enough as a hunter to have survived through the Dreamsinger's exile. Yet he was not a maverick by nature; he had challenged for position, and won acceptance in the pack that ran with the Wolfriders. Skyfire had fought him once, in the course of helping his master. She had gained the victory, but Song's submission had not cowed his spirit. His trust would be troublesome to earn, and time was of the essence. The Huntress understood enough of wolves to know that she must win Song over at once; otherwise loneliness would drive him to identify irrevocably with the pack.

The two moons lowered with the coming of dawn. Shadows turned vague and gray under the trees, and in that uncertain light, obstacles became difficult even for a keen-sighted elf to discern. A wolf, with better sense of smell, had less disadvantage. Song unavoidably drew ahead. Grimly Skyfire held to his trail. Exhaustion blurred her purpose; threat to her unborn cub merged with grief for her Dreamsinger. As she drove each tired foot into the next stride, the silver wolf who darted like a wraith out of reach came to symbolize the mate she had lost. If she could only catch up with the beast, if she could once touch its fur, something of the compassion she had learned through love might be recovered.

But Skyfire's persistent desperation won no ground. Song's intent to escape became all the more frantic. He did not understand the Huntress's motives; his strongest memory of her had been a fight, after which he had been forced to yield to her will. The wolf had let her run at her Dreamsinger's side out of submission, not goodwill. Now, with the master gone, Skyfire's pursuit keyed nothing but a primal instinct to flee. Years spent with an exile lent the wolf cunning: he was not habit-bound to any territory. Where a pack-raised beast would keep to familiar trails, his run a wide loop around a chosen area of forest, Song ran straight cross-country. He might not anticipate every twist in the terrain, or fallen log, or stone outcrop. He might be slowed by unexpected roots, or avoidance of a thicket too dense and tangled for running. Yet the Huntress who followed was equally disoriented; the safety of the cub she carried made her uneasy in strange country, where men

127

might prowl, and unknown terrain lead her into danger. Eventually her two legs must tire, and then Song could slip like a shadow into the wood to seek out his own kind.

Still, Skyfire had spent most of the summer season hunting without any wolf-friend to bear her weight. Spring's crop of cubs had already been weaned when Woodbiter died, and those that were inclined to partner an elf had already bonded. Aware her predicament must extend through the next turn of seasons, the chieftess had hardened to compensate. She did not quit, but continued, stumbling and pushing through the brush, until long after dawn. The sun blazed high overhead when at last she threw herself, panting, in a glade.

Song was footsore as well. His belly was empty of game, and his sinews too spent to hunt. Tail drooping, nose low, he sniffed out a small cave beneath an outcrop. There, he curled up and slept to recover his strength.

Although Skyfire was too weary to run, stubbornness would not let her quit. She tracked Song's footprints through last year's leaves, a briar thicket, and over the moist bed of a stream shrunken down to a trickle by summer. The heat of midday wore upon her energy, and hunger nagged her belly. Soon, for the sake of the cub she carried, she must stop for food and rest; but not yet. The impressions of Song's pads told of a stride no longer fluid. The wolf was tired also, and not so urgent in his flight. Presently Skyfire observed that his path began to meander, as he searched for a lair to take cover.

She paused then to wipe sweat from her face. If she found the wolf before he woke, she had a chance.

The cleft was situated beneath an outcrop of moss-caked stone. Spring water pooled nearby, protected by a stand of trees. Song's marks were plain in the mud by the bank. The darkness between the rocks held the warm scent of his fur. Certain the wolf had laired there, Skyfire retreated from the area with the care of a seasoned predator. She left no unnecessary scent, and made not a whisper of noise. Song must not awaken and discover her presence too soon.

The Huntress knelt at the spring and drank her fill, then wove a snare for small game. She retreated after that to wait. The sun on her back made her drowsy, yet she battled the lure of sleep; if she succumbed, and Song left while she rested, she would lose him. He had run too far through the night, well beyond the territory of the pack that ran with the tribe. This part of the forest was hunted by wolves unfamiliar with elves. Song would be forced to fight for a place among them, or move on as a loner who spurned others. His memory of the Dreamsinger's companionship would fade quickly, and Skyfire knew that success must depend on prompt action.

A ravvit jumped squealing into the snare. Huntress Skyfire started out of a drowse, shaken by the fact that sleep had taken her unaware. Quickly she studied the light. The sun's rays slanted just slightly lower; her attention had lapsed only minutes. Stretching stiffened muscles, the Chieftess arose and drew her dagger. She killed the ravvit with one deft thrust, but resisted the instinct to gorge. With the blood of fresh game on her hands, she set out to share meat with Song.

Her approach to the grotto was cautious as before, but the slight increase in moisture as the day waned made the scent carry. Blood-smell aroused the sleeping predator from his dreams of chase and the hunt. Skyfire heard the click of claws on rock as the great wolf bounded to his feet. She felt the gust of his breath as he sampled the air, then greeted her presence with a low growl of warning.

The Huntress froze instantly, ravvit flesh dripping between her fingers. She made no further move, but waited at the entrance to the cleft for Song to consider her gift.

The wolf made no effort to advance. Skyfire accepted his ambivalence in stride; she had expected no less. Wolves were distrustful by nature, and interactions between members of a pack were rigidly dictated by rank. She had bested Song, and by tradition, he could fill his belly only after she had gorged and lost interest. To share food without regard for hierarchy upset the order Song understood; and things not understood were to be feared.

Skyfire sensed the wolf's uneasiness. She held firm, even as his hackles rose, and a snarl furrowed his muzzle. Shining gray against the dimmer gray shadow of his head, the eyes of the wolf never left her.

Song. Skyfire put sending in the word. She offered reassurance in place of uneasiness, warmth in place of cold, food against the pain of hunger. She promised joy, and life, and the heady thrill of the hunt in full summer.

Song's snarl intensified. He remembered the past fight. That had ended with his throat bared to her mercy. His instinct was submission, but the close rock walls confined him, cut off his escape if this Huntress pressed her proven superiority against him. The ravvit promised nothing. The smell of its blood only drove the wolf to frustration, for he was hungry, yet dared not feed. Enraged by conflicting instincts, Song crouched on the hair-trigger edge of a spring.

"Song," Skyfire whispered. She shifted her weight slightly to ease a cramped leg; and that small movement tripped the balance.

Song lunged. Wild with fear, crazed to escape, he leapt for the elf in the entryway.

Skyfire could have dodged aside, let the wolf brush past to win freedom. But the name of the Dreamsinger's killer was a threat more dire than mauling. Her tribesmates must not run with a murderer unknown in their midst.

Tired, and slowed by hunger, Skyfire met Song's rush with braced feet. His weight slammed her, hips and shoulder, and his jaws snapped closed on her wrist. The pain was terrible. His teeth ripped down into muscle, and grated with bruising force against bone. Skyfire yelled, in part to distract him, but also to vent the shock and the agony of a wound that wrung her mind with faintness. Just enough awareness remained for her to hammer a fist at the wolf's gray eyes, Dreamsinger's eyes, shining now with the lust to tear and kill.

Song released her before the blow fell. He would not risk his sight; nor could he entirely forget his former defeat at the hands of this same elf. He had attacked, but she had neither given way nor succumbed to fear; either reaction would have invited further aggression. Yet since the elf met challenge with a savage intent to fight, Song backed down. Snarling, he lowered his brush and retreated to the farthest cranny of the lair.

Skyfire knelt, her shoulder pressed weakly to cold stone. The ravvit lay where it had fallen in the dirt between her knees. She cradled her injured forearm in her hand, wrung dizzy by the odors of fresh-killed meat and new blood. Somehow, through pain, she clung to her purpose. She must not leave the grotto, must not permit Song an opening to leave. The safety of her unborn cub depended on her steadiness now.

Teeth clenched, Skyfire worked off her tunic. She wrapped her wrist to slow the bleeding. She knew from past mishaps and remembered scoldings from Rellah: slashes were the least of her worries. More serious were the narrow purple punctures which cut deep, but did not drain. Without herbs to draw out the poison, these were sure to fester, slow her with sickness and fever until she lost her strength and died.

Dreamsinger's fall from the cliff had been a much cleaner end.

Skyfire squeezed her eyes closed. Such thoughts had no place, except to obscure one fear behind another far more dire. She had but one purpose: to win the murderer's name from Song before her tribe's future came to grief. Cautiously the chieftess shoved to her feet. Her shoulder scraped the rough stone, but she needed the support to rise, to stand straight as if she still had spirit to call challenge. Let Song once gain the impression that she could not fight, and the contest of wills was lost. At the slightest hint of helplessness, the wolf would attack and press for victory.

With a low growl of warning, Skyfire carefully, so very carefully, stepped back. She waited then, though dizziness skewed her balance. Song did not react. Skyfire clung to the stone. She thought of the Dreamsinger's music, now forever stilled; the anger that went with that memory helped to support her through another step, then still more slowly, another. Song watched, but offered no aggression.

Beyond the mouth of the grotto, the sun shone red in the treetops. The heat had eased, but Skyfire sweated in discomfort. Left no other alternative, she knelt at the entrance to Song's lair and trailed her injured forearm in the spring.

The icy water eased the ache and cleared her head enough for her to notice the emptiness in her belly. The meat dropped in the lair was lost. As twilight fell gray over the forest, she heard the sharp crunch of bones in the jaws of the wolf who had bitten her. Song had grown bold enough to appease his hunger on the ravvit. Skyfire wondered how long before he became restless, or desperate, or thirsty to the point where he challenged once again for his freedom.

Darkness brought stars and heavy dew. The sultry heat of day gave way to light breezes; frogs croaked in chorus with the crickets. Skyfire lay and listened to the night woods, her wrist soaking in the spring. Pain would not let her sleep. Light-headed with exhaustion, she reviewed each member of the tribe in her mind. Most were friends; all but the very oldest were forest-cunning, wise, and dependable in the hunt. All had shared through lean times, and bickered over trivia when there was plenty. True enough, there were factions, brittle tensions left over from Two-Spear's time. But the turn of the seasons had dimmed the old distrusts. Skyfire had taken pains never to show favor; always in council she had listened to any rider who spoke out. The fights over Dreamsinger's presence had caused the only open dispute since her chieftainship began.

Skyfire curled her fingers in the current, and winced. The pain of the bite had not lessened. The swelling had increased to the point where she could not effectively grip her knife or spear. Even the simple snare she had woven that morning lay beyond her dexterity. The Huntress rested her sweating forehead against the earth. Help and the Holt were beyond call. Yet even the threat of starvation could not turn Skyfire from her quest. That the hopes she had discovered through Recognition should be left at risk to a murderer offered hurt far worse than any wound. Song alone held the answer; only the wolf could reveal which friend, which Wolfrider, which elf under her trust still harbored enough hatred to deceive.

New day dawned humid and close. Birds flitted from the treetops to drink at the spring, but Skyfire could only follow their flight with her eyes. Song was awake and pacing. Fretful herself, Skyfire tried and failed to find a more comfortable position. Her arm had swollen to the point where only the icy water in the pool offered any relief. Her pain could be tolerated as long as she kept the wound submerged.

By noon, the sun fell full on the rocks. Song lay panting in the shadows, eyes fixed ceaselessly on the elf who kept him penned. Skyfire dipped water from the spring in a fold of her leather tunic. She offered to share with the wolf, but Song declined with a growl; irritable, restless, he arose and paced his prison.

Skyfire sweated with her back against the boulders. Reflections off the water hurt her eyes, and the wind which gusted through the treetops rushed unpleasantly against ears that rang with fever. Sickness only increased her determination. Periodically Skyfire checked the lair. Sometimes she saw the Dreamsinger's silver eyes, watching in silence from the grotto. Other times she saw only a silver-pelted wolf, vicious and surly with frustration.

"Who killed you?" she raged in delirium.

The wolf flinched away from the sudden croak of her words; the Dreamsinger refused to give answer.

Skyfire tossed fitfully. She dreamed in the throes of fever that fish with the teeth of predators came to gnaw at her hand. She awoke, screaming with pain, and faced the fearful certainty that her arm had festered from the bite. Rellah was going to be angry; except that Rellah and her bags of smelly herbs were too far distant to help. The thought somehow seemed funny, that the sour old female might wind up scolding bones. Skyfire laughed outright, while thunder growled, and a late afternoon storm showered rain on her head.

Lightning flashed, throwing white-edged reflections into the lair. The Dreamsinger's eyes followed her, shining gray in the shadows. "You're dead," Skyfire muttered, mad with torment and fever. "I will die, your cub will die, and an elf who kills other elves will shelter like a snake in the pack."

Her ravings were absorbed by forest stillness. Twilight darkened around dripping trees. Skyfire lay on her back in the mud, talking to stars that shone through sooty drifts of cloud. They did not bring her Sapling, as she asked; neither did they intercede to prevent the dream that racked her over and over: a staggering step into air, and a fall that ended in blood and pain on the rocky bank of a stream.

Night deepened, and another sort of darkness blanketed Skyfire's thoughts, until even suffering lay beyond feeling.

She awakened, ice-cold, and shivering uncontrollably. Night had gone gray with new dawn, and the wind carried promise of heavy rain. Skyfire opened her eyes. Weakly she attempted to sit up.

Hard hands shoved her back, crashed her bruisingly onto stone. The impact shot pain from her injury clear down her arm to her shoulder. Shock knocked the breath from her lungs. Through a sucking tide of darkness, she saw a face, and tangled hair, and a raggedy, leather-clad elf. His features were familiar. Through dizziness, Skyfire strove to remember.

"Stonethrower?" she murmured; and vertigo fell sharply away before memory. This elf was an outsider, an exile, not among the faces of friends who shared the howls at the Holt. Fear followed, thick enough to choke: Stonethrower had gone off with Two-Spear, his parting words an oath of undying vengeance for the plight which had befallen his chief at Skyfire's hands.

"You!" said Skyfire, recognizing through touch the memory of a sending that had ended in a fatal fall. "It was *you* who pushed my mate from the ledge!"

Stonethrower did not speak. But the flash of the stone

knife he raised above her body offered answer enough. He had returned only to kill her.

Skyfire rolled clumsily aside.

"Whelp of a starved she-wolf!" Stonethrower jerked her back. "You won't escape. You've strayed too far for sending to reach the others. They'll have no warning from you when I return and kill them, one by one, until there is no tribe left."

Strong and cruel and crazy, Stonethrower caught her hair, twisted her head to bare her neck to his knife.

Skyfire thrashed. Her reactions were muddled from fever, and sickness left her too weak to evade the blow. Still, she fought. Aside from threat to her tribe, her death would take the life of the cub within her belly, and the legacy of old magic bequeathed by the Dreamsinger might perish unborn. Frustration, grief, and an overwhelming sense of terror shaped a cry to a mate who was beyond all answer.

KYR!

Skyfire's sending framed the Dreamsinger's essence, just as Stonethrower struck downward.

A leaping streak of silver flew between. Song launched from the cave mouth with a growl of animal rage. He recognized the smell of his master's murderer, and Skyfire's sending rang over and over with echoes of the Dreamsinger's presence. Song's sense of loyalty blurred. He leapt for the hated attacker, bristling with a rending lust to kill.

Stonethrower sensed only movement; then the great wolf's charge overtook him. Committed to his thrust at the chieftess, he barely turned his head when the silver male's weight knocked him down. Jaws found his exposed throat and closed over gristle and windpipe with force enough to crush. Stonethrower dropped the knife. He never heard the splash as his weapon sank in the spring. His heels battered uselessly into stone as the wolf's jaws tightened and worried him, shaking elf flesh until the last scent of life was extinguished.

In time, Song tired of the corpse. He dropped it a short

135

distance off in the forest, shook his pelt straight, and returned to lap at the spring. Once his thirst was satisfied, he raised his dripping muzzle and sniffed the dawn air for game sign. A moan from behind made him turn.

The she-elf lay where she had fallen. The hand outflung from her body smelled overpoweringly of hurt. The wolf whined. A presence was missing from his side. Restless now, Song trotted a few steps back and forth. The scent in his nostrils meant trouble; the hunter who should partner him lay wounded. Drawn by the mystery of pack instinct, the silver creature stepped close, crouched down, and began to lick the still fingers of the elf-hand.

He still worked at the task past sunrise, when Wolfriders burst from the trees.

"She's here!" called Skimmer to the others. Rising wind and clouds heavy with rain served only to increase his concern. "Our chieftess is hurt. Sapling, run and fetch Rellah."

Song poised, ready on an instant to run, to abandon the tie so tenuously forged in the night. But a familiar pack surrounded him, and the habit of companionship was strong. As the Wolfriders hurried to succor their chieftess, Song raised his head. Holding ground at his elf-friend's shoulder, he growled challenge to any who might dare to interfere.

The Flood

by Allen L. Wold

It had been a rather wet autumn to begin with, and as all but the oaks and sycamores lost their leaves, it became absolutely soggy. There were no bad storms, no skyfire and thunder, no strong winds, just an almost constant rain that soaked the ground, the elves, the animals. Hunting was hard in this weather, especially during the last three eights of days, when there had been no letup at all.

But for some reason which she didn't quite understand, Graywing didn't care all that much about it any more. She had been feeling peculiar, a little different somehow, for the last few days, and had lost interest in hunts, weather, and the doings of people. She didn't know why.

All she knew was that today she wasn't going to do any work at all. After all, she was the oldest elf, she could take a day off if she wanted to. She didn't have a very clear idea of what she was going to do, but that didn't bother her, either.

She stood in the entrance to her den and looked out over the common yard, the clear space between the face of the clay cliff that gave Halfhill its name and the stream that provided them with refreshment, sanitation, and recreation—as well as good fish in certain seasons. The gentle slope of the common yard was muddy, with occasional puddles and little rivulets running down to the stream. There were trees on the banks of the stream, more on the other side than on this, but none in the common yard, which extended to the right and left almost to where the sides of the hill came down to the level of the rest of the ground.

All she wanted to do was sit and watch, but it was awfully wet out there. Graywing went back into her storeroom, where she rummaged around until she found the things she wanted—a large pigskin for a waterproof, two poles not quite as tall as she, three small stakes, a bit of gut twine, and a wooden spade. From her bedroom she got a cushion of sheep's wool, skinside out. Then she went outside, with the waterproof draped over her head.

The common yard was not perfectly flat, though it had been trodden on by elves for more hundreds of years than Graywing liked to think about at the moment. Near the cliff, but a dozen or so paces from it, and a bit to the right of the entrance to her den, was a place where the ground was just a bit higher, and thus drier. That was what Graywing wanted. She went to it and set to work.

It was a bit of a trick keeping dry as she dug a small channel around the uphill side of the mound, and even more so to stake out the back end of her waterproof while still under it, but she managed, and also managed to keep her sheepskin cushion dry. She set this down on top of the mound, sat on it, then pushed the ends of each pole into the front corners of the waterproof and the bottom ends into the ground so that the pigskin formed a tiny, personal lean-to tent.

She settled down and looked out at the gray and dripping world around her. It was morning, and there should have been lots of activity, but the rain was keeping people indoors. Fernhare and Glade came up from the stream and called out a greeting as they hurried back toward their den. They looked at her a little oddly, but Graywing didn't care.

Rain fell. Graywing found the sound of it on her waterproof soothing. It was a warm autumn, if a wet one, and she was comfortable. Silvercub, Ebony, and Dewdrop, almost grown but not quite, came out of their respective dens, wearing almost nothing. They glanced her way curiously, said good morning, then went down to the stream together, where they must have found something interesting to do, because they played there, half-concealed by the willows, for quite some time. Sometimes they dug, sometimes they moved rocks, sometimes they just splashed in the rising water. After a while Ebony came back to the dens, and reappeared a moment later with those children

138

and infants who had not gone off hunting with their parents, and took them down to the stream to join in whatever game it was the youths had invented. Graywing felt good just watching them.

After a while she noticed Two Wolves by his den, watching the youngsters down at the stream. He glanced at her and smiled, then went inside. Later he came out again, with Rainbow this time. Rainbow called Silvercub to her, and when he came running up handed him a small bundle like the ones she and Two Wolves were carrying. Off for a hunt. Graywing wished them luck, and watched as they went upstream and out of sight.

The young elves eventually tired of their game and went elsewhere. Other elves came and went. A few stopped to speak with Graywing, and though she was polite she did not encourage conversation, so they left her pretty much alone. Midday came, and everybody went in search of lunch, except Fernhare, who was down by the stream where the children had been, pacing up and down and kneeling to look in the water.

Fernhare was unremarkable as an elf, with one exception —she had had four children, by three different fathers, and none of them from Recognition. Graywing had once envied her the richness of her life, but now she saw it differently. Fernhare had had to endure the loss of two lifemates—only Glade still lived—and one child. Death was natural, a part of the Way, but Graywing had had only one mate in her long years, and only one child, still living, and so had had to suffer less than Fernhare had.

Graywing's thoughts must have taken her quite out of herself, because she was surprised to realize that Fernhare, the object of her contemplations, was kneeling in front of her, staring at her curiously. Water was streaming off her rain-darkened hair, puddling around her bare feet.

"Are you all right?" Fernhare asked.

"Goodness, yes, I was just thinking. I didn't mean to ignore you."

"That's okay. I was just wondering if you wanted something to eat."

"No, I don't think so."

"It's past time; the others have eaten."

"I know, but I'm not that hungry. I'll have something later. Could you figure out what the children were doing down at the stream?"

"Not very well. The water has washed most of what they did away. I'm kind of worried, Graywing. The stream has risen nearly two handspans since Glade and I first came out this morning. That's more than twice as much as it has risen in the last three eights of days. It looks like we're in for a flood."

"We could be, I guess," Graywing said, "though it's never happened before."

"There's always a first time," Fernhare said. "I'm going to talk to Freefoot about it. Are you sure I can't get you something to eat?"

"I'll be just fine," Graywing said.

The day went on, elves came and went, the rain continued to fall, gray and thin and not really the kind of rain that brought floods. If the water had risen as high as Fernhare said it had, then it must have come from the uplands to the south.

Graywing spoke when she was spoken to, but initiated no conversations. When at last she felt hungry she had young Dewdrop bring her a piece of meat. The meat was old, and the wet weather meant it had begun to spoil, but she had eaten worse before.

As she sat she thought that it really wasn't a very good day for watching the world go by, and wondered that she hadn't gotten bored by now. She had never been one to enjoy being inactive for very long. But today she seemed to be content just to sit and think. She wasn't really sure what she was thinking about, but she didn't worry about it.

With the sun always concealed by heavy overcast, it was hard to tell the time, but it was sometime after midafternoon when wolf howls came from the forest. In weather like this, the wolves were left to fend for themselves unless elves wanted to go hunting. A party had gone out before sunup, and it sounded now like they were returning. But there was a quality to the howls that boded ill, not howls of victory, but of grief.

For the first time since she'd come out this morning, Graywing found herself interested in something outside herself. The howls had come from downstream, where the hunters had gone, hoping to find some decent prey on Long Ridge. Graywing felt her stomach contract. Other elves came out of their dens, and stood around on the common yard, watching and waiting. The howls came again, and yes, it was the hunting party, Silverknife's wolf loudest of all—and most grief-stricken. Somehow the rain seemed colder and grayer than it had just a few moments ago.

It wasn't long before everyone's worst fears were confirmed. Out of the forest came Talon, Dreamsnake, and Stride, bearing between them a frightful burden wrapped in their waterskins. Their wolves slunk along beside them, wet, bedraggled, heads and tails down. Silverknife's wolf, Rakejaw, came behind, and howled again.

The three hunters brought their burden up to the common yard.

"Where is Stringsong?" Talon asked.

"He went out," Freefoot said, "shortly after you left."

Suretrail stood beside Ebony, and turned to the youth and told him to go find Stringsong. Ebony did not need to be told what message to take. He stared for a long moment at the burden the three hunters still held, gave a deep sigh, and then went toward the stream, and across it on the bridge tree, to find Silverknife's father.

The three hunters now took their burden up to the entrance of the den which Stringsong had shared with his daughter since Whiteraven, Silverknife's mother, had died, nearly a hundred years ago, when Silverknife had been just an infant known as Warble. There they put the body down, and the others gathered around.

Graywing's chest hurt, and not, she knew, from the weather. She had seen death many times before, usually violent, but this time it was different somehow. Carefully, so as not to upset the supports of her little tent, she got up from her seat and joined the others.

"What happened?" Freefoot asked. The full story would be told when Stringsong got here, but Freefoot was chief, and needed to know.

"We were on the south side of Long Ridge," Dreamsnake said, "just below where the boulders stick out. The rain must have washed a lot of the soil away. Silverknife slipped in the mud, put out a hand to steady herself, and the boulders above her fell."

No predator springing from ambush. No prey defending itself to the death. Just a stupid accident.

No more was said at the moment. The elves waited, and even the children and infants seemed to know that this was not the time to fuss or play.

At last Stringsong came, with Ebony beside him. The youth had told the elder elf the worst, and he was as prepared as he could be. The other elves made way for him as he approached. He knelt by the covered head, Dreamsnake beside him, Talon and Stride on the other side.

Only now did they take the coverings from Silverknife, the brightest and the best of the younger elves. Her body was crushed and broken, smeared with mud and blood. The rain fell on her and began to wash her.

Now Talon, Dreamsnake, and Stride told what happened, and this time they told the full story. By the time they had finished, Silverknife's body was clean. Stringsong, Dreamsnake, and Stride straightened the bent limbs, the crooked body, while Glade, Fairheart, Starflower, and Dewdrop went to the nearest trees and cut, as they would not have done on any other occasion, a few slender branches with which they made a light litter. Then they brought the litter to Silverknife, and put her on it, and carried her into her den. The other elves went, too, except for Graywing. She just stood in the rain for a long moment, then went back to her shelter to sit, and think, and watch the rain come down.

Graywing had not discovered what she was thinking about, nor figured out how she felt about Silverknife's death, or why she should feel the way she did, when the elves of the Holt came out of Stringsong's den. Had the mourning been that brief? No, the sky was darkening, it was late afternoon. Graywing had just lost track of the time. That was not like her, but she suspected that it would be more typical in the future.

Some of the elves, especially the youths and children and infants, went home to their dens, but others made up a special party. Stringsong took the lead, with his wolf, Striker, and Silverknife's Rakejaw on either side. He walked slowly toward the upstream end of the common yard, and behind him came Dreamsnake, Talon, Stride, and Freefoot, carrying Silverknife in her light litter. After them came Suretrail, Starflower, Fairheart, Moonblossom, and Treewing. Slowly they made their way around the western end of Halfhill and northward, into the woods. Every now and then Rakejaw howled softly, and turned as if to drop back to where her mistress was being carried, but Stringsong kept her beside him.

Graywing watched the funeral procession, felt the chill of late afternoon, of autumn, of senseless death. Silverknife would be carried deep into the woods, far from the Holt, into places where the elves seldom went, to a private place where she would be left to the care of her wolf and other wolves of the Holt. That was the Way. The weak die, and the strong die—oh, and surely Silverknife had been one of the strongest!—and life goes on.

Light faded from the gray sky, and Graywing finally decided it was time to pack up her shelter and go into her den. There she found a bit of something for her supper, and went to her bed, almost surprised at how good it felt to be warm under the furs. She hadn't been aware of being quite so cold out there on the common yard.

She lay in her bed for what seemed like a long time, though she knew that her sense of time was not to be trusted any more. She had lit no lights, so it was dark in her den, and quiet except for the gentle sound of the stream flowing past, which should have been shut out by the skins that covered the entrance. The water was so high, and getting higher. Graywing seemed to remember a couple of other times when the stream had risen, but she didn't care to pursue the thought at the moment.

143

Maybe she drowsed or maybe she didn't, but she was surprised to hear footsteps squishing through the mud outside her den, and soft voices. Wherever her thoughts had been, they came back to the present, and it took her a moment to realize that she was hearing the funeral party returning from their trek into the woods. It was after sundown then, but not all that late after all. Poor Stringsong, she thought. She knew he would take it hard. Somewhere off in the distance, a wolf howled. She turned over under her furs and went to sleep.

The next day was as rainy as before. Everyone at the Holt was getting more and more depressed, especially Catcher. She was the master woodcrafter, and traps were her specialty, and she liked to make them out in the sun. But for too long now she'd had to be content to work just inside the entrance to her den.

Today she was making trigger-drops. Catcher could make a trigger small enough to be hidden by a few leaves, but strong enough to hold a deadweight heavier than an elf; a trigger so stable that you could leave it for eight days, but so sensitive that a mouse could set it off; a trigger that would resist anything smaller than a pig, but that could be set by a child.

She liked to start early, and so she was already up and working when she saw Graywing come out of her den and set up her little skin shelter, as she had done the day before. Her movements were more hesitant today, her face was thinner, and the gray streaks in her hair, from which she got her name, were now white, and more than three fingers broad. The change had begun when the rains had. Catcher didn't understand it, and it frightened her.

Glade and Fernhare came out of their den to wash at the swollen stream, and said a word or two to Graywing on their way back. Then they came over to say good morning to Catcher.

"Is there something wrong with Graywing?" Fernhare asked.

Catcher put down the trigger upright she had been smoothing. "I don't know," she said.

144

"She's getting old," Glade said.

"I've never seen an elf get old before."

"No one has," Fernhare told her.

Aging like this was something beyond an elf's experience, though they knew it happened to animals, and the wolves who were their partners sometimes got old. Still, none of them really understood what old age meant. Changes occurred, to be sure, but they were slow and subtle.

Glade went off to go hunting with Dreamsnake and Two Wolves, and Fernhare went back to her own den. Catcher went on working. Several times she thought she ought to go and speak to Graywing but she could never work up the courage. She didn't want to see how much her mother had aged in just the last day.

At midday the rain slackened for a while. The clouds did not thin, the sun did not break through, but for a few moments the rain became just a drizzle. Rainbow, down at the stream with the children, hoped it was a good sign, but even as she sent the youngsters back to their parents and caretakers for lunch, the rain got heavier again.

Rainbow's main fear was flood. The stream was now more than six handspans above its normal level, and still rising, and the face of the cliff was soggy and running with thin streams of mud and dissolved clay. She washed the mud off her hands and went back to her den.

She got a piece of meat and a few white-roots that hadn't started to mold yet and brought them out to join Rillwalker and Puckernut, who were eating outside, in spite of the weather, under the branches of a blackwood tree, an evergreen broadleaf, at the upstream end of the common yard. Puckernut had woven some of the smaller branches together to provide protection from the rain. Catcher joined them a few moments later, bringing some dried red-berries and fuzzy-fruit. Graywing stayed where she was.

As they sat under the blackwood tree, they talked about the rain, and the rising water, and the soggy floors in some of the dens, and the face of the cliff which was being washed away.

"I think we need a drier place to live," Rainbow said at last.

Rillwalker agreed with her, but Puckernut did not. "Rain's rain," he said. "What's to worry about?"

But this was something that Rainbow had been thinking about for some time. Her idea, not clearly formed, was that the elves needed to find a new holt where they would be safe from the threat of flood, and she urged her companions to help her find such a place.

"We're just fine where we are," Puckernut insisted, and Catcher agreed. Rillwalker did not, and said so quite strongly, as if she, too, had been thinking about seeking refuge somewhere.

The conversation got quite loud, and Hornbird, eating alone in her den, heard the ruckus and came out to find out what was going on. She saw the four elves under the blackwood tree, and since she was more than a little bored decided to join them, bringing a double handful of dreamberries, slightly wrinkled now, to share.

She didn't think much of Rainbow's plan, however. "There's never been a flood before," she said.

"There could always be a first time," Rillwalker told her.

"I don't believe it."

The two sides were quickly drawn, with Rillwalker and Rainbow advocating the development of a new holt, and Hornbird and Puckernut insisting that their present holt was best even if it was damp. Catcher tended to side with Puckernut, but did not participate in the discussion.

It was not a serious argument. It was more interesting than sitting in one's den, or trudging through the mud on a futile hunt. Hornbird enjoyed it especially. But her high spirits washed away with the rain when, the others having things to do, she went back to her den alone, and passed Graywing on the way.

Hornbird was, after all, the second oldest elf. Would the changes that were happening to Graywing happen to her someday? She would rather die in a hunt.

Back in her den she gathered up her tools and supplies. Hornbird was the bonesmith of the Holt, and kept the elves

146

supplied with needles, hooks, small knives, bird-points, and so on, as well as decorative items. Her depression was not improved when her favorite bone saw broke a tooth and had to be discarded, and it got worse when a slither of mud and gravel came down from the face of the cliff beside her doorway. The Holt was old, too, and maybe it, like the saw, like Graywing, was worn out.

Hornbird wasn't the only one who felt depressed. Fangslayer had been grumping and fussing all day long, until Deerstorm, after their meager evening meal, finally got tired of it. "If you're so unhappy," she said, "why don't you do something about it?"

"I might as well," he said. "The water's going to get higher before it gets lower. We need to set up a temporary camp somewhere, until the worst is past."

"I think you're right," Deerstorm said. "I'm surprised it took you this long to figure it out."

Fangslayer had seen flash floods before, up in the highlands, and knew that streams and rivers could rise very high with frightening suddenness. He was surprised, in fact, that such a flood hadn't come already.

In spite of this, he wasn't confident about his decision, but he was determined to carry it out. What made it difficult was that he was afraid of the rising waters, and didn't want others to know that. When they went to bed for the night, the sound of the stream outside was far louder than he'd ever heard it before, and it made him nervous. Would others discover his fear if he proposed a temporary refuge? And what if the water rose no higher after all; would he look silly then, having gone out on a limb?

Best not to think about it until he had to, he thought, and tried to convince himself of that. He might have rested easier had he known how many other elves shared his fear, even some of those who professed the least concern. But they were no more eager than he to reveal what they perceived as a weakness. And so each struggled alone with private thoughts, until at last even the most wakeful elf slept.

It was morning, and toward the middle, but the overcast was so thick that Graywing had no idea at all of where the sun was. It was still raining, of course.

Down by the stream the youngsters were digging in the bank. Graywing thought about joining them, but never quite got up the energy. She could remember what it was like to play, though she hadn't felt that free for years, not since Prey-Pacer's time. Had she really been alive that long? How many names had she had?

Her thoughts drifted as far away in time as Prey-Pacer was, and she was badly startled when she realized that someone was staring at her, crouched only a pace or two away. But it was only Fangslayer, who moved back hastily and apologized when he saw her jump.

"Have you eaten yet?" he asked, as if he'd asked the same question before.

"Yes, I have, thank you," Graywing said. She smiled at him, and he smiled back, but he was not really content with her simple answer, and perhaps he had something else in his mind.

"Deerstorm and Ebony and I are going to find a dry place where we can go if the water gets too high," he said. "Would you like to come along?"

"Thank you, no," Graywing said. "I've got too much to think about." Fangslayer looked at her for a moment, then nodded and went away to talk with Freefoot about his plan.

Graywing thought that Fangslayer had a good idea; this weather was unlike anything she had experienced before, either here or at any other place where she'd lived in her long life. And just because it hadn't flooded before didn't mean it wouldn't do it now. In fact, she was rather convinced that it would. But even if it did, she had no interest in leaving.

Stringsong came out and walked halfway to the stream, then stopped, as if he had forgotten what he had come for. Graywing felt sorry for him. He had devoted his life to Silverknife. Graywing had felt before that Stringsong's devotion to his daughter was a bit overdone, for his sake if not for hers, and now she saw that she had been right.

There was nothing she or anyone else could do about it, however; it was something Stringsong would have to work out for himself.

After a bit Catcher came out, and with just a glance at Graywing, went up to Stringsong, put a hand on his shoulder, spoke a quiet word or two to him. Then they went off downstream together, to find something fresh to eat.

Graywing tried to remember if in fact she'd had a meal herself. She'd told Fangslayer she had, but she was hungry. She'd forgotten whether she'd eaten or not.

Fernhare came toward her from the stream. Graywing hadn't noticed her going down.

"The water's not rising so fast today," Fernhare said to her. "Maybe the worst is over."

"I certainly hope so," Graywing said.

"But you don't think it is?"

"It's still raining."

Fernhare looked upstream, then down. She looked across the stream into the forest, which now was more than a little boggy, and back at the cliff face which had eroded dangerously.

"What are we going to do?" Fernhare asked.

"I don't know," Graywing said simply, and since she didn't seem inclined to say anything more, Fernhare went away.

The morning passed. Other elves came and went, and some of them even spoke to her, but Graywing stopped paying any attention. Instead she thought about how Freefoot was going to handle this crisis, for crisis it would surely be. She did not know that he had already given his approval to Fangslayer's plan.

Graywing thought back about the other chiefs she had known. What would Freefoot's mother, Huntress Skyfire, have done in this situation? She'd never had the worry of floods like this to contend with. Skyfire's brother, Two-Spear, hadn't been chief long enough to have been tested like this. And Prey-Pacer, who'd been chief when Graywing was born, wouldn't have cared.

She could almost remember Prey-Pacer. She tried to conjure up his image in her mind's eye. Funny how sometimes she confused him with her father, Maplebrake, and sometimes with Hawk's Claw, her lifemate who had died before Freefoot acquired his adult name.

Why would that be? Prey-Pacer had been nothing like her father, and Hawk's Claw had been one of a kind; there'd never been another romance after him, not even a lovemate.

She must be getting old, maybe that was it.

Her thoughts came back to the present, and she noticed that there was a trickle of water near her feet. She used her little wooden shovel to adjust the drainage ditch behind her. That loosened her rain shield, so she tightened the stakes until it was just right.

That done, she looked around her at the rainy Holt, feeling as if she had just wakened from a nap. The common yard was soggy, the forest across the stream was boggy. The Holt certainly did look bedraggled.

Graywing had in fact been more than right about Stringsong, more than even *he* was aware. Death was, after all, a commonplace. His parents were dead, his mate was dead, her parents and brother were dead, so many others had died. So then, aside from the fact that it was his daughter, why did this death hit him so hard?

He couldn't help but think of the waste it was. Silverknife had had so much potential. The more he tried to shut the thoughts away the more he hurt. But if he let himself think, he became confused. He couldn't believe that she was really dead.

He didn't want to bother anybody with his problems, and couldn't see that Silverknife's death was everybody's concern. So he spent the entire morning wrestling with the truth, never winning, never losing, only miring himself down in unexpressed grief.

At last he couldn't stand sitting alone in his den any more, so he went outside to see if anything was going on. The only person on the common yard was Graywing, sitting under her tiny shelter. He went over and, squatting down in the rain, spoke to her. She answered, and for a while they talked, but all he could bring himself to talk about was the weather, the bad hunting, the rising stream. From the way she looked at him, he thought she knew what he was trying to say and was unable to, but he couldn't bring himself to mention death.

Very few animals died of old age, but Stringsong had seen a few, so he had a vague idea of what was involved. The trouble was that Graywing looked like that—grayed, weakened, thinned out, curled up. Death was too close to her, so he rambled on for a while, then felt foolish squatting in the wet, so he went back into his den.

He had to keep busy. Stringsong was the cordmaker, the thread spinner, the rope twister. That was what had given him his name, rather than his exceptional hearing, or his ability to sense talents in children.

He went to his shelves, extensive and deep, where he kept his raw materials. Gut wouldn't dry in this weather. Hair was frizzly. Leather was too damp, and rawhide wouldn't dry, either. Bark, grass, web-silk, none of them would work while the rain persisted.

It was futile, and a waste of his time, even to try exercising his craft. He went back outside and over to Two Wolves's den, but the other elf was still out hunting. Stringsong tried talking to Rainbow, but she could think of nothing but finding someplace else to live, with which idea Stringsong had no patience.

Maybe hunting would be a good idea after all. Even in the rain there was a chance he could run across something. He went back to his den and thought about which way he would go, what would he look for—deer, bear, pig, ravvit, antelope out on the prairie to the north? It had been a while since he'd gone out with Yellowtooth. But even as he decided not to use his bow because the string was slack with the damp, and picked up his spear instead, he lost interest in the project. He didn't feel like making the effort. He didn't want to go alone. It would take too long to get anywhere. He still had some food left.

He went back outside and down to the stream, which was not noticeably higher than it had been yesterday, to where the youths and children were playing. He stood for a while and watched as they made mudslides and waterfalls, dug channels in the bank which they blocked up and then opened up again. They'd dug an upper pool, which they filled with water, and then let it out through specially prepared grooves and tunnels. They were having a marvelous time.

But after a while their very youth made him sad. Dewdrop and Silvercub were not that much younger than Silverknife was—had been.

He turned away before his emotions could get the better of him and started walking slowly back up the gentle slope of the common yard toward the Holt. He saw Catcher, sitting just inside the entranceway to her den, and Hornbird in hers. Both of them were working at their crafts, making themselves useful. Stringsong felt useless, and a burden.

That wasn't true, he knew, but he had to talk to somebody about it, about his confusion and how he felt about Silverknife's death. And so he went to Catcher, who smiled at him and gestured to him to sit down beside her. He did so, and thought for a moment, and started to say something, but Catcher wasn't listening. He repeated himself, but her thoughts were elsewhere. After a while he realized that she was staring at her mother.

He silently cursed himself for his insensitivity. If he hadn't felt it appropriate to talk to Graywing about death, how much less appropriate to talk to Catcher. He gripped her shoulder gently to gain her attention, excused himself, and left. Maybe Hornbird would be better after all. She was the second oldest elf, and had helped other elves through times like this before.

But he didn't get very far with his conversation with her. She just wanted him to cheer up, grow up, accept life, accept the Way, and didn't really let him speak his mind.

When he left her, after only a little while, he went toward the downstream end of the Holt, so that he wouldn't have to pass Graywing and Catcher again, and climbed up the steeper slope here at the edge of the cliff to the top of Halfhill. He went along the edge of the cliff, treacherous now and almost crumbling, until he came to the place over his own den, then sat down and let his feet dangle over the side. The rain fell on him through the leafless branches overhead, but he didn't mind. Somehow it seemed appropriate.

From here he could see just how much of the land was flooded. There was water standing all over the other side of the stream, both upstream and down. The stream itself was much broader in places than it had been; low places were swamps, and marshy areas were almost lakes.

Maybe Rainbow was right. Stringsong watched as she went down to the stream, then came back with Silvercub. They stopped to speak with Graywing for a moment, too far away for him to hear the words, then went back toward their den. Had he leaned over, he could have seen the entranceway. He didn't bother. And if Rainbow was right, so what? It didn't matter, not to him at least. He just sat on the edge of the cliff, and the rain started coming down harder.

Fangslayer's camp was just up the backside of Halfhill a walk or so away, along the ridge to where a stand of small trees grew close together at the crest. The trees provided a framework from which Fangslayer, Deerstorm, and Ebony had stretched skins, forming a kind of wall-less tent. The ground sloped down and away from the tented area in all directions.

The three elves added more to the tent as the day wore on, using a store of skins which had been set aside for clothing. Each skin was hung so that the drip from one fell onto the next, leaving lots of light and space between the skins themselves. The design worked, however, only because there was no wind to blow the rain in under the overhangs.

Ebony, being the lightest, was up in the branches while his parents worked and rigged below. The rain started coming down harder, and they were almost out of skins, but before Ebony could come down he heard someone coming along the crest of the ridge from the direction of the Holt. A moment later Suretrail, slickered and carrying a bundle of skins and essential belongings, came toiling through the rain and mud toward them. He greeted them cheerfully enough.

"It's getting far too wet back there," he said. "The floor of my lowest room is getting muddy. I thought I'd come up and stay with you for a while, if that's all right."

"Of course it is," Deerstorm said. "Come in out of the wet."

Fangslayer led Suretrail into an inner part of the camp— it was surprisingly large for the work of just three people. There were fir boughs piled in one corner ready for making beds, and a pile of rocks for a fire-pit and a water trough. There he put down everything but the skins, which he carried back to where the others had been working.

Even though it was raining harder now, Deerstorm and Ebony went up into the branches, while Suretrail and Fangslayer worked below. At first it seemed to Suretrail that they were making a bit too much camp for four people, but Fangslayer assured him that, if the flood did come, he wanted to be ready for the rest of the people back at the Holt. And if the flood didn't come, at least it gave them something to do.

Fernhare also had found something to do, though she was less than sure of what it was, and was completely sure it served no useful purpose. With a skin draped over her head, she moved some stones by the bank of the stream, upstream from the Holt a ways, where the ground was especially low. Her objective was to block off the slowly rising water, to see if she could create an area lower than water level but dry—except for the rain, of course. She had gotten so involved in the project that she played like a child, fascinated and frustrated by her inability to control the water.

Graywing, sitting under her tiny shelter, had been watching her for the last couple hours. Though Fernhare was far enough away, and there were intervening bushes, that Graywing couldn't see exactly what she was doing, her movements were the same as the children's when they'd been digging in the bank nearer the cliff, so she assumed that Fernhare was doing much the same. Why, she had no idea, and didn't really care. Fernhare was enjoying herself, and that was all that mattered.

A little bit later Glade, Dreamsnake, and Two Wolves came out of the forest, carrying a deer. As they passed Fernhare she stopped moving her rocks, half-embarrassed to be caught playing like a child, but they didn't care. Their wolves, bedraggled but in high spirits, came with the hunters. Two Wolves was limping, and in some pain, but grinned at Graywing as they came to the Holt. He went into his den at once while the other two set the deer down in front of Graywing, to begin the job of butchery.

Two Wolves had just sprained his knee, but intended to rest for the remainder of the afternoon. Fernhare helped with the butchery, as did Rainbow and Hornbird. Graywing just sat and watched as the work went on in front of her. She accepted without comment the bits of liver, marrow, and brains that they gave her.

As they worked, Glade and Dreamsnake told about the woods, how wet and flooded it was already. It was boggy everywhere, except where the land was very much higher or rockier. Even slopes were showing a lot of runoff.

"I wish the Holt were a bit higher and drier," Fernhare said.

"There's always Bald Hill," Rainbow told her. "I think we ought to move up there."

"And leave the Holt?" Fernhare said. "I couldn't think of it."

"What if it floods?" Rainbow asked.

"I can stick it out. Besides, how high could the water get?"

"It can't get much higher," Dreamsnake said. "In fact, it seems to have stopped rising already. I'm going to stay right here, thank you."

"But what if it starts to rise again?" Fernhare asked. "Some of the dens are pretty close to the ground, they could fill up, what then? Maybe we ought to be ready to move out, in an emergency."

"I agree," Glade said, "if there is indeed an emergency. But there's no need to rush off right now, as Fangslayer and Suretrail have done."

"If we stay here until it's too late," Fernhare said, "we might as well stay here altogether, but if we're going to go, maybe we should go right now."

"Well, I'm not going," Hornbird said emphatically. "The Holt has never flooded before, and it won't now."

"I don't know," Fernhare said. "The stream *has* risen a bit today, about four fingerbreadths."

"That's not much of a rise," Hornbird snorted.

"Maybe not, but you never can tell."

Glade sighed in resignation. Fernhare just couldn't seem to make up her mind. It was partly to get away from her indecision that he had gone off hunting. His mate's vacillation was causing the others some frustration, too, he could see. But Graywing just sat and listened.

Catcher woke up the next morning feeling far from cheerful. Her bed was damp. She got up and dragged the furs into another room where the floor was dry, and although she would have liked to sleep in a bit longer there was nothing for it but to start the day. She got dressed and scrounged around in her larder for something to eat, but there was only a little bit of hopper meat left, and some prickly-pads that were very limp and wrinkly. She would have to go hunting today if she wanted more, unless she found something in her traps, which she doubted, since most of them had been set in places which would be flooded by now.

She heard voices outside, so she went to see what was happening. Rainbow, Two Wolves, their daughter Crystalmoss, and Silvercub were setting out bundles, as if they were going on a long expedition.

"Going up to Fangslayer's camp?" Catcher asked.

"That's just temporary," Rainbow said. "We're going to Bald Hill. It's dry up there, plenty of shelter."

"Not much drinking water," Catcher said. She glanced curiously at Two Wolves.

"There's a spring not far away," he said with a wry smile. He would go along with Rainbow's silly plan, for as long as she cared to try it, but his heart wasn't in it.

"It's not going to rain forever," Catcher said, "and when it stops it will dry up and we'll be comfortable here again."

"I don't believe it," Rainbow said. She hoisted her load on her back. Two Wolves and Silvercub did the same, but Crystalmoss hesitated.

"I'm not moving up there," she said to Catcher. "I'm just helping them carry stuff."

"Good for you," Catcher said, and started to go down to the stream, but Rillwalker came out of her den just then, carrying a bundle of her own.

"Are you going along with this?" Catcher asked her incredulously.

"The water's going to rise," Rillwalker said. "It's not the rain here, it's the storms in the uplands."

"But that's no reason to abandon Halfhill altogether," Catcher insisted.

But Rillwalker, like Rainbow, had her mind made up, and nothing Catcher could say would change it. At last Catcher gave up trying and let them go off on their way while she went down to the ever-deepening stream to wash up. She was more than ready to eat when she got back to her den, but her bowstring was limp, so she took two javelins and went out to see if any of her traps were still above water.

Meanwhile Rainbow and her party went north and west toward Bald Hill. When they got there they found their chosen caves still dry, and spent the rest of the day fixing up two dens, one for Rillwalker—and Puckernut when he learned the error of his ways—and the other for Rainbow, Two Wolves, and Silvercub. As soon as she could, Crystalmoss went back to Halfhill.

There were other elves, however, who held to a middle

ground. They had no desire to abandon Halfhill, but were tired of being soggy, and bored into the bargain. So it was that Brightmist, Broadhand, Longoak, and Stride all went up to the ridge-crest camp, bringing more tentskins with them.

The camp was becoming quite large by now. Suretrail and Ebony had their own private quarters, curtained off by blackwood branches laced together with willow. There was plenty of room for more, and once the new skins were strung, they would be able to accommodate anybody else who might come up later.

In the middle of the camp was the main fire-pit, lined with stones and kept burning day and night. Smoke escaped through the wide windows between layers of skins overhead. At the back of the camp was the water trough, into which the rainwater flowed from the tentskins. The overflow ran down a channel and behind some bushes.

It was altogether a satisfactory camp, and what with adding new tents and maintaining old, adding more privacy screens, and developing a better fire-pit, nobody had a chance to be bored any more.

Those elves left back at the Holt were not so lucky. Daytime at the Holt was usually spent socializing and working at the various crafts that each elf specialized in. That was hard to do in a constant downpour. The only alternative was to sit around in somebody's den, but the dens were not very large, and after nearly four eights of days of doing that, people were getting desperate.

Hornbird was having an especially hard time of it. For a while she visited Dreamsnake, along with Puckernut and Crystalmoss, who told them about her mother's strange ideas for making Bald Hill a permanent new holt. Puckernut and Dreamsnake were gentle in their ridicule of Rainbow, and Crystalmoss more or less agreed with them, on principle anyway, but Hornbird thought the conversation futile, and after a while excused herself.

Looking for someone else to talk to, she went to Freefoot's den, where she also found Starflower, and Bluesky, who was feeling especially lonely. Freefoot and

Starflower were convinced that everybody would have to move up to the ridge-crest camp eventually, and were glad that Fangslayer and Deerstorm had already done so much work against that time. Bluesky didn't care much one way or another, as long as she had some company, but Hornbird was determined to stick it out at Halfhill, no matter what happened.

When she tired of that conversation, Hornbird went to visit Fairheart and Moonblossom. Talon and Treewing were already there. They, too, were talking about moving to the emergency camp, and Hornbird lost her patience.

"There's no reason to go anywhere," she said. "Nothing is going to happen."

"It's already happening," Treewing said. "Suretrail's den has two fingers of water on the lowest floor, and that's not the only den that's wet."

"Then why haven't you already gone up to the ridge?" Hornbird demanded.

"Because our dens are dry, so far," Talon said.

They could see that her bad temper really had to do with something else, and tried to cheer her up, but Hornbird wasn't aware herself of what the true problem was. She was anxious, felt deserted, felt her judgment wasn't being valued—and secretly feared her judgment was wrong. She went back to her den, where she lay on her bed furs and listened as boulders moved downstream as the flood waters continued to rise.

By midday of the next day the stream had risen to the base of the cliff in some places. Graywing continued to sit on her cushion under her rain shield, in spite of this. Hers was one of the few "dry" areas left out on the common yard. The upstream end of the yard had flooded first, oddly enough, but the rest of the yard would soon be under water, too.

Catcher had brought her some meat earlier, and had asked her to come in, but Graywing had refused. She appreciated her daughter's concern, and thought she understood what was bothering her, but found it hard to worry about anything other than her own thoughts at the moment. She munched the meat slowly, not really tasting it.

The rain seemed to be letting up a bit, but the stream kept on getting higher. Graywing knew she would have to move eventually, but for the moment she was content to sit and watch.

Graywing knew that her presence here was giving the other elves some cause for concern, but apparently they had become accustomed to seeing her sitting under her shelter. When they did speak to her, she had to work either to respond with a smile or a word, or to ignore them. She sympathized with them, but really wished they would leave her alone. Maybe if she went inside they would.

She stepped out from her shelter and stood up, and for a moment she thought she was going to fall. She felt cramped, though she'd been there only half a day. It was hard for her to straighten up.

She pulled up the stakes, took out the poles, dropped the skin over her sheep's-wool pad, and picked the whole bundle up and carried it to the entrance to her den. She had to wade through muddy water to get there. There she tossed the skin, shovel, poles, and stakes aside and put the cushion down just inside her doorway. This was at least six handspans above the ground, and her den inside was higher still, so she wouldn't have to worry about the stream, unless it got a lot higher. Not like some others, who soon enough would have to seek refuge in the ridge-crest camp.

But there was no way Graywing was going to go there, as good an idea as it might be for everybody else. As for Rainbow's silly escape, Graywing hoped it was just a temporary aberration.

Stringsong was another matter. He would have to come to terms with Silverknife's death sooner or later, and the sooner the better. Graywing had known other elves in her time who had mourned too hard but not well enough, and who had followed the deceased into whatever realm the dead called their own. That was something she found herself rather looking forward to finding out about, but Stringsong, he was too young—indeed, as Silverknife had been.

For a while Graywing toyed with the idea of going up to the ridge-crest camp, if Stringsong would go with her, but she just couldn't bring herself to take the idea seriously. Stringsong had a long life ahead of him, but she knew her own remaining time was very short indeed, and she had to put her own interest above others, now, at the last. Moving to the ridge-crest camp would take too much effort, physically and emotionally. She had other, more important things to think about.

She looked out at the muddy, swirling water covering most of the common yard. From the stream she could hear the sounds of boulders and rocks moving with the force of the flow of the flood. From nearer at hand she could hear an occasional splash as some of the cliff face fell off. Rising water wasn't the only problem. The ground above the dens was waterlogged, and only the fact that the clay was mostly the kind that swelled up when it got wet kept their roofs dry. Even that wouldn't last forever, once water found its way down small cracks and crevices, as it had along the bottoms of some dens coming up. It was likely that the dens would drown from the bottom rather than from the top.

Graywing sat in her entrance a while longer, and then decided that watching the rain was both too tedious and too distracting. There were a few elves who had gone off on extended hunting expeditions, and whom she didn't expect to return for several days, maybe several eights of days yet, but that was the way that was. Everybody else, well, she'd said what she'd wanted to say to them. Time to think more about these other things that kept on intruding into the edges of her consciousness, into the background of her dreams. She didn't know exactly what they were, and wanted to find out.

She was surprised at how much energy it took to stand up. She was not at all premature in making this last move. She went into her bedroom, gathered up as many skins and

161

furs as she could carry, and took them into a far, inner chamber, high up in the back of her den. There she made a nest, which she amplified with more furs, as many as she had.

When that was to her satisfaction she went to her larder. She got several gourds of drinking water, and took them back to her nest, and put them in a niche near to hand. She would need no food.

The main chamber of every den had a fire-pit, and at this season of the year there was usually a small fire kept in it, for warmth as well as light. Graywing's fire had gone out several days ago, and she saw no reason to start another now. But she did think she'd like some light, so she worked with her drill until she got the tinder to smolder, and from it lit a lamp. Then she got a little extra oil, and a twist of wick, and took these, too, into her new nest chamber.

She stood in the doorway, looking at her arrangements, and felt that there was something still missing. It seemed to take her a long time to think of it. At last she wandered back through her den, from room to room, until she found, near the entrance, in its alcove, her spear, and a couple of good throwing stones which she'd been saving for a special need. Yes, she thought, that was what was missing. She gathered them up and took them to her nest.

And now there was just one more thing. In her bedroom, in the neat pile where she kept her clothes, at the bottom, was a belt, made and decorated by her mother. It had been repaired many times over the years, until at last it was too fragile to wear any more, and she'd put it away for safekeeping. Now was the time to take it out again. She took off the one she had been wearing—how loose it had become—and put on her mother's belt in its place.

That was all she needed to do. She went back and up into her innermost chamber, to where the tiny light glowed on her deep pile of furs. The spear stood by the door, the stones on the floor beside it, the water gourds and lamp in the niches in the walls. It was good.

She got into her nest and made herself comfortable. It wasn't all that cold, so she didn't have to burrow down in the furs. Or maybe she just couldn't feel the cold any more. She had no idea what time it was, at least by the sun, but she had no illusions about her own time. It was very near. She was going to die, and soon.

She was fascinated by the thought. She had survived every disease, every accident. Not only was she the oldest elf in the Holt, she was the oldest elf she had ever known or heard of. But now was the time for it to end, and it would be by simple old age. No other elf had ever experienced that before. Fascinating, she thought, and felt the other thoughts that had been teasing her these last few days gathering around the edges of her mind. Fascinating, she thought, and let those other thoughts come to her, if they would. Death was going to be a very interesting experience indeed.

Stringsong, on the contrary, did not think that death was interesting at all. In fact he found the thought so disturbing, so distasteful, that he had gotten himself involved in a project he would otherwise have avoided.

It had never been Stringsong's pleasure to dig in the dirt. But here he was, digging a trench in front of Dreamsnake's den, along with her and Fernhare. The stream came nearly up to the entrance here, and they were trying to see if they could dig a channel so that the water would run away instead of into the den. The only problem was, there was nowhere for the water in the channel to go, so it just filled up, forming a pool. The deeper they dug, the deeper the pool got, until at last they decided they'd be better to stop. Someone might come along and, thinking the muddy water no more than a fingerbreadth deep, step in it up to his knees.

"Think we ought to fill it in?" Dreamsnake asked.

"Probably," Fernhare said, kicking at the now-runny mud which they had dug from the trench. "It'll be awfully soft."

"Looks like we've made it worse instead of better."

"We should fill it with rocks," Fernhare suggested, "or cover it with strong branches."

"I never thought," Dreamsnake said, "that we'd have to have someplace for the water to run *to*."

"I did," Fernhare said, "and I'm sorry now I didn't say anything before."

Stringsong did not contribute to the discussion as they did their best to repair the damage. He was doing *his* best not to think at all. But as they filled in the trench and laid a stout section of branch across it, he noticed something missing from the common yard. There was a mound sticking up out of the water.

"Where's Graywing?" he asked at last.

The others looked up and noticed that the old elf was indeed gone from her place.

"I don't know," Dreamsnake said. "Was she there when we came out?"

"I don't think so," Fernhare said, "now that you mention it. Should we see if she's in her den?"

But Dreamsnake, though she was Graywing's granddaughter, was reluctant to intrude on the old elf, especially the way she had been these last few days, and suggested they talk to Catcher about it instead.

Catcher was working in front of her own den, by herself, piling rocks in front of the entrance. As the three elves went over to her, they could see that her idea was basically more sound than Dreamsnake's had been. By raising a barrier, well in front of the entrance, some of the water was being kept back. But it was hard to get the rocks to fit close enough together to keep all the water out, and when she tried to pack the spaces between with mud, the water just washed it away. She tried mortaring the rocks with clay, and that seemed to hold for a while, especially if she put down the clay before putting a rock on top. But eventually the water found a crack or hole and started leaking through.

Her main problem was that there weren't many rocks here, and Catcher had had to go far to the upstream end of the cliff to find those big enough to work with but small enough to carry.

The fact of her mother's departure from her accustomed

place was news to Catcher, and she had no explanation.
Now that it was brought to her attention, she was a bit
worried. "She's been getting frailer almost by the hour,"
she said. "I brought her some meat a little while ago, and
she looked like she hadn't eaten anything for eights of days.
I hope she hasn't wandered off somewhere."

"More likely she's gone inside," Fernhare said. "Should
we go and find out?"

"Well, I'm going to," Catcher said, "whether we should
or not," and she put down the rock she'd been holding and
went to Graywing's den. The others followed after.

Catcher stepped up into the entrance. It was dark inside,
and she could hear no sound. "Graywing," she called,
softly at first, then louder.

"Yes, child," she heard the answer at last. "What is it,
cubling?"

"Are you all right, Mother?"

"Yes, I'm resting."

"Can I get you anything?"

"No. If I need something, I'll call."

Catcher wasn't sure she believed her mother's
reassurances—she couldn't remember the last time
Graywing had called her "cubling." But she didn't want to
intrude, even though she was sure her mother was dying—
especially because of that. One did not fondle one's wolf
when it came time for it to die. And a wolf was the only
model Catcher had, so she sighed and came away to
reassure the others that everything was all right.

Fernhare and Dreamsnake went back with Catcher to
help her work on her dike, but Stringsong felt that the
whole business was futile. He walked away from the dens,
splashing sometimes calf-deep in water, and looked out
over the flooded land. Everything looked so different this
way. It was hard to believe that this was the home he'd
known all his life.

He turned back toward Halfhill. The face of the cliff had
changed, scarred by mudfall, gravelslide, and running
water. Besides Dreamsnake's den and Catcher's, three
others were in obvious danger of flooding—Suretrail's,

165

which was already wet, Fangslayer and Deerstorm's, and Two Wolves and Rainbow's. And none of them was here to do anything about it.

It was as if those three dens had been abandoned, though Stringsong knew it wasn't true. Other elves, whose dens were better situated, couldn't deal with the problems they had, and those who had worse problems weren't here to attend to them. Only a few elves seemed to care at all.

Far at the downstream end of the Holt was the den where Puckernut and Rillwalker lived. It was far enough away that Stringsong hadn't noticed Puckernut busy working in his own entranceway. Partly that was because Puckernut was completely inside his den, instead of outside. He seemed to have built a wall across the lower part of the entrance. For a moment Stringsong was curious. Then he noticed Fernhare staring at him, and turned away.

Fernhare had been intending to ask Stringsong to come back and help, but he had seemed so intent that she came away from Catcher's den and went to see what he had been looking at. When she saw what Puckernut was doing, she decided it was a good idea, and went to get the others so they could see, too.

For his part, Puckernut, as sour as he sometimes was, was glad to show off what he, with the help of Crystalmoss and Hornbird, who were inside, had accomplished. Rather than digging a trench or building a wall, he was carving down the ceiling above his lower chambers and using the dirt to raise the floor altogether.

Stringsong credited the irascible old elf with the only reasonable solution to the problem so far. But what a mess, and how much work, and what would happen if Puckernut scraped up through an impervious layer to soggy soil above? His den would fill with mud in a rush, and he'd be lucky to get out alive.

But Stringsong had to admit that his real objection was that his friends all seemed to have something useful to do, or at least were trying, while all he could do was to distract himself from his thoughts, thoughts which every other elf had had before, and had lived with. But Stringsong, for some reason, just couldn't shake off the pain.

He felt useless. He felt tired. He was soaked to the skin, though not muddy any more, and more than a little chilly. It was too cool to just stand around. So he went back to his own den, climbing up to the entrance on the rocks that formed his front steps, and went inside. His home, at least, was high and dry, his floors solid, and there were no leaks in his roof.

He knew he shouldn't go there, but he felt himself drawn to Silverknife's bedroom. Empty now. Soon, very soon, he would have to give her belongings away, or make use of them himself. It was a waste to just leave them there, good weapons, clothes, tools. But not now, he was not ready for that yet. He sat down on the edge of her bed, and put his head in his hands.

The next morning there was water standing all along the entire length of the cliff of Halfhill, and everybody except for a few diehards decided to go up to the ridge-crest camp.

Graywing didn't go, of course. She didn't even know it was morning, though she was awake, and had been for some time. She'd drowsed and waked all night long, totally unconcerned with what time it was, thinking her thoughts, pursuing the images that flickered still around the edges of her mind.

Puckernut didn't go. He might have if Rillwalker had stayed, or had wanted to stay, since he was a contrary fellow, and usually chose the other side in any argument, just for the fun of it. But then he might not have gone, either, since he was fairly sure his plan of rebuilding his den's floors would work, and he was enjoying himself, though he might not admit it.

Fernhare stayed behind, in large part because she had not been able to make up her mind whether to go or stay, and since staying was the default decision in a case of acute indecision, she stayed. But she, too, was enjoying herself, though she would have been surprised to have been told that. She spent a lot of time out in the wet, fiddling around with mud and rocks and ditches and dikes, not on the common yard any more, of course, since that was all flooded, but downstream near the base of the hill, at the edge of the risen stream, where she could actually experiment with the flow and retardation of water.

Hornbird remained at the Holt as well, of course. Her motives were perfectly obvious, or so she thought. Her belief that the Holt would not flood was not reversed by the present fact, since she had experienced a flood almost this bad once before, and that was the worst it had gotten. More important was the unconscious need to be right, having now committed herself so strongly, and stated her position so positively. She had to stay behind if she wasn't to betray her faith in herself.

And Dreamsnake was here, though she'd rather have gone. She was convinced that the Holt would flood, that the waters would rise, and her own den was in danger, with muddy floors and even a dripping ceiling in one storeroom. But her mother was staying, which in itself shouldn't matter, except for the concern her mother was obviously showing for Graywing. Catcher had been inordinately distracted during the last few days, ever since Graywing had first, and suddenly, started showing signs of advanced age. Dreamsnake understood that, and sympathized. She was determined to leave Catcher alone, but she wanted to be near at hand, in case the worst happened, as it had to sooner or later, to give Catcher the sympathy and support she would need.

And as for Catcher . . .

Catcher stood outside her den in the rain, feeling lonely, wet, and in some strange way frightened. The Holt was practically empty, and those who had remained behind were in their own dens where it was dry.

Everywhere she looked there was water. Trees standing from it marked the banks of the stream, now many handspans below the surface. Farther out the water moved, not just over the streambed, brown and muddy, littered with leaves and dirty foam and occasional small drowned animals and twigs and debris. Still farther on in the forest the trees were black and wet, leafless now, even the oaks and sycamores. The sky was a uniform gray, uninteresting, low. Behind her the cliff was a dark beige-gray, slick, pocked and grooved by water. Ugly, messy, wet, colorless world. Enough reason for feeling depressed. She didn't need the excuse of her mother's condition.

But that was the true reason, of course. Her fear was not born of the flood, or what might happen if the water got higher, but came of what was happening to Graywing. She tried to be rational about it, and it offered no solutions. One was supposed to take death in stride, but if one knew that a friend was about to do something that might kill him, and couldn't stop him, for whatever reason, then one would fear for the friend's life. The fact that Graywing was going on voluntarily did not ease the anxiety. She was going to die, and it hurt.

Catcher had tried to leave Graywing alone, but she'd felt compelled to take her something to eat last night. She'd found Graywing in her nest, all tucked away, and knew that things weren't right. She'd been trying to deny what she knew was true, telling herself that Graywing was just tired, maybe just sick, anything but dying. But seeing her mother there, in her innermost chamber, with only water, and light, and furs, and her special weapons, wearing her ancient belt—it was too obvious to deny any more.

But death was part of the Way. Graywing wasn't like Silverknife, young and full of potential not yet realized. She was old, so old, and had done everything an elf could hope to do, and more. Her very age made her almost supernatural, though most of the time nobody thought about it. It was time, perhaps, at last, for her to die. So why was Catcher hanging on to her so hard?

Graywing had been surprised when Catcher had brought her her supper, and a bit peeved, as if she would have preferred hunger in privacy. She had thanked Catcher for her consideration, asked her to put the meat down within reach—but by the door—and without pretense or apology, had said, "Will you please go now? I want to think."

169

So Catcher had gone, and would leave her alone. She tried not to feel peevish about it. It felt strange, unnatural, not to spend some time with Graywing every day. It wasn't right to just go off and leave someone all alone without stopping in now and then to chat and make sure things were all right. But Graywing needed her privacy, Catcher knew that, and understood it, intellectually at least, and so she was determined to stay away from her mother's den, no matter what she felt.

From where she was she could see the water standing in the entrance to Suretrail's den. She hoped he'd put things up before going off to the camp. The water was also over the floor of Fangslayer and Deerstorm's den, and of Rainbow's, too. Her own entrance was still dry, since it was a bit higher than the others, and taking ideas from both Fernhare and Puckernut, she'd built a solid dike, very broad at the base, of clay and rock together, and so far it seemed to be holding back the few fingers of water.

Puckernut, of course, was doing very well. He'd raised all his floors until the lowest, at the entrance, was now hip height, higher than it had been. He'd taken special care to use only the white clay, which swelled up when it got damp, so that even if water started creeping in from below, its very presence would soon seal the new floor off from further incursions. Catcher could just barely hear him, even now, working away inside. Rillwalker was going to have a big surprise when she got home.

Catcher was feeling decidedly lonely. Fernhare, Hornbird, and Dreamsnake had all gone off looking for something to eat. She couldn't talk to her mother, so that left only Puckernut, not the best of company under most circumstances. Catcher went over to his den and called to him.

He invited her in, and offered her some berries while he showed her how his work was progressing. Catcher tried to be interested, since it really was good work, and something she should do a bit of herself, especially where her floor was soggy, but somehow she just didn't have the heart for it. She stayed as long as she could, and then she excused

170

herself, which left Puckernut slightly confused, as he'd been in the middle of a sentence, and went back outside.

She was angry with herself for being so indecisive, and was about to call her wolf so they could go out to find something to eat when she heard other calls and howls. Hornbird, Dreamsnake, and Fernhare were coming back. So soon? Had there been more trouble? But no, they had just been lucky, had found a den of hoppers that had been flooded out and had culled their pick. Plenty to eat for all. Catcher called the news to Puckernut, then they all went into Hornbird's den, which was dry, to butcher the kill and eat the dozen or so small animals.

When they had finished there was still plenty left over, and Hornbird suggested taking a share to Graywing.

"I don't think she wants to be disturbed," Catcher said.

"I won't disturb her," Hornbird said. "I'll just take this in and give it to her."

"She didn't like me going in last night," Catcher told her.

"She won't even know I'm there," Hornbird said. She took up three hind legs and went outside. She was confident in her ability to make the gesture. After all, she'd known Graywing far longer than Catcher had, and had seen almost as much of life.

Still, she hesitated by Graywing's door, standing calf-deep in water. Graywing was dying, and it might indeed not be right to intrude on her during these last days. On the other hand, what if she lost her strength and needed help? She might be thirsty, if not hungry. Did her bed need to be cleaned?

Catcher would never go in to find out, if Graywing had asked her to stay away. But Hornbird had a bit more of a stake in the situation. She was younger than Graywing by two or three eights of eights of years, but that wasn't very much, given the time she had lived so far. If she avoided accident, predators, and disease, Hornbird herself might be facing the same kind of experience someday.

The thought sobered her. She did not, in truth, feel much older than when she'd met her lifemate, now long dead. It was a simple fact that elves, like many animals, grew until they were mature, then showed little change until very late in their life—if they survived at all. But when the time came, when age began to exert its influence, it came on all at once. Hornbird would very much have liked to talk to Graywing about it—when did she first notice a change, what did it feel like, what did she think about?

Hornbird wasn't sure that she wanted to grow old.

She had just made up her mind to go on into Graywing's den and quietly peep in, leave the hopper meat, and withdraw without speaking when she noticed that the water around her calves was no longer still, but swirling. She looked down and saw the muddy flood rushing past her legs. The broad expanse of water between the cliff and the line of trees where the stream had once flowed was not flat, but agitated, disturbed, twisting, splashing.

There was a change, too, in the subaqueous rumble of rocks being pushed around. It was louder, sharper sometimes, deeper sometimes as if even larger rocks and boulders were being forced from their places and jostled together. It was a most disquieting sound, though not all that loud, since it came up through the feet as well as in the ears.

Rillwalker, had she been here, would have been most fascinated. Rivers and streams were Rillwalker's special interest, and she knew more about the behavior of flowing water than any other elf. It did not help Hornbird's peace of mind any to remember that Rillwalker had gone away because of the rising stream.

There was a change in the quality of sound, not just more rocks, and Hornbird strained to listen. It was coming from far upstream, a complex rushing, splashing sound, a murmur that would have been as loud as a roar had it been nearby.

But it was not nearby, not just upstream where the tree trunks obscured further view, but very far away indeed, a very loud noise to be heard from such a distance. But if it was that far, it surely couldn't be anything to worry about at the moment, and Hornbird was reassured.

She was still three or four paces from the entrance to

Graywing's den. She took a step toward it, surprised that, in just the tiny moment of time that she had hesitated, the water was now almost to her knees. The rushing sound got louder, and she looked up and saw something odd about the broad expanse of water upstream. It looked like there was a slope to the water; the light reflected off it differently than it did nearer to the Holt. There were bushes in the water, swirling around, and logs, rolling, turning end over end. *End over end?*

Even as she watched, a good-sized tree leaned toward her and fell, its roots suddenly above the water's surface for a moment. What she had thought was a slope in the water was exactly that, a sudden rise—who knew how much?—coming down at her all at once.

She tried to take a step, against the current, toward Graywing's den, but the water pushed her back, and almost knocked her off her feet. She leaned against the flow, and looked around for somewhere to jump to, something to hold on to, but there was nothing within reach. The water was rising above her knees now, and pushing her downstream, cutting away at the cliff face at the same time, so that clay and mud and rocks fell from the cliff into the rushing flood. There was nothing for Hornbird to do but go back toward her own den.

Time seemed to stand still, while the water rushed on at full speed. Hornbird turned in place, struggled to keep to her feet. The water rose. She took a step toward her den, the water pushed her along. She stepped on something unstable and slick, and fell to her hands and knees—what had happened to the hopper legs?—and was drenched by water splashing up over her back. She lurched toward the cliff, grabbed the slick and crumbling clay, pulled herself to her feet, the water now well over her knees, and struggled down toward her den. But the cliff face gave way, the mud and clay slid down around her feet and knocked her down. The current was so strong, the flood swept her away, downstream, away from the cliff. Another mass of mud and clay fell, where she had been; had she stayed there she would have been buried.

173

She came up against something and was able to get to her feet, waist-deep now. She felt small rocks roll past her feet. Bushes, torn up by the flood, swept past her. The water grabbed her again, threw her down, and she fought to keep her head above the surface. She was spun around, saw a tree trunk splash by, then another, realized the trees were still standing and she was by the streambed. She passed under a branch, reached up, grabbed hold, and pulled herself up out of the water.

And then for the next few minutes she sat, on the branch, and just watched the water rise. Catcher, Puckernut, and Dreamsnake all came out to the entrance of Hornbird's den to watch, and were glad to see her still alive, though her tree of refuge was at the downstream end of the Holt.

The flood lasted only a few moments longer, then rose no more, and the water, though it still flowed quickly, became less agitated.

All the dens that had been in danger of flooding, with the exception of Puckernut's, had indeed flooded. Water stood in some of them waist-deep, and some of the lower chambers were completely full. It was going to take a lot of work to set things to rights again when the water went down.

Hornbird helped Catcher salvage what she could in her den, and Puckernut was giving Dreamsnake what assistance he could. Fernhare, still undecided about things, sat in the entrance to her den and watched the water. As for Suretrail's den, or Rainbow's, or Fangslayer's, there was nothing to be done until they got back from the ridge-crest camp.

Fernhare sat and thought about it. There had been floods before, but nothing like this since the Holt was founded, and there might not be another like it for as many years to come. But she wasn't satisfied with that thought.

She watched as another part of the cliff collapsed, saw how tree roots above helped hold the soil, how the grassy areas at the ends of the common yard upstream and down hadn't been disturbed except for the mud, rocks, and branches dumped on top of them. The water was moving more slowly now, was almost still, so Fernhare stepped down from her den to wade around.

The bank of the stream was invisible, marked only by the trees that bordered it. As she walked toward it the water got deeper, and she could feel the scoured and shaped ground underfoot. She didn't go all the way to the trees, some of which were leaning now, but she remembered how the tree bridge over the stream had come to be. That had been more than three eights of eights of years ago. The stream had risen to the tops of the banks, and the tree, much smaller then, had been undercut and had fallen over across the stream. Since then a side branch had grown up while what had been the main trunk had become the stunted branch everyone used as a bridge.

The trees that had rocky bases did better. She looked back at the cliff, saw how it had collapsed where there was sand, how the clay had seemed to hold, how the rocks sometimes held and sometimes didn't.

How about downstream? What if the water could drain away faster? No sense in blocking the water upstream, was there?

The more she thought about it, the more she began to think that something could be done to prevent any future catastrophe. It would take a while, and might not be needed, but it would be a rewarding project, even if nobody else was interested. She started upstream toward where the hill rose up from the waters. She wanted to find out what the flood had done to the slope.

The floodwaters remained steady all the next day. Those who had gone to the ridge-crest camp knew nothing about it. Those who had stayed at the Holt did what they could to clean up the mess, as best they could, under the circumstances and some twenty handspans of water, measuring from the stream's normal level.

Catcher had a rather hard time of it. She had resisted going to check on Graywing after the flood, had refused

175

Hornbird's suggestion to take her mother some supper, had stayed away from Graywing's den all morning, and by midday she could hardly stand it.

She ate her lunch alone in her main chamber. Outside she could hear Fernhare and Puckernut talking about controlling floods or something while thrashing around in the water. It seemed like a waste of time to her. Her den had not actually flooded, but the floor of some of the lower chambers, including her bedroom, was soggy, and nothing anybody could dream up could keep the water from rising up through cracks in the ground.

Catcher wished she had gone off with the others, but she knew she couldn't have stayed away; her concern for Graywing would have brought her back sooner or later. But what good was she doing sitting here? She knew her mother's den as well as her own, she could go over there quietly, just take a peek, make sure everything was all right.

But she was afraid. She didn't want to see what changes might have taken place in Graywing's appearance during the last day or so, didn't want to try to understand her change in behavior. The implications of age were not something pleasant to think about. All elves assumed, from comparing themselves to other animals, that barring accident, disease, and predation, they would live forever. Graywing's condition implied something else.

Maybe she was just sick. A disease, yes, perhaps that. But that did not change the fact of her mortality, or postpone the imminence of her death.

Besides, if Catcher tried to sneak in and find out how Graywing was doing, and if Graywing was all right, she'd know Catcher was there, and then there'd be awkward explanations.

Poor excuse, but better than none.

Catcher heard a splopping sound coming from an inner room. She went in and saw that the floor was muddy, even though it was higher than her main chamber, and there was a trickle of water running across it. Even as she watched, a crack formed in the floor and broadened, and the near wall, from which the water was coming, groaned.

She was suddenly frightened. She backed out of the room and stepped down into water that hadn't been there just a moment before. She turned around in surprise, to inspect the chamber, and heard part of a wall collapse where she had just been.

There was a sticky kind of feeling to the whole place, all the walls looked wrong, bits of clay fell down on her head. She hurried toward the entrance as part of the ceiling behind her collapsed and splashed her with muddy water.

From inside now came a flow of water, pouring down toward her entrance. She slipped in the sudden rush and fell, and one wall beside her slumped down, half covering her in mud. She could easily be buried alive.

She forced herself up to her feet and went as quickly as she could the rest of the way to the entrance, just as more roof fell in behind her, layer upon layer. As she reached the entrance the whole den seemed to cave in, and a wave of muddy water washed her out the door.

She floundered around for a moment, then regained her feet and stood, nearly waist-deep in water, and looked back at her den. From the outside it looked the same, except for the water coming out. Inside there was water and mud everywhere, but not as much roof had fallen as she had thought.

Then she heard a call from Dreamsnake, a frightened call that was suddenly cut off. She hurried to her daughter's den as quickly as she could, and when she stepped inside she saw that it was much the same there as at her own home.

"Dreamsnake?" she called. But the response was muffled.

Catcher's mind was paralyzed with thoughts of Dreamsnake being buried under tons of mud and clay, but that did not slow her as she plunged into the mess, and dug frantically around in the direction from which she had heard the sound. It was not long at all before she found where part of a wall and ceiling had slid down, covering a door. The mud was loose, and so wet that it was easy to dig the doorway out again, especially as physically charged up as Catcher was. She could hear Dreamsnake digging from the other side, and a moment later they broke through the barrier. Catcher grabbed hold of Dreamsnake's hand and dragged her through the hole, then hurried her outside.

They were both covered with mud, and the shallow lake outside the door was relatively clean compared to what was pouring out through Dreamsnake's entrance. They hugged each other with relief, and then set about checking to make sure that nobody else was trapped. They even called in to Graywing, but she called back that she was fine, and so they left her alone.

Which was just what Graywing wanted. She had to assume that her daughter and granddaughter had had a reason for disturbing her. Maybe it had something to do with that flood. It had been raining rather a lot lately. She could remember other times, some of them very long ago indeed, when it had rained like this. If she thought about it, the images came very clear. As for yesterday, she wasn't so sure. She'd lost track of how long she'd been here, snug in her nest. She still had plenty of water, wasn't at all hungry, and her thoughts were all the company she needed. The oil for her lamp was running a bit low, but that hardly mattered, for she lay with her eyes closed much of the time, anyway.

There was just a bit of light coming in from the room beyond her chamber, which meant it was still day outside —or another day perhaps. That was reassuring, in a way, though she didn't know why. She wasn't completely cut off from the outside world, though she had shut it out.

She drew her attention in again, and lost track of the time. The thoughts that had been flickering around the edges of her mind for the last few days had at last come clear a little while ago. It was the high ones she had been trying to think about, she didn't know why. All she knew about high ones were tales she had heard from the elders when she was a child, tales she had told herself many times to cublings in their turn. If she thought about it now—and she did, oh yes, she did—she realized that the stories she'd told most recently were not at all the same as the ones she'd heard first. She'd thought they'd been the same, but they'd changed over the years, with other people's tellings, with her "improvements." The old stories, how close to the truth were they, if they, too, had evolved with time? What were the high ones really like? Had there ever been any high ones at all?

Of course, there had to have been, or people to whom the elves had given that name, their ancestors before the time of memory. No creature came fully developed from nothing; every species had forebears. Her own stories had made the high ones seem more wonderful than those she had heard, so maybe the people whom the stories had been about had, in fact, not been anything special at all, had just happened to be alive when models were needed.

Or maybe not. She didn't know. All she knew was that it was the high ones who had been trying to get into her thoughts for some time now, and she could feel them, now that she had identified them, just *there,* just behind her sight, just beyond her perception . . .

Her imagination, of course. She was dying, and not suddenly, not by surprise, not in pain, but slowly, with full awareness, and it was special. Her imagination was providing her with images, telling her new stories, to help her during these last days and hours. Of course, that was all it was, nothing more.

Except that death was real, and the high ones were dead, and wherever their minds had gone, her mind would go there, too. And who was she to say that there wasn't some truth to the old tales?

Her thoughts took her on in this way for a long time. She saw, but did not notice, that the light outside her door was dimming, her den growing darker, as afternoon faded into evening. She did not even pay attention when her lamp at last ran dry, and the tiny red-and-yellow flame burned out. Not until some time later when she thought that, in darkness as complete and uniform as this, there should be no shadows.

But there were, and their presence roused her from her reverie, and she tried to see them more clearly, but it was, indeed, very dark in here, even for elf eyes.

But where was the source of light? Nowhere that she could see. And what was casting the shadows? There, by the door, in her chamber, were several figures, like elves. Had Catcher come to check on her? No, that wasn't it. What if, she thought, it were the high ones, come to take her away?

If she looked at the shadows in a certain way, she could almost see what made them, and could pretend that they were indeed high ones. As she built the images in her mind, at first they looked like this, but no, that wasn't right, and obligingly they began to look like that, and then, though it was no thought of her own, they began to look like something else, taller than elves, not as slender but not as strong, either. She wished she could make out their faces. She couldn't even tell how many there were.

For a while, trying to see the high ones was a game, but it stopped being that when it seemed that they were really there. She could not see them clearly, but she couldn't make them go away by just thinking about it. Indeed, they no longer just stood by her door; some of them now sat on the edges of her nest, or stood against the inner walls, and they all were watching her, though she still could not see their faces.

Had her imagination turned into madness? But she did not feel sick. How had they gotten here? That didn't seem to matter. All the high ones were dead, after all, and the dead could go where they wished.

And then it was as if her father were there with them. She could see him so clearly. He introduced the high ones to her, one by one. They were the parents of the parents of his parents. Not that many generations back. Her own life covered more changes than that.

That's exactly right, her father said. You have done much. It's time for you to go with them now.

Graywing thought she should feel sad about this, but she didn't.

180

She had seen no source of light before, but there was light now, coming from somewhere, a direction she couldn't define, but that seemed to be behind her. She turned and there was a passage, opening in the wall at her back, where none had been before.

The image of her father faded, along with that of his parents, and theirs, until only the high ones were left, a group of people, tall and fair, who somehow, without any change in her age, made her seem like a child, so mature were they. They stood in the entrance to the passage, and behind them, in the light, she could see what looked like wonderful caves—or maybe they were trees in a forest—or mountains, they were mountains and valleys . . . she couldn't tell, she just knew that, whatever this place was, it was their home—and hers, too, now.

Yes, she thought, her home, too.

She sat up straight. She felt good, healthy, happy. She stood, and felt strong, rested, content. The bright light of her tomorrow opened before her, and she stepped into it, and followed the high ones home.

Stringsong was more aware of the passing of that afternoon than Graywing had been, though in a way his mind was more in turmoil, and his thoughts more distracting. He sat, well back in his den and out of sight, but within view of the entrance, from which he'd withdrawn the curtain, so he could see if anybody passed by, anybody with whom he might wish to speak.

Few came by. There weren't many elves here, after all, and the water outside was still very deep. Not once did he feel the urge to call out, though he kept watch. What was he waiting for, what did he want?

As the afternoon wore on there was more than the usual amount of activity outside. He could hear voices and splashing, and at the same time the noise of the rush of water and rumble of rocks faded away. The rain was diminishing, too, and as afternoon faded into dusk, it almost stopped.

The worst of the flood seemed to be over, though it

would take a long time for the land to recover. Water like that moved much soil, tore up bushes, uprooted trees. Animals that depended on undergrowth for food and shelter would suffer most of all. Those that lived in the ground would be flooded out, drowned, or silted up. It was autumn, and winter was coming on, and it would be a hungry time for everybody. The elves would have to travel far to find food.

But they would survive, as they had before, and they wouldn't have to find a new home, either. It might be a lean winter, but it was the Way. The weak would fail, the strongest carry on. Of course, a flood like this took many that were strong otherwise. But those who were left were stronger still.

He couldn't help but be aware of the subtle optimism of his thoughts. As the gentle though devastating weather outside improved, so did his state of mind. Had he nearly succumbed to the flood, too, in his own way?

Silverknife had seemed such a promise of greatness. Yet she had failed to observe a treacherous terrain, had failed to react quickly enough to the first signs of danger, and had died. In spite of what had seemed to be strength, there was a hidden and fatal weakness. Had there been no storm, she might not have been tested. What if she had lived, and become chieftess, and then found her flaw exposed when it was not just her life but the life of the Holt that was at stake? Had she lived, such a thing might never have happened. The only truth was that, being tested, she had failed.

Her death was tragic, there was no denying that, unlike Greentwig's death. That poor child had never become an adult, had been a burden on the Holt for his entire life. Yet all had regretted his passing. How much more would they regret Silverknife's? But after they were dead, did it matter?

Whiteraven had died while Silverknife was still a child. Stringsong knew, now, that he had never come to terms with that. He had missed her so badly that, even when Silverknife had become an adult, they had continued to share the same den. She should have gone off and dug a home for herself long ago.

He had to live without her now. And as he thought that, he realized that he meant Whiteraven, not Silverknife. He'd carried grief for his lifemate all these years without knowing it. It should have passed as it had for his father and his mother.

It was getting dark outside. A flood washes away bad as well as good, and brings in new. Stringsong should have given up Whiteraven on her death, and he was sorry that it took Silverknife's death to make him realize that. Such a hard lesson to learn.

Now was the time to let them both go. The best die, and the worst, and those who live must go on, so that others might live, too. That was the Way.

Outside, from somewhere, he could hear voices— Hornbird and Puckernut, splashing around, checking out other dens. Stringsong got to his feet and went out into the early night. It was already quite dark, though there was just a hint of color to the west, signifying that the clouds were beginning to break up at last.

He listened for voices, heard Hornbird and Puckernut over at Suretrail's den, and went there to join them. "How bad is it?" he called out.

"Not as bad as it might be," Hornbird answered from inside.

"Need any help?"

"Not much to do," Puckernut said as he and Hornbird came out. "Catcher's the one who needs help, and Dreamsnake. Their dens caved in earlier this afternoon."

"Let's go give them a hand," Stringsong said.

The next morning there was an actual sunrise. Hornbird was the first one to see it, and she also noticed that the water level had begun to fall, though it still lapped the bottom of the cliff.

Which was a mess, with piles of mud and clay and rocks at its base where the face had fallen in. Fortunately none of the dens had been exposed.

Out in the common yard—or where it would be when the water went away—were drifts of gravel and mud, broken branches and torn-up bushes, bobbing logs, and boulders that must have come a long way. It was time to start clearing up.

Soon other diehards began to come out of their holes. Catcher and Dreamsnake had spent the night with Puckernut, and were eager to start cleaning out their dens. Fernhare and Stringsong got to work near the base of the cliff, while Puckernut and Hornbird worked farther away, taking advantage of the buoyancy of the water to move some of the larger boulders into slightly more suitable places. When the ground finally dried out, it was going to look very strange indeed.

A little later Fangslayer, Deerstorm, and Ebony came back to the Holt. Their den had nearly filled up with water, but at least the roof had remained intact. It was going to be a long time before they could sleep dry again. Puckernut showed off what he had done with his own den, and Deerstorm thought it an excellent idea, so they got to work at once, raising the floor by raising the ceiling.

One by one the other elves returned, some of them bringing back their belongings, others leaving them at the camp until their dens were dry. Even Rainbow, Rillwalker, Two Wolves, and Silvercub got word of the passing of the flood, and decided to come back, after all.

The water continued to recede, and by night Stringsong could walk the whole length of the cliff without getting his feet wet. He got his feet plenty muddy, of course. He had been out and about the whole day, still a bit reserved, a bit tender, but he was on the mend, and everybody was glad to see it.

But even Stringsong's recovery couldn't alleviate Catcher's fears. She kept her worries to herself until the evening meal, and then she had to let others know how she felt. It had been two nights ago that she had last seen Graywing, and she was afraid that her mother was dead.

The others agreed that, in spite of Graywing's expressed wishes, they should go find out if she was all right. They all went to Graywing's den, and Catcher called in to her. There was no answer.

Catcher was afraid to go inside, afraid of what she might find. The worst would be if her mother had been very ill, or in pain, and had suffered alone. Or maybe her roof had fallen in and she was trapped. The thought made Catcher fearful, for not having intruded in spite of Graywing's wishes.

So as she hesitated at the uncurtained entrance, Dreamsnake came up and put her arm around her shoulder. "Would you like me to go in?" she asked.

"Yes, please," Catcher whispered.

Dreamsnake went into the darkness of the familiar den, and felt it somehow strange. Graywing was her grandmother, and more than eight times an eight of eights of years older than she, but Dreamsnake felt the parent now. She was the child-tender, after all, with only two children of her own but mother to every child born. Graywing had become a child, and even Catcher seemed a child, too, now. Dreamsnake was the elder, it was up to her to do the hard thing and be brave.

Though she had no light, she knew where Graywing's nest was, and had no difficulty finding her way. Much to her surprise, Brownsides, Graywing's wolf, was lying in the doorway to the inner chamber. Brownsides raised his head as Dreamsnake neared, whined softly, then put his head back down again.

Dreamsnake didn't need to go any farther, but she did. Carefully, gently, with soft words and a few soft touches, she stepped over the wolf and into Graywing's nest. Only the faintest of light found its way in from the outer door, but it was enough for her to see the pile of furs. Dreamsnake dropped down on her knees at the edge of the nest, and felt out with her hands. There was Graywing, cold. A faint scent of death came to Dreamsnake's nostrils. She'd not noticed it before, not wanted to, though she'd known it would be there.

"Mother," she called over her shoulder. "Bring a light in here."

185

Catcher understood, from the term, the tone of voice, what she was going to see; not suffering, not entrapment, just death. Someone—she forgot who—handed her a lamp, already lit, as if they had anticipated its need. She went into Graywing's den and to her nesting place. Brownsides whimpered when he saw her. It would be harder on him than on her.

The two elves grieved their ancestor for a moment, and then they carried her outside to the others. Hornbird came up and touched Graywing's face. "I am the oldest now," she said.

"It is the Way," Stringsong said. "Death for the young, death for the old. Life goes on."

At the Oak's Root

by Nancy Springer

He was an unremarkable cub, and he knew it, even at the barely-yet-aware age of seven summers. His parents had given him the stolid name of Oakroot because of his brown hair, brown eyes, plain face; he had no special beauty. Nor did he yet show any special gifts, whether in the hunt, or healing, or shaping, or at the howl. It did not matter. Being a Wolfrider was enough. And there were few in the tribe, since Two-Spear's madness; cubs had never been many, even before, and always every cub was prized.

A cub lost in the Everwood, then, would be searched for long and hard.

And scolded hard once I am found, Oakroot thought. He felt more afraid, more disconsolate, thinking of his father's anger than he did because of his predicament. He deserved punishment, he knew, for letting himself fall behind the tribe. The Wolfriders, journeying on one of their frequent nomadic ventures to different hunting grounds, would waste two whole days of cold, tiresome wintertime travel because of his foolishness.

But, whatever it was, it had tugged so at his heart . . .

Oakroot sighed, wandering through the bare, sturdy boughs of his namesake trees as easily as if on the leaf-strewn forest floor beneath him. There was no danger in the trees except that of falling and, in the summertime, snakes. Poisonous serpents half again as long as an elf frequented the trees in this part of Everwood, close to Muchcold Water. But this was wintertime; the snakes were asleep in the mud of the lake bank. Far safer to stay in the trees when alone, on account of humans—Oakroot gave the wisdom of his elders that much obedience, though there was little fear of being sighted by humans this deep in Everwood. The tall hunters stayed on the outskirts.

187

Oakroot knew he should stop his meanderings, stay in one place, make it easier for the Wolfriders to find him. But he had not yet found whatever had pulled him away from the tribe.

Tall, dark evergreens ahead. Instinctively Oakroot altered his course, preferring the oaks to the pines, the chestnuts, the elms or beeches, because he felt more at home in them. Sunset touched the twigs at the top of the forest; soon it would be dusk. Less need to be concerned about humans then, so near to nightfall. Oakroot let his half-grown, reed-thin legs carry him lower, down to the comfortable shadows already gathering beneath the oaks. Though the Wolfriders, in his brief lifetime, had sometimes traveled or hunted by day, Oakroot preferred the night and twilight, even in the chill of wintertime; that love of the stardark under two moons was in his blood.

The tug felt stronger, nearer to the ground. Nearly tangible, nearly a scent, a whisper it was. Scent, faint but sure, and sound as well. The scent, that of fear and fur. The sound, that of something young and lonely. Once his pointed ears had pricked and swiveled toward it, Oakroot could hear it clearly. Soft, but audible in the hush of twilight, he heard the whimpering of a pup, a cub like him.

He felt sure then what it must have been that had made him lag behind the tribe and turn aside from the trail. "My wolf-friend!" he whispered aloud to the world beneath two moons. For since he had been old enough to understand, he had been promised that sometime after he had seen his seventh summer a wolf cub would call him, would bond with him, would be his first wolf-friend, to grow along with him and carry him, once it was large and strong, through the dangers of hunt and battle. Not that he very much looked forward to either hunt or battle (something he had admitted to no one), but to have a wolf-friend would be wonderful.

In the twilight he saw the windfall, the tangle of roots and large tree butt, under which the cub had taken hiding. "Come out, little friend," he urged softly. "I am here."

Nothing happened except that the pup's low-pitched

plaint abruptly ceased, leaving only shadows and the misty hush of dusk.

Creature-friend, Oakroot sent, **come out, let me greet you.**

Nothing, except that the faint odor of fear on the air increased.

Seven years is a hard age for an elf to be. Though half the height of his elders, Oakroot had less than the hundredth part of their experience, for many of them were older than the oaks towering above him. Though independent enough to walk beside the wolves on the journey, ranging the length of their line, instead of having to be carried like the youngest cubs, Oakroot was yet far from clear on some of the basic tenets of the Wolfriders' Way. Much of what his elders told him was without reality to him, as insubstantial as his dreamings. Though he had heard it said often enough, he did not truly understand that a wolf-friend could come only from the descendants, however scattered, of the pack Timmain had joined. He did not know that he should have been able to call his destined wolf-friend to him with a few friendly words.

Instead, he sat down on the leaf-brown ground, in the chill of the oncoming night, and looked into the dark hollow beneath the windfall tangle—his eyes widening hugely to catch the faint light, enormous in the twilight—and hunched his thin shoulders against the cold, and bent all the strength of his young will on bringing out of hiding the young creature he had heard.

Little one, he sent, **I heard you crying, I know you are alone, I felt you calling me. Now I am here. Don't you know me? I am Oakroot.**

The name felt false to him. Someday he would have a truer name, and a soulname as well.

I am a cub, too, he amended. **I am alone. I am cold.** It had only just then occurred to him that he was, indeed, cold, and the night would get colder, and that he must somehow survive it. Coarse salt-cured hides were so stiff and heavy that he had gone without his cloak that day, preferring to shiver, but he missed the wretched thing now.

189

And his parents would only just now, at the end of the day's journey, be missing him. Until then they would have thought he was with tribesmates at some other portion of the line. Even if the whole tribe started back at once, without food or rest, he could not expect them to find him until the middle of the next day at the earliest. The thought made him feel suddenly, crushingly alone and added vehemence to his plea.

I am cold. I am lonely. I need you. Come out. Come out. Come out!

He felt the strength of his willful summons clash against the resistance of the creature denned under the windfall. Then he heard the faint scrabbling of small clawed paws. His ears moved to catch every sound, his eyes hurt with peering. The creature stayed in the shadows. Oakroot could catch only a glimpse of a pointed nose, staring eyes, furry ears cocked at an uncertain angle. But as if the glimpse had been enough—or as if the animal had given a wordless sending back to him—Oakroot understood suddenly how shy the cub was, and how shivering (not with cold but with fear), and how frail.

"Oh, little friend," he whispered aloud. "Please do not be so afraid. I will never hurt you."

Step by soft step, the animal ventured into the moonlight.

It was not like any wolf Oakroot had ever seen, whether cub or weanling or adult. It was too delicate of build, too dainty of step; paws small, unlike a wolf's spreading pads; face nearly like that of a fox, with none of a wolf's strength of jaw; eyes dark and soft instead of the eerie yellow of a wolf's. Yet he could not say it was not a wolf. He did not know what else to call it. And he knew it was his wolf-friend, a soul-friend, nearly a double. It was awkward and leggy, half-grown, like him. It was alone, like him. It was very thin. The runt of the litter, a wretched hunter, it had been driven out of the pack. Looking into its eyes, he knew that; the bond told him.

"Never mind," he told it. "Be with me. I will never turn on you."

Its eyes were the same deep brown as his own, the rich

brown of last year's oak leaves under water, on the bottom of a deep, spring-fed pool. Its fur was the same soft brown as his own hair, the brown of the deep-lobed leaves that cling to the oak tree all winter.

"Winterleaf, I will call you," Oakroot whispered, and he sent, **Winterleaf!**

The little wolf cried aloud, as if he had sent a dart to its heart. Then, the last shred of its reticence gone with the name, the sending, it sprang into his arms, licking his face and his four-fingered hands, whimpering. Oakroot hugged it close to his narrow chest, and it nestled its short, pointed muzzle under his chin, pressing against him.

Winterleaf. Wolf-friend.

Two cubs together, they spent the cold night under the windfall, huddled close to one another, curled into a tangle of thin bodies and gangly legs, warming each other and the hollow around them. Oakroot slept warm and well and achingly happy, that first night of his life apart from his parents, slept better than he would have thought possible. In the morning, when he crawled out of his shelter, Winterleaf went with him.

Oakroot kept to the ground, a stone in his hand, trying to down himself something to eat. He felt terribly hungry, and happy in spite of it every time he looked down at the soft-furred brown head at his side. He did not ask Winterleaf to hunt something for him to eat. Somehow he knew that the wolf cub was as wretched a hunter as he. Fat mouse-gray doves sat in nearly every tree, and Oakroot tried to stalk them, but the few times he came close enough to knock one down, his stones flew far wide.

"Puckernuts!" Oakroot gave it up at last.

Something crashed in the distant underbrush. A deer, probably, startled by his oath. Oakroot paid no attention.

"Double puckernuts! We'll both starve if we have to depend on me. I wish my people would come."

Standing stiffly, whining low in his throat, the little wolf did not offer the sympathy Oakroot had come already to expect. Winterleaf bristled in the direction from which the crashing sound had come, then turned and nipped the elf's shaggy furred tunic for attention. Startled, Oakroot looked down into dark eyes and felt all the blunt force of Winterleaf's knowledge: **Humans. Danger.**

No time for thought, only for reaction. Like a treewee, Oakroot leapt for the nearest trunk, sped up. Not until he had reached the safety of the high, muscular oak branches, broad enough to hide his thin body from the loutish humans below, did he think of his wolf-friend. Winterleaf! Was the half-grown starveling cub swift enough, strong enough to get away?

Single file and grumbling in the cold, six human hunters in furs even more stiff and rotting than those the elves wore clumped below Oakroot's perch. If the humans sighted Winterleaf, they would try to kill him. Humans tried to kill everything. Gulping, Oakroot barely restrained himself from a mind-cry, from calling Winterleaf's name, which would only summon the little wolf nearer. And he barely restrained himself from yipping aloud, from falling off the oak limb that supported him, when a small, wet tongue touched his ankle.

Winterleaf was right at his feet, in the oak with him.

Winterleaf! You climb trees?

It was a useless sending. Winterleaf could not understand or respond to his surprise. Of course Winterleaf climbed trees. Climbing trees was part of what he was. The rest of that morning, after the human hunters had gone on their way, he followed Oakroot lithely through the branches, padding along on his small paws and leaping as deftly as a wildcat. Of what use was surprise? No matter that Oakroot had never known a wolf to climb trees.

Light-headed with astonishment and hunger, Oakroot judged by the sun and worked his way in what he thought might be the direction from which the Wolfriders would come. He hoped the right direction. He hoped they would come soon. The day was not yet past the mid; he did not dare to hope much, though expectation thumped in his heart in spite of his thoughts.

Oakroot! Son!

The sending came from far off, faint, urgent. Oakroot's breath caught for a moment before he gathered himself and sent for all he was worth.

Father!

Oakroot! He could tell by the tone of mind, relieved and focused and angry all at once, that his father had heard him.

Here I am!

Oakroot's sapling-thin legs carried him, apparently without the direction of his mind, down to the ground and toward his father, running hard. Winterleaf ran along with him, and Oakroot snatched up the pup and clutched him to his chest; he needed something to hug. Winterleaf's lanky legs trailed, but the wolf was a starved runt, light enough for the cub to lift. He let himself be snuggled in Oakroot's arms.

So it was that the Wolfrider search party found them, a few moments later, Oakroot at the foot of a huge oak tree with a draggle of bones and fur in his arms.

The cub's father was the first to burst from the underbrush on his huge mount, the fierce old pack-leader, Blackjaw, and Blackjaw's first act was to snarl at Winterleaf. His rider paid no attention.

"Son! Are you all right?"

Oakroot gulped and nodded. The scolding, he knew, would come in a moment. It would be years before he understood how his often gentle and loving father felt he had to be harsh at times, was conscientious to a fault in the discharge of his duties, one of which was to teach his son the Way. Meanwhile, quickly, before his father could gather his anger, Oakroot blurted, "Father, this is my wolf-friend! Winterleaf."

That Oakroot had found a wolf-friend should have been cause for rejoicing. But neither in his father's face nor in those of the other elves gathering around on their strong wolves, larger than other wolves, could Oakroot see anything but doubt.

"I heard him calling me. Felt, I mean. That's why I got left behind."

The older elf shook his head. "Son, that can't be your wolf-friend. I'm not even sure it's a wolf! It is not of our pack, and it will never be large enough or strong enough to carry you to the hunt or battle."

193

Oakroot could scarcely believe what he was hearing. How could his father attempt to deny what was so obvious to him, Oakroot: that he and Winterleaf were meant to be together? Lacking better words to describe the bond, he protested, "But he kept me warm all night, and warned me about the humans, and—"

Humans! There are humans hereabouts?

Oakroot winced at the force of the dismayed sending. His mind gave his father the image of the human hunters walking under his tree.

Why did you not tell us at once? We could have blundered right into them, in our eagerness to find you!

It had not occurred to him, a cub, that his father could be anything less than always careful, always right, always perfect. In confusion more than shame he hung his head, and the next moment his father's strong arms caught him around his bony chest, swinging him onto Blackjaw. Startled, Oakroot dropped Winterleaf.

Back to the others! Oakroot's father ordered urgently. The wolves sprang into their swiftest run.

Oakroot twisted in his father's grip to look for Winterleaf. **Father! Winterleaf cannot keep up.** Already the stunted, sharp-muzzled wolf, weakened by hunger, was falling behind.

He will have to catch up later. Hard. Oakroot knew that hard tone in his father; anyone who opposed it did so at his peril. Only the ache of the bond between him and Winterleaf, sending him nearly into panic, could have made him argue with his father after that sending.

But he might never catch up! He is hungry, like me. Father, please, stop just for a moment! He is my wolf-friend, truly!

The older elf gritted his teeth and gave an order; Blackjaw did not stop, but slowed to a trot, and Winterleaf surged alongside, running hard, his ribs heaving painfully. Oakroot leaned over, straining against his father's strong grip, and opened his arms. A leap later, Winterleaf was in them, then slung across Blackjaw's shoulders, riding in front of Oakroot. The big wolf sprang to a run again, seeming scarcely to notice the extra weight.

194

For half the afternoon the elves rode fast and in silence. Winterleaf rode limply. Oakroot did not mention hunger, his or Winterleaf's, again. The scolding had not yet been given, and he wondered why. Dimly, puzzled as always by the ways of adults, he understood that he had somehow fallen beneath scolding into something worse, some form of disgrace too obscure to be put into berating words. Oakroot felt that he should have been able to down himself a dove to eat. He had not acquitted himself well at all. His father had given up on him, was ignoring him.

His mother, the beautiful Starflower, she would feed him. Where was she? He had been surprised not to see her riding her big bitch, Striker, in the rescue party. To his silent father he ventured, **Where is Mother?**

She's ill with chills and fever.

Winterleaf moved on his uncomfortable perch and whined, perhaps sensing the young elf's painful lurch of heart. Oakroot said aloud, forgetting himself, "Is she—is she going to be all right?"

Hush. We all hope so. His father's tone, gentler. **But she cannot be moved or defend herself. And worrying about you has made it worse. And if there are humans about . . .**

The humans had been heading the other way. Oakroot did not see why his father had to always fear the worst. As long as his mother was going to be all right.

Which she was. But for several days after getting back to the tribe, until Starflower's fever had abated, Oakroot was not allowed to see her where she lay in a makeshift shelter. His father was distant (worry made him so; again, years later Oakroot understood), and everyone was on edge, keeping guard against humans, for the tribe could not travel until Starflower was better. There was nothing for Oakroot to do except eat the meat the hunters brought, sharing his portion with Winterleaf.

It was as Blackjaw had warned: Winterleaf had not been taken into the pack, and could not even begin to hold his own at the kills from which the pack ate. He was half the size of the yearling wolves.

The odd little tree-climbing leaf-brown wolf spent his

195

time inseparably with Oakroot, sharing whatever hollow the cub chose to sleep in, shadowing Oakroot's heels when the youngster was awake and about. Within a few days an older elf, Rainbow, noticed how the cub was sharing his meat with his wolf-friend and gave Oakroot some of hers. "Stop starving yourself," she grumped. "There's plenty. Though there might not always be," she added.

Oakroot took what she offered, but nodded, accepting her hint. After the meal, and for days afterward, he set himself grimly to learning how to bring down birds and snare ravvits. He learned how to stalk the doves at dusk after they had settled to roost. Once every day or two or three he downed one. It was not enough, nor were the few winter-thin ravvits he snared. He continued to share his food with Winterleaf.

The dainty, fox-faced animal, once he had gained in strength, was as playful as any wolf pup but in a different, graceful, infinitely amusing way. Winterleaf would chase oak leaves in the wind, leaping like a dancer to follow them on the eddies of the air, twisting, patting at them with swift paws. He would pounce at the long shadows of tree limbs moving on the snow. He would play with anything that moved, but his favorite targets were things that swung and slithered: tunic fringes and boot lacings hanging down, pelts trailing from a hunter's arms. Once, only a few days after his return from his misadventure, Oakroot winced to see Winterleaf leaping with kittenish charm and sinking his small teeth into a pair of brand-new fur mittens— which were, at the time, dangling from Oakroot's father's hand.

Oakroot hurried to disengage his wolf-friend from Winterleaf's inappropriate object of attack. "Sorry," he muttered, eyes downcast, holding the squirming wolf pup in his arms. He did not care to look at his father, who had not yet scolded him; to Oakroot the silence was worse. His father examined the damaged mittens in dour silence, then spoke. "That wolf is useless," he said. "He can hunt mittens; why does he not hunt his own food?"

Oakroot, no great hunter himself, did not find Winterleaf's lapse hard to understand, but kept his eyes down and his mouth closed.

The pack was right to cast him out. He is good for nothing except to eat hard-hunted food.

Oakroot heard the unspoken words, that Winterleaf was as useless to the tribe as he had been to the pack. Ought the tribe, then, to cast him out as well? Oakroot said to the ground between his two bony feet, "He is my wolf-friend."

"He can't be, I tell you, lad!" His father suddenly hunkered down, seizing the cub's chin and making the youngster meet his eyes. "He is not of our pack. I'm not even sure he is a wolf. He acts more like a cat."

Oakroot's father had been aghast the first time he had seen Winterleaf climb a tree to curl up in the hollow with his son.

Cat, indeed. Oakroot knew wildcats, and Winterleaf was not one. To Oakroot, there seemed only one way by which he could justify keeping Winterleaf. So, although himself not at all sure what the little creature was, he stubbornly shook his head. "He is my wolf-friend," he repeated.

"No, he is not. He is your—I don't know what he is." And what the older elf did not know, he did not much like.

Winterleaf, held against Oakroot's chest with his long legs dangling, grew tired of being talked about above his head as if he were not there, opened his mouth and yowled, showing his bright pink gullet as if he were a baby bird. The older elf's gaze wavered to the pup with distaste, then back to his son again.

"You are too thin," he said to Oakroot, feeling the sharp bone of the boy's chin in his hand. "You are to give no more of your meat to this useless one here. Let him learn to hunt his own."

Oakroot's deep-pool-brown eyes locked on his father's, defiant, intense. "I am of no use," he said, his voice shaking. "I am not a hunter. You have to feed me. Why do you not cast me out? Why did you come looking for me when I was lost?"

His father met his gaze, his words, with a blank and angry look, then got up and walked away.

Oakroot could not disobey his father's order, that he was not to give Winterleaf any of his dinner. He hunted desperately through what remained of that day, with no success. But he need not have worried. The other elves continued to share their food with Winterleaf, not only Rainbow but many of the others, and none of them seemed to mind. Though the concept of "pet" was unknown to them, for some reason they felt they could not let this pert and playful creature suffer. Often they smiled on the little wolf, even when he exasperated them by pouncing at their feet as they walked.

Trying to keep Winterleaf out of trouble, Oakroot made a braided rope out of scraps of the raw hides in which the hunters brought home the meat. He took to swinging the rope or snapping it or dragging it for Winterleaf to chase. The little wolf dashed at this long object in greatest excitement; it became at once Winterleaf's favorite object to attack. Oakroot could amuse him all day with the rope, and wear himself out until his thin arms ached, and Winterleaf—who had exerted ten times the effort, chasing the flying tip of the thing with teeth and leaps and reaching paws—would still be standing with shining brown eyes, begging, pattering with his sensitive forepaws, the soggy-wet, much-chewed rawhide rope draped limply from his mouth.

When Oakroot was told it was all right for him to see his mother, of course Winterleaf went with him, and Oakroot took the rope to busy the wolf.

"Cubling!" Starflower embraced her son from her bed of furs, looked at him with glad eyes, teased him. "So here is the youngster who has been causing all the trouble. You're thin."

She was thinner, but her happy acceptance of whatever she had heard about him was like cool water on scraped skin to Oakroot.

"And there is the other mischief maker!" she exclaimed. "Winterleaf."

To amuse her and make her laugh, Oakroot flipped the rope for Winterleaf to chase. The little wolf darted after it and trapped the writhing thing between agile paws, at the same time biting it with teeth like the needles Rainbow made of bone. Oakroot showed his mother how Winterleaf could leap after the flying rope, twisting his body in midair to follow its wild path. Starflower did more than laugh. Her eyes widened.

"Oakroot, he is so quick, so clever with his paws and teeth. I cannot believe he is as useless as your father says. And what is this I hear, that you say you are useless also?"

"I am," said the cub.

"You will grow and find your use and your Way, and so will Winterleaf."

It had been a bad fever. Starflower was slow to mend; then those who had nursed her came down with fever as well. No elf died of it, but the tribe stayed in that place, chosen at first for a single night's camping, through deep winter and into early spring. It did not matter, for game was adequate, though more plentiful elsewhere—but because the humans had followed the large herds of deer, they did not blunder into the elves. That worst of disasters, to an elf, did not happen.

But a nightmare nearly as bad did occur. The serpents came up out of the thawing mud.

Never before had spring caught the Wolfriders near this portion of Muchcold Water, where the snakes came up from the shore by fours and eights. And though they did not have a human's irrational fear of snakes (for the elves respected all animals, fearing none for fear's sake and killing none for killing's sake), they knew from summertime mishaps, years past—a single snake encountered by a hunting party or by a sheltering family in a tree hollow at night—they knew what the poison of these snakes could do. Cubs, bitten, would die at once, within instants. Adult Wolfriders would convulse, suffer, lie helpless, dying more slowly but just as surely.

The onslaught started one day at dusk, as the tribe sat at its daily meal, and Oakroot ate his share under his father's watchful glance, and Winterleaf sat nearby, hopefully gazing at Rainbow with soft brown eyes. A single hoarse shout went up, turning to a scream; the first serpent was in camp before anyone had seen it. The same fleshy brown as

199

an earthworm, but muscular, whip-quick, and longer than an elf was tall, it came surging onward, its blunt lance-shaped head up and swaying, inexorably bound toward some inland tree and a mate. With high, birdlike screams the elves scattered before it. Some hunters raised spears or stones, but the snake moved too quickly, almost quicker than sight; to strike it without surely killing it would be only to anger it and endanger every elf within its long reach. Better to get out of its way . . . but Dewberry, Rainbow's younger daughter, could not get out of the way! Taken by surprise, the cub crouched helpless, caught between the serpent and the tree trunk against which she had been sitting.

"No!" Rainbow's cry hung in the air. Oakroot, stone in hand, did not dare hurl it. Everyone seemed frozen, still as death, except the slug-brown serpent swaying its head in front of the cub in its way—

—and a leaf-brown flash. Joyously, lithely, as if he had been doing nothing but attack snakes all his life, Winterleaf leapt. His small body changed course in midair, quick, quick, finding its mark. His two deft forepaws pinned the serpent to the ground just behind the head; its powerful body writhed wildly but could not throw him off. His small jaws struck as quickly as any serpent's head; his needle-sharp teeth bit neatly into the snake's neck just behind the skull, severing the spinal cord. The serpent convulsed a moment longer, then lay quiet. Winterleaf stood prick-eared, happy-tailed, and proud a moment, his kill trailing from his jaws, then started to drag the snake off to eat it.

Tumult for a moment. Rainbow had snatched up Dewberry. Wolfriders were comforting both of them, exclaiming to each other, looking around them with lifted weapons. "So that is what Winterleaf is good for!" Starflower called to Oakroot. "He's a snakecatcher."

The cub's father was standing at the alert, and if Winterleaf's feat pleased him he did not yet show it; his pressing concern was for the future. "There will be more snakes," he said. He lifted his head, howling a warning to the wolf pack in the forest. Blackjaw would take them out of danger; they could not help the elves this night. They

200

were strong-jawed, big-boned, large of padded paw, but not one of them could dart as snake-fast as Winterleaf.

And Oakroot went to his wolf-friend. "Winterleaf!" he called. "Eat later. Listen." He heel-sat, taking the jaunty fur at each side of Winterleaf's foxlike face in his two hands so that he faced the animal's brown eyes with his own; stare met stare, forehead nearly met forehead, and Oakroot sent, trying to mesh his own thoughts with the far less complex animal images. **Snakes come hurt my people. Snakes kill elves.**

Snakes kill Oakroot? Winterleaf understood; he whined in consternation.

Oakroot told him, **Maybe. You make snakes go.**

Winterleaf snakecatcher, the wolf agreed. **Winterleaf good bounce on snakes.**

You make snakes go or dead. No dead elves.

Winterleaf not let snakes hurt elves.

No sooner had Oakroot turned to his father and nodded than the shout went up again.

The elves were prepared this time. The hunters and warriors had ranged themselves between the lake and the shelters where two of their tribesfellows lay sick. But even to the wide-eyed, night-sharpened vision of an elf, the mud-brown serpents were difficult to spot in the failing light. Nor did the snakes make any sound; they rippled over the moist springtime ground with scarcely a whisper of scales on dead leaves for warning. The snakes were almost on them before the elves saw them. Nor was it a single serpent, but six or eight this time; the first one had been but a precursor.

The shout went up, stones flew, and faster than the stones flew Winterleaf. Huddled behind the line of battle with the cubs and the mothers of nursing cubs, Oakroot gulped, afraid for the little wolf; he knew Winterleaf's flashing speed, had not feared for his wolf-friend against the single serpent, but there were so many—

Oakroot's four-fingered hand found a stone on the ground. He broke away from the huddle of cubs, shot past the nearest warrior, saw Winterleaf clinging to the back and neck of a huge, writhing snake, biting deep, saw the next snake coming fast—and threw his stone. The oncoming serpent flattened its head, faltered in its course, and an eyeblink later Winterleaf jumped it. But Oakroot stood stupid with surprise. His stone had hit its mark. He had become a better hunter, after all.

Someone shouted and thrust him back, away from the battle, and a moment later Winterleaf was licking his hand. Oakroot need not have worried about his wolf-friend. Four snakes lay dead on the ground, three killed by Winterleaf, one by an elf's swinging spear; and the others had passed by, turned aside from their course.

"Must we go on killing them?" asked Starflower. Elves killed no animal without need, and the serpents were not attacking them, but merely taking the straightest way to their breeding grounds; anything in the way risked being bitten.

"Perhaps not," said the chieftain. "Spread out the bodies like a barrier."

Gingerly some elves took the dead serpents by their tails, the most recent four plus the one Winterleaf had killed before, and arranged them into a line between the Wolfriders and the lake.

"'Ware!" shouted a watcher. More worm-brown bodies were approaching.

They hesitated at the line of their dead comrades, bowing their blunted spear-shaped heads, flickering their forked tongues. Then, after all, they crawled over. The barrier had done nothing more than slow them for the warriors and Winterleaf.

That was a long night. By dawn, when the waves of serpents finally slackened, then ceased, Winterleaf lay panting, for once too weary to play, too weary even to eat the serpents strewn around him. Oakroot went and sat by him and gathered him into his arms. Other elves stood numbly, holding one another; at a small distance Rainbow wept. Two Wolfriders had been killed in the course of the night by venomous stings; one of them was her lifemate, Two Wolves.

Oakroot's father came and heel-sat by his son and Winterleaf, carrying the most choice remains of yesterday's kill, the sweetmeats that had been reserved for the ailing elves. On the palm of his hand he offered juicy bits of liver. But Winterleaf hung his head, closed his bright brown eyes, and would not eat.

"Is it just that he is tired?" his father asked Oakroot.

The cub took his wolf-friend by the head and willed Winterleaf to open his eyes. After a moment the animal responded. Gaze met gaze.

Winterleaf failed, the little wolf sent. **Elves died.**

Without you, we might all have died.

Winterleaf remained unconsoled. **Winterleaf promised. Winterleaf failed.**

I was wrong to ask so much of you.

But not until Oakroot's father, sensing what was the matter, went and spoke with Rainbow, and Rainbow came and offered the meat on her own hand, would Winterleaf eat.

"We are all in your debt," Rainbow told him softly. "You are a brave wolf. As was my lifemate." The tears in her eyes were more of triumph than of sorrow. "As someday my little Dewberry will be."

Though guards stood all that day and night in apprehension, no more snakes came. Like locusts coming up out of the ground, all had come up out of their wintertime stupor at once. Now they were in the trees somewhere—in the forest in which the Wolfriders must hunt, under which the Wolfriders lived, through which the Wolfriders must pass in order to travel elsewhere.

Every Wolfrider went through those days with fear slithering cold on the spine, and Winterleaf had changed in the single night from the tribe's most useless hanger-on to its most important safeguard. He prowled round and round the camp, dozens of times every day, and climbed the trees overhead as often, on the watch for snakes. He gave himself little rest, and although he ate well— Oakroot's father saw to that—he grew thin.

Before any elf went to a tree hollow to rest, Winterleaf went first, to check for serpents, and sometimes he found one. Then he would leap into the hollow, straight for the back of the neck, and his teeth would fasten at the base of the skull, and the snake would writhe, convulsively biting at whatever came within its reach, until it died.

One day (for with the coming of warmer weather, the elves had turned fully from daytime to nighttime wakefulness), near sunset, sleeping in his own small treetop hollow as he often did, Oakroot awoke to find himself not alone. Sometimes Winterleaf slipped in to curl up with him, furry-warm, for an hour; that would have been wonderful. But he knew even before he fully woke that the lumpish mass atop him was not Winterleaf.

Careful not to move in any other way, he eased his eyes open. He could see nothing except, near his face, a bulge of brown-scaled muscle. A snake lay warming itself on him.

He shut his eyes quickly. Crying out in the panic he would not allow his body, his mind called, **Winterleaf!**

Then he waited. *Still, I must lie very still*, he instructed himself. *Like a sun-warmed stone. A snake won't bite a stone.*

Not daring to open his eyes in case he might move his head, he sensed rather than saw the silent approach of his wolf-friend. **Winterleaf?**

A low whine. Oakroot could send to Winterleaf, but unless they could eye-lock, Winterleaf could not communicate with him mind-to-mind. Oakroot knew nothing but that his wolf-friend was there, standing on the narrow bough outside the hollow. He lay quiet, trusting the animal to do what was best for him. He knew that the snake's head lay somewhere entirely too near him (in fact, it lay by his ear) and that when Winterleaf leapt, the snake's convulsively snapping jaws, if they met his flesh, would pump poison into him. But if Winterleaf did not leap, the snake might stay on him all night, for warmth. Oakroot did not know if he could lie stone-still all night. Or another elf might blunder near, coming to wake him for meat, and rouse the snake. Then two elves might die instead of one.

Oakroot felt movement. The snake was stirring. He did not know how Winterleaf had patted its tail with a cautious paw. When the head reared, Winterleaf leapt. Then Oakroot's dark, still, tree-hollow world exploded into a nightmare of writhing coils, a snake's long body flailing at him. He opened his eyes, trying to make sense of the mayhem, but blinked, and in that eyeblink snake and snakecatcher and convulsing chaos disappeared. Winterleaf, throwing all his body's small weight against the strugglings of the snake, had rushed both of them out of the hollow.

There was no way for him to find footing in the confusion of tree branches while fighting. Oakroot looked out just in time to see the snake going down, like a long, limp stick amid the branches, perhaps already dead, with Winterleaf's teeth still gripping its neck, Winterleaf falling, falling . . .

"No!"

On the bottom branches the snake's body caught for a moment, swung, then slithered off. Winterleaf hit the ground first, with scarcely a sound, as if he were indeed as light as a falling leaf. Then the serpent, with a thump, landed in a mass of coils atop him.

But before Oakroot, frantically scrambling down the tree, could reach the wolf, Winterleaf struggled up, shook himself, and sniffed the dead snake with a satisfied air. And startled elves were running to see from several directions, and Winterleaf seemed not to understand what they were exclaiming about, or why his young elf-friend was hugging him so.

That night the howl met, and a decision was quickly made. The two elves who had been sick were well enough to travel, though barely, and the Wolfriders felt half-frantic to leave the snakes behind. All was quickly made ready; there were few things to pack. At dawn, the wolves were summoned and started off with their riders. They traveled by day, even in the early-summer heat, because the dirt-brown snakes were hard for even a Wolfrider to see in the shadows of night. And traveled slowly, for the sake of those still weak from fever. Winterleaf needed no ride this time; he frisked alongside, and Oakroot ran with him.

Within the first day an elf died. Sky was killed by a serpent while hunting with a few companions, far ahead and aside from the body of the tribe. Riding hard on her wolf-friend, she had brushed her head against the sagging belly of a snake resting on the low branch of a tree. Winterleaf was nowhere near; he could not have prevented the death. But his head drooped when the Wolfriders howled their grief; he took the mishap to heart.

"Winterleaf, it is not your fault!" Oakroot tried to comfort him.

The little animal voluntarily eye-locked with Oakroot. **Winterleaf sorry.**

You shouldn't expect to save all of us!

Winterleaf promised.

Oakroot puffed his young cheeks in exasperation. **It doesn't matter. We are going where there are no snakes.**

No snakes? When?

Soon. In a few days. Then you can just rest and play and be useless again.

The cub meant the thought fondly. But Winterleaf did not understand the elves' sense of humor. Useless again. Which was worse, to be useless, or to fail, always fail, always elves dying, no matter how hard he tried? Winterleaf trotted through the next day of the journey without eating, no matter how Oakroot coaxed him, and without a playful bounce, not even one.

That evening Oakroot took him by the head, met his eyes. **Winterleaf, what is the matter?**

Winterleaf not know what to do.

Oakroot whined, inquiring, as troubled as his wolf-friend, and Winterleaf tried to amplify. **Elves go back where snakes are, ever?**

Puckernuts, no! We'll never let ourselves be caught in that place again.

Then Winterleaf always be no use to elf-friend.

Winterleaf . . .

There were no words Winterleaf could understand which would let Oakroot protest as he would have liked. The animal continued his thoughts.

Winterleaf no good to ride. No good to hunt anything but snakes. Just eat elves' food. No snakes for Winterleaf to eat?

Winterleaf, you know we will feed you as long as you live! Gladly. Elves don't forget.

But still the little wolf hung his head. And the next dawn, when Oakroot looked into his eyes again, Winterleaf said, **Winterleaf had dream, what must do.**

And a few moments later Oakroot ran to find his father, tugging urgently at the fur of the older elf's tunic. "Father! Father, talk to him, please, tell him to stay! He says he is going away!"

The cub was crying and scarcely coherent. His father, busy mending a skin bag, put it down and crouched, taking his son into his arms. "Easy. Talk with who? Who says?"

"Winterleaf! He says he's going to where—far south, in the wet woods, where the big snakes are. He says he had a dream."

"If an elf or a wolf has a dream," said Oakroot's father slowly, "he should follow it."

The cub pulled away from his arms in a tearful fury. "You don't want him to stay! You never wanted him in the first place!"

"Oakroot, no! Listen to me—"

"Never mind!" cried the cub fiercely. "I'll take care of it myself!" He turned his back and darted away. And that day, traveling, watching Winterleaf trot along beside the far larger wolves of the pack, Oakroot's father grew thoughtful. No longer a cub, this little animal. Though not much larger than he had been the winter before, he had obviously grown to his full size; he was no longer leggy, but neatly compact, precise and quick in all his movements. Yet the watching elf did not think it was because Winterleaf was grown that there was none of the former kittenish bounce in his step, that his ears lay folded back against his head and his plumy tail hung low. Studying the tired, sad-eyed little animal, Oakroot's father knew what Oakroot had done, and knew that something had to be corrected, and promised himself that when the tribe reached camp he would attempt it.

But that dusk, when the Wolfriders assembled, Oakroot and Winterleaf were gone.

This time Oakroot's father did not bother with anger. He had been thinking hard most of the day, and he believed he knew where the youngster might be. He mounted Blackjaw again—the strong wolf-pack-leader had plenty of run in him after merely a day of slow travel—and, by himself, set off.

The path of the Wolfriders' journey had led them to very nearly the same part of the Everwood where Oakroot had wandered off on that other journey, months before. By midnight the cub's father had picked up his scent, and by daybreak—his legs rubbed raw by riding so long in the crude, smoke-cured hides he wore, but his mind and heart still calm, controlled—by daybreak he had found Oakroot sitting at the edge of a forest pool, with Winterleaf at his side.

Oakroot looked up without surprise or fuss as his father came riding up, and the older elf said merely, "Well?"

"Strange, Father." Oakroot swallowed. "I thought it was Winterleaf who had called to me that other time. But I felt the same call again today, when Winterleaf was right beside me."

Oakroot's father nodded, slipped off Blackjaw, and sat down by his son's side. It was as he had said; Winterleaf was not, strictly speaking, a wolf-friend. The little animal was something else, something rare and beautiful. Perhaps the cub would realize on his own.

"So I went to see what it was that tugged at me so." And of course Winterleaf had followed. "You are not angry, Father?"

"A little. You could have told me you were going."

"I didn't think you'd understand."

"I don't, entirely," the older elf admitted. "What called you?"

"This."

Oakroot sat staring into brown water. The pool, deep and gleaming as the cub's eyes, lay half-hidden at the foot of a huge oak, where it was fed by the seepage that came through the roots and the many years' worth of fallen leaves. The water smelled richly of brownness; not mud, not earth, but the good brown essence of bark and wood and leaf. The father elf looked at his cub, then reached out quietly and got a swallow of the water in his hand, sniffed it, tasted it. The water itself was indeed brown, and did not merely appear so because of the wealth of fallen leaves in its depths. And it tasted of its brownness.

Oakroot turned and looked behind him. At no great distance hulked the windfall where he had found Winterleaf one cold winter's dusk.

He said, to the Everwood or his father or himself, "So it was a mistake. I felt this, and heard Winterleaf, and I thought it was Winterleaf calling me, but he wasn't. Not really. I forced him to come out to me."

His father said, "No need to call it a mistake. We are all honored to have known Winterleaf. He has found his gift; he is a snakecatcher. And you have found yours, or one of yours. You are a bonder with animals."

Oakroot said with shame in his voice, "Today I did the same thing. I forced my will on him. I bonded him to stay with me."

At Oakroot's other side sat Winterleaf, loyal but no longer happy. Oakroot stared at the brown pool rather than turning to meet his creature-friend's troubled brown eyes.

The older elf said quietly, "I see you are learning fast, how a gift is a knife that can cut many ways."

Oakroot turned and met Winterleaf's gaze, brown eyes to brown eyes. For silent moments the two minds met, Wolfrider cub and—what? No one of that tribe would ever know for sure.

Oakroot said, perhaps to his father, perhaps to himself, "Winterleaf loves to fight snakes. He loves me, too, but he should not have to live where there are no snakes to fight."

Silence. The older elf sat waiting, nearly breath-holding, unwilling to tell his cub to do what the youngster might do by himself.

Oakroot said, "He saved my life. Twice at least, maybe more. I owe him."

Silence for another moment. Then Oakroot reached out, ruffled the fringe of hair below the young creature's sagging ears, hugged him around the neck once, then let go. "I release the bond," Oakroot said aloud.

Winterleaf sprang up and licked the elf cub's face, dancing kitten-light on small padded paws; his brown eyes shone, his ears pricked jauntily upward, his tail waved high. He would go to test himself against great snakes, the greatest snakes in the world of two moons. And if he lived, perhaps he would see Oakroot again someday; elves lived long, and release of the bond did not mean love had ceased.

Farewell, little wolf-friend, Oakroot wished him. **And good hunting.**

And the little beast, who had never given voice like a wolf, yipped once in farewell and flashed away.

Oakroot sat where he was, with his father, watching long after the small brown running thing had ceased to be a spark of movement in the forest and was gone. "What will he eat?" the cub muttered at last.

"He is like you," said his father. "He will learn to do what he has to do."

"Yes." Oakroot sat silent a small while longer. "Perhaps he will not always be alone," he said finally. "Perhaps there are other snakecatchers in the world, and he will find them."

"Perhaps." His father hoped it also, that Winterleaf would be happy.

Oakroot looked up, his eyes glimmering, wet as the pool at his feet. "Father—what is it about this place? What calls me here?"

"I don't know. It is your special place; you must find its secret. Someday you will understand."

The youngster was still very much the cub; he wanted comfort. He rested his head against his father, and his father put his arm around him.

And so it was that Freefoot, chieftain of the Wolfriders, sat through sunrise with his son at the edge of an oakroot pool—his son who had once thought himself of no use, with no distinction, no gifts; his son who would be Tanner, chieftain of the Wolfriders for eight hundred years, and who would learn the secrets of tanning fine leather from oak trees and tannin-brown water.

And who would never in all those years forget what it felt like to be a cub, and never forget Winterleaf.

The Fire Song

by Diana L. Paxson

Goodtree crouched in the dry grass as if she had been rooted there, her skin browned by the scorching sun and bright hair dust-coated until she was the same lion-color as the endless, rolling plain. The faintest of breezes set stiff stalks to rustling. Elf ears pricked, but there was nothing moving out there, only the wind. The spear was growing heavy, but she dared not lay it down. When they came it would be fast.

If they came . . .

Goodtree sifted powdery soil through the fingers of her other hand, sent her awareness down the grass stalk into the earth. But the roots were dry, too, only an occasional flicker of life where once an interconnected mat of rootlets had connected all the plain—nothing here to tell her where the game was feeding now. There was little nourishment in the grass, and the animals had worn white trails to the muddy centers of cracked craters that had once been waterholes.

But Lionleaper could track a leaf on the wind, and where there was scent, the wolves could follow. He and Fang would start the chase, and Acorn and Twitch-ear and Leafchaser would herd their prey toward the fold in the plain where Goodtree was waiting.

Of the three of them, Acorn was the best runner, and in the seasons since she found her soulname, Goodtree had practiced what she had never allowed her mother to teach her, until, of them all, she had the best aim with a spear. The old jealousy between her two lovemates was by now long forgotten, and the harmony between the three of them made them and their wolf-friends an unequaled hunting team. The hunters would find something, they *had* to . . .

Goodtree's belly growled painfully, but she suppressed

211

awareness of her own hunger. A dry winter had sent the Wolfriders early from their dens in the Hurst to the wandering life of the plain. The spring hunt had been good, but when the great surging herds of branch-horns had eaten their way northward across the grasslands there was little left for others, and no rain had fallen to renew the land.

The mad-horns and serpent-noses had all moved on somewhere, southward, maybe, to that other forest Goodtree had once seen. *We should have gone with them,* she thought. *I'm chief. I should have understood how it would be.* But it was too late. Too many of the Wolfriders were too weak to survive such a journey now. Hunger gnawed in her own belly constantly. But Goodtree knew that she could endure—it was the cubs at the encampment who must have food.

Soon—soon, she promised herself, shifting her grip on the spear. *Soon the branch-horns will come back again, and there will be enough for all.*

For a moment her weight rested on her other hand. Goodtree felt the faintest of vibrations and stiffened. There was something—a light, irregular tremor—not a serpent-nose, then, or even a moon-horn—something that moved in frantic bounds. Senses strained outward . . .

Sound came first, a swift drumbeat on the hard ground; then wolf-senses caught the mingled scents of wolves and a springer, its sweat soured by fear. She was downwind then. Parched lips drew back in a grim smile—wolf-scent was stampeding the springer toward her. The stretched muscles in her bent thighs quivered with tension.

Then a swirl of dust and a blurred shape coming. Goodtree uncoiled from the grass, spear arm swinging back and over. The spear arced through the air. The springer leapt straight up, squealing as the spear scored its side. Goodtree howled her frustration, groping already for her knife as the beast landed running. But there were two wolves before it. Panicked, the springer turned. Another lance flew. She glimpsed Acorn through dust.

Get back! she sent frantically. **It'll leap over us!**

Wolves ranged outward. The springer plunged and snorted, shaking sharp horns.

Goodtree grabbed Acorn's spear and pulled back again with a warning howl as their prey headed for the momentary opening. The springer's gaunt flanks heaved as it whirled in place. Goodtree hefted the spear, panting. If she had been in top condition, she would not have needed to catch her breath this way. But if the springer had been stronger, they would not have been able to bring it to bay!

Lionleaper! Surprise had failed—they would need all three spears. His answer came more strongly than she had expected. He was close, then. **Leafchaser, Twitchear—keep moving . . .**

It was all coming together now. Goodtree was aware of the two males as she felt her own limbs, moving together in instinctive harmony, as they did sometimes when the tribe danced beneath the moons. Even in the instant of action, she savored that perfect balance, the unique bond that the three of them had found.

Acorn, can you get my spear? Goodtree edged forward.

The springer took a nervous step back. In motion, one saw only the flex and spring of powerful haunches as the beast soared. Now all she could think of was the length and sharpness of its horns. Then Fang's dark muzzle poked through the grass. Lionleaper slid from his wolf's back, and Fang sat down, tongue lolling. Peripheral vision showed her something dark moving; Acorn darted in, grabbing for the fallen spear, and the springer swiveled, head lowering.

Watch out!

Acorn started to roll away as Lionleaper dashed forward to help him. Goodtree cast Acorn's spear, but the springer was turning. The weapon slammed into its shoulder; suddenly Lionleaper was in front of it, the beast squealed and swung its head in agony, horntips slashed, and the sweep of the horns splattered bright blood through the air.

"Lionleaper!" Shock tore the shout from Goodtree's throat. The springer's head jerked up at the sound. Acorn, still rolling, brought his spear up under the beast's belly;

Twitch-ear darted in and powerful jaws clamped one hind leg; Leafchaser seized the other, and then Fang was at the springer's throat, bringing it down.

But Goodtree saw only Lionleaper falling; she gasped as the sharp blood scents of prey and hunter mingled in the dusty air.

Wolves growled as they pinned their prey, lapping the lifeblood that poured from its torn throat. Lionleaper's blood was still welling from twin gashes across his belly, scarlet against the white of old scars. Goodtree knelt beside him, trying to press the torn edges together with her hands. His breath came in hoarse gasps that grew fainter as he continued to bleed. Lionleaper had been gored before, turns ago, but not like this. His eyes were closed, his skin chill despite the heat of the day.

"Help me bind the wounds—" Acorn's voice seemed to come from a great distance. Goodtree blinked and saw that he was haggling at his jerkin with his knife. Worn leather tore, and she lifted Lionleaper as Acorn passed the strip beneath him. "Now the next one—" Part of the leather made a pad, reddening as blood soaked it.

"I think we're catching it," Acorn went on. Lionleaper's skin had paled to a sickly yellow. Had they stopped the bleeding in time? Goodtree's sight blurred, tears slid down her cheeks to her lips; she reached up to wipe them away and tasted Lionleaper's blood mingled with her own tears.

Emotion slashed through her as if she were the one who had been gored. She bent, gripping his shoulders, and sent her spirit questing after his.

You cannot die . . . I won't let you! Listen to me— *Lleyn—Lleyn*! Her grip tightened. Acorn was saying something, but she could not hear. For a moment she felt a feather-touch like a distant call. Awareness spiraled downward, inward, pursuing that contact into a red darkness in which it was the only reality.

And then there was suddenly more, flooding her entire consciousness with his, and borne on that cool tide, the single question of her name . . .

Neme?

Lleyn, you are going to live, for me! She opened her

214

eyes, and saw his fixed on her face, saw the moment when his heart took up its steady beat again. He would live—and to that inner awareness was added a sudden overwhelming sense of his physical essence, and pulsing from her loins through every vein, the awareness of her own.

And it was only then that she realized by what name she had called him, and how he had replied.

"Goodtree—we'd better send one of the wolves back to camp with a message," said Acorn. "We'll need help to carry him, and—Goodtree, are you all right?"

Dazed, she looked up—saw Acorn's dark eyes round with anxiety, the dust in his brown hair, every beloved line and angle in his face tight with concern. *Beloved* . . . With a whimper, her gaze went back to the other elf, always beloved equally, in his own way, and now—she forced herself to see him with a healer's eye. A little color had come back into Lionleaper's face; golden eyes searched her own.

It's happened, came his sending. **We were right to fear!**

She nodded. They had been so sure that Recognition was only a mindless reproductive urge, easily satisfied. They had assured each other that if it happened they could handle it, that nothing could destroy the unique bond that the three of them had treasured so. But what she was feeling now was like being shaken by a whirlwind.

To be aware of another being breath by breath, cell by cell, to know that he felt her every emotion, too . . . *No! I won't be compelled this way! I am more than an animal!* Panicking, she forced her fingers to let go of him, and as she did so, heard his thought again.

Neme—we must never let Acorn know!

Goodtree closed her eyes. "It was the . . . shock . . ." she said with more truth than Acorn knew.

Neme . . . leave me . . . I can't resist both you and the pain . . . came Lionleaper's sending.

"I'll go with them—we'll need a litter—the wolves couldn't explain."

"I can go," Acorn said. "He needs you here."

She shook her head. That might be true, but Acorn

needed her, too. Lionleaper had said it—if she stayed, neither of them would be able to resist Recognition's compulsion. Maybe later, when he was healing and she was over this first shock that had left her spirit naked, maybe then they could dare to be together once more.

"You've had a long run already. I'll go faster now."

"That's true," came Acorn's reply at last.

Shivering with reaction, Goodtree got to her feet. "Take care of him. Take care of him for me . . ." She dared not look at Lionleaper again.

Taking a deep breath, she forced her legs into motion and left the two males she loved most in the world behind her on the dusty plain.

For quite a long while there was only pain.

Lionleaper welcomed it. In his lucid moments he knew that when his body began to heal itself he would have a worse torment to deal with. He clung to the ache in his belly and tried to shut out that hunger of the spirit that was so much harder to bear than the emptiness within.

"Here, brother—I've made broth for you."

Lionleaper opened his eyes and saw that Weaver was holding out a vessel she had made of rawhide and sealed with resin. Obediently he opened his mouth and swallowed, trying not to wonder what it contained. It was tasteless stuff, fit only for cubs and invalids, but he did not have the strength to chew fresh meat even if there had been any. After a few swallows he lay back again, panting.

"Shall I lift you?"

He shook his head. Weaver's amber braids swung forward as she bent over him. Her face was like a fairer mirror of his own. She was as stubborn as he was, too.

"Lionleaper, you have to try! Don't you want to get well?"

That was a good question. Dying would have been so much easier. But Wolfriders did not give up life easily. He felt his body taking strength from the broth he had swallowed and knew he was healing.

"Maybe Goodtree can make you listen. She can't be off hunting all the time."

"Don't ask her." Lionleaper winced as he got himself up on one elbow. Weaver set the cup to his lips again.

"Why not? For turns you've been lovemates, but she hasn't come to see you since you started getting well again. Did you quarrel? Don't tell me she has other responsibilities—you've always found time for each other before."

"Don't blame Goodtree," he whispered. "There are reasons."

She eyed him suspiciously. "I don't believe you, but if you drink the rest of this broth I'll let it go for now."

Lionleaper got the cooling liquid down in one long swallow and then collapsed back onto the furs. His belly hurt, but he was still conscious. He saw the sunlight flicker through the woven canes of his shelter and remembered the gold of Goodtree's hair. Even in his weakness he could feel his body's response to the thought of her.

"I don't want to see her." He was glad they were not sending. His sister would have known he lied.

Is Recognition worth it? he wondered. There were those lucky ones who Recognized their lifemates, like his sister and Briar. To some it never came at all. And for the rest it was as enjoyable as an evening with the dreamberries— and except that it brought cubs, it meant no more.

He could have mated with anyone else, anyone but Goodtree, and it would have made no difference. She had a horror of being forced into things—she had run from the chieftainship like a stampeding branch-horn. If he made her give in to this compulsion she would hate him.

And Acorn—in an odd way Acorn was his lovemate, too, and Lionleaper measured his friend's pain by his own. He closed his eyes. He could not see the end of this trail—all he could do was to keep following it.

As soon as I can travel I must get away from here, he thought.

The wolves were hunting—a moment of quivering stillness, then a sudden pounce into the dry grass that brought up a frantically wriggling morsel that disappeared down the gullet almost too quickly to be seen.

217

"At least *they* won't starve," said Joygleam bitterly. "But we can't live on squeakers until our hunters return."

"Do we have a choice?" asked Goodtree. "The thought doesn't excite me, either, but if wolves can eat them, so can Wolfriders! We'll get the wolves to sniff out their burrows and then dig them out ourselves. Over by the river the ground's full of their holes—what used to be the river, anyway."

She eased back under the shadow of the hide they were using for a sunshade, squinting out at the glare. In the heat of the day, most of the Wolfriders huddled under rude tents cobbled together out of old pelts, or lean-tos of woven grass. In one of them, Longleaf was telling the cubs a story. In another, Lionleaper lay resting while his sister, Weaver, tended him. Goodtree did not have to look in that direction to know that he was watching her.

"It's better than starving, I suppose," said the huntress, "but those little naked tails revolt me."

"Well, I won't ask you to lead the hunting party!" Goodtree grinned sourly. "Snowfall can take some of the cubs over there in the morning. Why don't you and I try the mudhole by the red rocks again? There might be a moon-horn or two left around."

"Pity Lionleaper is still too weak to track for us," said Joygleam.

Goodtree could feel the hot color rising in her cheeks, betraying her.

"I'll be glad when he recovers. The tribe needs his skill," the huntress went on. "Though why he should want to get better when you keep avoiding him I do not know. You act as if he had the froth-madness instead of a belly wound."

"There are reasons," Goodtree said stiffly. "He understands." She kept her gaze on the wolves.

"I'm sure he does . . . farts and fewmets, Goodtree!" snapped Joygleam. "Do you think we're too stupid to have figured out what is going on between you two?"

Goodtree stared at her. She had tried so hard to keep her secret. But Joygleam and Longreach and some of the others must have seen it all so many times before. Why had she even tried? She shook her head with a sigh.

"You can be very like your mother sometimes!" the old huntress went on. "Stormlight never wanted to accept Recognition, either, but at least she did her duty and produced you! Is it pride that's stopping you, or what? I thought you liked Lionleaper!"

Like! Goodtree shook her head, suppressing the urge to howl. She was not refusing Recognition for lack of liking, but because she loved too well.

"I'll take your advice on hunting, Joygleam," she said between her teeth, "but this is none of your affair!"

"You're chief of the Wolfriders," the huntress answered wearily. "And always supposing we survive this summer, your cub may be our leader one day. Your mating is everybody's affair."

"That's why I didn't want—" Goodtree swallowed the rest of her words. She hadn't wanted to be chief, but she had accepted the responsibility. Yet she had a responsibility to Acorn, too, and she wanted to be able to face him when he and the other hunters returned.

Someone is going to suffer no matter what I do, she thought. *At least for the moment, let it be me!*

She looked up at the huntress, and her green eyes held the dark gaze of the older elf in a long wolf-stare. It was Joygleam who first looked away.

"As you say, first we have to survive," Goodtree said quietly. "Now, are you going to come with me tomorrow?"

The moondance was finishing another round when Acorn came back again. With Oakarrow and Brightlance, and Briar, Evenstar, and young Fern, he'd been off southward, scouring the plain for game. They were not coming back empty-handed, but Acorn felt ashamed when he saw with what joy the Wolfriders who had stayed behind eyed the dried strips of springer meat that they were carrying in, the half-smoked haunch of moon-horn, and the gutted ravvit carcasses strung on thongs. Wolves howled back and forth in greeting, frisked around elf-legs like cubs, made playful snatches at the game.

He glimpsed Goodtree's bright hair and grinned. She waved back, but there was no joy in her smile. She looked strained, even thinner than she had been before. And he could not see Lionleaper anywhere.

Acorn felt as if *he* had taken a belly wound.

The other end of his pole was dropped suddenly. He turned, saw Briar with his arms around Weaver, swinging her around and around. But there was no sorrow in her eyes.

"Weaver, is your brother—" His eyes finished the question.

"He's mending," she answered when Briar let her go. "But I'm glad *you're* here!"

Acorn frowned. What an odd thing to say. Then Briar picked up the pole and they carried the meat the rest of the way into the camp.

Dusk was casting long shadows across the plain before he was able to get free long enough to go and visit his friend. He had made a song to help them forget the long marches, and of course his companions wanted everyone else to hear it. They were still singing as he padded through the dust to the shelter where Lionleaper lay.

> *"Faint the trail that we must follow.*
> *Long the chase and hard the way.*
> *Trailing dreams into tomorrow.*
> *Hunting memories today."*

Lionleaper was a deeper shadow in the darkness of the shelter. Even elf-eyes could make out little beside the dim blur of face and arms. Acorn hunkered down beside him. Keen ears caught the change in the other's breathing. He was awake, then.

"I've brought you some of my kill. Can you eat it?"

There was a sound that might have been laughter, then Lionleaper sighed. "I'm healing. You know how it is. What doesn't kill you quickly makes you stronger."

Acorn handed the meat to his friend. It was a piece from the moon-horn, smoked to the consistency of leather. He heard sharp teeth worrying, a tearing sound as Lionleaper got a strip free and began to chew.

"Why aren't you at the celebration, then? Goodtree is there."

"I'm not quite ready . . . for reveling."

"Goodtree didn't seem to be enjoying herself, either," said Acorn thoughtfully.

> *"Seeking something fair as star-sheen.*
> *Soft as misty veils of rain:*
> *Or distant shapes that move afar, seen*
> *In mirages on the plain."*

Suddenly he pushed the woven mat aside. Elf-eyes gleamed in starlight, and he saw agony in them. Not of the body—Lionleaper was devouring the moon-horn too eagerly to be in physical pain—but of the soul. He had seen the same sadness in Goodtree's eyes.

"Have you had a fight with her?"

Lionleaper shook his head, still chewing.

"Weaver says you must have. She says that Goodtree hasn't come to see you, not once, since I've been gone!"

"My sister has nursed me like her own cub, but I wish she'd keep her nose out of what's none of her concern!" muttered Lionleaper.

"And what about me? Is it no concern of mine? You're my friend . . ." There was no answer. Acorn snarled. "Lionleaper, answer me!"

"I *can't* tell you! In the high ones' name, let it be!"

Can't, or don't dare? Suddenly Acorn felt cold. Did he really want Lionleaper to tell him what was wrong? In their circle, the Wolfriders were still singing.

> *"Herds we may hunt down, yet never*
> *Find the truth that's hid within.*
> *Shall we follow dreams forever?*
> *Where's the wonder we would win?"*

Full-fed he was, and yet Acorn's heart felt hollow. The love that had sustained the three of them was shattered. How or why, he did not yet understand, but the tribe lived

221

too close for such a secret to be kept forever. Soon, perhaps too soon, he would know.

Goodtree glared at the strip of springer meat in her hand. Wolf-senses told her to eat and grow strong, but starving had kept other feelings more or less at bay. The sun beat hot against her back and released the scent of the food. She was salivating already, wanting to worry the tough meat with her jaws as she wanted to taste the salt savor of Lionleaper's skin, needing the nourishing solidity of food in her belly as she needed the hard strength of his body joined to hers. There were moments when all she could think of was that pure intensity of need.

A bitch in season, she thought then. *Is that all I am?*

She and Lionleaper had chosen this abstinence out of loyalty to Acorn, but now Goodtree had other reasons. How could she lead the Wolfriders when she couldn't even keep her own body under control?

We are more than just bodies—we must be—or why not lose ourselves in the wolfsong as Longreach tells us the Hunt did so many turns ago?

But she would never solve this problem if she starved. The high ones had chosen to live in physical forms, and on her spirit quest, so had she. She tore off a piece of meat and began to chew.

Then Goodtree felt coolness on her back, someone was standing between her and the sun. For a moment she was simply grateful for the shade.

"I have to talk to you."

Acorn . . . the meat Goodtree had eaten lay in her belly like a stone. *Go away,* she thought, but she neither spoke nor sent. Ever since Acorn had marched in with the other hunters the day before, she had known this moment must come.

"Everyone says you and Lionleaper have been avoiding each other. Can you tell me what's wrong?"

"Ask him." Goodtree stared at the meat in her hands.

"He won't tell me, either, but there must be something. Are you blaming him because he got hurt? That's silly. It could have happened to anyone. And besides, it was my

222

fault. I was the one who missed my cast. He got gored trying to protect me when I went in after that spear."

"*I* told you to do that," muttered Goodtree. "I don't blame you or him."

"Well, if that's not it, then what is it? Are you too worried about the tribe? Wolfriders have survived worse, Goodtree, and it'll be easier if you let Lionleaper and me help you. When he finishes healing, that is—*if* he heals . . ."

"He is getting better," Goodtree said wearily. "I've kept a regular check on that."

"Because the tribe needs him? What use is it for his body to heal if you kill his soul?"

An emotion too sudden and violent for her to name brought Goodtree to her feet.

"What do you know about it?" she snarled. *It's my own soul I'm killing, and all for you, for you!*

"I don't understand." Acorn was shaking his head, dark eyes wide. "I thought I knew you, but the elf I loved would never act this way."

"That's why—" she began, then shut her lips and turned away.

"*What* is why?" A hard hand closed on her shoulder, whirled her around to face him again. "You are going to tell me, Goodtree!"

For a moment she stood it, then reached up and with a sudden exertion of her own strength, struck his hand away.

"Don't touch me! Don't try to force me—into anything! I won't be compelled, Acorn, not by you, not by Lionleaper, not by anything!"

"*Anything* . . ." His voice wavered. She saw him swallow, trying to master it. "But it is *something*, isn't it, Goodtree? What could frighten you, anger you so badly that you can't tell me . . . that *he* couldn't tell me . . ." It was no longer a question. "I was stupid, wasn't I?" His gaze fixed on the endless dun swells of the plain.

"Recognition," he went on. "When two elves get into such a state about each other, what else can it be? I suppose everybody else figured it out long ago."

They stood in silence. The warm wind stroked the dry

223

grass like an invisible hand, and Goodtree clasped her arms, trying to still her trembling.

"And you're fighting it," Acorn said finally, "because of me. *That's* stupid, Goodtree. Do you think it will make it easier for me to know that you're unhappy, too? Recognition is the Wolfrider Way! Why not get it over with, and then maybe we can all go back to the way things were before."

Goodtree shook her head. "You don't know what you're talking about." The bitterness was too great for her to spare him now. "It will never be the same, but you're not my only reason for resisting it any more. They all keep telling me how wrong my mother was to fight her bond with Tanner. When I was a cub the only thing I ever wanted was for her to settle down and be a mother to me. But I'm beginning to understand her now."

"You're not Stormlight!" He reached out to her and she stepped away.

"I'm her daughter! Don't you understand? My mother fought against accepting the Way until the struggle killed her. But why were her only choices to be unhappy or to give in? I will not accept this just because elves always have."

"Even if it hurts everyone you love? Even if it hurts the tribe?"

Acorn's voice had always reflected every fine shade of emotion. It was like being dragged through a field of fire-thorn, listening to him now.

"What makes you so sure Recognition is *good* for the tribe? Wolfriders are supposed to be free!" Goodtree cried.

Lionleaper drew back his arm, wincing as the motion stretched half-healed muscles and tender skin, and threw the spear. It did not hit the target he had set up for himself, but it was closer. Each day his muscles toughened and more strength returned.

He trotted forward to pick up the spear. Soon he would be able to—what? Hunt again? He and Acorn and Goodtree had hunted together for too many turns. There would be little joy in going alone.

The weapon dragged behind him as he returned to his mark. Then he straightened. Joygleam was waiting for him. As he came up to her, she nodded approvingly.

"You're recovering, I see."

He shrugged. "I'll be ready to hunt with you by the time the branch-horns come."

She looked at him oddly. "If they come. Did you lose track of time completely while you were ill? It's the middle of the time of Long-necks Flying. The herd should have been here by now."

He stared at her. The days were still warm, but it was true that the last few nights he had needed his sleeping fur. He should have known. He had been too bound up in his need for Goodtree's survival to notice. That, as much as the threat to the tribe's survival, made him afraid.

"Why, Joygleam?" he whispered. "Has this ever happened before?"

"I don't know. Maybe the heat has fooled the branch-horns, too. But if they wait till the white cold is upon them to start south, it will catch them, and us, here. Still, that's not my greatest fear . . ." Her brown features grew more pinched as she looked out over the plain.

Lionleaper followed her gaze. "The plains have been eaten to the bone, is that what you mean? Are you wondering whether the great herd will come this way at all?"

Joygleam nodded. "Easy to say that the tribe should follow them, but do we have the strength for it now? The branch-horns have got to come this way—some of them, anyhow, or this season will be worse than ever the hot has been!"

When the huntress had gone, Lionleaper stared after her, wondering why she had said all this to *him*. It was Goodtree she should be talking to!

And what if she is suffering as much as I am? the thought came to him then. It was all he could do to bear their separation, and he had no responsibilities. *Goodtree can't act as chief because of me.*

It had been a mistake to even think of her. He felt the

225

familiar stirring in his flesh, and reaching for the bowl of ointment Moss had made for him, started to rub it into the scar tissue on his belly, pushing hard, welcoming the distraction of pain. Elves who hated each other had Recognized in the past, but had there ever been two for whom it had spelled the death of love?

Branch-horns—that's what I should be thinking of. Lots and lots of branch-horns . . . Where can they be? He forced his imagination to bear him away from the dust of the camp over the endless undulations of the plain. He wanted that empty freedom almost as much as he wanted Goodtree, and suddenly he understood why she had run away so long ago. It seemed like the only solution sometimes.

If he could find the branch-horns, both of them would be too busy to worry about mating. Maybe full-fed, the frustration would be easier to bear. Anyway, they couldn't go on this way. He had to leave, Lionleaper told himself, for the good of the tribe . . .

Two days had passed, and the hunter was packing a few fragments of dried meat into the pouch that already held his kit and spare spearhead when he became aware that someone was watching him. He thrust the pouch beneath his rolled sleeping fur and turned.

Acorn was standing over him, leaning on his spear. Lionleaper saw his friend's gaze move from the fur to the bow and arrows laid ready beside it.

"Does Goodtree know you're going away?"

Lionleaper flushed. "No," he said shortly. "Nor will she." *Joygleam might guess,* he thought then, and wondered if that was why she had come to him. But she would not give him away. "Don't try to stop me, Acorn. I'm going to find out where the branch-horns have gone."

"Stop you?" Acorn's dark eyes widened. "I'm going with you!"

Now it was Lionleaper's turn to stare. Then, slowly, he smiled.

"What about Goodtree?" he asked. Acorn's eyes were on the pattern he was scuffing into the dust.

"She feels angry every time she looks at you," he said, "and guilty every time she looks at me, but she'd never forgive me if I let you go alone!"

"We'll slip away tomorrow, then, when everyone is resting at noon."

Lionleaper sat back on his heels, watching Acorn saunter away. *Who could have figured it?* he thought. But suddenly he was glad.

The great herd was like a forest, as if the Everwood had taken root in the high plateau. But this forest was moving. Mighty horns tossed like branches in a high wind, shaggy backs jostled, and then the whole mass was flowing downhill. Acorn let his breath out with a sigh and straightened. The branch-horns would not notice his movement now. Twitch-ear got to his feet beside him, tail quivering.

Is time? the wolf's eagerness came clearly.

Not yet. Wait for Lionleaper's signal—wait!

Acorn's gaze went back to the branch-horns, and he shuddered with the same surge of emotion that shook him sometimes when he was starting a song, but this experience was still too new for him to transform it into poetry. Acorn had been hunting branch-horns with the Wolfriders since he was a cub, but always from the plain. The high plateau was broken by upthrusts where the bare stone poked through earth's hide. For the first time he saw the herd as a whole.

The multitudes of animals that he knew were there had become a single being, a mass of life too vast, almost, for comprehension. The herd become a forest, and the forest a brown river that flooded toward the plain.

Lionleaper's whistle brought Acorn back to self-awareness. He realized that even now he had been trying to use images to somehow control what he saw. He shook his head to clear it. He should be seeing the branch-horns as meat—meat for the tribe.

Lionleaper whistled again and trotted down the slope, Fang at his side. Acorn left the protection of his boulder and started after him.

For several days they ranged along the edge of the great herd, coming down from the plateau to the beginnings of the great plain. When their food ran out, they let the wolves cut out a straggling cow from among the others and brought her down. She was stringy, probably past calving, but her flesh was life to them and the wolves.

Tearing into a piece of haunch, Acorn eyed his companion. Lionleaper was gazing into the little fire they had built to warm them, for the nights were beginning to grow cold. His meat lay forgotten in his hand.

"Do you think the herd will reach the plains before snowfall?" Acorn asked brightly. Lionleaper blinked and looked up at him.

"What?" His eyes were wide, dazed. Acorn decided his question had been a stupid one.

"Lionleaper, what do you see in that fire?"

The other elf shivered as wind gusted around them again, drawing out the fire into long streamers of flame.

"I see Goodtree's bright hair . . ."

Acorn sighed. The constant physical demands of the journey had numbed his own need for her, but clearly for Lionleaper it was otherwise. They were both thin from short rations and hard traveling, but how could he have missed the pain that twisted the other elf's face, the feverish glitter in his eyes? For the first time, he was grateful that it was Lionleaper whom Goodtree had Recognized. It was hard enough to be at the mercy of the music that pulsed within him, without being subject to this overwhelming physical need.

Recognized couples often separated after mating; this was the first time Acorn had seen what happened if they did so before consummating their bond. *It cannot go on,* he thought then.

"I'm sorry." Lionleaper gave a hopeless little shrug. "I can't forget her. I don't know what to do . . ."

"Go back to her," Acorn said harshly. "Survival is more important than anyone's feelings."

"Even if the thing that made you love life is gone? If I force Goodtree, she'll never forgive me, and I think the

228

spirit that makes her a good chief to us might be destroyed as well. Then the tribe would never forgive me! If the only thing I have to look forward to is a lifetime of her hating me, I'd rather die now!" He was shaking. Acorn started to say something soothing, but Lionleaper shook his head.

"I don't have your way with words, Acorn. The only thing I know how to do is to stick to what I know is right, to follow a trail. I agree with Goodtree—if Recognition makes you betray everything else you believe in, then it can't be for the good of the tribe."

Lionleaper grimaced. Then with a visible effort he pulled himself together, became the hunter again. "But if the branch-horns don't head eastward, it won't matter what Goodtree and I do, because nobody is going to survive. Acorn, we'll have to turn the herd somehow."

"Two elves and two wolves against all that?" Acorn gestured out at the great shifting mass of the herd.

"Two elves and two wolves—and fire!" Light glittered crazily in Lionleaper's eyes as he thrust a new branch into the flame.

Goodtree is stepping carefully through a field of fire-thorn, stepping carefully and slowly, because she is looking for something that she's lost . . . or was it something that she threw away? Guilt stabs her as she tries to remember; an unwary step sends pain stinging up her leg and she stands still.

Someone is moving on the other side of the field. She strains to see, but the dark clouds are gathering. She cannot tell if his hair is brown or tawny, but the lithe grace of his movement starts a fire in her gut that burns worse than the thorn.

Clouds race overhead; thunder startles her into motion. Thorn catches at leggings and tunic, tripping her, stabs through thin leather until her whole body is ablaze. But she must reach . . . him? The male she was looking at is gone. Where she saw him before, now she sees other figures—a brown-haired cubling, another with hair as vivid a gold as her own, and more.

229

She forces herself forward, ignoring the pain. Then bright-ness stabs downward from the heavens, and the fire-thorn erupts into real flames. Goodtree cries out as she is cut off from the cubs by a wall of fire.

"Goodtree, Goodtree! Come see—the prairie is on fire!"

Goodtree whimpered as the cry merged with her dream. But hard hands were shaking her. Groaning, she opened her eyes.

For a moment she thought it was Lionleaper. Then vision cleared and she saw Weaver bending over her, and pointing. A wall of shadow was billowing up against the afternoon sky, and she caught the reek of smoke. *I smelled it in my sleep,* she told herself. *That's why I dreamed of fire . . .*

Even as she thought it, she had rolled to her feet. She blinked the last sleep from her eyes. She had spent a lot of time sleeping lately, but what she was seeing now brought her wide awake, with alarm prickling through every nerve. As she watched, the clouds of smoke reached higher, their underside glowing luridly. The horizon sparked with the first bright flickers of advancing flame. She licked a finger and held it high, waiting for the first coolness to show her the direction of the wind.

Red flower coming fast. Leafchaser's nose poked her side. **Go quickly, get away!**

Not yet, Goodtree answered. **Wait as long as you can.**

"Joygleam says the flames should pass us." Weaver was saying. "If the wind doesn't rise, if the fire hasn't spread too widely by then—"

Goodtree nodded. Once she had commanded trees to keep floodwaters from washing the tribe away. But there was not enough live vegetation left on the plain for her to talk to, and even if she could have put a forest in the path of the fire it would only have fueled the flame.

As she stared, through the soles of her feet she felt a vibration. She straightened, feeling the wind on her right cheek. Flames were racing across the prairie, leaping skyward, then reaching greedily for the grass before them.

The air shuddered with the crackle of the fire. The wolves had retreated to the far edge of the campsite, whining, as love for their friends fought the instinct to flee.

But that was not what had alerted her. Now she could see dark spots against the brightness. Of course any animals that were left on the prairie would be fleeing the fire, but what she saw was *many* animals, a mass of moving figures like a storm-tossed wood whose flailing branches scored the sky . . . branch-horns . . .

"Well, now we know where the herd is," gasped Joygleam, coming up beside her. For a few moments Goodtree watched in silence.

"I think the fire is going to miss us, but the branch-horns are coming this way. Get everyone to call their wolves—everyone who can run, or ride! We'll go out to meet them, try to turn them before they overrun those who can't get away."

She tipped back her head and let out her breath in a long howl. Dimly she sensed Leafchaser's panic, and strengthened her sending until terror became confusion, and confusion a nervous obedience to her will.

Others were doing the same around her. In a moment she felt a cold nose thrust into her palm, the wolf's shaggy warmth pushing against her, the long tremors that shook Leafchaser's body even as she obeyed.

We're going hunting, old friend. Goodtree tried to make her sending eager, to project images of excitement to replace the fear. **Fresh meat, good meat—we have only to go after it!** She stroked the rough fur until the wolf's trembling eased, then flung a leg over Leafchaser's back and got a good grip. **See them? Feel them? They're coming. Let's get them now!**

The wolf barked sharply, catching her excitement. Goodtree howled, and suddenly everyone was giving tongue. They were moving, fear transformed into a hysterical energy that sent them hurtling through the smoke toward the stampeding herd.

For the branch-horns, too, one fear battled another as leaping forms and bared teeth appeared suddenly in their

231

path. Outrunners swerved, caroming into the mass of their fellows. The edge of the herd disintegrated into a confusion of plunging individuals. Snarling, the wolves leapt in to nip at their flanks; stone spears pricked them to new panic. But the weight of the herd still pressed them forward.

Goodtree and Leafchaser raced alongside the branch-horns, shaken by the vibration, deafened by the rumble of thousands of hooves. She caught glimpses of the others: Joygleam waving her spear and yelling, Oakarrow and Brightlance close behind, and then another Wolfrider, so grimed with ash that she only realized it was Acorn after he had gone by.

There was no time to wonder. Suddenly the fragile shelters of their camp were before them. She urged Leafchaser onward, stabbing with her spear. Branch-horns shoved into each other, bellowing, bounced outward again, and crashed into the outermost lean-tos. Had any elves still been inside?

A young branch-horn bull, maddened by a thrust from a herdmate's horn, careered off at an angle from the rest. Others began to follow him. Goodtree shrieked warning and leaned over Leafchaser's neck, calling the last strength from her friend.

Now the bull was thundering toward Snowfall's shelter. Goodtree yipped and the beast's head came round. She flung her spear with all her power, and as the bull swerved, the spear pierced his broad chest. It was a perfect cast, but the branch-horn's mighty body did not yet know it was dead. Leafchaser tried to leap away, but she was going too fast. Goodtree was thrown off just as the branch-horn reared. One flailing hoof grazed her head as it fell . . .

"Goodtree, I didn't know this would happen. Look at me, please!"

That voice was familiar. Goodtree groaned. She could still feel the earth trembling beneath her, and her head was throbbing in time to it.

"Get the furs under her, that's right—carefully, now! We don't know how badly she's injured."

232

The hands that lifted her were gentle, but she almost lost consciousness again as they eased her onto something soft and warm.

"I tried to stop him, Goodtree, but it was too late," said another voice.

"Be still—this is no time for excuses," said Moss sharply. "Goodtree, can you tell us where you're hurt?"

Carefully she opened her eyes, then gasped. They were surrounded by flame! But a cool breath of wind soothed her forehead. Blinking, she realized that she was seeing a sunset ignited by the smoke in the air. She let out her breath in a long, shuddering sigh.

"Hit my head," she whispered. "I'll be all right soon. The herd—"

"—has gone on by, and so has the fire."

Goodtree saw Acorn silhouetted against the sunset, and realized that his was the second male voice she had heard.

"And the branch-horns that nearly trampled us are spreading out over the plain," added Joygleam. "Lion-leaper's plan didn't go completely wrong. We'll be doing our fall hunting soon."

Goodtree tried to sit up and was pushed gently down again.

"If you want to go hunting with them, you'll lie still for now," said Moss.

"Listen to her, Goodtree!" snarled Acorn, "and for once, will you listen to me? You, too, Lionleaper!" He reached out and yanked the other elf to his knees beside Goodtree. She saw that the hunter was pale beneath the ash that blackened his skin, and he was trembling. But Acorn's face was flushed with fury.

"The two of you not only nearly got yourselves killed, you almost wiped out the tribe!" He paused to draw breath, and the other Wolfriders sat back, staring. "But I'm not going to let you torment yourselves and the rest of us any more!" Acorn grasped Lionleaper's shoulders and shoved him down into Goodtree's arms.

Instinctively she held on to him, breathing in his scent, feeling the hard strength of his body against hers. For one stunning moment, everything was astonishingly *right* once more. Then Goodtree passed out again.

The Mother moon had risen, red as if she, too, had been scorched by the fire, when Acorn saw Goodtree's eyelids flutter at last. Oakarrow and Brightlance were guarding Lionleaper, but the other elf had made no resistance. He sat in sullen silence with his head resting on his knees.

"Leave her alone, Songshaper," Moss whispered. "She's been injured."

"Yes, and I'm hoping that branch-horn knocked some sense into her," he answered grimly. "That's why I'm doing this now. We don't dare wait until she has her full strength again!" He glanced at the circle of elves around them. They were eyeing him as if he had gone crazy, but nobody had tried to stop him. The moon dimmed, obscured by drifting cloud, then brightened once more.

Maybe I am crazy, he thought. *This is my lovemate, and my chief!* But nobody else could help her. None of the other Wolfriders would even try! He looked back at Goodtree. Her eyes were open now, and she was watching him warily.

"You and Lionleaper are mates, Goodtree," he said. "And you're not going to fight it any more."

"Not against her will." The hunter shook his head. "I told you I'd rather die."

Goodtree was still pale, but her eyes glittered in the bloody light of the moon. "Do you think you can force—"

"I'll tie the two of you together if necessary," he said brutally. "You know what will happen then!" *I'm killing your love for me,* his soul wailed, *but I'm saving your life, Goodtree, and maybe the tribe!*

She sat up, glaring, "I'm your chief, Acorn Songshaper."

"Are you?" he snarled back at her.

His dark gaze caught hers and held, will straining against will in sudden challenge. He could not have done it if she had been well; the force that makes a pack-leader was not in him, only a desperate love. But he could feel her wavering. Grimly he held on.

"You can win this battle," she whispered at last, "but

don't you see what we will lose? Not just me—all of us. We are the high ones' children! Are we to have no more power over our passions than the beasts who rut in the woods? The wolfsong has no answers, and the elfsong is lost!"

She lay back, offering the long sweet line of her throat. And there was enough wolf in him to be disarmed by her submission. Abruptly his anger was gone. A rush of pity shook the heart in his breast, pity for her and for Lionleaper, whose misery showed in his eyes.

"Go free, then," he answered, "and may the high ones help us all!"

"Songshaper, find another way for me! You are the only one who can do it now!"

Goodtree's whisper was a challenge. Acorn shivered. Once, a creature he called Shadowshifter had taught him another song. Suddenly he was painfully aware of the fires deep within him from which his music came. But since Shadowshifter, Acorn had tried not to waken what lay there. It frightened him, for he could not be sure if it was madness or power.

"I was going to force you. How can you trust me?" he asked Goodtree. "And Lionleaper—what about you?"

"You gave me the freedom to choose again." Goodtree's eyes met his, and he trembled.

"We love you," said Lionleaper painfully. "What do you want us to do?"

Something blazed up within him, and Acorn knew suddenly that it was not madness, and not power, but if he had the courage to embrace it—love. He took a deep breath.

"Get up. Weaver's shelter wasn't damaged. Go to it, together, and I will find a new song for you."

They heard the first notes of the flute as they lay down.

Acorn's judgment had brought them this much grace, thought Goodtree; their joining would not be the frenzied mating of animals. Weaver had borrowed furs from half the tribe to make a soft bed for them, and Moss had scrubbed off the worst of the soot and combed out her hair. The scent of the fire was still on both of them, but Lionleaper had also suffered a rough cleansing. She could feel him trembling beside her. She knew that she was trembling, too.

"I fought as long as I could, Neme," he whispered. She reached out to him, and her breath caught as his lips touched her hand.

The flute piped cheerfully, and despite her fear, she found her mouth beginning to curve in a smile. "We didn't fail, we chose to trust Acorn's song." She laid her fingers across his lips. "Listen to it." She recognized a melody she had heard once through a dreamberry haze.

She laid her head upon Lionleaper's shoulder with a sigh. Clouds had covered the moons, but she did not need sight to know his every movement. The slide of his hand through her hair was a downward trill of the flute. He pulled her closer, and she quivered to a cascade of melody.

> *The hunt goes on, the body's yearning*
> *Seeks to understand the soul . . .*

Oh, Lleyn! She was beyond speech suddenly. But the music said it all. The pain of this terrible summer was in that music, yet it held all the splendor of the Everwood in the spring. She had thought she knew every span of her lovemate's body, but their explorations were transmuted by the music into something entirely new. Joy and sorrow gave each other meaning, flesh and spirit united in wondering harmony.

> *Deep magic sets the spirit burning,*
> *Till what was sundered is made whole.*

They came together in a climax of music, but the spasm of delight that should have ended it led instead to a long climb to some other region where they and the music were all part of the same thing. Consciousness expanded, encompassing Neme and Lleyn and the thing that united them . . . the music that resolved itself into a third name—*Mirj* . . .

Awareness fountained outward, separated itself into three parts, fell back toward ordinary reality in a shower of joy.

The last sweet notes of the flute faded away. In the stillness that followed, the only sound was the gentle pattering of rain.

Coyote

by Richard Pini

This was in the days when Mantricker was barely grown
from cubhood, when he was full of piss and dreamberries
and the will to test the new name he had given himself, and
before he learned the subtle difference between games of
fun and games of seriousness.

If he felt any fuller of himself than he did, he would
surely burst. That's what the young elf thought as he ran
lightly from branch to branch. Seeming light as a treewee,
legs as tight as a springfrog's, he bounced and bounded
through the new green leaves. Sunlight dappled him, crisp
late-morning air flushed his face. Let the others attend to
the day's business; not even his wolf-friend accompanied
him on his romp. At this moment, the forest was his and
his alone.

Behind him, deeper in the woods and far from any open
spaces, was the Holt. His tribesmates, the Wolfriders, had
come to live there many turns of the seasons ago. It was a
good place, well hidden. Humans, whenever they migrated
past the wood or camped in the bordering plains, avoided
it. They gave it wide berth. They knew, from the words of
their own storytellers, that the forest was the stamping
place of demons. All of which was well and good, for game
was good in the forest, a stream of fresh water ran through
the Holt, and the elves had no desire to have anything at all
to do with humans.

The young elf's mother, chieftess Goodtree, had taken a
great and ancient tree at the center of the Holt and crafted,
by skill and magic and over a long time, a place where the
elves might live. The Wolfriders called it the Father Tree,
and it was a wonderful maze of nooks and tunnels within

238

the living trunk. Goodtree still shaped the wood with her green magic; she often said with a smile that the Tree would never be finished as long as there were Wolfriders to live in it. Standing like a giant in the leafy embrace of other forest monarchs, surrounded by bits of color growing wild in the filtered sunlight, watchful over the quiet stream that flowed over its deep roots, the Father Tree was a marvelous warren for Wolfrider cubs to play in and around.

But not for the solitary imp who leapt from branch to branch—not today. Word had buzzed around the elfin encampment for days and days. The word was: *humans.* Humans, the tall ones, the five-fingers, had camped just beyond the edges of the forest, closer than they had come in, well, in more turns than anyone knew for certain. Stories by the eights had been told of humans, spun by Acorn and Longreach the talesingers to the eerie and beautiful music of wolfhowl on moonlit nights. Wolfrider parents whispered warnings of humans into cubs' ears by the glow of flickering deer-fat lamps.

The trouble was that all the talk and stories and warnings were of phantom creatures who had made life difficult for the Wolfriders in seasons long ago. *Besides,* the scampering elf thought, *I don't believe those stories of fighting and killing, anyway. I'll bet these are silly, stupid creatures, perfect for playing tricks on.* And on the heels of that idea came another. The youngster grinned. *I'll make my own name,* he delighted, *now, and not wait for someone to give one to me.* It would be fun. Enough of stories. These humans were here, now, and they were close. Close enough to see. And Mantricker, newly self-named, just at the age to feel his blood sing and muscles quiver, and to go against every bit of advice he knew, wanted to see them.

Why the five-fingers had chosen that spot to set up their camp Mantricker could not guess. He knew from the tales that the enmity between elf and human was said to be old, older than the eldest Wolfrider he knew. Humans were supposed to think of the elves as beast-eyed monsters, the young chief-son understood. So why then did they settle so close to the monsters' forest? Maybe these ones did not fear the elf-demons so much? Mantricker pondered this briefly as he spied from his comfortable branch at the edge of the clearing.

The camp still had the look of newness about it. Some of the ugly hide-covered dwellings were finished and obviously in use; several others were still clusters of branchless sticks poked into the ground. There was a large one going up in the center of the clearing. Cookfires sent stenchy gray smoke into the air, and Mantricker sent contemptuous thoughts toward the stinkmakers. Animals that reminded the young Wolfrider of small wolves, though they were mangy scruffballs compared to the fine companions of the elf tribe, yapped and nipped at each other's necks.

As he observed, Mantricker began to learn some things about these human creatures. They seemed to come in all sizes. There were large ones, some old and grizzled. Mantricker wondered how they could stand it with their skin all hanging in loose folds like that. There were very young ones that mewled and waved arms and legs in the air, and reminded the young elf of dirty grubs found beneath stones and rotted logs. There were some that looked like they might put up a good run or fight, though Mantricker knew from the tales and from his own belief that all humans were slow and clumsy.

He watched the comings and goings for a while longer and then, impatient, disappeared back into the cool, leafy green of the forest, hopping from branch to branch. All in all, he thought, not terribly worthy of the stories the Wolfriders wove about them. *But,* he brightened, *worthy of tricks.*

A day went by and then another, and Mantricker put the humans and his plans for them in the back of his mind. He told no one of his spying adventure, and spent his time sharpening his skill with the knife.

Now, while it was true that not every Wolfrider was a hunter, every hunter was an expert with one weapon or another. Some of the elves, male and female both, used the bow, some the spear, and some were skilled with snares. And that was because while the bringing down of a sleek

black-neck deer or gruffling wild boar generally meant full
bellies for the entire tribe, the elves still knew how to
appreciate squirrel or ravvit.

So there were scattered throughout the woods
surrounding the Holt clever snares and nets, all but invisible, and every so often one elf or another went to check and
see what had been caught. This day was Spinner's turn to
make the rounds. His traps were the best, for no one could
match the delicate, darting movements of his slender
fingers as he plaited vines and hair and sinew into intricate
devices. He was proud of his skill and always looked forward to bringing back the small treasures for his tribe.

No one, however, expected the Spinner who returned,
gentle face flushed with angry blood like a swollen thunder-
cloud, a handful of snares clenched tightly in his fist.

"Look at this!" he spat, throwing the lines and nets to the
ground. "Every one, ruined! Cut!" And as the astonished
Wolfriders poked through the tangle, they could see the
source of Spinner's upset. It was subtle work. Here, a loose
knot set to tighten around a ravvit's leg had been untied;
there, the weave of a bag-net had been sliced ever so slightly
so that the weight of a captured animal would tear it
through.

"Who could have done this?" Spinner demanded of no
one and everyone. No Wolfrider was beyond playing a
small prank now and then, but this was hurtful, and
immensely frustrating.

"The humans?" someone suggested. It was the easy
answer, but it was barely spoken when Spinner snarled, "I
thought of that! How could I not? They're close by, closer
than ever if you believe the stories. But smell these!" He
thrust the snarl of lines beneath the noses of several of the
elves. "You know how the humans stink; you can scent
them eight arrow-flights away." The snares smelled of
leaves and earth, and nothing else.

Spinner threw the useless tangle as far as he could.
"Nothing!" he growled. "And you know how clumsy the
five-fingers are. If one came into the forest, don't you think
we'd hear him crashing about like a giant mudwart?"

Mantricker, remembering back to his observation of the

241

human camp, thought that the image Spinner painted was quite funny, and he snickered out loud. Goodtree hushed him.

"It is a mystery," she said, her voice soothing, "but the hunting's been good. At the very least we're not depending on the catch the traps would have made." It was an attempt to salve Spinner's feelings, not a very good one, and Goodtree knew it as she spoke. Still, it was something.

"It's not the humans, as far as we can tell," she continued, "and it's none of us. There *are* tales—could it be an elf unknown to us?" She turned to the stormy-faced weaver and took his hands. "Make your nets again. Set them out. Perhaps if we watch we'll find an answer."

In his mood, Spinner was tempted to say, "I lay out three times as many snares as there are Wolfriders. Just how will we keep eyes on every one at every moment?" But he kept his tongue still and simply nodded.

Mantricker, however, had an idea. *Now* he would study them, closely. It was time. Trouble had been made, now he would make trouble. It didn't matter to him who or what had tampered with the traps; he was full of his own energy. He knew just one thing: the humans would be such *easy* prey.

For several days Mantricker watched the human camp from his high secret place. He even brought a deerhide blanket to wad into the crotch between two branches to make a comfortable place to sit. He began to learn some of the habits of these five-fingers. He saw how they slept and when they hunted and how they ate. He came to understand how to tell when a hunt had been successful and when not. He found he could even tell the humans apart, and who ranked high in the group and who ranked low. He saw one young human who seemed different from the others, almost delicate. This one seemed not to go on hunts with his mates, but spent long times inside his hide-covered dwelling. There was a female who seemed to be nimble with her black stone knife, skinning hunt animals with incredible deftness. Mantricker watched an older woman who worked with herbs and powders. To his surprise, he saw that some of the hunters managed to move with speed and grace.

He overheard bits of conversation among the humans. And he even understood a little of what he heard, because from the time of Two-Spear and Skyfire the elves had kept alive some knowledge of their enemy's language.

One day (for even though the Wolfriders preferred night to day, they did not shun the sunlight, and Mantricker was determined to study his victims-to-be when *they* were about) he saw some of the adult humans bring back from a hunt a black-neck deer, its hooves tied together, slung from a pole. He saw how the whole tribe gathered round. He listened as the hunters spoke of the herd nearby. He watched as one of the humans, one of the old, wrinkly ones, threw his arms in the air and capered around the deer, chanting all the while. Perhaps, Mantricker thought, this one was some kind of shaman or spirit man. He saw the old human take a stone knife and swiftly cut the deer's throat so that the blood gushed and the humans murmured happily. And Mantricker got a wonderful, wicked idea.

Now, it was true that for as long as anyone could remember, the Wolfriders had tried very hard not to take life unless it was cleanly in the hunt or in defense of one's self or one's tribesmates. That was the Way. But it was also true that every now and then in an unthinking moment an arrow flew from bowstring or a stone shot from sling and a small animal fell. And early on a certain day when he was as sure as he could be that the humans would hunt deer, Mantricker, while he was thinking about the prank he was going to play, forgot about the Way for just long enough to quickly and carefully kill an unsuspecting whitestripe.

Bentclaw was Mantricker's first wolf-friend, a burly ruffian who had once gotten his paw caught between two boulders. Elf and wolf seemed suited for each other, for Bentclaw was also a merry trickster who played long and hard with the rest of the pack, bowing and nuzzling and nipping.

Bentclaw was a smart beast. Even so, it took the better

part of the afternoon, and left Mantricker brain-tired, to put the elf's plan into the wolf's mind. But now, as Mantricker watched from his spying tree, his excitement humming within him, he smiled. The human hunters were returning to camp and yes, they had a fine, fat doe hanging from their carry pole. It was going to work. Bentclaw waited at the foot of the tree. If everything went right . . .

Now! he sent with all his might to the wolf.

Like a silent shadow cast by a flickering campfire Bentclaw ran along the edge of the forest, keeping just out of sight. At that moment, the hunters entered the circle of huts from the direction of the hub star; all the human tribe was on that side of the camp to greet them. So far, so good; Mantricker knew things would happen that way. So Bentclaw raced as fast as he could in the other direction and, unseen as Mantricker hoped, reached the boundary of the camp that was away from all the hubbub.

The deer was hung up and made ready; the old human grasped the stone knife.

Now Mantricker held his breath, felt gently for the small leather sack that hung from his belt, and sent again.

Now!

If the five-fingers did not believe in demons before, they surely had reason to now. A snarling, gray-furred fury of bared fangs and flashing claws tore into the ceremonial circle, running rings around the shock-frozen humans. Bentclaw scrabbled to and fro in the dust of the camp, snapping at everything that moved, scattering the yapping dogs, running between the old shaman's legs to bowl him over.

In moments the camp was in chaos as mothers grabbed children and ran to hide in the huts and yammering men tried to spear the apparition weaving like a windstorm among them. Later, some would notice that no one in the camp had been hurt by the beast, but at the moment the camp was a shambles of fear and outrage.

Then Bentclaw broke away from the melee and scurried through the encampment the way he'd come. The old shaman, red-eyed with fury, barked a command and every hunter—which was to say every human who had not hidden, shivering, in one of the huts—ran shouting with spears waving after the wolf.

For a moment—perhaps the barest of moments, Mantricker knew—the doe hung unattended, ignored.

And, chortling to himself like a grinning wolfling, the elf seized that moment with both hands and leapt from his hiding place.

Later Mantricker would swear to himself that his feet never touched the ground as he ran into the clearing in the human camp. He felt certain that no one had seen him, for the hunters were still tangling with Bentclaw and all other eyes were shut tight and hidden away within the dwelling. So the elf set to work, quickly but calmly, for it was a delicate task.

Kneeling by the head of the doe, he reached into the leather carry sack and carefully closed his hand about the moist parcel within. Just as carefully, he stuck the fist he'd made into the doe's mouth and up into the still-warm throat. He had to guess a bit, for he had no sure way of knowing where the old human would cut, but he knew where the big tubes were that carried the most blood, and gambled that that's where it would be. Twisting his hand, he opened his fingers and deposited the fragile package within the doe's throat and then, without a backward glance, ran like the stormwind back to his tree.

Once there, Mantricker scampered in two leaps up to his favorite watching place, and then howled—"AYOO-OOOAH!"—which was the signal to Bentclaw. As easily as if he had been romping among a fluttering covey of frightened quail, the wolf shot from the human camp, leaving behind sweating, panting hunters, a yowling old man, and a slowly settling cloud of dust. Mantricker watched as the wolf scampered into the woods away from where the elf sat in his tree; he knew the beast would circle around to him shortly, but now all he wanted to see was if his trick would work.

Well, it took some moments for all the excitement to die down, and for the shaman to call all the others out of their lodges, and for all the yammering to stop, but shortly all was as it had been. The old one cleared his throat, wound up his voice and made the noises again, and took the stone knife in hand.

In his tree, Mantricker leaned forward as far as he dared and screwed up his eyes for the clearest sight; he wished he could be right there in the camp, watching.

Like a flash of skyfire the knife fell and slashed the throat of the doe. Like a fat raincloud bursting, the blood, thick and warm, spurted and gushed over the arms and chest of the old man as a murmur of approval went up from the assembled camp. Then . . .

The shaman noticed it first, and Mantricker had to grasp the tree limb he sat upon with both legs, for he needed both hands to keep the laughter from rushing from his mouth. The human's face wrinkled horribly; first he sniffed the air, then himself, and then he shrieked and ran to and fro, trying to outrun his own skin. But no one would help him, for now all the humans had caught the gagging scent and they all scattered, holding their noses. The odor had even made its way to Mantricker, as far away as he was, and the elf rocked back and forth in merriment, holding his sides, laughing as quietly as he could. It had worked—it had *worked*! He'd placed the whitestripe's stink-pouch just right so that the shaman's knife sliced it open as the doe's throat was cut.

He *was* Mantricker!

As the elf scampered back to the Holt through the trees, he wondered if the humans knew just how long the stink would last. If they didn't, he could imagine the old human trying and trying in vain to wash the smell from him, and being shunned by the entire camp until it wore off only after many days. It was a hilarious image. If the humans *did* know about whitestripes, then they were already aware that life was going to be miserable for quite a while. *Either way,* Mantricker thought, *it worked! Timmorn's Eyes, these humans are fun!*

Life, of course, even for an elf of Mantricker's bent, was not just a series of pranks. There was the hunting, and there was the crafting, and there were all the things that fill a

Wolfrider's day. Spinner had found no more of his traps tampered with, and the tribe had just about forgotten the incident. Mantricker did think of it from time to time, but came to no conclusion. So it was almost a full dance of the moons before the young elf again gave thought to the humans. He recalled the joyous feeling he'd experienced at the successful conclusion of his first trick, and decided that it was time to try something new.

It was evening when he made the journey back to the edge of the woods where his favorite spy-tree was. He needed an idea, so he decided to watch what they did at the end of their day and see if that would spark anything within him. He knew that even though the humans kept fires burning through the night, they mostly kept to themselves during the dark time, and did little other than sleep. Perhaps there was something in that . . .

The daystar had been below Land's End for a little while when Mantricker reached his tree, but the sky was still light, and so the elf had no trouble seeing his way to his sitting place.

Timmorn's Blood! His heart froze.

Someone—or something—*had been there.*

It was a shock beyond imagining.

For long moments the elf did not move, but hung motionless in exactly the position, one hand here, one leg outstretched there, that he'd been in when he made the discovery. He was glad that Bentclaw had not come with him, for if someone knew about the spy-tree and it was no longer safe, that someone might not see Mantricker come and go, but that would certainly spot the wolf.

Finally the elf moved, slowly, ever so slowly, down into the crotch where his deerskin blanket was still wadded. He looked everywhere in the fading light; with one exception, everything was as it had always been. He sniffed everywhere and wished for the extraordinary senses of his wolf-friend, but found no scent of anything other than what should be there.

Except . . .

Except for the glittery stone, hanging by a thread from a

247

higher branch, right where he used to sit and watch the humans. Very slowly, the stone spun around and around at the end of its cord—and did nothing else.

Well, this was a mystery, and a far greater one in Mantricker's mind than the mangled traps. His brain buzzed with questions seeking answers. What *did* he know? He knew that someone had put the thing here; it was tied with a knot and not even the most clever bird could do that. It had no scent, nor was there any odd scent around it—and that in itself was strange, because *everything* had an odor of one kind or another, humans especially. This was truth to the Wolfriders as much as anything was. What else? The thing seemed to be some kind of stone, but it was unlike any stone or rock that the elf had ever seen. That was strange, too.

Finally Mantricker put out his hand and very gently, with the tip of one finger, touched the stone and then quickly pulled his hand away. The pendant swung gently back and forth a few times and then came to rest, just like any stone on any string. It did nothing else.

Slightly bolder, the elf touched it again, and then took it between two fingers so he could hold it and look at it more closely. It was not quite stone; it was just the slightest bit crumbly at the surface. If he dug with a fingernail, Mantricker could pry loose some of the glittery flakes that gave the stone its sparkly appearance. He looked at the thread; it was ordinary, made from the hair of some animal, he guessed. He decided not to try tasting the stone.

What to do?

For a long while Mantricker sat in his tree, listening to the sound of his own breathing. He pondered the alien object as the evening grew darker and darker. In the human camp, the cookfires were tended, the meal made, the sleeping mats unrolled—all while the puzzled elf sat and racked his brain. *Could this have come from them? But how? The five-fingers? No* . . .

At last the youth got up, took hold of the odd stone with one hand; with the other he took the black flint knife from his tunic to cut the thread that had suspended it from its branch, and set out back to the Holt. *My brain is full to bursting with this thing,* he thought; *maybe Acorn knows a story about things like this—or something. This is too much for me.*

Of course Goodtree and the other elders were not happy to learn that the chief-son had been spending time so close to the human camp.

"What were you trying to do?" asked his mother, knowing that he had taken his new name and suspecting what it could mean, to him and to the entire tribe.

Mantricker answered, "I want to study them. I've heard all the stories that Acorn and Longreach have told. I just want to see for myself." It wasn't an actual lie, he told himself; it just wasn't every bit of the truth. The effects of the difference he would learn someday. "They seem to be pretty harmless—kind of funny, if you look at them the right way."

A few of the elder Wolfriders smiled at this, a few frowned. Each of them had a tale about some personal encounter with humans; some of them could be thought of as humorous, some not. It was all part of the whole of Wolfrider life.

Acorn spoke then, a gentle voice; he was still close to Goodtree after many hands of turns. Young as he was, Mantricker knew some of the stories that were woven about his mother and Lionleaper and Acorn; in a tribal history that often spoke of hardship and violence, the thread of that enduring love was a welcome change.

"The humans have been here as long as we have," he said, "maybe longer. For all that time the best we've been able to hope for is that they pay us no heed, and allow us to do them the same favor. If the youth wants to watch them, and causes no trouble to them, and thus to us"— Mantricker squirmed just a bit here, but no one noticed— "then perhaps he might learn something that will be of use. For now we have a different question . . ." and he turned toward the odd stone which sat in a clay dish, doing nothing.

"It's too bad there are no rock-shapers among us," said Far-Touch, a young hunter about Mantricker's age. "I remember the story about . . . about . . ." He faltered.

"Windwhisper," aided Longreach. "Yes, she would be able to touch this stone and tell us much about it, were she not gone these generations. And there has never been another who could mold the rock as our chieftess molds living plants."

"Well, I want a better look at it," said Far-Touch, who was in his way as headstrong as Mantricker, "and it's too dark." And with that, he went to get one of the fat-lamps from the Father Tree. The Wolfriders shunned the use of campfires, but the little flames provided more than enough light for the night-sighted elves.

Far-Touch returned and set the lamp next to the clay dish. He picked up the stone and, bending over, held it close to the flame, turning it over and over. "It sparkles so beautifully," he murmured, "like the stars in the sky or the fireflies in the trees when the air is warm and moist." The hunter seemed almost hypnotized by the bits of light he held in his hands, and without realizing it he let one edge of the fragment rest in the lamp's flame for just a moment.

The stone exploded.

Actually it didn't so much explode as it burst into a flare of light as bright as the daystar. Far-Touch bellowed and dropped the rock to the ground, where it flared and hissed and spat foul-smelling smoke. The brilliant light cast hard shadows everywhere of Wolfriders, blinded, diving every which way to escape the . . . whatever it was. The Holt was all and completely ascramble. Mantricker was thrown backward by his own surprise when the stone ignited; someone landed on top of him in the harsh glare; he couldn't see who it was and at the moment didn't care. He just wanted to get away from the light and the smell and the horrible knowledge that *he* had brought the cursed thing into the Holt.

The rock burned for several hands of heartbeats, and then, with a final hiss and sputter, went out. Darkness returned to the Holt, a darkness aggravated by the fact that the Wolfriders' sensitive night vision had been destroyed by the dazzling brightness. It took a while for sight to return. It took somewhat longer for the night breezes to clear the swampy stink from the air.

No one spoke; except for the sound of coughing, silence reigned. Mantricker knew that no one blamed him outwardly for what had just happened. He also knew just as well that questions burned in every mind. *Where did he get that thing? Is there some connection to the humans? Tell us what you know. Is there something you haven't told us?* He could feel their eyes on him, sense the concern in Goodtree's heart as he turned to spend the night alone in the deep woods.

Morning found him back at his spying tree, chin resting in cupped hand, trying to make sense of what was happening. He didn't know if whatever had left the flaring rock in the tree knew that he was there, but at the moment he didn't care. He had no reason to think that the humans were responsible for the object that had thrown the Holt into such turmoil, but somehow he sensed that there had to be a connection. He just didn't know what it was.

There was no one else in the forest when Spinner's traps were destroyed. Then I played a trick on the humans, but I'm sure no one saw me. Then someone put the stone in this tree, so someone knew I'd find it here. I've gotten close to the human camp. Could whoever put the stone in the tree know about the Holt? There's got to be some sense in it somewhere!

Mantricker fretted and fumed, but the pieces still would not come together for him. So he got an idea. If the humans were responsible somehow, he'd get them to give themselves away. If they weren't, then he'd have some fun. He wasn't going to let this mystery stop him from being who he was.

It was time for another trick.

This time the elf had to wait for the proper weather. Fortunately it was the right season, and Mantricker knew that skyfire storms and heavy rains were more common at this time than at any other. So he waited, and he watched, and he prepared, collecting old animal skins wherever he

251

could, and he brooded. And finally his patience was rewarded.

The day he'd waited for dawned gray and heavy, and Mantricker knew that before long water would come pouring from the skies in torrents. He was ready. He would have to sacrifice the hides he'd gathered, but that didn't matter. He knew the five-fingers' habits; he was certain his trick would be successful. And he was ready to see after that just what was what between the humans and the Wolfriders, no matter how long it might take.

It was sometime after the daystar, had it been visible, passed overhead that the rain started. What began as a sprinkle quickly became a cold downpour that Mantricker knew would last a long time. Within moments of the storm's arrival, all the humans scurried to their huts just as the elf knew they would. Most of the humans took refuge in the big central lodge, and smoke started puffing through the single opening in the big shelter's roof as the day's interrupted activities were resumed inside.

Mantricker smiled grimly as the rain washed over his face and the thunder boomed overhead. It was time. Gathering the bundle of hides to him, he made his way from the edge of the wood to the camp. He took some care that no one saw him; he was almost certain that everyone was concerned with indoor things, and not with looking out into the storm. But a small part of his mind wondered . . . Then: *Ah, well, back to the task at hand.*

He reached the corner of the great lodge without incident. It would be an easy climb to the roof, and even if he made some noise, the wind and thunder would mask it from the humans' insensitive ears. He made his way to the top.

It was almost too easy, he thought. He unrolled the bundle he'd brought and, as best he could in the wind, spread out the sheet of stitched-together hides. It was easily large enough to cover the hole from which the smoke was coming, and several stones tied to the sheet's edges would ensure that the wind didn't blow it away.

As quick as it was to think of it, the prank was done, the

252

smoke-hole was covered, and Mantricker was away from the lodge and running back to the trees. It would take a while, he knew, before the smoke built up inside the shelter. He had time to make good his escape.

This time he had prepared a different hiding place, another tree off in a different direction from the first, from which he still had a good view of the camp. He wasn't certain that it would do him any good, as his other vantage point had been discovered, but it had to be better than no effort at secrecy. And besides, he still didn't know if the humans had anything to do with the exploding stone.

He heard the tumult before he saw it—voices raised in alarm, coughing, wails of fear. He had to admit, he thought to himself with a smile, it was a good joke. *They're still a funny bunch.* Almost immediately humans young and old came stumbling out of the lodge, wiping their eyes, gasping for breath. The old shaman was helped out, held up by two hunters. As soon as he looked up to the roof of the shelter and saw the blanket that covered the hole, he began to dance about, yowling and shrieking. Mantricker couldn't make out anything that the human said, but it was an amusing sight.

Someone, a young boy, was sent up to remove the hides. Smoke once again plumed out of the hole to be whipped away by the wind, and life in the human camp went back to normal.

All right, Mantricker thought as he bundled himself against the storm, *I've pricked their wrinkly skins again. Now the waiting begins.*

Well, the son of Goodtree was determined. For an eight of days the elf did not budge from his spying place. He watched the humans as they came and went. He stayed awake as long as he could, and then sent to Bentclaw to stay on watch while he caught fitful snatches of sleep. He ate while he observed, and had tribesmates—Far-Touch and others, who did what he asked but who did not understand —bring him food. For that many days nothing happened.

And then on the evening of the eighth day, as he watched

253

all alone, Mantricker spotted what he hoped he had been watching for. It was a dark evening; the day had been cloudy and the daystar had shown its face only now and then. But even in the murky darkness the elf's keen eyes followed the hint of the shadow that detached itself from the campsite and stole away into the woods off to his left. He didn't know who or what it was and he didn't know what it might mean, but in all the time that he'd spied on the humans, not one of them had gone into the woods, and this was reason enough for Mantricker to follow.

So follow he did, or tried to. He leapt from limb to limb through the trees to arrive at the spot where he'd seen the shadow enter the woods. But when he got there—and he was certain that *this* was the place—he could find no sign at all that anyone had passed that way. There were no broken branches; there was no human smell.

Mantricker was baffled. The shadow had come from the human camp; the camp had not been in any uproar; therefore the shadow must be a human. It was the only conclusion. But humans were big and clumsy and smelly, and never had there been a human who could enter the forest without the elves knowing it. So it must be a human and it couldn't be a human.

Mantricker cursed. He felt as stupid and as helpless as he had the night of the burning stone. Mystery piled upon mystery; it fueled his anger but gave the anger no outlet.

He decided to pursue a shadow. Since he had no trail, no scent to follow, he did the next best thing. If the creature was heading toward the Holt, and there was no reason for the elf to think otherwise, then he would go in that direction himself. Surely he knew these woods better than something that lived in the human camp. Perhaps he could intercept it.

So, silent as a shadow himself in the starless dark, he began working his way back to the Holt, moving from tree limb to tree limb, traveling in a straight line when he could, zigzagging when he must. He knew he must move both quickly and carefully; if the thing was there he had to catch it, but he couldn't let it know he was trying to follow.

Always he kept his eyes on the ground, pausing now and again to scan every bit of forest, every bush and path, every rock and . . .

There!

Even though there was just the barest light in the night air, Mantricker could see the double patch of black that was too big to be just the shrub he was looking at. As he watched, the blackness moved, shifted just a bit; he couldn't tell what it was doing. There was no sound, no scent—but the elf was certain that this was his prey.

The dark creature was too far away for Mantricker to drop onto from where he was. He looked about—yes. If he moved from this tree to that one to the other, he could put himself almost directly above it. No animal that he'd ever tracked required the silent skill that he needed now, for somehow he knew that this beast would know he was there if he made the slightest noise. He wondered if it could hear his heart beating, for that seemed very loud in his ears.

Barely breathing, a fingerbreadth at a time, Mantricker began to make his way to the place he wanted to be. The shadow stayed where it was, moving slightly now and then as if occupied with some private task. Getting to the spot he wanted seemed to take days. Mantricker felt his entire body tensing; he realized his teeth were clenched painfully. He had no idea what this thing was, and he was going to leap onto it as if it were a newborn black-tail. *What* am *I doing . . . ?*

He was there. The creature was below him, perhaps three elf-heights, and a little to Mantricker's right. An easy leap, one he'd made many times before—under totally different circumstances. At the last moment he remembered his flint knife, slipped it from his tunic, gripped it tightly in his hand—

—and with a bloodcurdling snarl, leapt straight at the shadow-beast.

Later, much later, Mantricker would recall that, except for the grunts of labored breathing and throaty growls, there was no sound during the fight. At that moment, however, it seemed that the entire world was awash in

noise and light as Mantricker landed on the creature's back
and the two beings thrashed wildly in battle. The knife was
lost in the first moments. Whatever the thing was, the elf
discovered, it was wiry and strong, for it flopped about like
a jump-bug, making it nearly impossible for Mantricker to
get a grip. It almost seemed that the creature was shaped
like Mantricker himself, for he could swear that it wrapped
arms and legs about him if he gave it the slightest chance.
The two scrambled and flailed in the leafy damp of the
forest floor, straining, neither gaining an advantage.
Mantricker had never fought any animal like this one and
he began to wonder if he would survive the encounter;
surely one of them had to tire first.

It was pure luck that, as the two combatants rolled about
on the ground, Mantricker's hand banged into his flint
knife. He grunted at the flash of pain, then managed to grip
the weapon by the blade, cutting his palm. He feigned
weakness for just a moment; his opponent, mistaking the
ruse for victory, eased its own pressure—and in that
instant Mantricker swung the butt of the stone knife
around and cracked it hard against the side of the shadow-
beast's head. The creature went limp and Mantricker lost
no time in heaving its weight from him. The elf threw the
creature to its back and, breathing heavily, held the point
of the knife to its throat.

The clouds parted, and faint moonlight filtered down
into the forest. At last, Mantricker was able to see his
enemy. His eyes went wide.

It was a youth. A human boy.

This is the fearsome shadow-beast? he gaped. *A five-finger
child?* Then the elf realized, no, not just any human
boy—he'd seen this one before. Where . . . ? Mantricker
racked his memories. Yes—the delicate one, the one who
did not go on hunts. But this one was such a fighter, and he
walked the woods leaving no track and no scent—even
now, after as strenuous a battle as he'd ever been in,
Mantricker could barely catch the human scent on the boy.
More mystery.

The boy groaned and started to stir. His eyelids fluttered

256

and he began to rise. Mantricker increased the pressure on the stone knife so that the human, even groggy, got the message. *Stay still, don't move.* The boy opened his eyes and stared into Mantricker's.

There was silence as the two took each other in.

The elf's curiosity got the better of him. He shaped the human words as best he could and asked, "What do you want in our woods?"

The boy's eyes flickered wide for only an instant.

"You are a good fighter," he replied. "Take the knife away. I won't run."

He compliments me!? Mantricker held the flint blade where it was for a long moment, searching the young human's face. It was a test, he knew, but of whom and how to tell the winner he had no idea. Finally he pulled the knife back slowly and returned it to his tunic. The boy sat up and rubbed his throat.

"You cut the traps," said Mantricker. It was a statement, not a question. The human nodded.

"Why?"

The boy thought a bit, then answered. "It was a test for myself. I am not a hunter; I don't fit there, so the others ignore me. We know these are demon woods. If I could prove myself another way, things would be better for my family. If I could walk among demons unnoticed, the others would respect me."

"You found my tree as well. There was no scent. How did you fool us?"

The boy smiled. "My mother knows every plant that grows. She made a"—he searched for the word—"medicine. Some of it I drank. Some other I rubbed on my body. It makes me invisible to those who scent, to you and your wolf demons. And you are not the only ones who can learn to move lightly through the forest."

Mantricker grunted; he'd learned the truth of that. This stripling had led him—and the Wolfriders—on more than one wild chase after shadows. He'd have to think again about "clumsy, smelly" humans.

"And the glittering stone in the tree?"

The boy grinned hugely. "My mother knows so many things to make. It was a good joke!"

Joke?

Joke!?

Mantricker leaned forward, his face a study in conflicting emotions. "What were you doing here tonight?"

The boy hesitated, then pointed to the remnants of a device made of bone and sinew, bits of leather and stone. It had been fairly demolished by the struggle.

"It would have been even better than the last," he said with pride. "Better than the traps, better than the stone." Mantricker groaned; a prank. The boy continued, "Better than the stinkstuff in the deer's throat."

Mantricker was no longer surprised. "You knew," he said. The boy just grinned.

What do I do with this one? the elf wondered. *He's an enemy, and yet he's a worthy enemy.* Mantricker stared at the youth for a long moment.

He decided. "Get up," he said. The boy did so. "I know you, and you know me. That"—he pointed in the direction of the open plain, toward the human camp—"is yours. This," and he swept his arm in an arc that included all the forest and the Holt, "is mine. We know each other now. Test yourself out there, not here. I will—test—myself here. Do you understand what I say?"

The youth took a breath, and then nodded.

"Go, then," Mantricker said. The boy turned away and started to leave.

"Wait," said the elf, just before the human melted back into the shadows. The boy hesitated.

"What is your name?" Mantricker asked.

"I—I call myself Demontricker," came the answer.

Demontricker! It was the final joke, and Mantricker could not help but laugh out loud, forgetting the dark, forgetting the fight he'd just had, forgetting everything in the ironic moment.

The boy just smiled, and disappeared into the night.

The Phantom of the Berry Patch

by Mercedes Lackey and Richard Pini

"Gone?"

Bearclaw had, until this moment, been lounging idly in the dreamy half-sleep of a wolf nap, luxuriating in the warmth of a patch of sun that had found its way down into a well-worn and comfortable crotch of the Father Tree. Now he sat bolt upright, awake and outraged, bits of bark catching on the leather of his tunic.

"What do you mean, *gone*?" he demanded of the gray-clad hunter standing below him. With the grace and start-stop speed of a squirrel, Bearclaw leapt from his resting place and hopped lightly to the ground. "Those bushes were covered with berries last night. They'd have been just ripe today!"

Not a child any more, and yet, somehow, not truly an adult—in maturity anyway, for he had the turns of seasons —Bearclaw was one of the taller of the Wolfriders. Physically it might be said that he had a bit of a way to go, for while it was clear that he would in time be devilishly handsome, all dark brown angles and bright grins, he still had a roundness to him, a touch of softness. But he had reached his full height, and now and then he took advantage of that when he faced another Wolfrider.

He also knew quite well how to take advantage of the fact that he was the chief's son. It wasn't the Way, really, to skirt the edge of insolence with one's elders, but in Bearclaw it was usually tolerated, for it was not overdone. He was, generally, a merry sort, though hints of a black temper were beginning to show now and then. Too, times were good for the Wolfriders, and the tribe as a whole was relaxed. Mostly.

The short, stocky elf who faced Bearclaw, however, had just returned from a fruitless and frustrating hunt. Far-Touch had been at it all night; he had *almost* brought down the black-tail but somehow it had gotten away from him; he was tired, sweaty, dirty, and very low on patience.

He shrugged, an eloquent, disgusted gesture. "There's nothing I can do about that, cub," he said as he scratched his chin with the flint tip of the short javelin that was his pride and skill and, indirectly, the source of his name. "They're all gone today. Only green ones left. Maybe birds got 'em."

Bearclaw snorted with scorn. "At night?" he retorted.

Far-Touch sighed as a morning breeze tousled his auburn hair and the leaves of the Father Tree above them. He rolled his eyes up and shrugged again. "Bears, then, or foxes," he said without conviction. He wanted the conversation to be over; he wanted to clean up and rest, but he owed some courtesy at least to the chief-son. His wolf-friend Windwhip, however, felt no such need, and paced back and forth, clearly wanting the chatter to end so he could pad home to his cozy lair and sleep.

"Bears. Foxes. This close to the Holt? Bearclaw replied contemptuously.

"Look here, *cub*," Far-Touch snapped, his small store of patience now quite exhausted. Chief-son or not, Bearclaw *was* younger than he. "Don't you take that tone with me. I'm tired, I'm hungry, I want very much to be washing off in the stream over there, and it's only because I said earlier that I'd look at that blamed bush that I bothered to talk to you this morning!"

Bearclaw, his own anger deflected, turned his eyes away and muttered an apology.

The hunter humphed. "If you'd ever had the patience to think to ask," he went on, "Longreach or any of the elders could have told you that something's been stealing dreamberries for as long as elves have lived in this forest— and cleverly, too. I don't know what's doing it, and frankly I don't much care. Whatever it is, it's been here longer than we have—maybe if Goodtree were still here she could tell us a thing or two—and the way I see it, it's welcome to its share."

"But . . ." Bearclaw began.

"But nothing!" Far-Touch interrupted, thrusting his face close to Bearclaw's. "Aside from Longreach, you're the only one in the Holt who gives that much of a hoot about dreamberries. Longreach I can understand. If you want to find out what's filching 'em, you do it yourself!" He turned on his heel and stalked away toward the stream, Windwhip trotting at his side.

Bearclaw slumped down into one of the hollows formed by the Father Tree's great coiled roots. He felt deflated, but his lazy-morning lethargy was gone. He crossed his arms over his chest and brooded, scowling, gray eyes fixed on his own brown boots.

"What's the matter—have you lost your best friend?" The melodious voice came from above.

Joyleaf swung lightly from the branches above him and landed gracefully beside him. She made almost no sound as her feet touched ground, she was so light and airy-seeming. In fact she could almost be said to be his opposite, sunlight where he was dark earth, fluid curve where he was sharp angle, calm where he was storm.

Bearclaw smiled in spite of himself; she could always bring him out of his worst moods. She'd been his friend for a long time; they'd played silly cub-games as younglings and somehow the friendship had stayed intact through the turns—despite Bearclaw's shifting moods.

"What a *sour* face!" Joyleaf teased, dancing lightly about him as he sat. Her sunny-golden hair lifted in the breeze, wreathing her smiling face in a bright cloud of color like the cup-flowers that blossomed at the end of the cold season. Bearclaw watched as she moved, noting—as he'd done a lot lately, he realized—how her red and brown tunic and breeches clung and molded themselves to her figure—a figure at once youthful and mature, and full of promise.

She halted her dance and bent over him. "You look like you've just swallowed a mouthful of green dreamberries," she teased.

261

"That's about *all* there are," he grumbled. "Green. And I'd counted on having enough to . . ." He hesitated. Why *had* he thought that he wanted a bushful of the potent purple berries all to himself? He enjoyed them, that was certain. Far-Touch was right in that; did the entire tribe know? Unlike Longreach, who carefully dried the berries and used them to help him in the remembering and telling of stories, Bearclaw preferred the fruits raw, savoring the giddy buzzing it brought to his head. "To . . ." he tried to continue.

"To finally have your fill and send your head off into the starry sky?" she jibed, her wide, midnight-blue eyes sparkling with mischief. "There's a wager, you know, between Brightspear and Hawk that you'll never have enough dreamberries." She giggled, a low trill as musical as any bird's. Bearclaw flushed; well, that answered *that* question. He wondered how secret his "secret love" had ever been.

"No," he replied, trying another tack. "No. I, uh, wanted them—to share with you. Sometime. Tonight. To spend some time. To talk. About, uh, things . . ." he finished lamely. *Now, why did I say that—and stumble all over it to boot?*

"Oh!" Joyleaf was taken aback at the turn of Bearclaw's words. By the surprised look on her face, it was clearly not an answer she had expected. She didn't know that it was an answer he hadn't planned on giving. The game was taking a different turn all of a sudden.

Bearclaw gazed into those wide and startled eyes and felt lost, just for a moment, but he knew that something was changing. He couldn't put a name to it, but he saw her in a new way. For a moment he wondered if this was that Recognition thing that others of the Wolfriders occasionally talked about, and sometimes felt, but then realized that if he was able to ask the question, the answer was no. Nonetheless, something was changing, growing, evolving between them.

It was Joyleaf who looked away first, blushing and confused as well. Bearclaw's stare hadn't been a challenge, she knew, but still she felt easier breaking the contact.

He coughed, ending the awkward silence, and kicked at the bark of the Father Tree. "Anyway," he said, "Far-Touch says there aren't any ripe berries to be found—nothing but green ones."

She crouched down, balancing easily on the balls of her feet. "But I thought there was one whole bush full, at least, nearly ripe, over by the spring . . ."

"There *was*," Bearclaw interrupted. The dreamberry bush was a solitary plant, growing where it would; they were scattered far and wide throughout the Holt. The berries, too, appeared and ripened at different times on different bushes, so there was no way to predict when the fruits would be ready. The only way to harvest dreamberries—if harvesting it could be called—was to patiently and painstakingly go from bush to bush, checking each day, taking those few berries that were ripe, and leaving the rest for another time. Longreach and Bearclaw knew this; most of the others didn't care.

"There was," the chief-son repeated angrily, pounding at the root with his fist. "Something stripped all the ripe ones last night—and it was one of the fullest bushes I've ever seen. Far-Touch said it was probably birds or foxes."

"But there aren't any berry-eating birds that fly at night," Joyleaf pointed out with patient logic, "and the wolves wouldn't let foxes this close to the Holt. Besides, if a fox *had* eaten that many dreamberries, he'd still be there this morning. Somebody would have a new hat, and the fox wouldn't care!" She giggled again.

Bearclaw had to laugh at the image she conjured. "Only . . ." he said when their shared laughter had subsided, "what's eating the dreamberries, then? Far-Touch said it's been happening for as long as we've been in the Holt."

Joyleaf was thoughtful. "I don't know," she said. "I don't think anyone has ever bothered to find out. If the dreamberries aren't ripe, well, you just wait until they are. There always seem to be enough. It just isn't that important"—she grinned mischievously, and touched him on the tip of his nose—"to most of us."

Bearclaw didn't smile at the affectionate gesture. "That's what old Far-Touch said," he replied slowly. "But don't you see what this is *really* all about?" His voice took on a note of excitement and concern. "There's *something* getting in close to the Holt without our ever seeing it— without the wolves even noticing it! So maybe all it's done so far is pick dreamberries—but what if it decides to do something else? What if it decides it doesn't like having to share the berries with us? What if it doesn't want to share the Holt with us at all? What if it wants to attack, to chase us away?"

"Oh . . ." Joyleaf's eyes darkened, and she rose to her feet. "I hadn't even thought of that. If it can get to the berry bushes without being seen, and some of them are close by, what's to stop it from coming right up to the Father Tree?" Her face was troubled, suddenly shadowed with doubt and uncertainty. "But Bearclaw," she went on, "how will you convince the elders of that? Surely someone else has thought of this. They'll just say that the berries aren't worth getting that upset over, that there's never *been* any trouble so there won't *be* any. How will you argue that?"

Bearclaw grinned and sprang to his feet. "Ha! I won't have to. Far-Touch, all of them, they're always talking about how impatient I am. Well, I'll show them all—I'll show them just how patient I can be!"

Crest yawned, displaying a formidable mouthful of strong white teeth. When Bearclaw glanced over at his wolf-friend, she sighed heavily and put her head down on her paws, the very image of bored tolerance.

Bearclaw scratched her thick, soft ruff. He didn't blame her; he was bored nearly out of his mind himself. He echoed Crest's sigh and rested his chin on his knees.

Big Moon, overhead, was a day or two past full, and Little Moon was farther down the sky, well on its way toward hiding its face entirely. The orbs had been in nearly the same phases eight hands of days ago when he'd first had this notion.

Bearclaw sighed again restlessly. *If I'd known it was going to take this much patience I think I'd have let the dreamberry thief go on stealing the blamed things to its heart's and gullet's content.*

The plan really was a simple one; at least it had that going for it. All Bearclaw had to do was to wait by *one* berry bush until the thief came around to it. Stay with that bush, because the unseen presence never stole from the same one two nights in a row—Bearclaw had learned that after several fruitless days of trying to discern a pattern to the thief's depredations. Go to that bush faithfully every night and stay until dawn, for the thief also never seemed to strike during the daylight.

So that's what he'd done for two dances of Big Moon, turning down invitations to go on hunts, declining to listen to Longreach's stories, missing the chances to go fishing with spear and torch at moondark. He'd even been absent at a howl . . .

. . . and all to sit in the middle of a patch of poking, scratching branches, to stare at a stupid dreamberry bush until his eyes crossed (and not even eat one berry, for he must have his wits about him), to think evil thoughts at the bugs that bit him.

Owl pellets, he grumbled inwardly.

It was such a lovely night, too. The seasons were turning again; new green was giving way to warmth and riotous growth. The air was balmy, gentle with breezes, and bright with moonlight. The silver light washed over the shrubs, touching the leaves with a frost of paleness, tipping the grass with sparkles. Overhead, stars shared the unclouded night sky with the moons, more hands of stars than Bearclaw could count. Somewhere a mocker-bird woke and filled the night with his song. Crickets chirped cheerfully from the grasses around him, and frogs chirred off in the direction of the stream.

But where he sat, sharp little branches poked through his tunic and into his ribs, and twigs tangled in his long hair every time he moved, which was not often, for he didn't want to scare the thief—whatever it might be—or give away his position. There was a rock or root digging into his rump. Something bit his ankle. His legs were cramped.

What am I doing here? he asked himself for the eighth time that night. *I should be out hunting, or with Joyleaf. This night is too nice to be wasting like this!*

But he knew that if he gave up, he'd appear the fool before everybody. What was more, he'd prove what the elders had said about him, that he was impatient and flighty and reckless, and that he'd never make a good chief when it was his time. They thought that he was unaware of their criticisms, or else they thought he paid them no heed. But they were wrong; he did know and he did listen. He just chose to do it in his own way.

It was hard to be the son of a chief—harder still to be the son of Mantricker.

Mantricker, it could be argued, was the most solitary chief the Wolfriders had ever had. Many of the elves thought that his courage was dangerous, bordering on foolhardy. Some of them even suspected that his lonely campaign to frighten any and all humans from the area of the Holt was actually a dubious bid for glory. And no one except for his son and his lifemate knew why he did what he did; Mantricker confided in no one else, took no counsel except when it was forced on him by the elders, asked no advice. He made his plans and carried them out alone. He had his reasons, and he believed them to be good ones.

But the other Wolfriders didn't see things that way. They felt that it was their duty to share risks, and some saw it only as their chief's pride that he would not let them do so. They also saw it was their privilege to share the fun of harassing the humans—an attitude Mantricker would like to have beaten out of them, if they only knew—and they resented that he did not let them share in that, either.

A fair number of the Wolfriders saw Bearclaw likely to grow up just like his sire.

They called him reckless, for the pranks that he played, and headstrong and bad-tempered and selfish. Not often, and rarely to his face, but he knew their thoughts. And the truth of it was that, to an extent, he knew they were right—but they just didn't see all sides of him.

Yes, occasionally his jokes got on the reckless side, he admitted it—he winced at the memory of one that had left him stranded and alone in the far lake country, with a tribe of spirit-worshipping humans between him and the Holt. But his pranks could be fun, too—though he supposed they would be funnier if everyone shared his sense of humor, and saw the laugh where he did . . .

He would have to try to do something about his temper, he mused. He did go off easily sometimes, and cooling down was long and difficult afterward. Joyleaf was good at calming him down; he always felt better when she did that.

And so what if he was selfish now and then? True, a chief must live for the tribe, but it ought also to be true that the tribe should allow the chief to have a bit of his life for himself. Certainly a chief had to set a good example, but one never really learned about something unless one tried it first . . .

Bearclaw shrugged mentally—to do so physically would make the prickly twigs snag him. Sitting around in dreamberry bushes through the night was making him as moonsick and philosophical as old Longreach. What he needed right now was to *do* something!

Hunt now? Crest sent the image full of hope.

Not now, the elf replied. The wolf sighed again and closed her eyes.

Then, abruptly, she lifted her head from her paws and sniffed.

Something, the wolf thought. **Coming close?**

Where? How? Bearclaw craned his neck carefully over the bushes and peered in all directions. There was nothing. **I don't see . . . **

He sniffed the air. Nothing there, either—no, wait. He inhaled long and deep. Yes, there it was. A faint scent, almost imperceptible, that had not been there before—so subtle, no wonder no one had caught it before. It wasn't elf,

Mercedes Lackey and Richard Pini

it wasn't human. In fact it wasn't any animal or bird or reptile that Bearclaw recognized. He drew another deep breath through his nostrils. There was something about the scent of freshly turned earth . . .

On an impulse, he looked down. At the base of the very dreamberry bush next to which he sat, a round plug of earth and sod, perhaps two or three hands across, was slowly and quietly moving. Back and forth, back and forth it twisted in near total silence, and then as if by magic it began to rise out of the ground. With the slightest "plop" it fell over next to the hole it had left, and as Bearclaw watched, eyes huge with surprise, a hand came up out of the hole and plucked a fat, ripe purple dreamberry from the branch nearest to it.

The hand was large, larger than an elf's hand. It was human-sized, but not human-shaped, for it had three fingers and a thumb, the same as elf hands. But it wasn't an elf's hand, never mind the size. It was hard to tell in the uncertain moonlight—all colors tended to fade to shades of gray—but Bearclaw thought that the hand had a most definite shade of—*green.* The fingers had nails that were as long and cracked as talons, and the skin was covered with warts.

The hand took its juicy treasure down into the ground and came up again, reaching for another berry, one a little higher up in the bush. One a little more plump than its unripe neighbors.

Whatever this thing is, it knows dreamberries, Bearclaw thought, grinning, as the hand withdrew and returned a third time.

This time he was ready.

"AYOOOO-HAH!" he howled as he leapt and caught the hand before it could slither back down its hole. Crest yipped with excitement beside him as he dug both heels into the ground and held on with all his might. The owner of the hand put up a fine fight, twisting and turning and trying to drag the appendage back below ground, but Bearclaw had it in an unbreakable grip.

268

Howl, sister, howl! he sent, and Crest obliged him
with glee. **Call the pack—we'll see what kind of strange
land-fish we've caught here tonight!**

In almost no time several of the wolves, digging frantically, had enlarged the hole enough so that several of the
Wolfriders could force the strange, lumpish creature
Bearclaw had caught to climb out into the moonlight. For
long moments no one spoke as it stood there, slowly
turning from side to side and glaring defiantly at its
captors.

It seemed to be as ugly all over as its hand was. The face
was hairless, with a huge nose like a waterskin, two piggy
little eyes, and a mouth that was a great, frowning slash. It
had a torch with it, and by the feeble light Bearclaw could
see that, yes, its skin *was* green! He gave silent thanks that
most of it was covered by a shapeless kind of garment that
covered the creature from neck to knee, with a hood to
hide most of the head. Remembering his earlier thoughts
about Joyleaf, Bearclaw found that he had no curiosity
whatsoever about what the thing might look like under its
clothing.

Mantricker looked the creature up and down, his eyes
wide with surprise—and a portion of amusement, for he
could not somehow consider it a threat—and said, "All
right, whatever you are. Can you understand me? Who are
you, *what* are you? And why have you been stealing our
dreamberries?"

The creature looked at the elves holding sharp spears and
the wolves that surrounded it, and it seemed to wilt just a
bit. It spoke in a voice that reminded Bearclaw of two
boulders crushing over each other.

"You wouldn't hurt poor, weak, helpless Old Maggoty,
would you?"

Another moment passed in surprised silence. So, it—
this Old Maggoty thing—did understand them and could
speak.

"That, I suppose, depends," Mantricker replied levely,

"on just how old, weak, and helpless you really are, and what you were doing besides stealing dreamberries."

A familiar sending touched Bearclaw's mind. **Maggoty —phew! It's certainly a good name for her.**

Bearclaw welcomed Joyleaf's presence in his thoughts as he felt her touch his hand. **How do you know it's a her?** he asked.

Well, it's shaped like a female. Sort of. And it smells like a female . . .

Sort of, Bearclaw agreed.

Old Maggoty was talking again. "I wasn't *stealing* your berries," she grated haughtily. "What you don't own can't be stolen, and you elves don't own the forest. We *trolls* were here first."

Trolls? thought Bearclaw. *What are trolls?*

"That may be true," replied Longreach, who was the oldest elf of them all, "but we've never seen you, or any of your kind. For all we know, you could be lying to save your own skin. Besides," the elf smiled, "if it weren't for Goodtree and the other tree-shapers there wouldn't be any dreamberry bushes here. We brought them, and we helped them to grow, as you should well know *if* you were here before us. So we do, I think, have a claim to those plants and their fruit."

"You still haven't answered my first questions," Mantricker added, "other than your name. Perhaps we ought to have a long chat, far away from this hidey-hole of yours. We could wait until daybreak so that we could get a good look at you . . ."

"Day . . . break?" Old Maggoty gulped. "You mean— sunlight?"

The troll collapsed where she stood, caving in until she was little more than a trembling huddle within her shapeless cloth robe. Whatever defiance she'd shown earlier was gone, and she groveled at Mantricker's feet.

"Ohhhh, you've got Old Maggoty in a bad way," she whined. "Ask whatever you want. Just don't let me be out here when the cursed sun comes up . . ."

* * *

270

The moons wheeled across the sky, and words poured from Maggoty's mouth. The Wolfriders soon realized, however, that as frightened as the troll might be, she was still a master dissembler, because for every bit of useful information they extracted, Maggoty added her own weight in trivial ramblings. Bearclaw happily left the questions to the elders, listening with only half an ear, until he heard a word that made him sit up and take notice.

"Metals," she had said.

"Wait a moment," Bearclaw interrupted, pushing his way among those who were questioning the troll. He had an idea. He wasn't certain that others of the Wolfriders hadn't had the same idea, but he wanted to be the first to express it.

"You said 'metals'," he went on. "Do you or your people make things of metal?" Bearclaw knew of metal things, as did all the Wolfriders; they still owned a few bits of the precious stuff that had been handed down over generations but there had been no way to get or make more—until now.

"Oh yes," Maggoty answered slyly, seeing that at last she'd snared the attention of her captors. "All kinds of things. Spear points that won't chip the way stone ones do. Arrowheads. Knives and swords for your hunters. And other things, too. Axes that make much better choppers than a knife—even pretties to wear, like this." She fondled a collar of gold plates that had been hidden by her hood. "And if you'd just let poor Old Maggoty go . . ."

Bearclaw had another idea. "If we let you go, that's the last we'd see of you, no doubt. But what do you"—he pointed to her, and then to his tribesmates, including them in the question—"think of this?" He turned back to the troll. "Your people like our—*our*—dreamberries enough to steal them. Do you like them enough to trade honestly for them?"

Old Maggoty's eyes narrowed in thought; her expression grew crafty. "Maybe," she replied slowly. "Maybe . . ."

"And how about other things," Bearclaw went on, "like furs, or good tanned leathers . . ." He glanced down at the

271

size of the troll's paunch and hazarded a shrewd guess about where her real interest lay. "Or fresh, red meat for your bellies?"

Bearclaw could practically hear Maggoty's mouth watering, and decided to press his advantage. He looked around, saw the smiles twitching on the faces of several of the Wolfriders, got the slightest of nods from Mantricker. "And how about goldfruit?" he went on. "I'll bet you don't get that often, so sweet and ripe the juice runs down your chin when you bite into one."

The other Wolfriders joined in, as eager to play the game as to tip the balance in their favor for new weapons and metal goods.

"Pheasant—and ring-neck," added Longreach, closing his eyes in mock ecstasy. "Meat so tender it melts off the bones . . ."

"Fresh fish," chimed in Far-Touch, who was as good with his javelin in water as on land, "flaky and firm . . ."

"And nuts," said Hawk quietly. "They keep well, too— and herbs to add flavor to your food such as you've never tasted."

Maggoty weakened with every new delicacy mentioned until she was prepared to give them whatever it was within her power to give, and to promise them anything else. Of course, Bearclaw had no illusions about *that*.

Nor, from the calculating look on his face, did Mantricker.

The chief put one foot on a rock, rested his elbow on his knee, and leaned over so his face was level with the troll's. "All right, old one," he said firmly. "Let's bargain."

Five good metal knives for Old Maggoty's freedom— that was the first price to be paid. That, and the pledge to leave the dreamberry bushes alone. And the Wolfriders would accompany Maggoty to get the knives . . .

The moons were down, but there was enough predawn light for the elves to see without difficulty. The troll led them on a twisting trek that took them into parts of the forest that were less familiar to them, and that ended at the side of a hillock. Cleverly concealed in the sloping ground was a door that looked just like a rock, but which gave forth a metallic clang when struck. Maggoty banged on the door with a stone until from within there came a creaking and clanking and the roughly circular portal swung open a bit. Another troll, who was even uglier than Maggoty, stuck his head halfway out.

"Maggoty?" he rumbled. "What in the pits are you doing coming in this way instead of by the . . ."

Then the doorkeeper saw who accompanied the troll female, shrieked, and tried to slam the ponderous door shut.

Far-Touch was faster, however, and jammed the door open with the butt end of his spear, giving Maggoty the chance to browbeat the cowering troll.

"Scurff, you blubbering coward," she yowled, "don't you dare lose this opportunity for me! These little beasts are ugly but they've got something . . ." and then she whispered the rest into the doorkeeper's ear. Soon after, the troll scuttled away.

Shortly, a bigger, even craggier troll came to the door. He carried the knives, finely wrought and sharper than a sliver of flint, and laid them outside the tunnel. "I'm Picknose," the troll said, "and I'm the one in charge." And then he added, "Except for the king, of course," when he saw Maggoty's eyebrows rise. "Here's your knives, now let Maggoty go."

Mantricker replied calmly as Bearclaw scooped up the weapons, "We'll let her go before the sun comes up, but we've got something else for you to think about. Tell him." He gestured to Maggoty.

She did, and as the elves watched and chuckled silently, they saw the litany of food-temptations working the same spell on Picknose as it had on Maggoty.

The burly troll wiped his mouth with the back of his hand. "I'll have to check this with Greymung." He swallowed. "But the king ought to go for it. Don't go anywhere yet—I'll be back."

Picknose's word was good, for he was back in a very

short time indeed. With him was the ugliest troll yet, who was wearing some sort of metal thing on his head. The "king," Bearclaw supposed.

With his arrival, the Wolfriders turned Maggoty loose to vanish down the tunnel. Then the bargaining began in earnest.

By dawn's first light, when the trolls made it clear that they were going to close the tunnel door, the agreements had been made. Each side had tried to get the better of the other, and each felt that it had succeeded. Bearclaw, who had mostly watched, was satisfied, although privately he thought his father had gone too easy on the trolls.

But . . .

He sat on a rock on the edge of the forest that held the Father Tree, and ran his thumb along the edge of his new metal knife. By unspoken but unanimous agreement among the Wolfrider elders he'd been given one of the ransom-blades since it was his stalking—his *patient* stalking, he'd reminded them—that had gotten Old Maggoty caught in the first place.

It was a marvelous blade. Human-made weapons of flint and stone would chip and break against a blade like this. Bearclaw grinned fiercely at the thought, and swung the knife over his head. He held it up to catch the golden light of the rising sun, and smiled at its sheen. And if Bearclaw was any judge, this fine weapon was only a promise of what might be wrangled from the trolls in turns to come . . .

Admiring your new toy? The sending held a wry, dry amusement that was unmistakable.

And why not? Bearclaw answered his father. **I spent two full dances of Big Moon sitting in that cursed dreamberry patch, being devoured by bugs. I think I've earned it.**

"You've earned more than that," Mantricker said aloud, gazing off to the horizon where the sun was half-risen. "The tribe has called you many things that I don't think they'll call you again"—the chief chuckled—"at least for a long while. Reckless, headstrong—there are worse things to

274

be." Mantricker grew momentarily pensive, and then sent, **Especially if you are chief . . .**

Bearclaw laughed. "Well, if they call me these things, they call my father the same, and I can think of many worse things than to be compared with you."

Mantricker looked at his son, grinned evilly, tousled his hair, and said, "You're right!"

THE BEST IN FANTASY

☐ 53954-0   SPIRAL OF FIRE by Deborah Turner Harris $3.95
     53955-9   Canada $4.95

☐ 53401-8   NEMESIS by Louise Cooper (U.S. only) $3.95

☐ 53382-8   SHADOW GAMES by Glen Cook $3.95
     53381-X   Canada $4.95

☐ 53815-5   CASTING FORTUNE by John M. Ford $3.95
     53826-1   Canada $4.95

☐ 53351-8   HART'S HOPE by Orson Scott Card $3.95
     53352-6   Canada $4.95

☐ 53397-6   MIRAGE by Louise Cooper (U.S. only) $3.95

☐ 53671-1   THE DOOR INTO FIRE by Diane Duane $2.95
     53672-X   Canada $3.50

☐ 54902-3   A GATHERING OF GARGOYLES by Meredith Ann Pierce $2.95
     54903-1   Canada $3.50

☐ 55614-3   JINIAN STAR-EYE by Sheri S. Tepper $2.95
     55615-1   Canada $3.75

Buy them at your local bookstore or use this handy coupon:
Clip and mail this page with your order.

Publishers Book and Audio Mailing Service
P.O. Box 120159, Staten Island, NY 10312-0004

Please send me the book(s) I have checked above. I am enclosing $_____
(please add $1.25 for the first book, and $.25 for each additional book to
cover postage and handling. Send check or money order only—no CODs.)

Name _____

Address _____

City _____ State/Zip _____

Please allow six weeks for delivery. Prices subject to change without notice.